Ride The Ranger Winds

By Richard Womack

iUniverse, Inc.
New York   Bloomington

Ride the Ranger Winds

iUniverse books may be ordered through booksellers or by contacting:

iUniverse
1663 Liberty Drive
Bloomington, IN 47403
www.iuniverse.com
1-800-Authors (1-800-288-4677)

ISBN: 978-1-4401-5004-3(pbk)
ISBN: 978-1-4401-5003-6 (cloth)
ISBN: 978-1-4401-5005-0 (ebk)

Printed in the United States of America

iUniverse rev. date: 6/10/2009

TEXAS RANGERS

The Rangers were recruited from the ranks of the toughest men available – men who could not only shoot straight and fast, but could ride hard and long. They had to patrol great distances on horseback and sometimes they exercised their own judgment as to methods of law enforcement.

RIDE THE RANGER WINDS
By Richard Womack

Chapter 1

The sun was slowly disappearing over the tops of the cactus and Ranger Laughlin McFarland knew it was time to stop and set-up camp for the night. He had made this trip several times while making his South Texas Patrols and the Frio River was just ahead. Sam, his big dapple gray stallion, was going to appreciate the cool water in the Frio and sweet grass growing along the banks of the river. They had been traveling several days and were headed to Laredo to investigate the murder of a rancher and his family.

As they reached the Frio, Sam walked in for a much needed drink then Laughlin rode him across, dismounted and started building a campfire for coffee. Tonight's meal would be jerky and coffee. He promised Sam oats, several blocks of hay and a nice stall when they reached Laredo. For himself he was thinking about a hot bath, dinner and a bed. After eating, and drinking his coffee, he laid his saddle on the ground for a pillow and spread out his bed roll. It was May, with hot days and cool nights. He looked up into the heavens at all the stars and fully realized there truly was a God.

Laughlin awoke at sun-up, it was cool during the night and he had covered himself with a blanket. As he moved his arms to remove the blanket he heard the distinct sound of a rattlesnake. It was lying next to him to absorb his body heat. He knew he was in a life threatening situation just as much as if he was in a saloon facing down three outlaws. He could not panic; he had to control the situation. Beads of sweat were popping out all over his face and body. He knew he couldn't move fast enough to get away from the snake and chances of a passing rider were unlikely. He realized he must lie perfectly still until the sun heated the snake's body then maybe it would crawl off in search of food. What seemed like hours went by, finally the sun was directly above him and he was getting hot from the sun's rays. He felt movement as the rattler's head appeared at the top of the blanket by his left shoulder and slowly crawled across his throat and off his body stopping about six inches from his face. The snake was at least five feet long and coiled. Looking straight at Laughlin's' head it began to rattle.

It was as though the snake was challenging Laughlin to move so it could strike. The Ranger's body was burning and aching, he hadn't moved in almost five hours and wasn't sure he could even if he tried. Suddenly the snake turned its head directing attention to movement and noise. It was Sam coming to check him out. The big gray evidently sensed something was wrong since Laughlin was not up yet and Sam was still unsaddled. Seizing the moment, Laughlin rolled quickly, pulled his 44 pistol from its holster lying next to his saddle and put three quick shots into the snake killing it instantly. With a sigh of relief, Laughlin got to his feet, walked over to Sam, patted and rubbed him while telling him thanks for saving his life; then he kissed him on the forehead fondly remembering how he had acquired the big horse from Herman Fox, a rancher who lived in the valley.

Laughlin just happened to ride by and see the young colt in the corral. He was bigger than normal for his age and well defined. He was strong and fast; just what Laughlin needed for his job as a Ranger. The rancher could sense how much Laughlin wanted the colt. Laughlin was sitting on the top rail of the corral when Herman walked over and started a conversation. He said, "You know I've got too "gol durn" many studs and gelding, what I need is more fillys and mares. I would be much obliged if you took this colt off my hands when you ride off on your route." Laughlin looked Herman in the eyes, nodded his head and said, "I'm obliged." Great men don't have to say a lot, they understand each other.

Laughlin put his foot in the stirrup, swung his leg over, and took the lead rope that was secured to the halter on the colt. The colt tugged a little bit and Laughlin said, "Hey little feller, you are as strong as that fellow in the Bible, I guess I'll name you Samson." As the years passed the bond between Laughlin and Sam became unbreakable. Then as Laughlin's thoughts returned to the present, he broke camp, skinned out the rattler knowing the dried flesh of the viper would be a welcome addition to his daily ritual of jerky and coffee.

It was late evening when he and Sam rode into Laredo a typical Texas border town: dirty, crime infested, violent and unpredictable. Laughlin pulled his pistol from the holster, checked the load, spun the cylinder and holstered the big iron. He rode into the livery stable and told the young Mexican boy that was caring for the horses to give Sam a clean stall, oats and a rubdown. He gave the young boy a dime and he knew his horse would be well cared for and protected this night. Laughlin walked down the wooden sidewalk slowly and carefully. He was a Texas Ranger and though he had many friends, he knew he had made enemies during his seven years as a Ranger. He remembered since becoming a ranger at twenty one, he had been shot three times, once in the left shoulder and twice with a shot gun at long range. He knew A Ranger had to be on the alert every minute, plan his activities and be in control at all times.

When he reached the hotel he stopped, looked in the windows then entered. He had his 44-40 rifle in his hands, cocked and ready. He would be leaving the rifle in his room when he went to dinner. It didn't look obvious, but it was a well planned safeguard. He checked in a room at the end of the hall, one window with no porch access. He didn't want someone to climb up to the porch and shoot him thru the window nor did he want someone in the lobby to be able to see him coming out of his room. All these things had been taught to him by Captain Beasley once Laughlin became a Ranger. Prior to that He had been a rough and rowdy cowboy, fast with a gun, stood 6'2", weighed 225 pounds and loved a good fight. Captain Beasley probably decided it would be best to have Laughlin on his side, otherwise, one day he may be sent to bring him in.

After a shave, bath, and a change of clothes from his saddlebags, he brushed the trail dust off his Stetson, looked in the mirror and adjusted his hat. The mirror reflected back a handsome, but manly image. He was tall, well built with dark hair, high cheek bones, square jawed and steel blue eyes that could put fear in an outlaw or love in a ladies heart. He sat at a table waiting on his meal when an elderly, raw boned, weathered man with a handlebar moustache walked over to the table and sat down. It was Luke Starrett, an old friend and the town marshal.

"Hello Laughlin, got a telegraph telling me you were on your way. What a shame about the killings out on the Rawlings Ranch. Still a mystery how it happened." said the marshal. Laughlin replied, "Hopefully we can ride out there in the morning and look around." The meal was served; they talked and enjoyed their meal. Laughlin tipped the waitress, paid for the food and, they started on their way to the saloon, a place called 'Opal's'.

It was around 10:00 p.m. and Laredo was gearing up for the night. Loud noises were coming from the saloon as a single shot pierced the evening. McFarland told Luke to go in the front door and he would go in the back. As Laughlin eased in the back door he could see a young sandy haired cowboy no more than 20 years old holding a gun on Luke. There was a body on the floor, shot through the head. It appeared the cowboy had shot the local card shark. It was evident by the way he was dressed. It was the end of the month and the boy probably had his wages for the month, too much to drink and got cheated at poker. The cowboy had the drop on Luke and was telling him to unbuckle his gun belt. Laughlin stepped around in front of the bar, told the young man to put away his gun and at the same time exposed his Ranger Star on the vest under his coat and said, "I'm Ranger McFarland. The cowboy looked at the star then stated, "You're Ranger McFarland, Laughlin McFarland?." As Laughlin was walking, he was talking, "That's right young man, put your gun away. I can still take you." With his gun still in the holster and his steel blue eyes burning into the boys' soul, Laughlin reached over, took the gun, led him to Luke and said, "Lock him up." Then he walked out the door and back to his hotel room as he thought back to his younger days and Captain Beasley.

Laughlin woke up the next morning in the hotel after a restful night in a real bed. After meeting Luke for breakfast they saddled up and rode to the ranch where a family of three had been slain. The ranch was on the northwest side of Laredo in the direction of Uvalde. It was a typical working cattle ranch of about six thousand acres. When they arrived there were several members of the family at the ranch, including the slain wife's younger sister from Uvalde. The sisters' name was Melissa; she was about twenty-three years old and not married. She had long brown hair, beautiful hazel eyes and a beautiful body. Laughlin was very taken by her looks and mannerisms. Luke and Laughlin introduced themselves, told them they were there to investigate with hopes of finding clues to help them find whoever committed the crime.

Luke told Laughlin there had been four strangers in Laredo recently that were dirty and rough looking. They stayed two nights drinking, visiting the ladies and then all four of them rode off together. About two days after they left town the bodies were discovered at the ranch. The ranch was a half day ride from Laredo and the four drifters had ridden towards the ranch and Uvalde.

Of the three victims it appeared the woman was by herself when she was raped and killed. Her naked body was found in the bedroom on the bed. She was badly bruised and had been shot in the head and private area. The father and son were found in the yard in front of the porch. It appeared they had returned while the crime was in progress and were shot from the house. While the woman had been killed with a small bore weapon, the father and son were shot with a large caliber, probably a rifle. Laughlin circled the house for tracks. Sure enough he found hoof prints from several horses traveling together towards Uvalde. Laughlin told Luke, "I'll try following this two week old trail and when I get to a town with a telegraph I'll wire you and keep you informed." Luke replied, "Be careful, there are four of them and they've already killed."

Laughlin returned to Laredo for supplies; he knew he could be on the trail for several days. His food supply would be pretty simple; lots of jerky, coffee and one dried rattler. Since he was pursuing four men, he purchased more cartridges than normal for his side arms, a 44-40 rifle and matching caliber pistol allowing him to shoot the same cartridge out of both weapons. He always kept Sam in mind and made certain not to overload; he kept everything except ammunition to a minimum. Laughlin mounted Sam and started out of town to the ranch where he could start tracking. He found himself thinking about Melissa and hoped she had not left the ranch to return to Uvalde.

When Laughlin arrived at the ranch it was vacant except for a couple of the Mexican vaquero ranch hands. After relocating the tracks, he started his journey riding slow and carefully following the trail left by the horses. On the second day he found an abandoned camp site left by the riders. This puzzled him. Why would four men who had just killed, take the time to camp and rest. The trail was leading directly towards Uvalde, not across the border into Mexico as he had expected.
On the third day he reached Uvalde, a neat, clean and profitable town. He went directly to the sheriffs' office and was welcomed by Oral Fox, the sheriff and brother of Herman Fox, the rancher who had given him Sam. Oral told Laughlin that the bank had been robbed by four men two weeks ago and they got away untouched. He and a posse had pursued them for three days but lost their trail close to Del Rio. The outlaws had been following the Rio Grande and it appeared they had crossed into Mexico.

Laughlin decided to stay in the hotel one night, get refreshed, care for Sam and get ready for the long chase. After registering at the hotel, bathing and grooming, he went to the local diner. Walking toward the place he got close enough to read the freshly painted sign which read 'Melissa's Diner'. For a moment his heart stopped, could this be the same Melissa? He entered and sure enough there she was, taking an order at a table. She looked even more beautiful than he remembered and his heart began to beat a little faster. As she turned and saw Laughlin her face lit up with a beautiful smile. He could feel the excitement in his body just by seeing her.

He selected a table and sat down. Melissa came over, welcomed him, took his order and went about her duties. When she served his food she said it was slowing down and could she join him for dinner. Laughlin was thrilled and in his mannerly cowboy way said, "It would be my pleasure to dine with the most beautiful lady I have ever met." She blushed and rushed away to prepare her plate. They had a wonderful dinner, pleasant conversation and it seemed they were the perfect blend. She had married a young man when she was twenty years old. Her husband had inherited a house, the Rocking Horse ranch, where they were raising thoroughbreds as well as range horses for the army. For a moment, hearing she was married, he could feel his heart pounding once again." Then she continued.

"One day he went to the corral to feed several thoroughbred colts he was keeping. It had been raining, the ground was muddy, and he was carrying a bag of oats to the feed trough. The colts were hot blooded and very high strung. They smelled the oats and in their efforts to be first at the oats they knocked him down and he was trampled, killing him instantly." She told him she tried to continue and manage the ranch, still owns it, but is letting her foreman and ranch hands operate the ranch until she sells it or gets someone with horse knowledge that can continue to breed quality horses and bargain with the army. She came to town and bought the restaurant. They had only been married for seven months when the accident occurred.
Although Laughlin felt a little twinge of guilt, her husbands death had returned his pulse to normal and prompted him to ask; "Have you ever considered re-marrying; is there anyone else in your life?"

He held his breath while waiting on the answer. She replied, "I have never met anyone that interested me and no, I do not have anyone special in my life." Laughlin looked into her beautiful hazel eyes and said, "Well," with a pause, "You now have someone that's interested in you and hopes to be a special person in your life." Melissa blushed again and said, "Laughlin, you have peaked my interest, so please be careful when you leave in the morning. I'll be anxiously awaiting your return." She got up from the table, kissed him on the cheek and said goodnight.

The next morning when Laughlin saddled up and rode off to start trailing, life was different. He had a warm feeling in his body that he had never experienced and he could still feel her kiss on his cheek and smell her perfume. Sam walked steady and slow. They stayed on the trail until it turned and went into the Rio Grande. The river was very shallow from there all the way into Del Rio. Sheriff Fox and the posse had turned back at this point, thinking the robbers had gone into Mexico. This didn't make sense to Laughlin, there was nothing for days if you took this route, they would need to go deep into Mexico before they could party and spend their money. Laughlin continued on to Del Rio.

Del Rio was much like Laredo: dirty, crime infested and violent with numerous range wars going on between the Texas and Mexican ranchers. As usual, his first stop was at the sheriffs' office. The sheriff and his deputies were riding the border in an effort to halt border wars and rustling. Laughlin went to a gun cabinet in the sheriffs' office and, with his key, unlocked the cabinet. Inside was a sawed off 12 gauge side-by-side, loaded with double ought buck. It was Laughlin's' riot or crowd control gun and he left it in Del Rio; it wasn't a trail gun.

It was mid-afternoon when he started walking toward the 'Water Hole' saloon. As he approached, he looked at the horses tied to the hitching post. There was only one horse in a group of seven that looked trail weary. Laughlin cradled the 'scatter gun' in his left arm, pulled his pistol from it's holster, spun the cylinder and replaced it. He wore his holster high on his hip very close to his belt with the barrel slightly pointing forward. When making a quick draw he didn't reach low for his pistol and then point it out
 in front of him at arms length and fire, instead when his pistol cleared the holster, it was pointed and fired directly above it. This is the style that made him fast and deadly.

He walked thru the saloon doors and quickly surveyed the room. At a table next to the side wall was a young man with two Mexican girls in his lap and two more at the table. Only a big spender would attract this much attention. He walked toward the bar carefully watching the man in the mirror behind the bar. When he reached the bar, the bartender immediately recognized him and in a loud voice said "Ranger McFarland, good to see you. What kind of drink can I get you?" Without taking his eyes off the mirror and watching the man at the wall table, he replied "Whiskey." Laughlin was sure the man heard the bartender call him "Ranger". The girls all left the table and the man got up and started toward the door. Laughlin turned and commanded, "Stay right where you are, don't go any farther."

The man stopped and faced Laughlin. He was a large man, dirty looking with a beard attempting to hide a massive scar on the left side of his face. Laughlin's eyes were fixed on the man's eyes and he said, "I need to talk to you about a bank robbery and three murders." The man hollered out, "I ain't afraid of you Ranger, you'll never take me." He then reached for his pistol; it was barely out of the holster when three shots were fired from Laughlin's' pistol. A Ranger is taught when you pull your weapon – shoot to kill, don't take a chance. The three shots had struck the man in the middle of his chest, probably heart shots. Laughlin, with gun in hand eased back to the bar and asked the bartender, "Was he by himself? Are there others upstairs?" The bartender answered, "There were three more but they left and rode west yesterday. The man you just killed wouldn't leave the girls and whiskey, so his two brothers and another man left him."

Laughlin walked over to the dead body, tore open his shirt exposing a money belt. He removed the money belt from the body, laid it on the bar and counted the money. There was a little over two thousand dollars in the belt. The bank reported ten thousand dollars stolen, a four way split of the cash would just about equal what the dead man had in the belt. Laughlin walked across the room and noticed how the smell of gun powder, blood and the presence of death overpowered the ever present smell of liquor and tobacco; then he went back to the shcriffs' office and looked at the wanted posters. The man's name was J.W. Lockett, he and his two brothers were wanted for rustling over in Beeville, Texas. Laughlin wired the sheriff in

Laredo, told him what happened and informed him he was continuing his search.

Realizing he was traveling into one of the most desolate areas of Texas, he restocked his provisions. Laughlin also, due to pursuing three men, tied his shot gun on top of his bedroll. He apologized to Sam and they rode west. About three miles outside of Del Rio, Laughlin met the stage coach. The driver, Bob Bell, was a long time wagon man, had been on a number of wagon trains and was now driving the stage. He was around sixty year's old, green eyes, handle bar moustache, full beard and hair down to his shoulders. He was well liked and respected by Laughlin. Bob loved to talk and this was very helpful to Laughlin because Bob drove the stage all over Texas.

They exchanged greetings and then Laughlin told Bob he was looking for three men that robbed the Uvalde Bank and killed a Laredo family. Bob always had a large chew of tobacco with drippings running out the corner of his mouth. Bob spat off the side of the coach and said, "Could be you're looking for those three fellers over in Pecos. When I went thru there the feller at the post office said they showed up a day ago and had been drunk, dancing and shooting in the streets, but finally had calmed down and were bedded up with the local whores." Laughlin thanked him, wished him luck and rode off toward Pecos.

It was hot, no water, no shade, all the things that made traveling slow. It appeared the outlaws felt as though they had lost the posse at Del Rio and no longer thought they were being pursued. Laughlin knew he didn't have to push Sam; he would soon catch up to them.

Pecos was a town of only two or three buildings with a Post Office/ General Store combination and of course the saloon. It was also a place where people wanted by the law could gather, kinda like an outlaws roost. Laughlin knew he could be facing more than the three he was trailing. No telling what kind of a congregation could be in the saloon. He had pulled the wanted poster of the two remaining brothers, Carl and Olin Lockett, so he knew what two of the men looked like. Waiting until about 9:00 PM in hopes he could get all three of them together, he tied Sam down the street away from gunfire so he could silently walk to the saloon then charge through the front door. He couldn't go behind the saloon where the girls had their little shacks for entertaining; he would probably be seen. He cocked both barrels on the scatter gun, eased up on the porch, quickly stepped thru the door opening and said in a very loud voice, "Texas Ranger, nobody move." The shot gun was at his waist and he was scanning the room. Much to his amazement only two men were in the room, the Lockett brothers. Evidently they had run everyone out of the saloon. He pointed the shot gun directly at the brothers who were sitting at a table surrounded by girls. He told the girls to go out the front door and run, he then told the two brothers they were under arrest. One of the men said, "Let's take him." They both started up from the table while drawing their pistols. The report from both barrels of the shot gun being fired at once was deafening and deadly. One of the brothers was knocked backwards into the wall. He was almost cut in half. The other brother was hit more on the left side and he was spun around, as he was falling he tried to get a shot off at Laughlin, but a shot to the head from Laughlin's pistol ended the shoot out.

Both men were dead – where was the one remaining man? Laughlin quickly reloaded and positioned himself to watch the door. He expected the last man to come charging thru the door to try and help his partners after hearing the gunshots. He never appeared although he had heard the shots from one of the girls' shacks and panicked before riding off to escape being killed or caught. Both dead men had money belts, with less than the first belt recovered. They must have been partying hard.

Laughlin knew that the last member of the gang did not have time to prepare provisions for his escape. Evidently he ran out of the shack when he heard the shots, jumped on his horse and rode away with escape being the only thing on his mind. Laughlin knew he now had the advantage, one on one with provisions to last a couple of weeks and a fresh trail to follow. He felt safe enough to spend the night in Pecos and get a fresh start in the morning. He bunked on the floor of the post office while the postmaster stood guard all night.

Without water or food, and probably on foot, Ft Davis was out of reach for the outlaw; his only hope was to stumble on to a Mexican camp and that was unlikely. Laughlin figured he would catch up to him on the third day. As he and Sam were approaching the Davis Mountains, it was as if they were uninhabited. Laughlin rode Sam at a walk, the trail was easy to follow and as he suspected, laying in the trail was a dead horse. The rider had ridden the horse fast and hard until he literally dropped dead, then, utilizing an old Indian method for staying alive; he had opened up the horse with his knife,
ate the heart and liver, and drank as much blood as possible. Probably, to sustain himself, he had a canteen full of blood and part of the horses' hips cut into strips, much like jerky. Advantage was still to Laughlin. It was just going to take a little longer and he had to avoid an ambush. Maybe the man had a rifle, hopefully he didn't. It would be much easier if all he had was a six-shooter and limited ammunition.

Laughlin figured the outlaw could make maybe five miles on foot in his present condition and, even if given the chance, he wouldn't shoot Sam. Instead, he would try to setup an ambush for a clean kill, take Sam and make his escape into Mexico at Presidio.

Laughlin decided it was too risky riding out in the open into an ambush. He would bring the prey to him. He rode about four miles, stopped to setup camp, started a big campfire, boiled coffee and heated the rattler to create the smell of food. While he ate the dried snake, he threw some green foliage on the fire much like the Indians did when sending smoke signals. He wanted the outlaw to see the camp before dark figuring it would lure him in. Just before sunset, Laughlin placed his saddle standing on its end on a rock by the campfire. Then he dropped his blanket over the saddle and propped a stick up against it to set his hat on. This created an image of a man sitting on a rock by the campfire. He then took his shotgun, laid down on the ground behind some bushes about twenty yards from the fire and waited.

It was almost dark as the sun set. Laughlin had only been waiting for about an hour when Sam's head suddenly rose up and looked into the dark surrounding camp. Thanks Sam, you told me where he is, thought Laughlin.

POW – POW – POW – POW, four shots rang out and with each shot the saddle jumped from the slugs hitting it. Come on, Laughlin thought, shoot two more and you'll be empty. Suddenly the outlaw stepped out of the darkness into the light of the campfire. Laughlin aimed the shotgun and said, "Texas Ranger, you're under arrest. Throw your pistol down or you're dead." The outlaw cried out, "Don't shoot! I'm surrendering." "Throw your gun in the fire", said Laughlin. The man cooperated and Laughlin rose to his feet, walking toward the man. All the time he was thinking, now I have one of them alive and I can get some answers. It was dark, the fire was flickering and he didn't see the belly gun stuck under the outlaw's empty gun belt, but, when Laughlin exposed himself from the darkness, he saw the outlaw reach for it. The gun was out and in the act of being pointed when a single shot from Laughlin struck the outlaw in the chest. He dropped immediately as Laughlin rushed to him and kicked the gun away before grabbing the man's head and saying, "Don't die! Don't die! Tell me why you killed that family in Laredo." The man whispered with his dying breath, "They were dead when we got there." He gasped for air several times; then he died.

Laughlin laid the man's body close enough to the fire so that he would be protected from animals during the night. He was too far from a town to try and return his body for a proper burial. As he laid down his saddle for a pillow; he realized a new one would be necessary since the old one had extensive damage. All four of the outlaws' shots had left their mark. Being too tired to think, he immediately went to sleep.

The next morning Laughlin took the man's body to an elevated area, laid him down on his back, crossed his arms and covered him with heavy rocks. After saying a short prayer asking God to forgive the man, he 'mounted up' and headed toward Uvalde.

It was hot; he kept Sam at a slow walk and asked himself a question, 'What if the outlaw had told him the truth?' If so, then who killed the family? He rode for three days and his time was spent on thoughts about the murders and Melissa. He would have lots of questions to ask when he got back to Laredo.

Chapter 2

Laughlin finally reached Uvalde. It was midday and he didn't want to attract a lot of attention. He just wanted to get a room, have a chance to bathe and make himself presentable before going to Melissa's Diner. Didn't happen, as soon as he rode down the street to the sheriffs' office, a crowd gathered inquiring if he had caught the outlaws or had gotten their stolen money back. Ignoring their questions, he closed and locked the door behind him. Sheriff Fox was there so he filled out a report and turned in the money he had recovered. Ten thousand had been stolen and he was returning about eight. Laughlin could hear the crowd outside the door anxiously awaiting the sheriff's report. Suddenly the door was being kicked, beaten on and pulled almost hard enough to open. Oral said he would quite them down but, as he opened the door, he was almost run over by Melissa. She charged across the room, grabbed and kissed Laughlin saying, "Are you alright? Are you injured?" Laughlin gave her a big hug and said, "Now that I have you in my arms everything is fine." Melissa was crying.

The sheriff said he would telegraph a report to Sheriff Starrett in Laredo and then have his deputy take care of Sam. "I know", said the sheriff, "extra oats."

On the way to the hotel with Melissa, Laughlin told her he was going to bathe, wash his clothes and when they were dry, he would come to the diner and join her for dinner. She told him to hurry and reluctantly returned to her restaurant.

Laughlin soaked and scrubbed in the hot bath water and then washed his clothes and hung them up to dry. He had just lain down on the bed when there was a knock on the door. With his cocked pistol in hand he approached the door and asked, "Who's there?" It was the deputy. Laughlin opened the door and the deputy handed him a new shirt, britches, socks and undergarments. Melissa had purchased them from the general store. The deputy said, "I also have a message for you" and handed Laughlin a note. It read, 'Please hurry, I miss you.' Laughlin's heart raced and his legs felt weak. Melissa had given his life a new meaning. He had never loved before, could it be possible that he was falling in love?

The shirt was a perfect fit, solid black with double breasted button front, red bandana and new dark blue jeans. With a wet rag he wiped down his black Stetson, tried to reshape it and placed it on his head. His hair had not fully dried and it was naturally curly, extended to his shoulders, in long curly strands. He picked up his gun belt and holster, strapped it around his waist and made the proper adjustments before walking back to the mirror and checking his appearance. Dressed in the black shirt and black hat, he smiled and thought to himself how much he looked more like a desperado than a Ranger. He pinned his Silver Star on the left side of his chest; now he felt like Laughlin McFarland, the eight year veteran Ranger.

After slowly descending the hotel stairs and visually scanning the lobby, Laughlin crossed the street, stepped up on the wooden sidewalk and walked toward 'Melissa's Diner'. He was followed by several of the youngsters that lived in town. He stopped in front of the restaurant door, turned and addressed the group of seven or more young boys. Laughlin said, "You boys honor me by showing that you support me and the Texas Rangers. Hopefully some of you will become a Ranger. Texas is growing fast and it needs fine young men like you." He tossed each kid a cartridge from his gun-belt as he turned and walked into the restaurant. Laughlin thought, 'I haven't seen her yet and my heart is racing just from the expectation of spending time with her this evening.' Out of habit, he sat down at a table facing the entrance.

Melissa entered the dining room from the kitchen. She was dressed in a beautiful crimson full skirt, a low cut white blouse with lace, matching necklace and earrings. Her beautiful brown hair was long and curly, hanging past her shoulders and her hazel eyes were sparkling and dancing when they met Laughlin's steel blues. When he stood up, they embraced, then Melissa took a step back and said, "My, my, what a handsome Ranger you are Laughlin." He blushed and said, "It's just the clothes madam. You know, they say clothes make a man. Thanks, I'll repay you but it's the first time in my life that a woman dressed me." He was laughing playfully. The food and wine were excellent. The crowd was slowly disappearing and soon the room would belong to Laughlin and Melissa. They sipped wine, continued to talk and explore the lives of each other.

Melissa began by telling Laughlin that she and her sister were born in San Antonio. It seems that Helen, her only and older sister had married a rancher from Laredo then moved there to start a family. Melissa met her husband while he was in San Antonio selling horses off his ranch.

Then Laughlin asked Melissa about her relationship with her sister. Melissa told him they were close, very close then slid her chair closer to Laughlin, put her hand on his hand and said, "Laughlin, can I trust you with something very personal between the two of us?" Laughlin nodded yes. Then Melissa told Laughlin that about a month before she was killed; her sister rode the stage to Uvalde and spent a week with her. During this time she told Melissa that things had not been going well at home. She was very unhappy and had been seeing someone else for about three months. She told Melissa that she had come to her senses, realized how much her family meant to her and was going to end the relationship. Melissa said her sister didn't tell her who the other person was and she hadn't pressed the issue. Then she said, "I still have no idea who it might be." "Enough about me," she continued, "Now tell me about this Ranger McFarland. Where you're from, why a Texas Ranger, You know."

"Well, it's a long story," said Laughlin, "But here goes." "I was born in Austin; My Dad, Wayne, was shot in the back while serving as a deputy there and my mother died giving me birth. I was heading in the wrong direction at full gallop when Ranger Captain Wilford Beasley entered my life. I remember when I turned twenty I was in a barroom brawl with three of John Chisums' drovers. I had two of them out on the floor and was chasing the other one out the door just as Captain

Beasley was entering. A sharp blow to my head from the Captain's gun butt ended the fight.

The next day I found myself in jail and Captain Beasley asked if I could make bail. Of course I didn't have bail money and couldn't pay a fine or any court costs. It appeared I would be in jail for quite a while. Beasley must have known how my father died and had silently been observing my life while I was growing into manhood. He apparently figured it was time he got more involved with me before it was too late. Here is where my life changed. The Captain offered to release me in my own custody and dismiss all fines if I would consent to be his deputy for one year. During that year, I would carry a badge and a gun then, if I so desired, I could become a ranger. On my twenty-first birthday, Captain Beasley administered the oath to me
and I've been serving this star (Laughlin proudly pointed to his Ranger Badge) ever since.

Melissa listened intently then replied, "You speak of Captain Beasley almost as if in reverence, tell me more about him."

Laughlin took a deep breath, stuck out his chest and said, "I'd be proud to tell you about Captain Beasley, he's been my mentor and champion for a long, long time." He then related the following stories about his hero to Melissa. "As I was growing up I heard many stories about Ranger Captain Beasley. He was one of the original Rangers and had fought the Indians daily up until the Civil War. During the war he fought for the South as an officer, served proudly, and was decorated for heroic deeds. He has killed many Indians while protecting the settlers and it was said the Indians called him 'White Man with many lives". It was reported he had been wounded seventeen times while Indian fighting; all due to being shot, stabbed or being hit with arrows. He was responsible for rescuing several white children kidnapped in raids and was viewed with respect by the Indians for his bravery and the ferocious manner in which he fought.

Once he was traveling alone close to Fredericksburg when a raiding party of thirty or more Indians gave chase. He rode to a large rock that covered a section of land north of Fredericksburg called 'Enchanted Rock'. He climbed to the top where he was unreachable. Then he commenced to pick off the Indians with his rifle as they attempted to climb the rock. Now, the Indians would not attack at night because they thought the rock was inhabited by their gods. The Captain held them off for four days before they gave up and left. It was reported there were fourteen dead Indians found on and around the rock. Outlaws and gunfighters alike feared him due to the swiftness of his draw and the accuracy of his aim. Legend has it he never lost a man when he went after him. As a kid I kept up with tales about him and nourished a desire to someday become a Ranger myself. So you're right, I guess I'll always look upon Captain Beasley with a certain amount of reverence."

Laughlin and Melissa continued sipping wine and exchanged a few more pleasantries then realized it was after midnight and the restaurant was empty except for the two of them. Since the restaurant had living quarters Melissa lived there while she was working in town. Laughlin told Melissa that he had enjoyed the evening, and how sweet she was for getting him the clothes.
He stood up, reached for her hand and walked to the front door. As he put his arms around her, she tilted her head back and Laughlin kissed her affectionately. After the kiss, he said, "Melissa, I care very much for you." He then turned and opened the door stepping out onto the porch and said, "Goodnight."

Laughlin and Melissa spent a lot of time together for the next week. He had promised her he would not report for Ranger duty so he could spend more time with her and then go back to Laredo to complete his investigation. Laughlin knew he was falling in love with Melissa but was exercising one of the Ranger rules: Don't let your emotions overrule good judgment.

After a week Laughlin and Sam were well rested. He didn't want to leave Melissa, but he had questions that needed answers. As he rode back to Laredo he carefully, in his mind, laid out all the pieces of the puzzle. The whispering voice of the dying outlaw, 'They were already dead' kept repeating itself in his mind. None of the four outlaws had a small caliber weapon on them or in their saddlebags. Where were the weapons used and most of all, what was the motive?

Laughlin finally reached Laredo and went directly to the saloon. Not because he was thirsty, but because bartenders are told everything. He stood at the bar, sipped on whiskey, talked for about an hour; nothing valuable came out of the conversation with the bartender. He then went over to the corner table facing the door and sat down. Laughlin was deep in thought when Nathan, the town drunk, came in and tried to get a drink on credit. Nathan was handicapped, he was peg legged. He had lost part of his leg due to infection from a musket ball. Alcohol dominated his life. He tried to do odd jobs for the merchants in town, slept in the livery stable or wherever he passed out. Laughlin always gave Nathan some change when he saw him. As soon as Nathan spotted Laughlin he headed straight for the table and asked for money to buy a drink. Laughlin said, "Sit down, talk to me and I'll buy you a drink." Nathan sat down and started asking about the bank robbers. He wanted to know details much like a kid.

Laughlin told him he wanted to talk about the cowboy and gambler killing and was he in the saloon when the gambler was shot. Nathan said he was working, sweeping and cleaning up when the argument started. Nathan said, "Wesley, the gambler, had been drinking heavy for over a week, was short tempered and mean." Nathan said Wesley had hit him with a chair and cut his head. He pointed to the scar above his left ear and said, "He got what he deserved. The young cowboy won a pot; he called the boy a cheat and started to draw a derringer from his vest. The boy was quicker and beat him to the draw." Laughlin asked Nathan if he had told anyone this and Nathan replied, "Ranger, nobody's gonna believe me, I'm a drunk. You're the only person that talks to me. No one liked Wesley and even the pretty lady that came down the alley late at night didn't attend his funeral." "Pretty lady?" asked Laughlin. "What do you mean?" Nathan replied, "I would be sleeping in the alley under a stairway, and several times I saw this pretty lady, late at night walk down the alley and go up the stairs to the back door of the hotel where Wesley lived. The last time she came to visit she was only in the room for about thirty minutes when she ran out crying and Wesley was cursing at her from the top of the stairs."

Laughlin said, "Nathan you have been a big help. I want you to consider yourself my unofficial deputy, and keep me informed of anything you hear about the dead gambler." Laughlin gave Nathan a silver dollar and said, "Nathan, consider that your first days pay. A ranger earns a dollar a day and as far as I'm concerned, you just gave me a day's work," then Laughlin added, "Keep yourself straight and there may be many more silver dollars in store for you. I see a real man in front of me, not a drunken saddle bum." Nathan grinned, put the dollar in his pocket and walked away thinking, "How 'bout that, I'm a deputy for the Rangers, and all because I'm sober."

Laughlin walked back to the hotel, laid down on his bed and started pondering over what he knew so far. Then it hit him. Melissa's sister had told her she was having an affair but was going to end it. Suppose the affair was with Wesley. He was a gambler, card shark and a ladies man. So she comes to town whenever possible and secretly meets Wesley in his room without being seen, except for Nathan. During her last visit, Wesley is told the relationship is over and to stay out of her life. They argue, she runs out the back door, down the stairs and flees with Wesley cursing at her. A couple of days go by and as Nathan had said, Wesley was drinking heavy and was violent. He gets drunk, rides out to the ranch during the day thinking the husband and son would be out on the range tending cattle. Wesley finds Helen alone, roughs her up, and rapes her, all the time thinking she would not end the affair. Rather than feeling affectionate for Wesley after being raped, Helen screams at him that she is going to tell her husband that he raped her and she would see him hang. Wesley panicked; pulled his
32 caliber two shot derringer and shot her. Once in the head and once in the private area as if to say, 'If I can't have you, no one else can.'

The husband and son heard the shots and came to help when they were killed. They were shot with a rifle. Where the rifle came from and its' whereabouts is unknown.

The next morning Laughlin got up early and rode out to the ranch. When he arrived he went to the corral where a couple of vaqueros were shoeing a horse. He asked the cowboys if Mr. Rawlings had any rifles in the ranch house. Pablo, one of the men shoeing the horse, seemed anxious to talk to Laughlin and told him that Mr. Rawlings kept a Lever Action Henry Rifle loaded and mounted above the mantle over the fireplace. Although it was a lever action, Helen had been taught how to use it and it gave her several shots to drive away unwanted visitors; but, it never left the house.

Laughlin rode back to the ranch house, went inside and looked above the mantle at the vacant pegs used to hold a rifle. Speculating that the killer, Wesley, grabbed the rifle, ran to the front door to shoot the father and son; but, did he shoot from inside the house or from the porch. Laughlin looked carefully in the area where a cartridge would have been ejected if fired from inside the house. Having no luck, he stepped out on the porch, lined himself up as if shooting and imagined where the ejected hulls would have landed. Then he crawled under the porch and sure enough, there laid two empty cartridges.

Except for the whereabouts of the rifle, Laughlin was pretty sure he had all the pieces in place. After shooting Helen with his derringer, Wesley grabbed the loaded rifle and shot the father and son as they raced toward the house. Realizing he had no more ammunition for his pistol, he grabbed the box of rifle ammo on the mantle and rode back to town. If needed, he had the rifle and ammo should he be pursued. As he approached town he threw the rifle away, probably in the Rio Grande, which separates Mexico from Texas on the south end of Laredo.

Then Wesley began drinking, became angry and quick tempered. Probably when the young cowboy in the saloon beat his hand at poker he challenged the cowboy and was outdrawn in a fair fight. Laughlin grinned, he didn't want to see the cowboy hang, and Nathan's testimony would clear him. The cowboy didn't know it but he probably served justice by killing Wesley.

Laughlin rode back to Laredo, went to the sheriffs' office and filled out his report. It read: Rancher and two members of his family murdered. Bank robbery in Uvalde, believe all responsible parties are dead and bank money has been returned.

CHAPTER 3

The next morning Sam and Laughlin started for Uvalde. Laughlin had a lot on his mind and his life had changed since meeting Melissa. For the first time in his life he felt loved and it felt good.

Laughlin and Sam arrived in Uvalde only to find that Melissa had gone to her horse ranch for her monthly financial meeting with her foreman. Laughlin was given directions by the cook at the restaurant and a message saying Melissa was anxiously awaiting his arrival. When he walked out of the restaurant, untied Sam and started to mount, he heard a loud voice shouting in his direction. The voice was coming from the saloon porch saying, "Hey! Ranger, I hear you're fast. Just how fast are you? Come on out in the street and lets see how fast you die."

Laughlin slowly started walking toward the evening sun that was setting low in the west. When he got to the position he wanted, his back to the sun, he stopped walking and turned. He was directly in the middle of the street. The man had also crossed to the middle placing them some eighteen steps apart, about sixty feet. Laughlin looked at the man and knew he was a gunslinger, not a drunken cowboy. He was dressed well, long sleeve shirt, vest, black leather gun belt with a pearl handled forty five and a quick draw tie down wrapped around his leg. He was clean shaven, except for a moustache, and had a fine Stetson cocked back on his head. Laughlin thought to himself how glad he was that Melissa was not in town to witness this shoot out.

Laughlin's eyes started changing color, from warm blue to dark steel as he gave the man his death stare. The gunslinger said, "My name is Clint Bellows and I hate Rangers. Let's see how brave you are by yourself. Two of you Rangers killed my brother in Abilene." Laughlin responded, "I was there. He was crazy drunk, wounded the bartender and was shooting up the bar. He had a buddy that was just as drunk. My partner went in the back door and I came through the front. Both were told they were under arrest, but your brother drew and I beat him. His buddy decided not to draw and surrendered."

"Now, Mr. Bellows, if you want to see how brave and fast one Ranger is, this is your chance. Just be aware it's the last thing you'll ever see." Bellows said, "I'm a bounty hunter and I've killed five men in gunfights. All you Rangers are cowards and back shooters. You're dead Ranger." He went for his gun. They carried Mr. Bellows to the undertakers, he had two holes in the center of his chest – his gun had not been fired.

The gunfight would delay Laughlin's departure for Melissa's ranch until tomorrow. Riding out the next morning he put Sam in a slow gallop; he needed to see Melissa. Yesterday was heavy on his mind so he decided not to tell her about the gunfight. He soon found the ranch, it was beautiful: water, green grass and well stocked with horses. Laughlin loved horses and had earned a living when he was fourteen breaking horses and making them saddle ready.

He rode up to the beautiful white ranch house, trimmed in brown, with a wrap around porch and a fenced in yard. Melissa ran out the door and met Laughlin before he dismounted. He quickly stepped down; hugged and kissed her several times before walking up onto the porch. Laughlin said, "Let's sit on the porch swing." It was cloudy and cool due to the chance of rain and it felt good to feel the cool wind.

Laughlin sat on the swing while Melissa went to the kitchen and got Sam an apple. When she returned, she gave Sam the apple, stroked him and said, "One of these days, Big Boy, you're gonna give me a ride." Melissa then turned and came back onto the porch, sat down in the swing and cuddled next to Laughlin.

"Laughlin, everyone is grateful to you for recovering the lost bank money and serving justice on those men", said Melissa. Laughlin had decided that no one but him would ever know the truth about her sister. He wasn't going to allow Melissa's sister's reputation to be ruined. He had not lied in his report. He let everyone believe the four men had committed the murders. The young cowboy had served justice and it would always be his secret, not to be shared with anyone, not even Melissa. Laughlin looked her in the eyes and nodded.

She looked Laughlin straight in the eyes and said, "I've got to tell you my feelings toward you. I think of you every minute that I am awake and when
I'm asleep, I dream about you. When you're away or out of my sight, I'm sick. I'm in love with you and I've never felt love like this before in my life. I want to bear your children and be your wife for the rest of my life. I don't think I could live without you now that I've found you. I know it's too soon, but my feelings will never change. I love you with all my heart."

Laughlin held Melissa close, kissed her and said, "I have the same feelings. You are always on my mind and I have thought about life with you here on the ranch, and it would be good. If we marry and I don't quit being a Ranger, it would be unfair to you each time I rode off. You would be worried not knowing if I was going to come back alive. Being a Ranger is my first love, it made a man out of me and I enjoy life as a Ranger. Texas is growing and there's a need for men like me. I can't explain why I love being a Ranger, it's dangerous, lonely and the pay is poor, but there is pride in being able to say I am a 'Texas Ranger' and will be a part of history."

Laughlin said, "Melissa, I love you, but I also love being a Ranger and I don't see how I can have both at the same time. I need time to think. I'm on my way to Abilene to meet two other Rangers. We'll be trying to catch a gang of rustlers. It's a long way to Abilene and I'll have time to think about our lives." Melissa was crying as Laughlin got up from the swing. He took her by the hand and walked her across the porch, down the steps and stopped where Sam was tied to the hitching post. Laughlin knew he couldn't talk anymore; he was fighting to hold back his own tears. He hugged Melissa with both arms, gave her a long kiss and then mounted Sam.

Melissa was still crying as she watched him ride away. She had heard it said that when someone is leaving and loves you, they will always stop, look back and wave. Melissa was saying out loud, "Please, Laughlin, please stop, look back and wave." As Laughlin was topping the hill, he stopped, turned, looked back and waved. As Laughlin turned back around, he couldn't hold back his tears. It started raining and as the rain hit his face he looked up to the heavens, and said, "God, I guess you're crying too."

As Laughlin rode away from Melissa and the ranch, the rain continued. The cool air and the gentle rain made Sam frisky, he wanted to run, and he had to be held back. Laughlin was hoping for a slow uneventful ride to Abilene, he had lots to think about. He had to compare a life with Melissa as his wife, living on the ranch raising horses and children to a Rangers life. Laughlin knew only a select few could live the life required of a Ranger. You had to
be disciplined, fair and firm yet very tough. Most of your time is spent in the saddle, sleeping on the ground, facing danger and death every day.

It's unfair to try and share your life while being a Ranger. He was torn apart, he loved Melissa and he loved the Rangers. At night, when he bedded down he prayed to God for guidance. Each day Laughlin traveled farther away from Melissa, he found himself thinking more about his job in Abilene.

The telegraph received in Uvalde said he would be meeting two more Rangers. One was a veteran named Jim Weaver and the other was not identified.

When Laughlin arrived in Abilene, he was exhausted, hungry and needed a nice long hot bath with plenty of soaking time; as always he took care of Sam first and made sure he got extra oats. Abilene is a cattle town where herds are driven to the stockyards, sold and shipped to other areas of the country. It's a rough and rowdy town with gunfighters, drovers from the cattle drives, local outlaws and ranch hands.

Gamblers, girls and drunks keep the local sheriff and his deputies busy.

Laughlin walked from the livery stable toward the hotel. He had to cross the dirt street to enter the hotel. As he crossed the street a group of riders at full gallop came down the street directly at him. They were firing pistol shots in the air and 'hooping and hollering'. Laughlin had to get out of their way in a hurry, and then he stood and watched as they rode to the 'Bent Elbow Saloon'. He counted seven riders as they dismounted and entered.

Laughlin resumed his walk to the hotel and entered in his customary way: rifle in hand and pistol fully loaded. He went to the 'Desk Clerk' and asked for a room upstairs and at the end of the hall. As he signed the register he found Ranger Jim Weaver's name and just below it was Wilford Beasley – his Captain. Laughlin identified himself and asked the clerk if they were in their rooms. He was told they had gone to the saloon about an hour ago and he was to meet them for drinks when he arrived. Laughlin was thrilled. It had been a year or more since he had seen Captain Beasley. The Captain worked out of the Ranger Headquarters in Waco and rarely went in the field.

Laughlin hurried to his room, bathed, dressed, left the room and walked quickly toward the saloon. He entered the bar, spotted Jim and Captain
Beasley sitting in the back of the bar at a table facing the entrance. Laughlin started toward the two Rangers, when Brenda, one of the barmaids spotted Laughlin. She was sitting in a drovers lap and quickly jumped up to embrace him. The drover grabbed her by the arm, threw her to the floor and said, "You ain't going nowhere, I've spent a lot of money on you." The drover then threw a 'round house right' at Laughlin. Laughlin ducked, as the punch went over his head and from a semi crouching position, threw a vicious left hook to the man's liver.

The drover bent double and fell to the floor from pain. Laughlin turned around and two more drovers were in front of him, one lowered his head and charged, Laughlin drew his pistol and delivered a hard blow to the man's head, knocking him out. Laughlin then stuck the pistol in the other mans face with the barrel pressing in his eye. "Texas Ranger" shouted Laughlin while displaying the Ranger badge with his left hand. "This can end here with nobody going to jail or it can continue and you **will** die. Tell your men to drop their pistol belts to the floor, now!!!" The drover with Laughlin's' pistol barrel still pressing against his eyeball was trembling and stuttered as he said, "D do do what he says or he'll bl blow my head off!" Laughlin said, "You men pick up your two buddies, you can get your guns tomorrow at the sheriffs office. Get on your horses and get out of town – don't let me see any of you in town tonight."

After the men left the bar, Laughlin walked over to the table where the Rangers were sitting. They were grinning at Laughlin and had never left the table while the fight was taking place. Laughlin said, "Thanks for all the help. Couldn't you see there were three of them on me at one time?" Captain Beasley's grin increased in size and he said, "Laughlin, any Ranger can handle three men. As good as you are, we were waiting till all seven of them were in the fight." Laughlin grinned, shook Jim's hand vigorously and then embraced Captain Beasley.

Brenda, the barmaid, came over to the table and said, "Laughlin, it's so good to see you. It's always exciting when you are around. By the way, Linda is over at the hotel, she heard you were on the way and she's very anxious to see you." Linda owned the "Bent Elbow Saloon" and also the hotel. Laughlin met Linda on his first trip to Abilene when he was twenty-one and making his rounds through the state.
The three Rangers sat at the table sipping on whiskey for the next hour. Captain Beasley said there had been a lot of rustling for the past six months. Some of the ranchers had reported heavy losses and a couple of cattle drives had been hit on the trail to Abilene. They decided to meet the next morning at the sheriffs' office for more details and then ride out to the Double J Ranch. It was one of the largest ranches in the area and owned by J.J. Fox, the older brother of Herman Fox; the same rancher that gave Laughlin Sam.

They started walking to the hotel and when they reached the front door Captain Beasley asked Jim to excuse them so he could speak privately with Laughlin. Captain Beasley laid his hand on Laughlin's' shoulder and said, "Son, you're making a name for yourself and you're considered the best of all the Rangers in the field. You make me proud; keep up the good work."

When they walked into the hotel, Linda was sitting in the parlor. She was a beautiful woman with dark brown hair, blue eyes, high cheek bones and beautiful lips. She was about five foot five, an extremely small waist, with full rounded hips. She had a smile and mannerisms that could capture the heart of most men. She hugged and welcomed Captain Beasley, then she turned to Laughlin and said, "Laughlin you are more handsome every time I see you." With that said, she kissed him on the lips. Captain Beasley said, "I'll leave you two alone, big day tomorrow with an early wake up. Goodnight."

Laughlin asked Linda to sit with him in the parlor. The desk clerk brought them drinks and left the area, giving them privacy. Linda reached over and took Laughlin's hand. She said, "Laughlin, are you ok? You seem different." Laughlin turned his head, looked into her blue eyes and said, "Linda, there's something I need to tell you." Linda's body tensed and then she said, "Please do, you know how I feel about you." Laughlin said, "Linda, I've met someone and have fallen in love. She's not placing any demands; she loves me and just wants to be in my life. I am torn apart; I love her and want to be with her, but not as a Ranger. I don't know if I could be happy not being a Ranger and I could become resentful in a marriage?"

Linda lowered her head and tears rolled from her eyes. She said, "Laughlin I want you to be happy, but I love you too and I also want you in my life." "You love me?" asked Laughlin. "You never told me." "Laughlin, I knew not to press you and I hoped one day you would say you loved me too", answered Linda. Laughlin was overwhelmed, he didn't know how to react, and he didn't know what to say. Linda got up off the sofa, said "Goodnight" and left the room.

Laughlin walked out onto the porch of the hotel, took a deep breath and started walking toward the livery stable. He entered the stable and walked over to Sam's stall, found a bucket and sat down. Sam walked over, nudged Laughlin with his nose wanting to be petted. Laughlin laid his hand on the top of Sam's head and said, "Sam, this time I've got myself in a mess and I can't shoot or fight my way out. Don't ever let me introduce you to a mare or a filly."

The next morning the Rangers met at Sheriff Cletus Meeks office. Cletus was about thirty-five years old, six feet tall, and one-hundred eighty-five pounds, well groomed and commanded respect in a silent way. He had been a deputy for Wild Bill Hickok while Bill was in Abilene. Cletus was said to be fast with his pistol, a veteran of many disturbances in Abilene.

After their meeting, the Rangers saddled up and started their ride to the J.J. Fox Ranch. It was a half days ride to the ranch house, a slow ride since it was July and hot. They arrived at the ranch and immediately noticed all the activity. As they were tying their horses to the hitching post, Mr. Fox stepped out of the house and out onto the porch. In a loud and semi gruff voice he said, "Welcome Rangers, I've been waiting on you boys." He turned to a young Mexican boy at his side and said, "Pablo, take care of their horses, feed them well and spend extra time brushing them down. The Rangers will be spending the night." Laughlin responded with, "If you don't mind, give the big gray extra oats." Fox nodded OK and the boy led the horses towards the stables.

Laughlin had heard stories from Captain Beasley about Mr. Fox and was anxious to become acquainted. Fox had started building his ranch before the civil war while he was already in his fifties. He had fought Indians, rustlers, carpetbaggers and many times had taken the law into his own hands.

As they walked up to the porch, he shook Laughlin's' hand. The old man's hands were calloused and he had a very strong grip. He was about the same height as Laughlin, lean, broad shoulders, thick head of gray hair, weather beaten face, a gray handle bar moustache and the most piercing eyes Laughlin had ever seen. No gunfighter he faced had eyes to compare with Mr. Fox's.

They went to an area in the house that had a large stone fireplace decorated with antiques from all the eras of Mr. Fox's' life. It was the type of setting you could spend hours asking questions and admiring all the things from guns, buffalo mounts, rugs, Indian and Civil War artifacts and such.

When the men were seated, a young Mexican boy brought them whiskey. Mr. Fox looked at Laughlin and said, "Son, I feel like I already know you. You could ride with me and my boys anytime." Laughlin nodded in appreciation as Fox continued, "Times are changing. We're trying to build some windmills and stretch some wire. We need to rotate our herds and not overgraze. At the present time I have about fifteen thousand head with them spread out all over the ranch in designated herds. The rustlers are taking the smaller herds of around two hundred and fifty, killing drovers and the herds are disappearing. There also have been reports of two small cattle drives that disappeared, cattle and drovers. Evidently they are stealing the cattle, altering the brands and then driving them north to be sold."

After a little small talk and a well prepared dinner, they turned in for the night. The next morning they met for breakfast along with plenty of coffee and conversation. The Rangers had talked in the bunkhouse before going to sleep and had come to the conclusion this was not just some men rustling cattle, it was organized and there was a headman or maybe a group of ranchers involved.

The next morning the Rangers rode back to Abilene and Laughlin went directly to the telegraph office and sent Melissa a message informing her that he didn't know how long he would be gone; he missed her and sent his love.

After dinner, the three Rangers went to the saloon for drinks and more conversation and planning. As they were talking a young cowboy with a familiar face walked into the saloon. It was the cowboy that killed Wesley, the gambler in Laredo. The cowboy went to the bar and ordered whiskey. He was standing at the bar enjoying his drink and had not seen Laughlin at the back table.

Laughlin told Captain Beasley about him and said, "I have a good feeling about that youngster and believe he could become a Ranger." Before Captain Beasley could comment a man at the table across the room got up and went to the bar. The man definitely wasn't a drover; he was a gunslinger or gambler. He walked up behind the youngster, grabbed him by the shoulder and spun him around as he threw a roundhouse right. The cowboy stepped to the side letting the punch go over his shoulder. Then he answered with a hard straight right of his own hitting the man flush in the face. The blow broke the man's' nose and blood flowed from his nostrils as he fell to the floor. The fight had ended as abruptly as it started. Captain Beasley said to Laughlin, "Bring that young man to our table – reminds me of you."

Laughlin walked over, flashed his badge and said, "Fights over." Some local ranch hands carried the man out the door. By now the young boy had recognized Laughlin and joined them at the table as requested. Introductions were made and then Captain Beasley asked, "Who are you and what was all that about," referring to the fight. The cowboys name was Glen Ray Porter, born in Ft Worth and he had been a drover since he was twelve; he was now twenty. "There was a horse race down in Bandera about a year ago and I beat this fellow's prize horse", muttered Glen Ray. Then he added, as he motioned towards the door, "That man's name is George Barrett, a gambler and horse owner. There's getting to be more and more horse races and with a good horse you can make some real money. There's going to be a race here next Saturday and I guess when Mr. Barrett saw me, he decided to try and run me out of town." Glen Ray looked at Laughlin and continued, "I want to thank you for what you did in clearing me of that shooting in Laredo. I've heard stories about you, and never dreamed that one day I would be facing you. Thanks for not killing me."

Captain Beasley said, "Boys, I'm turning in, gotta catch the stage back to Waco in the morning. Laughlin, you and Jim know how to handle the problem out here, suggest you get a little help," then he winked at Laughlin.

The two Rangers and Glen Ray continued to sit at the table after Captain Beasley left for his room. Laughlin informed Glen Ray how he became a Ranger and said, "The same deal is being offered to you. Only a few men are good enough to be a Ranger. Now Remember, Rangers are married to the State of Texas; don't ever embarrass yourself or the State." Glen Ray beamed with excitement and pleasure then said, "I accept the offer."

Laughlin then thought about Melissa and what he had just said. As his thoughts returned, he and Jim made arrangements at the hotel for Glen Ray before deciding to meet for breakfast at 5:00 AM.

Laughlin went to his room and took advantage of a hot bath and then went to bed. His thoughts went back to Melissa and how beautiful she was. He could see her smile and how she looked when she told him she was in love. Laughlin remained torn apart not knowing which direction he should take. All the things the Captain had said, calling him his best Ranger, the comment J.J. Fox had made about how he could ride with him and what he had just told Glen Ray. All these things made him proud, but, he found himself thinking of Melissa often.

About 2:00 AM a sudden noise jarred Laughlin out of a deep sleep. He pulled his pistol from under his pillow, cocked the hammer and aimed at the dark outline of someone standing beside his bed. "Don't shoot," said a voice, "it's me, Linda." As she moved closer, Laughlin could see she was dressed in a robe. She walked directly to the side of the bed and in one motion reached up and slid the robe off. She was naked as she eased into the bed along side Laughlin. She said, "Laughlin, I know you must have feelings for me, please make love to me."

Laughlin had to fight hard to resist the feeling aroused in him by a beautiful naked woman lying next to him but he replied, "Linda, we must talk. I have strong feelings for you and I have to admit that I desire you as you lay here with me." Linda said, "Please let me make love to you, I will change your mind." Laughlin answered, "Please don't confuse me more than I already am. It's Melissa, the Rangers and now, you. I must have time to think, then make my decision, please honor my request." Linda looked at Laughlin and said with tears rolling down her checks, "Laughlin, you must really care for her to turn me away like this. She's a very lucky woman. There are few men like you anymore. I'll honor your request, but please remember, I love you and if you change your mind, I'll be waiting for you." With that said she left the room. Laughlin did not sleep the rest of the night.

CHAPTER 4

The next morning, Captain Beasley boarded the stage and asked Bob Bell if he could ride up top so they could talk. He had known Bob before he was a driver for the stage lines. The Captain asked Bob if he had seen anything out of the ordinary along his route. Bob said, "Funny you should ask. I've seen where large amounts of cattle are being driven across the road north instead of following the road to Abilene."

It was beginning to make sense to the Captain. The rustlers were hitting the areas where Fox had his herds separated into small groups for grazing purposes. The drovers were being killed; cattle were driven to a box canyon, branded and then put on the trail to be sold up north instead of Abilene.

The next morning Laughlin, Jim and Glen Ray rode out to Fox's ranch. Mr. Fox was sitting on the front porch with them when Laughlin asked him, "Do you have any enemies, anyone that doesn't like you?"

Mr. Fox said, "The only person I know would be Abe Silas, a small rancher north of my ranch." "Why would he dislike you?" asked Laughlin. "Well, about thirty-five years ago, he and his brother came to Abilene to start ranching" said Fox, then continued, "The two of them were bad, had no business ranching. One night someone stole eight horses from the Remuda (a herd of horses) at one of our grazing pastures. Me and some of my boys trailed and caught him. He was by himself, with the horses. His name was Bob Silas; we hung him and left him hanging right where we had found him with the horses. Then rode over to Abe's ranch and told him what had happened. Abe became violent and said one day he would get me for killing his brother. Then he continued to rant and we haven't spoken since." Mr. Fox explained that stealing a horse is a hanging offense; there were no judges and law enforcement, so ranchers took it on themselves to enforce the law.

Laughlin told Fox that he was going to Abe Silas' place and ask some questions and if he, Fox, had someone who could ride with them that knew the area. Fox replied, "Start riding out the south gate, Fred will catch up with you."

It was very hot and it was only noon. They walked their horses while waiting on Fred. They had not traveled far when Glen Ray said, "Look behind you, look at that horse run and look how that rider sits a horse." The rider and horse continued at a full out pace and just when it appeared he would ride by the Rangers he 'reigned up'. The horse dropped his rump almost to the ground, and dust flew from his rear hoofs and his front legs were straight. He came to a beautiful stop, something to be admired by cowboys.

In one easy motion the rider dismounted, held onto the reins and removed his sombrero. He said, "My name is Fred Ramirez and I am supposed to ride with you Rangers. It is my honor." With that he put his hat back on and with one hand on the horn of the saddle he remounted. He was Mexican, about thirty years old, long black hair hanging to his shoulders. He had on all the things of a working vaquero: sombrero, long sleeves, gloves, chaps, high top boots and big Mexican rowel spurs. He flashed extremely white teeth when he smiled and women would consider him handsome. His horse was a black stallion with high withers, long body and muscular rear end. Fred was sitting in a high candled working saddle with a lariat tied on and a scabbard with what looked like a sharps rifle.

Laughlin said, "Glad to have you riding with us." He could see Glen Ray sizing up Fred's' mount. You could bet there would be a race coming soon.

As they rode along, conversation was directed at Fred about his horse. Fred said "He's a two year old and Senor Fox gave him to me." Then added, "His name is Diablo; he is a smart horse, reins well and is mucho rapido, fastest horse on the ranch." Glen Ray was all ears and from looking at the horse he knew Fred was not bragging.

Laughlin asked Fred if that was a sharps rifle he was carrying in his scabbard. Fred said, "Si, Senor Fox gave it to me. It was one of his rifles and I am honored by a gift like the horse and rifle. El Jefe is a good man."

Laughlin asked, "Why a long range big caliber rifle?" "Senor Fox," said Fred, "Gave it to me for when I am hunting coyotes, mountain lions and other varmints that kill our stock. No coyote is too far and no rustler can ride away from me." Laughlin liked Fred.

About three hours later Laughlin reigned up, dismounted under a tree and told the boys to take a water break or at least that's what they thought it was. Laughlin had been looking for a spot to do some shooting. He wanted to see how fast and accurate Glen Ray and Jim Weaver were with their pistols.

After about a ten minute water and jerky break, Laughlin walked over to a large sandstone rock and with another rock in his hand he scratched two Ex's about chest high and a couple of yards apart. Glen Ray knew what Laughlin was doing and was anxious to show his skills. Laughlin said, "Jim, the one on the left is yours and the one on the right is yours Glen Ray. Face your target and when I say draw, pull your pistols and fire six shots."

They lined up and Laughlin hollered, "Draw!" Jim fired two shots after Glen Ray emptied his pistol. Jim Weaver, among the Rangers, was considered fast. Now, Laughlin could see how the gambler in Laredo had no chance, even though he pulled out a hideout derringer. Laughlin walked out to the rock and you could draw a twelve inch circle around the group and both men would be inside the ring.

Fred said, "Let me get my pistol." It was in his saddle bag, a working cowboy rarely wears his pistol. It gets in his way while working cattle. Laughlin watched as he strapped it on, much too low thought Laughlin. Laughlin hollered "Draw!" and Fred put six shots inside Jim Weavers circle. Laughlin figured Fred was every bit as fast as Jim and

Jim is fast. With a few adjustments of raising the holster, not extending the arm, firing over the top of the holster and ..., then Laughlin remembered, Fred's not a Ranger. Someday I could be facing him and I will not have my edge if I show him what I was just thinking.

They rode on for about an hour when Fred jumped off his horse, tied his rein tight to the d-ring on the saddle, pulled out his sharps rifle and said, "Porcupine. We try to kill them. A calf smells them and gets the needles in his nose and then the cow won't let him nurse and the calf dies. Mr. Fox wants to rid the ranch of them." Fred sat down on his butt, crossed his legs under him, laid his rifle on his lap, elevated his rear sight, and said, "Hold your horses" as he put his elbows on his knees bracing the rifle and aimed.
Laughlin finally saw the porcupine about three hundred yards out and walking slowly. BOOM! The rifle shot rang out, the porcupine exploded, a direct hit. Fred looked up and grinned. Laughlin was impressed by all three of his companions; they could be deadly when needed.

About an hour before sunset they reached the Abe Silas Ranch. The ranch was cluttered and rundown. Abe met them at the porch with a shotgun in his hands. He was in his seventies, a very thin man with snagled teeth, stubble beard, dirty and generally unkept. He had tobacco juice running out the corner of his mouth and down his chin. He was a disgusting sight with a red face associated with overuse of alcohol and was wearing filthy coveralls with only one strap hooked, long handle underwear and no shirt. Laughlin identified himself and the others, and Abe said, "Don't make any difference who you are. Get off my place. You don't have any business snooping around here and get that Mexican off my property. He works for Fox and I **will kill** any of his men on my place."

Laughlin put on a stern face, looked Silas in the eyes and said, "This Mexican happens to be my deputy. If I have to arrest you and take you to the Abilene jail for questioning, I will. It would be a lot easier for you to talk to me now." Silas' challenge had been met, he knew Laughlin meant business. Laughlin started asking questions about cattle being rustled and Silas wouldn't listen. All he did was talk about how Fox hung his brother and was trying to run them off the land. He said Fox was lying, that no one was losing cattle. He also said Fox had always wanted his ranch because of the water. Laughlin didn't buy anything that Silas had said and he didn't seem smart enough to be directing rustlers.

As they were leaving, Laughlin asked Fred why Silas didn't have a productive working ranch. Fred said, "He's lazy, loco and a drunk, but won't sell the ranch because his wife and brother are buried on the ranch."

Laughlin asked if there were any box canyons on Silas' place. Fred said, "Si, a big one over by the river, but its miles from the ranch house and stage road." Laughlin decided to make camp. They had watered the horses at the stage stop and there was good grass here for the horses. They drank coffee, ate jerky then laid down for the night. After he laid down, Laughlin was still thinking about Melissa, Linda and the rustlers. Having a feeling the rustled herds were being held in the box canyon, He said, "Fred, tomorrow I want to see that canyon."
They were up at sunup, more coffee, a bite of jerky and then back in the saddle. After about a two hour ride they approached the box canyon and heard cattle. They dismounted and climbed a cliff to a vantage point overlooking the canyon. It was full of cattle, at least two hundred fifty head. They counted seven cowboys; they were using a running iron and were hastily branding cattle.

Laughlin said to the others, "I think that's the seven cowboys that were in Abilene. They stole the cattle from J.J. Fox, drove them to this box canyon to change brands and then move the herd. I don't believe Abe Silas knows they are on his ranch." Laughlin continued, "He only has a few cowhands, he's drunk all the time and never out on the ranch. Someone is directing this operation. The question is who and where are they taking the herd."

They secured their horses behind the hill, setup camp and kept one man on the hill watching the activity below. Laughlin believed they were going to move the herd when the last steer was branded. He pretty much had decided they were driving the cattle to the Chisholm Trail. The trail ran north and south just west of Ft Worth. They probably were selling them in Ft Worth for a big profit then they would join a legitimate herd going to Kansas. Any cattleman would buy two hundred and fifty head at a good price to put into his herd.

Laughlin said, "We'll stay here tonight, out of sight, and hope their boss shows up." The next morning about two hours after sunup, a lone rider appeared on the trail going to the camp. It was George Barrett. It made sense; he didn't have a job, had gambling money, bought expensive horses and gambled heavily. Laughlin figured he had hired the seven boys to rustle, kill the drovers and then drive the herd to Ft Worth.

Laughlin told Fred to get into a position where he was elevated and could pick off anyone leaving the canyon. Then he said that he, Jim and Glen Ray would ride in hard and strong about 50 yards apart with Jim on his left and Glen Ray on his right but needed to avoid a stampede if possible. So they started in slow. Laughlin wanted the fifty yard gaps so the rustlers would have to go between them if they tried to ride out of the canyon. If they got by the three of them, Fred was ready on the edge of the canyon with that sharps.

Three of the men were branding and three were roping. The other cowboy was with George Barrett, apparently getting directions. Laughlin's' adrenalin was flowing; he gets a high out of dangerous situations. He held up his Ranger badge, they rode in fast and hollered, "Rangers, you are all under arrest!" The three riders that were mounted broke for the mouth of the canyon. The three that were branding tried to get to their horses. Two were on Jims' side and one was on Glen Rays' side. They never reached their horses; Jim dropped two of them with his pistol and Glen Ray got the other one. Laughlin heard three rifle shots; he knew the riders had reached Fred and wondered if they had escaped.

George Barrett had a big bandage on his nose that fell off as he ran for the rocks along with the remaining drover. Laughlin had to laugh and turned to Glen Ray and said, "Go get him, I want him alive. I'll take the drover." The drover had almost reached the cover of the rocks when Laughlin dropped him with his 44.40 rifle while on horse back at about one hundred yards. The Rangers knew that Barrett didn't have a rifle so they stayed back out of pistol distance and watched Glen Ray go to work.

Glen Ray hollered up to the man, "Give it up, you're the only one left." All the time Glen Ray was walking to the base of the hill, Barrett was on the side of the hill about twenty yards away and hiding behind a rock. All of a sudden, Barrett jumped out from behind the rock with pistol in hand. Glen Ray put a bullet in his right shoulder knocking him to the ground then climbed the hill and brought him down.

There was a wagon in the camp so they hitched up some horses, took all the guns off the bodies then unsaddled and removed the bridles from their horses and loaded the dead bodies in the wagon.

While this was being done, Laughlin rode out to the mouth of the canyon and Fred was off the ledge, on horseback and checking three dead bodies. "Good shooting" said Laughlin as he estimated one shot being four hundred yards. Fred grinned and said, "Remember, no coyote is to fast and no rustler can ride away."

The wagon was loaded, horses turned loose, George Barrett was made to drive the wagon as they headed back to Abilene. Cletus met them when they rode in and said there were reports to be made by Laughlin and that he would like to join them for dinner. Laughlin told them to go to their rooms and get ready for a seven o'clock celebration.

After taking care of business with Cletus, Laughlin went to his room and he saw a note pinned to his pillow. He crossed the room and picked up the note. He hesitated before opening it and thought to himself, do I read this or throw it away. The note read, 'Laughlin, I'm glad you are safe. Love, Linda'. He started to crush the note and throw it away, but he hesitated, then folded the note and put it in his wallet.

They had a nice dinner, drinks and congratulations from Cletus to all four men and then Laughlin toasted his three men for a job well done. They were tired and knew the 5:00 AM breakfast would come early so they turned in.

The next morning during breakfast Laughlin told Jim to take Glen Ray to Ft Worth and try to find out who was buying the stolen cattle. He told Fred that he was returning to the Fox Ranch with him and he'd give Mr. Fox all the details about the rustlers.

During the ride to the ranch, Laughlin and Fred talked. Fred said he was honored to have ridden with the Rangers and to have been a temporary deputy. He said he greatly admired the Rangers and it was his pleasure to have ridden with the best, Laughlin McFarland.

They reached the ranch gate and a rider from the corral was riding at full gallop towards them. Fred said, "Here comes Mr. Fox, look at that, I hope I can ride like that when I'm over seventy years old." "Howdy boys," said Fox, "lets ride up to the ranch house. I want to hear all about it." The three of them sat on the porch and Laughlin gave Mr. Fox the full report.

They talked for an hour or more and then Laughlin asked Fred to leave, that he needed to speak with Mr. Fox in private. They both shook Fred's hand and patted him on the back. Fred grinned then nodded and touched his hat, mimicking Laughlin. Laughlin broke into a big grin and said, "Get out of here amigo."

Mr. Fox and Laughlin sat down in the living room and Laughlin said, "Tell me about Fred." "Well," said Fox, "he was born on this ranch. His entire family lives and works here. He has three brothers and two sisters. Sisters cook for me and do housework, have been since my wife died. Brothers are vaqueros for me and top notch, not as good as Fred, but good."

"Fred is the best I've ever seen with horses. He breaks all the horses, oversees all the working horses, veterinarian, you name it, he can do it. I've been around Indian trackers for the army, they can't compare to Fred, and he's got a gift. He can track a man, horse, animal, and absolutely will not give up on a trail. He is a marksman with that sharps 45.70 and lightening fast with his six gun. One man can't handle him in a fist fight. My wife and I weren't able to have children and Fred is like the son that I never had. Now don't go telling me that you want him to be a Ranger." Laughlin grinned and said, "The Rangers would love to have him, only a few have what it takes and he qualifies. However, I would never ask him without talking to you. The way he speaks of you tells me there is a strong bond between the two of you."

Mr. Fox looked at Laughlin and said, "If he wants to be a Ranger, I will approve of it. I want Fred to be happy." Laughlin said, "No, I won't ask him, but if we ever need someone to track, I may send for him." Mr. Fox said, "That's fine, feel free." Laughlin looked Mr. Fox in the eyes, grinned and then said, "What a shot, four-hundred yards, rolled him off that horse and you won't let me have him as a Ranger." They laughed; shook hands and Laughlin mounted up and headed toward Uvalde. Laughlin wondered as he rode off if one day Fred would own the Fox Ranch. The trip from Abilene to Uvalde seemed longer than he remembered, but he knew it was because he was anxious to see Melissa.

Laughlin and Sam arrived about 2:00 PM, it was hot, dry, and they both were ready for a rest. He had wired Melissa before he left Abilene to inform her when to expect him and had barely dismounted when Melissa ran out the door, leaped into his arms, hugged and kissed him. Then she said, with excitement in her voice, "Thank God you are alright. I've been so worried, especially after learning of the shoot out in the street before you left for Abilene. Why didn't you tell me? Never mind, you can tell me later. You're going to the ranch and spend some

time with me. Wait right here." She turned, rushed into the restaurant, returned quickly with a box lunch and a big apple in her hand. She went to Sam, gave him the apple and rubbed his nose. She then turned to a beautiful Paint Horse tied to the hitching post and swung up and onto the saddle and said, "Lets' go, I've been waiting on you. Got my riding pants on, a picnic lunch and we're going to the ranch."
Laughlin didn't have time to say he would like to bathe, shave, and change clothes. He could see he was in a woman's world now and it didn't matter about the trail dust on him. Melissa was happy having him back.

A short distance outside Uvalde they stopped near a shaded creek with a nice area for their picnic. Laughlin loosened the cinch on Sam and Princess' saddle so they could drink and graze. Melissa spread the food on a tablecloth: fried chicken, potato salad, beans and for dessert, pudding. They sat partially on the plush grass and on the tablecloth and prepared to eat. Laughlin grabbed a big juicy looking drumstick, Melissa looked at Laughlin and said, "Can we bless this food and will you do it?" Laughlin was startled, he had never blessed food or prayed out loud. He didn't want to say no to Melissa, so he tried. He didn't know what to say, he hesitated, then he prayed. "God, thank you for the food that we are about to receive and for bringing Melissa into my life – Amen." He was shaking but he felt good, real good. After eating lunch they mounted up and galloped to the ranch. Melissa was an excellent rider and Laughlin was sure that Sam thought Princess was pretty.

When they reached the ranch, Melissa told Laughlin to make himself comfortable, take his bath and she would have Candido, her ranch fore-man, take care of the horses, "I know, extra oats for Sam." Candido's wife, Maria, cooks for Melissa when she is at the ranch and she was going to prepare dinner and serve. Candido and Maria live in a nice little house built especially for the foreman and his family. They worked for Melissa's father-in-law and stayed on when he died.

Maria prepared a wonderful Mexican dinner: rice, beans, tortillas,

chicken mole with a dessert called flan and wine to drink. After dinner they sat in the swing on the front porch, enjoying the breeze and conversation. Melissa was very concerned about the shootout in front of the restaurant. "How many more men are out there with grudges?" she asked. "Laughlin, you didn't tell me about the shoot out; I heard about it when I went to town after you left for Abilene. What happened in Abilene? Were you involved in more killings? What's going to happen tomorrow?" Laughlin looked at Melissa; she had tears running down her cheeks. Laughlin firmed up the tone of his voice and said, "Melissa, I'm a Texas Ranger, danger and death ride with me every day of my life. I know you're concerned about me, but please, don't press me. I might not make the decision you want." "Laughlin, I am so sorry", sobbed Melissa, "it's just that I love you. I
promise not to confuse you more. I will accept you as a Ranger or as a rancher, just as long as I'm with you." With that said she took Laughlin by the hand and led him to the bedroom.

When Laughlin awoke the next morning, Melissa was cuddled next to him with her head lying on his arm. He kissed her closed eye lids and she awoke. She said "Good morning" and gave him a kiss. Then she said like an anxious little girl, "Today I'm going to show you around the ranch." They had coffee and jelly toast while Maria prepared a boxed lunch. In a few minutes Candido brought Sam and Princess to the hitching post in front of the house and notified them the horses were ready. Sam looked very handsome and Princess was tantalizing him by biting him on the neck.

The ranch house sat on the north end of the property that covered approximately fifty thousand acres. It was a horse and mule ranch, the government had signed a long term contract with Melissa and it was honored as long as she could meet their demands. Laughlin could see into the future and if for some reason the demand for horses expired, it could be a great cattle ranch. It had water and good grass with easy delivery of a herd to Abilene.

He had been observant as he rode throughout Texas and had seen windmills, fencing, and pasture rotation to prevent over grazing thereby producing a heavier beef. Exactly what Mr. Fox was doing on his ranch could be done on Melissa's' ranch.

As they continued to ride Laughlin made sure to take occasional breaks for Melissa's' benefit but when he requested a fourth break, Melissa looked at him and said, "I know what you are doing and I am not tired." Then she said, "Catch me if you can, let's ride Princess." She nudged Princess with her boot heel as they broke into a full gallop.

Laughlin was caught by surprise; the picture was pretty as she raced off. The paint horse and Melissa, leaning forward in the saddle, her hair blowing back and urging Princess on with her quirt. All of a sudden Laughlin realized that she was getting farther away and Princess wasn't a slow horse.

"Let's go Sam!" and he responded, almost rolling Laughlin out the back of his saddle. Sam wanted to catch that little filly and the race was on. The terrain was level with a good surface and after a mile Sam had closed a one hundred yard gap down to about thirty five when Melissa reigned up. When Laughlin rode up beside her she looked over at Sam and said, "Sam, it's a good thing there's no lady outlaws, you never would catch them" and she laughed heartily. Laughlin could feel his love growing; he had never been around a woman like her.

When they returned to the ranch house it was almost sundown. They rode by the corral where several vaqueros were breaking horses so they stopped and watched the rodeo. The ranch was well situated for horses, with corrals, stalls, blacksmith shop, hay barns, bunkhouse and foreman's quarters. Laughlin could see how this ranch could work for horses, cattle or both. They left the horses with Candido and walked back toward the ranch house. As they walked, Melissa held on to Laughlin's arm as if he might try to get away. He asked, "Why are you holding on so tight?" She said, "I'm afraid you are going to leave; today has been the best day of my life."

Candido and Maria had prepared grilled steaks, baked squash and baked potato for dinner. After bathing and preparing for dinner, Laughlin asked Candido and Maria to join them. He wanted to ask Candido some business questions. After dinner, Candido and Laughlin went to the porch and talked. Then, after about thirty minutes of questions and answers, Laughlin said to Candido, "I was concerned about some of the things I saw today. For example, the stalls needed cleaning. Horses should never be kept in a filthy stall. I also noticed that more attention should be paid to the working horses, their hooves look bad. A horse is only as good as his feet. This place has been left unsupervised except for you. The ranch will reflect your attitude. If you clean this place up and put your men to work, you'll have a good opportunity here don't let it get away." Laughlin paused, looked Candido directly in the eyes and growled, ""nuf said?" When Laughlin returned to the house, Melissa asked, "What did y'all talk about?" "We discussed the girls in the saloon back in Uvalde" said Laughlin with his boyish grin. "Oh yeah," said Melissa as she reached for Laughlin's' hand. "Come with me and I'll show you what a real woman is like."

The next morning was a typical Texas summer day. Laughlin was up at four-thirty but he had left Melissa sleeping while he went to the front porch and watched the birth of a new day. It was peaceful and beautiful watching the sun come up slowly over the horizon. He felt blessed and said a prayer of thanks for the new found blessings in his life. He was sitting on the porch with his feet on the steps and deep in thought when Melissa kissed him on
the cheek and handed him a cup of coffee. She sat down beside him, laid her hand on his and said, "Laughlin, I love you." Laughlin turned to her and gave her a kiss on the lips.

The front gate was about a half mile from the ranch house. Laughlin could see a rider followed by a dust trail riding fast and coming through the gate. Melissa saw the rider and she knew Laughlin was being called for duty. Her heart cried but she held back the tears.

The rider met them in the yard and said, "Telegram for Ranger

McFarland." Laughlin opened the telegram and it read '**CAPTAIN BEASLEY SHOT – ALIVE – IN WACO – CALLING FOR YOU**'. Melissa was at his side holding onto his arm, she could see it was bad news by the look on Laughlin's' face. He turned to her and said, "I have to go, Captain Beasley's been shot." Laughlin's' face had turned almost to stone and the look in his eyes was cold and hard. She knew Laughlin would get the person responsible. She had never seen that look in his eyes; it was scary, now she knew why men were afraid of Laughlin.

Melissa helped him prepare for the long ride he was about to take. He was in a hurry. Sam was saddled and brought to the house. Laughlin tied on his saddle bags, bed roll, rifle and poncho. He hugged Melissa tightly, kissed her passionately, told her he loved her and rode off at a gallop.

When he was out of sight, Melissa ran into the house, fell across the bed, cried and prayed. She prayed for Laughlin's safety and for Captain Beasley. She could hear Laughlin's' words, 'Each time I ride away could be the last time you see me alive. It's not fair to you being a Rangers wife.' None of that mattered; she knew without Laughlin, she had no life.

Chapter 5

As Laughlin rode to Waco his head was spinning; he was concerned, angry and prayed to God for Captain Beasley's' recovery. He rode Sam hard and he responded as if he knew they were in a crisis. When Laughlin rode into Waco, Sam was heavily lathered and very tired. He rode straight to the livery stable and gave instructions for Sam to have plenty of oats, lots of water and to walk him until he cooled down, then brush him dry. He also asked for another horse to be used while in Waco, hopefully this would give Sam time to rest.

After taking care of Sam, he went to the sheriffs' office. There he found Ranger Jim Weaver, Glen Ray, and Sheriff Steve Ballard. Jim and Glen Ray immediately started walking Laughlin to the doctors' office where the Captain was being treated. As they walked Laughlin was filled in with the available information about the shooting.

Captain Beasley had been on his way to Ft. Worth on a personal trip to see his newly born grandson. He was riding the stagecoach when it was held up by three men. The stage wasn't carrying any money, just the mail, passengers and their luggage. They took all the personal items from the passengers: watches, cash and jewelry from the female passengers. For the safety of passengers Captain Beasley was co-operating in order to avoid a shoot out. As they were searching the Captain they found his Ranger badge. He was held and severely beaten. After mounting their horses' one of the men shot the Captain three times as he lay face down and unconscious in the dirt. Bob Bell, the stage coach driver, loaded the Captain in the stage. Since Waco was the closest, he turned around and brought him back there for medical help.

They walked into the doctors' office; it had a treatment room in the doctor's back bedroom. The doctor, an elderly and distinguished looking man named Abe Greene, greeted them and gave them an update on Captain Beasley's condition. He said, "Captain Beasley is a tough and strong man, but it will take everything he's got to survive. He's been

beaten badly, has some broken ribs, a concussion and three gunshot wounds. One shot in his leg,
one in his shoulder and the other high in the back, narrowly missing his lung." Pneumonia, infections and loss of blood was his concern and the next three days would determine his fate. "Son," the doctor said to Laughlin, "he's been asking for you since they brought him in."

Captain Beasley was awake when they entered the room. Laughlin was shocked when he saw how bad he had been beaten. His eyes were almost shut and his face was swollen like a pumpkin with purple bruises on his lips and ears. Laughlin stood next to the bed, grasped his hand and said, "Ranger McFarland reporting," with a smile. The Captain tried to smile and squeezed Laughlin's hand. Laughlin told him that he knew the details given to him by the sheriff and asked, "Do you know who it was?" The Captain whispered, "Howard Spotted Horse, Charlie Little Elk, and Shorty Hendricks." Laughlin knew them; they had broken out of the penitentiary and were on Wanted Posters.

Laughlin told the Captain to rest and he would see him in the morning, then they returned to the sheriffs' office. The sheriff, Steve Ballard, a long time lawman was bald, with a full white beard and heavy frame. He was a strong man with a good reputation. Laughlin briefed everyone about the men. Howard Spotted Horse was the leader of the gang. He had been captured during an Indian raid and raised by Indians until he was twelve. Soldiers found him in an Indian camp, brought him back to live with his people, but it never worked. He was wild, dangerous and had been sent to prison for knifing a rancher while looting the ranch house. He hated anyone with authority and should be considered extremely dangerous. Charlie Little Elk, a half-breed, was riding with Spotted Horse when they were captured and sent to prison. Shorty Hendricks had also been sent to prison for robbery and cattle rustling. That's where he had met Spotted Horse and Little Elk; they all broke out together.

For the next three days the Rangers stayed in Waco and watched over Captain Beasley. His condition seemed to be improving daily. Laughlin told Captain Beasley that they were going to Ft Worth to try and find the gang. He vowed to the Captain that he would find the trio and bring them back "Dead or Alive". The Captain nodded and tried to smile. Laughlin laid his hand on top of the Captains hand and said with tears in his eyes, "You are the Father I never had. What I am today is because of you. I love you." Tears rolled from the Captain's swollen eyes and down his cheeks.

Laughlin asked Jim and Glen Ray to get the horses and meet him at the telegraph office. He sent a wire to Melissa: **Captain is better – Going to Ft Worth in pursuit of three men – Love and miss you – Sam said tell Princess that he misses her too.**

Sheriff Ballard rode with them and pointed out where the hold-up happened. According to Bob Bell, the stage driver, the group rode off in the direction of Ft Worth. The trail was too old for tracking so they rode at a gallop. It was a two day ride, ninety miles to Ft Worth which was known as a "cowtown" with a large stockyard about two miles from the town. Lots of money changed hands in the area of the stockyards: hotels, saloons, and brothels. Drovers, ranchers, buyers, bankers and outlaws walked the streets around the stockyards. Laughlin knew the trio would be in cheap saloons, brothels or in one of the make shift hotels that slept fifty men or more on the floor, hallway or wherever they could throw down a bedroll.

Laughlin, Jim and Glen Ray checked into one of the better hotels then met at the Cattlemen's Restaurant for dinner. Laughlin knew one of the waitresses, her name was Jeanette. She was a long legged, attractive blonde that always flirted with Laughlin when he was in the restaurant. Jeanette spotted Laughlin when he came in and quickly seated them in her area so she could wait on them. They ordered and enjoyed their meal. After dining, Laughlin asked Jeanette to join them. She sat down at the table and Laughlin noticed that Glen Ray was admiring her.

Laughlin told her of the three men they were looking for and why. Jeanette said, "Sounds like you're looking for three men that were involved in a shooting night before last. The men were rolling cowboys down on Exchange Avenue. They were hiding between saloons; when a cowboy left the saloon and was walking on the boardwalk, they would grab him, take him into the alley, knock him in the head and take his poker winnings. They did this several times then got all liquored up. When it started raining they went to one of the flop houses and were recognized by one of the cowboys they had rolled. There was gun play in the flop house and the cowboy was killed by one of them. They all shot at him. The sheriff rode out after them toward Weatherford but lost their trail when the rain washed away their tracks." Laughlin tipped her, thanked her for the information and rose from the table. Glen Ray, who didn't get up, said, "I'm going to stay a little longer if Jeanette doesn't mind." She looked pleased.

The next morning they met with Sheriff Jim Elick. He told them that information had just been wired to him saying Shorty Hendricks was born in Brady, TX and the group might be going there to hide out with his kinfolk. They went to the livery stable, picked up their horses and purchased a four year old Gelding, named Trailer for a pack horse. He had gotten his name because he would trail behind you even without a lead. Trailer was a bay with a blaze face and three white feet. He would be used to pack for three riders; they would be out for long periods at a time without a chance to buy more supplies.

They rode west and reached Stephenville on the second day. As usual, first stop was the livery stable. Laughlin told them to take care of Sam, have him re-shoed and ready to go in the morning. He told the boys to go to the hotel and get a room; then he wired Melissa, gave her the direction they were traveling and his love. Immediately afterwards, he sent a telegram to Waco inquiring about Captain Beasley. The return telegraph read: **Captain Beasley died three days ago – Collapsed lung and pneumonia.** Laughlin could not believe what he read, he read it again.

When Laughlin walked into the hotel room it was evident by the look on his face there was something wrong. His jaw was squared, his face was as if it was made of stone and his dark steel blue eyes were on fire with anger. He handed Jim the note and asked him and Glen Ray for some privacy. They silently left the room. Laughlin walked over to the bed, sat down, put his face in his hands and cried hard, very hard.

Laughlin told Jim and Glen Ray they were going to Brady, find Shorty's relatives and pressure them for Shorty's whereabouts.

They saddled up and rode southwest toward Brady. It was August; the days were hot so they rode slow. Laughlin had to discipline himself, he wanted to ride hard and quickly avenge the Captains' death. It was all he could do to exercise his training; his anger was growing more each day.

Brady was a very small town. The combination Post Office/General Store had the most activity. The postmaster told Laughlin that the Hendricks place was about fifteen miles south of town towards Ozuna. The ranch was very small and had not been worked in years. It was occupied by Mr. & Mrs. Hendricks and yes they did have a boy, Charley; he was no good and mean. The last they had heard he was in the penitentiary.

When they arrived at the Hendricks place it was late in the day, overcast and misting. Dogs started barking and nipping at the horses hooves as they approached the house. The dogs had done their job; there was no chance of surprise. They rode up to the front porch and were met by an old man dressed in bib overalls, no shirt, just his long handle underwear serving as a shirt, britches tucked in boots that came to his knees, and a heavily sweat stained felt hat with no shape. His sleeves were stained with snuff where he had been wiping. He had a double barrel shotgun in his hands with both hammers cocked. In the doorway stood his wife, gray uncombed hair, no teeth, snuff dripping from her mouth as well and a worn out dress that probably hadn't been washed in six months.

Laughlin introduced himself as a Texas Ranger and told the man he wanted to talk with Shorty. Old man Hendricks blurted out, "He ain't here, don't know where he is." Laughlin said, "We think he is here, and we're going to find him. Put your shotgun down; don't make us take it from you. You don't want a shootout and neither do we." Laughlin figured the group might have split, especially since Shorty, Spotted Horse and Little Elk were old friends. Laughlin got off his horse, stared the old man down, walked up and took the shotgun away from him. Laughlin said, "I'll go in the house and flush him out. Y'all cover each side of the house." Nothing happened; he had to be in the storm cellar or in the barn if he was here. They approached the storm cellar, raised the door, it was empty. About that time they heard a horse run out the backside of the barn. It was Shorty and he was riding hard. "Go get him but don't kill him," shouted Laughlin, "bring him to me." Glen Ray spun his horse, sod flew from his hooves, the horses' ears were laid back, Glen Ray was leaning forward in the saddle and Laughlin knew he would have Shorty soon.

Laughlin and Jim walked their horses in the direction that Shorty had taken. In about twenty minutes they saw Glen Ray trotting his horse. Shorty was running behind with a rope around his waist. Laughlin rode up to Shorty and asked. "Who shot the Ranger?" Shorty shouted, "I don't know what you're talking about! I don't know anything about any Ranger being shot!" Laughlin dismounted, walked over to Shorty, removed the rope and said, "You three boys like to beat up on a Ranger. Well, I'm going to give you a chance to beat up one now." Shorty pleaded, "I don't want to fight you, haven't done anything." Laughlin walked within punching range and Shorty threw a punch. It was the last punch he would throw; Laughlin hit him with a right hand that crumpled Shorty. He then picked him up off the ground, held him up with his left hand and sunk his right hand into Shorty's stomach and rib cage at least ten times. It was evident that Laughlin had lost control. While holding him up he looked Shorty in the eyes and said, "He was my best friend," then he threw a vicious right hand that spread Shorty's nose all over his face and he began to bleed profusely. The blow knocked Shorty to the ground and landed him on his back.

Laughlin straddled him, put a thumb in each corner of Shorty's mouth and said, "Tell me who shot the Ranger, if you don't I will tear your face apart." Jim and Glen Ray were fearful of him. Then Laughlin seemed to gather himself as he stood over Shorty and said, "Tell me who shot the Ranger and where they are. Tell me the truth or this dance starts all over again." Shorty was barely conscious and struggling to breathe, his nose was badly broken and no telling how many ribs. Shorty said, "Spotted Horse is crazy, he shot the Ranger. We heard he died and we headed for Mexico at Del Rio. I had to get away from them, they stay crazy drunk and I left them at Brady. I thought they were going to kill me when I wanted out, but they didn't." Laughlin said, "Put him on his horse, tie his hands behind him, I'm going to hang him before we get to San Angelo. Want him to think about it awhile." Shorty started crying and begging; Glen Ray and Jim looked at each other but dared not challenge Laughlin. They camped that night and Shorty begged and cried, "Please don't hang me; I'm sorry for what we done." He wheezed and gasped for air all night and Laughlin would say to him, "Don't die before I can hang you."

It was late in the evening and they were about a mile from San Angelo when Laughlin spotted a good hanging tree. They rode up under the tree; Laughlin stopped and said, "It's time. Let's get it done." Then he took his lariat and made a hangman's noose. Shorty screamed, cried, begged to the Lord for forgiveness, "Please don't hang me!" Laughlin rode under the tree limb and threw the rope over the limb. Glen Ray and Jim watched without saying a word, they were scared of Laughlin. He looked sternly at Shorty and said, "Glen Ray, bring his horse over here under that limb. Jim, tie the other end of the rope around another tree." With that done he slipped the noose over Shorty's head and around his neck. Glen Ray was holding the reigns on Shorty's horse to keep it from bolting and hoping Laughlin wouldn't do it. Shorty was pleading and trying not to scare his horse. Shorty was on the verge of passing out, he had pissed all over himself. Laughlin rode over beside Shorty, looked him in the eyes and said, "One thing and one thing only is stopping me from hanging you and that is the Ranger code; we are to enforce the law, not take the law in our own hands. As much as I want to hang you, I won't. The law will do the job for me."

"Jim, take him off his horse and set him on the ground. Glen Ray, put the noose around his ankles." Laughlin had the rope around his saddle horn and rode forward lifting Shorty into the air up side down. He tied off the rope and rode on in to San Angelo. Laughlin went to the sheriffs' office, told the sheriff where and why Shorty was hanging, to cut him down, put him in jail and wire Waco to have the Rangers come pick him up for trial.

They ate in the restaurant that night and not a thing was said about Shorty. The trip to Del Rio was discussed and they hoped they could catch up to Spotted Horse and Little Elk before they left town. They finished their meal and Laughlin wanted to go check on Sam. When Laughlin was far enough that he couldn't hear them, Jim looked at Glen Ray and said, "What a Ranger!" Glen Ray looked at Jim and said, "No, what a **Man**!"

Laughlin sat in Sam's stall and talked to him about Captain Beasley and how he had taught him to be a Ranger. He told him how much he was going to miss his Captain and how he wished he was with Melissa and in her arms. He just needed someone to talk with and console him. The next morning they rode out of San Angelo toward Del Rio at a slow walk. It was hot, dusty and windy. Jim rode up beside Laughlin and asked, "Are you alright?" Laughlin nodded. That's what he liked about Jim, he didn't say much, but you could count on him. They camped early that evening at a clear stream, had coffee, beans and bacon for their meal, and sat around the campfire.

Laughlin took advantage of the early stop to brief Glen Ray and Jim. He said he had seen Wanted Posters of Spotted Horse and Little Elk. "Little Elk is a half breed about thirty years old, five foot eight inches tall, one hundred seventy-five pounds, dark hair to his shoulders and a little bit of facial hair on his chin. He is uneducated, very quiet, and good with a knife and rifle. His pistol is usually a hideout gun. Liquor is his down fall, always drinking and if available he will drink till he passes out. He is very good on horse back and hard to find if you are trailing him. He is sneaky and dangerous; you must think the way he does, if necessary be prepared to bring him in dead."

"Spotted Horse is around thirty years old, white man raised by the Indians, six feet tall, broad shoulders, narrow waist, one hundred eighty-five pounds. Has dark shoulder length hair, bad temper, especially when drunk, likes to fight and uses a knife. Wears a pistol, but prefers his rifle. He has no conscience, hates everyone, and very brutal with some of his victims – reverts to the Indian way, likes to torture before killing." "Since the three of them escaped over a year ago, it's believed they've killed fourteen people, sometimes just for a watch or a horse. Don't kill Spotted Horse, he's mine", said Laughlin.

"We'll ride into Del Rio after dark, if they see us before we see them they can cut us down in the street. Conceal your Ranger badges and stay together. One hotel room, one man on watch all night, they may come to us, remember, they know Indian tactics." They went to the hotel, checked in, told the clerk not to mention they were in town then paid him to take the horses to the livery stable.

The night was uneventful and Laughlin was certain they had gone straight to Mexico. They could be recognized easily and Shorty said they heard the Ranger had died. These factors made it certain they had crossed the River. They knew the Rangers would be coming mad and mean.

Laughlin said, "Boys, take off your badges, put them in your saddle bag. We're going on a sight seeing trip in Mexico."

They crossed the Rio Grande into Acuna. Acuna's life depended on the river, it consisted of make shift shacks next to the river. The best building in town was the cantina. It was a roost for outlaws, prostitutes and had no law enforcement except for the gun on your side.

They rode to the cantina. There were no horses tied in front or rear. They entered the cantina and immediately were rushed by the young

Mexican prostitutes. Laughlin asked, "Who speaks English?" One of the girls spoke broken English and was able to communicate. Laughlin held some money in his hand and said, "Yours if you tell me where the two men have gone." The girls name was Carmelita and she told Laughlin the men had a campsite on the river about two miles downstream. She said they were dressed like vaqueros, but they weren't Mexican. She also said they had been coming to the cantina the last two nights, drinking and partying with the girls.

Laughlin decided to wait in the cantina in hopes they would come to them, but they didn't. Maybe they were told about the Rangers and had decided to move on. The two outlaws knew the Rangers were out of their jurisdiction in Mexico, but they had killed a Ranger and the Rangers would not honor any rules.

Jim and Glen Ray met with Laughlin to discuss his plan. He said, "It will probably be a long chase assuming they know we're here. We must avoid an ambush; they'll shoot our horses out from under us to put us on foot. Today we'll ride down river, find their camp and try to pick up their trail. We have to be very careful they don't ride in a circle and come up behind us." The Rangers had plenty of provisions since they had loaded Trailer's packs before leaving Del Rio. They filled their canteens and carried extra water in goat skins. If the trail took them deep into Mexico, water would be unavailable except in villages or Missions with a well.

They left Acuna mid-morning. It was hot and windy with desert like terrain. They found where the men had camped and picked up their trail; it headed south. The trail looked to be two days old. Laughlin knew the chance for an ambush would increase the next day. The terrain would change and they would be going thru some passes. When they camped that evening, no fire was built and Laughlin again reminded Jim and Glen Ray, the men will be using Indian tactics, protect your horses. They bedded down with one man on guard duty and a total of three bedrolls spread out; Laughlin's was empty.

After everyone was in bed, Laughlin went out about one hundred yards in the direction they were traveling, sat down under a mesquite tree, pulled some small limbs over him and laid his double barrel shotgun in his lap. His plan was to surprise the killers if they came back to attack the Ranger camp.

Chapter 6

About two hours before sunrise Laughlin heard horses, it was a moonlit night and he could see them get off their horses about fifty yards away. They crouched low and started sneaking up on the Ranger camp. One of the men was coming directly toward Laughlin and carrying a rifle. When he was about ten yards away, Laughlin, while still sitting, said, "Drop your rifle." The startled man fired his rifle toward Laughlin; the bullet went high over his head. Laughlin pulled both triggers on the shotgun, fire flew from the barrels lighting up the area and Laughlin could see the full load strike the outlaw in the face. He quickly loaded the shotgun; then he heard a horse ride off. About that time he heard a horse from the Ranger camp, it came riding by Laughlin. It was Jim Weaver. He was after the other man that was already on horseback. Then he heard Glen Ray running thru the brush and hollering, "Are you okay? Are you okay?" Laughlin hollered out, "Over here, I'm fine!" The Rangers heard several rifle shots and then silence. Glen Ray said, "Jim cinched up his saddle that was still on his horse and was gone in a flash after the rider."

In a short time they heard Jims' voice, "It's okay; I'm coming in. I think I got Spotted Horse." He came thru the brush dragging a man, head first with his rope under the armpits. You could tell damage had been done to him other than being dragged thru the brush. He had at least a six inch cut on his eyebrow and his eye was swollen shut. His front teeth were missing and his upper lip was cut completely thru and only one side was holding it on. Jim had removed his right glove, it was bloody and his hand was swollen as if he had stuck it in a beehive.

Laughlin was looking at Spotted Horse as he lay on the ground and he felt cheated. Jim walked over to Laughlin and said, "I'm sorry, but me and the Captain go back a long way. He was my best friend just as he was yours. Me and Glen Ray can ride off with Little Elk's body and leave you here with Spotted Horse if that's what you wish." Laughlin looked at Jim and said, "Thanks. A man can't always do what he wants.

He has to follow his oath. That was taught to me by Captain Beasley and he would have wanted me to bring Spotted Horse in for trial. We'll see him hang in the proper way."

With that said they shook hands and hugged one another. Glen Ray had watched and heard. He was learning why it was special to be a Ranger.

They rode back to Del Rio, left Little Elks' body for burial, had Spotted Horse patched up by the doctor, stayed overnight and left the next day for Uvalde. Laughlin would stay in Uvalde, Jim and Glen Ray would take Spotted Horse to Waco for trial. A week before he was put on trial, Laughlin and Melissa would travel to Waco for the trial and hanging. After that they would go to Austin and visit Captain Beasley's' grave.

Once in Uvalde they put Spotted Horse in jail under constant supervision. Someone spotted Laughlin and told Melissa that he had just ridden down Main Street to the jail. As he came out of the jail she flew into his arms, kissing him and said, "Thank God you're safe." She would not let Glen Ray and Jim stay at the hotel; they all went to the ranch. Sam and the other horses were glad to have stalls, oats, hay and fresh water. Princess was in the stall next to Sam, they had missed each other.

The Rangers were very tired; they ate dinner, drank some wine and retired for the night. Laughlin and Melissa laid down, and while he was telling her about the chase he went to sleep. She smiled, held him tight and went to sleep with him in her arms.

The next morning they had breakfast then Glen Ray and Jim saddled up for their long trip transporting Spotted Horse to Waco. Laughlin told them to be careful and wire him when they got there. As they rode out thru the gate, Laughlin felt different than in the past. He wasn't sorry he wasn't going with them. He turned to Melissa, gave her a kiss and said, "Take me into your custody."

Several days had passed when Laughlin told Melissa that he realized he had not been acting like himself and he was sorry. She said, "Laughlin, while you were on the chase, you were angry. Now that it's over, you are starting to grieve. Captain Beasley was like a father to you, you loved him. Go ahead and grieve, cry if you feel like." Laughlin said, "I have a hurt that I never felt before. Thank you for being here for me. I love you."

Laughlin received a telegram from Jim; he said they were in Waco. Spotted Horse was in jail; jury had been selected and had a trial date in ten days.
While preparing for the trip Laughlin included the trial, the hanging, and a trip to Captain Beasley's grave. This would expose Melissa to things she had never seen or encountered before. Laughlin hoped it would not be too much for her. The next day the two of them caught the stage in Uvalde. They would go to San Antonio, Austin and then to Waco.

They went thru Austin, but couldn't stop to visit Captain Beasley's' grave site. They would have to get off the stage and it would be a week before another stage would arrive. Laughlin did not want to miss the trial and the hanging. He was coming back to Austin on the way to Uvalde.

Waco was filled with people that had come for the trial and to see the man that killed the famous Captain Beasley. Some people had traveled more than a hundred miles. The hotels were full; people were sleeping in their wagons, and some on the ground. It was almost a carnival atmosphere. Jim reserved two rooms at the hotel. Laughlin and Melissa weren't married, so he figured he would let them make the decision. Laughlin and Jim shared a room and Melissa stayed alone.

The trial only took a few hours. The passengers on the stage and Bob Bell, the stage driver, all identified Spotted Horse as the killer. The jury found him guilty then asked him to stand to receive his sentence. He stood and showed no emotion as he was sentenced to be hung by the neck until he was dead.

Melissa was in the courtroom for the entire trial. It was the first time she had ever been to a trial and exposed to a killer like Spotted Horse. It scared her even more now that she could see the type of men Laughlin had to bring to justice. She was scared and prayed to God for him to get out of the Rangers.

The next day Laughlin went to Spotted Horses' cell. You could hear the gallows being built outside the window. Laughlin pulled up a straight back chair outside the cell. He turned the chair around, sat in it with his forearms resting on the back of the chair. He looked at Spotted Horse; who was looking out the cell window and watching the gallows being built. Laughlin said, "You know I'm glad Jim ran you down, this way you can look out the window and count the days until you hang. You killed my best friend and I was going to drag you to death. Thank God Jim brought you in and I didn't reduce myself to your level. The law will hang you tomorrow and I never thought I could say this, but, may God have mercy on your soul." Laughlin got up and walked out; Spotted Horse never turned around from the window. The next day at eleven-thirty, Laughlin, Glen Ray and Jim went to the jail to prepare Spotted Horse for his twelve o'clock hanging. He stood up when they opened the cell door; Laughlin said, "It's time." Spotted Horse's hands were secured behind his back and he was led out of the jail. They paused on the front porch, the streets were full of people, kids had climbed trees, people were sitting on roof tops, and every one wanted the best view possible to see the outlaw and watch him die. He was led to the gallows, up the stairs and his feet were positioned on the trap door. Laughlin asked if he had anything to say; he looked at Laughlin and said, "I killed the Ranger and sorry I didn't get more of ya'll, especially you. It gave me pleasure to know I had killed a Captain." Laughlin was trying not to show his anger. He asked, "Do you want a hood?" "No," said Spotted Horse, "I want everyone to see my face and remember the Ranger killer." The noose was slipped over his head and snugged against his neck. He was still cursing the rangers when the trap door swung open. You could hear the neck snap when the rope caught his fall. Suddenly there was absolute silence; the crowd stared silently at the hanging body. They had just witnessed death and justice.

The body continued to hang until he was pronounced dead. One of his eyes popped out of its socket and was hanging on his cheek, he was purple, had lost control of his bowels and kidneys, not a pretty sight, but one to be remembered. He was cut down, taken to the undertakers, prepared, laid out in an open coffin, and propped up for viewing in front of the funeral parlor.

At the end of the day the Rangers and Melissa met for dinner. Laughlin proposed a toast. It was simple, "To you Captain Beasley, the best of all Rangers. We are going to miss you." They emptied their glasses and ate. After the meal, Laughlin said, "Melissa and I are going to Austin and then back to Uvalde. I'll be inactive for awhile, but I will stay in touch."

Laughlin could tell by looking at Melissa that this day was like no other day in her life. She looked scared, almost as if in shock. As they walked out of the restaurant toward the hotel Melissa said, "Arrest me; take me to your jail." Laughlin said, "Don't worry, neither one of us will be alone tonight."

The next day was cloudy, cooler and a few sprinkles were falling. The stage driver was once again Bob Bell, he had been a witness in the trial and the
stage had been held over for the hanging. It was full so Laughlin rode up top to give the passengers more room. As they traveled Bob told Laughlin some Captain Beasley stories; about him in his younger days. But Laughlin already knew why the Captain was a legend and that his legacy would live forever.

The cemetery was on the north side of Austin and it was well kept with lots of live oak trees making it quite and peaceful. Laughlin and Melissa walked hand in hand until they arrived at the grave. It was covered with flowers and the marker read: Texas Ranger – Captain Wilford

Beasley – Leader among Men, The Best of The Best.
They stood at the foot of his grave and Laughlin removed his hat. He then said a prayer, "Heavenly Father, I thank you for allowing me to have known this man. He was like a father, my mentor and my best friend. He will be missed but his memory will always be alive in my heart. Someday we will be reunited and ride the streets of gold in heaven – Amen."

Laughlin looked at the grave and said, "Captain, I owe my life to you. You gave me a chance to be a Ranger and you were my mentor and hero. Everything I did was to make you proud. You believed in me. You taught me to enforce the Ranger Code. When we caught your killer, I wanted to drag him to death, but your teaching kept me from doing it. Justice was served your way, the right way. You were the only person I ever loved, now you're gone and God has given me Melissa."

As everyone gathered around him, Laughlin said softly, "Today the trail has come to an end. My last chase may be over. I think I'll hang up my guns and put my star away." He kissed Melissa and said, "Let's go to Uvalde and raise some horses and kids."

Chapter 7

It had been about thirty days since Spotted Horse, Captain Beasley's killer, had been hung. Jim told Glen Ray its' usually quiet after a hanging, people are impressed and become law abiding citizens for a while. A telegraph came for Glen Ray and Jim; it was from Laughlin. They were informed that, although Laughlin had intended on retiring, he was promoted to captain and would be taking over Beasley's territory. The last part of the telegram read 'Congratulations, Glen Ray, you are now officially a Ranger. As Captain, making you a Ranger was my first official function." Glen Ray became a Ranger ten days before his twenty-first birthday.

The peace and quiet did not last long. A telegram was sent to Sheriff Ballard saying Shorty Hendricks had broken out of jail in Austin. He and Spotted Horse had purposely been separated to avoid a jail break and Shorty was scheduled to be tried in Austin. Whoever broke Shorty out tied ropes to the jail cell window bars during the night and pulled the window and part of the wall down with horses.

The Rangers figured Shorty and his buddy or buddies would head straight to Mexico. The shortest way would be thru Laredo. Just across the border was Nuevo Laredo and they could hide in the hills or maybe join with some bandito gangs. The banditos come across the border to rob, steal, murder and then flee across the river to hide out and avoid being caught.

Before leaving Waco, Glen Ray went to the gun shop and picked up a Winchester Lever Action 44-40 with an extra fold up rear sight for long range shooting. He bought an American Arms 12 gauge double barrel shotgun. He also had the barrels cut down for faster handling and wider blast pattern. He then selected a Peacemaker .45 with cutaway trigger guard, which saves the shooter a split second in reaching the trigger. The guns were courtesy of the Texas Rangers. He elected to keep his saddle and horse. His horse, a three year old Roan Stallion with a long mane and flowing tail was named Whiskey. He was the color of whiskey and was extremely fast. Glen Ray had won lots of races on him and collected some good prize money.

After getting provisions, the two Rangers set out for Laredo. Jim said when they reached Laredo they would wire Laughlin in Uvalde and bring him up to date. It was mid-October; they were hoping that Laughlin wouldn't join them on the hunt since he and Melissa were getting married on the first of December. Maybe Shorty could be captured quickly giving the rangers time to attend the wedding.

As they rode to Laredo, Glen Ray and Jim talked about life as a Ranger. Jim said, "It's a very dangerous life and you have to think survival at all times. You'll find most people resent law and authority. Some people will smile and treat you with respect until you ride away, then they'll curse you." He continued, "You have many towns that are governed by vigilantes. They know they'll hang without a trial so they're very dangerous, especially drunk. Pick out the leader, stop him and the rest will turn away. Vigilantes, bounty hunters, rustlers, horse thieves and paid gun men in range wars are what you'll mainly be facing. The cowboys and ranch hands don't get paid to fight, however; the men in range wars are mostly paid gunmen."

Glen Ray asked if he would have any problems since he was young and looked even younger. Jim said, "In the beginning, but the reputation you build will soon make you known. Everyone knew who Laughlin was, only the crazy ones dared to try him. As a Ranger you must always be in control and not let anything be a surprise. To answer your question, look at Billy the Kid, most of the outlaws are your age."

Glen Ray said, "Jim, I feel much older than I look. I was born in Ft. Worth, the son of a cowboy. My dad left me and my mother when I was eighteen months old. Never seen him. My mother raised me while working at any job available. I went on my first cattle drive all the way to Montana when I was fourteen. Spent most of my time breaking and training horses. One of the drovers on a ranch who considered himself a retired pistolero, taught me to draw and shoot. I learned to shoot the rifle by hunting coyotes and cougars. The first time I killed someone was that gambler in Laredo. It was self defense and happened so fast I didn't have time to be scared. I want to be a Ranger and want to be like you and Laughlin."

Jim laughed and said, "You've got what it takes, just be careful, watch out for the alcohol and women", then he winked. With that, Jim said, "Let's see
how fast Whiskey can run. Last one to that big tree on the right pays for tonight's dinner in Austin."

Jim got a jump start of about fifteen yards. Whiskey soon caught Jim, blew by him and was first to the tree by thirty yards. Jim pulled up and said, "Kid, first town with a horse race I'm going to make some money off that horse." Glen Ray flashed his boyish grin with dimples and said, "Thirty two ounce steak tonight, on you, courtesy of Whiskey."

Glen Ray turned his horse and galloped away. Jim sat for a minute and watched him. Glen Ray was slender built, six feet tall, one hundred ninety five pounds, long blond curly hair, light blue eyes, and was probably what every mother wanted their son to look like. Jim spat, shook his head, spun his horse and said, "Oh, to be young again."

They arrived in Austin, took care of the horses, went to the hotel and prepared for dinner. As they left their rooms Jim looked at Glen Ray. He had on a blue shirt, buckskin vest, freshly brushed and re-shaped buckskin colored hat. Jim said, "Boy, you clean up pretty good. Stay close to me and I'll show you the big city." Glen Ray grinned and they walked to the restaurant.

The restaurant was crowded and when the Rangers walked in, people looked up and made others aware Rangers were in the house. Jim noticed the women looking at Glen Ray. The waitress, a young pretty girl, showed them to their table and you could see she was quite taken by Glen Ray. When she came back to take the order, Jim said, "Ma'am,

I'll order for the kid. He's deaf and dumb, that's a play gun he's wearing and that's not a real badge. All of us Rangers kinda look out for him and we let him pal around with us on occasion." The waitress looked at Jim and said, "Ranger, if he's a problem and you want to get rid of him, me and the other girls here will gladly baby sit him at no charge." Her name was Sandra and she was too sharp for Jim. She bent over, gave Glen Ray a hug and said, "Poor baby."

During dinner Sandra came back to the table. Glen Ray found out she was originally from Hondo, and was living in the boarding house. He asked if he could walk her home when she left work and she happily consented. They left the restaurant and walked down the boardwalk towards the boarding house. It was around ten thirty and they had to walk past the saloon. About ten yards before reaching the entrance of the saloon, two drunks came out
and immediately saw Sandra and Glen Ray. They were young cowboys with too much to drink and they started talking to Sandra. "Hey sweetheart, let me give you a hug, get rid of your kid brother and come with us." Just before they were close enough to grab Sandra, Glen Ray stepped forward blocking the men from her. One of the young men was at least six feet six inches tall and weighed about two hundred sixty five pounds. Glen Ray told them to step aside and let them pass, they didn't want any trouble. The cowboys hadn't seen the Ranger badge; it was dark and they were drunk. The smaller cowboy said, "Big Willie, get rid of the kid and let's show her a night on the town."

Willie swung; Glen Ray ducked the punch, and sunk his left arm in the man's belly, drew his pistol and hit him over the head while he was bent over. He fell to the ground, out cold. Glen Ray stuck the barrel of his pistol between the other mans eyes and said, "I'm a Texas Ranger. Willie's seen all of the town he's going to see. Unbuckle your gun belt and get Willie's; your guns will be at the sheriffs' office – you can have them in the morning when you're sober. Don't ever let me hear that you have so much as looked at this girl. If so, you'll have me to face and you will not enjoy our second meeting. Now drag Willie boy out of here and give him my message when he wakes up."

Sandra and Glen Ray walked to the front door of the boarding house. They stopped and Glen Ray asked if he could see her when he was back in town. She said yes, squeezed his hand and went inside.

The next morning Jim and Glen Ray mounted up and headed south. It took six days to reach Laredo. When they arrived they went to Marshall Luke Starrett's office. As they walked into the jail there was Nathan, the town drunk, wearing a deputy's badge. Luke told them that when Laughlin made him his unofficial deputy, Nathan stopped drinking, sobered up and asked Luke if he could work in the jail. He sweeps, cleans, works as the jailer and sleeps in the jail for his pay. Luke said, "He has progressed to the point that he's been made my official deputy." Luke said Nathan had a breakdown after the Civil War, became a drunk and gave up on himself, then quickly added, "He's as good as any deputy I've had: smart, honest and loyal. I wouldn't hesitate to send him with you boys on a search. I gave him a shotgun and he's my backup when needed. Two days ago we walked out of the saloon with six men wanted for rustling and now they're in a cell waiting to be tried." Both Rangers shook Nathan's hand, congratulated him and told him they would make Laughlin aware.

That night the Rangers invited Nathan to dinner and started getting a plan together. Knowing that outlaws can't resist bragging after drinking, the first thing they would do was go to all the cantinas in Laredo. Shorty will be scared and careful. Whoever broke him out might start bragging. The Rangers would need to question all the girls to see what they had heard.

After dinner Nathan went back to the jail and the Rangers went to the saloons and brothels. They weren't able to get any leads, no one was talking.

The next morning Nathan walked into the restaurant where they were having breakfast and said, "I have some information for you. Two of the men that broke Shorty out of jail are not only brothers, they're also his cousins. Their names are Buck and Ben Blackwell. Wanted for armed robbery, they're small time criminals, the kind that would brag." "Nathan, how did you find this out?" asked one of the Rangers. "I went to the jail and told the rustlers all about hanging and how they were all going to hang because the Hanging Judge was coming for their trial. I told them if they knew who it was and where they were I could get whoever tells me a twenty year sentence rather than a hanging. Three of them told me the same story. The six rustlers were across the border in a camp when three men joined them. After they all got drunk, Buck told them who Shorty was and how he and Ben broke him out of jail. He said there were four or five Mexican girls in the rustler's camp where Shorty was." Nathan said, "I know where that camp is and I can take you there."

Jim told Nathan "You're needed to lead us across the border, but I'll have to appoint you as a Deputy Ranger." Nathan's chest swelled, he sat up straight and tall in the chair at the breakfast table and said, "Proudest day of my life. Me, a drunk, riding with the Rangers." Jim said, "No Nathan, you were a drunk. You had some bad things happen in your life and you were knocked down, but you didn't stay down. We are glad to have you riding with us. Take us to Mexico, let's go catch us some outlaws before your friend Laughlin does it for us."

Chapter 8

They mounted up and headed south riding across the Rio Grande into Mexico, where the only law was that of the six gun. There was a lot of activity along the river. At the crossing you could see poverty and all its creations. Young girls were selling themselves. There was stealing, and violence from drunken banditos; it was not a safe place for Rangers. Nathan led them about five miles south of the river into a desolate area. He said there was a fallen down mission just ahead and, because it had a well for water, it was used as a cantina by the banditos. Only outlaws and prostitutes would go there. The Rangers rode into the old courtyard, tied up and carefully went into the three walled cantina. A door had been placed on some stacked rocks creating a bar and jars and bottles of whiskey sat on the floor. A skinny, dirty Mexican man was the bartender. He had a stubble beard, long moustache, balding in the front and hair in the rear to his shoulders. His sleeves were rolled up and you could see raw sores on his forearms. There were three young girls in the room and they immediately approached the Rangers and asked for drinks. One of the girls was pulling Glen Ray by the arm toward the back door. Outside you could see several beds of straw and blankets. Jim bought one of the girls a drink and sat with her at a table.

Jim told the girl he was looking for three of his friends. She said three men had been there and a "loco" called Shorty had bragged about how mean he was. Said he had killed a Ranger in Waco and was going to Uvalde to kill another one. He got crazy drunk, took one of the young girls outside and when she didn't do what he asked, he hurt her very bad. He broke her arm then slashed her face and breasts with his knife. The other two men knew her brothers were part of a bandito gang and if they returned they would be dead along with Shorty so, they mounted up and rode off. The girls' brothers and the other banditos came in about six hours later and rode after them. She told the rangers they had better go back across the river where the banditos couldn't follow them because, when they return, gringos like them would be killed and drug out in the hills for coyotes to eat.

Jim said, "Let's go boys, we've got our information. I'll wire Laughlin with the news then it's time to get out of here." As they walked out the door Nathan stopped inside to adjust his peg leg. Five men on horses came galloping up to the mission and it was evident who and what they were, banditos. The leader pulled up on his horse stopping him about ten yards away from the Rangers. In broken English he said, "Ola, gringos. What you doeeng here in Mexico? We no like gringos, you hurt our weemen, we maybe gonna hang or choot you, maybe cut u troat and bleed you like a peeg."

Nathan heard what was happening and the men had not seen him. He had made a holster for his sawed off shotgun and it was strapped to his peg leg. He pulled the shotgun out of its holster, stepped thru the door, and aimed it at the bandito doing the talking. He said, "Hey, hombre, you doing all the talking, what you said may be true, but you'll never see it happen. Both barrels loaded with double ought buck are aimed at you and the hammers are cocked. If any one of you boys makes a move you're a dead man. Now if they don't understand me, you better start talking to them. You got an option, have your boys throw down their pistols, go in the cantina and wait patiently while you ride with us to the river. We'll go on across the river and you can return to your boys. The second part of the option is try us and I will cut you in half with this scatter gun. Now, be smart or dumb, it's your choice."

The bandito was talking fast to his men. Jim said he was saying do what he says, don't try anything, he will kill me. The bandito turned back to Nathan and said, "Gringo, we go in and have a dreenk okay, maybe u meet my seester. I am sorry. I no mean all the theengs I say. Let's have some tequila." Nathan stepped forward about two steps and said, "I've said all I'm going to say. Get those guns with your left hand and get them on the ground or the fiesta starts." The bandito told his men to drop their guns and go into the cantina. After the men dismounted Glen Ray fired two shots in the air causing their horses to run away. The Rangers mounted up and rode to the river along with the bandito leader. As promised, the bandito was released and he rode back toward the mission.

After they crossed the river, nothing had been said. The horses were walking and Glen Ray said quietly to Jim, "What color were the eyes of that little girl you were talking to?" Jim said, "They were dark brown. What color were the eyes of the one that had you by the arm pulling you in that room?" "They were brown, really dark brown." said Glen Ray. They rode on for about a minute, then without turning his head Glen Ray said, "By the way, what did you think of our deputy?" Without turning his head Jim said, "I guess he'll do, but he's not much of a ladies man." With that said, Glen Ray and Jim spurred their horses and headed back to Laredo leaving Nathan behind.

By this time, in Uvalde, Melissa and Laughlin had hitched up the buggy and were riding to town for supplies. As they came down Main Street towards the general store, the telegraph agent ran into the street and stopped the buggy. "Ranger McFarland, I have a telegram for you." Melissa cringed, she feared bad news. Laughlin silently read the telegram, and then he looked up, squared his jaw and said, "Shorty broke out of jail." Another long pause, then he said, "Glen Ray and Jim are going into Mexico trailing him and two of his cousins." Melissa said, "Laughlin, please don't go. I know Shorty was involved in Captain Beasley's death, but, please don't go. You are not in the field and we're getting married." Laughlin was sitting on the seat of the buggy, elbows on his knees and looking at the floor. He raised his head, looked at Melissa and said, "I want to go and help, but if I do, I'll be interfering with Jim and Glen Ray. So I'll show respect and allow them to do their job; but if I'm called, then I must warn you, I will go." He then raised her chin with his hand, looked into her eyes, smiled and said, "I have been on lots of outlaw chases, but I've never been married before. You think I'm going to miss out on that." She grabbed him and said, with tears in her eyes, "Oh Laughlin, I love you so much." They completed their supply run and headed back.

It was a beautiful south Texas morning when they returned. Laughlin and Melissa had breakfast then he picked up his pistol and rifle, went to the front porch, sat down and started cleaning the weapons. Melissa was watching through the screen door. Once finished, Laughlin strapped on his gun belt and with rifle in hand, walked to the barn. In a few minutes he came back riding Sam. His rifle was in the scabbard and full canteens were tied on. Laughlin led Sam to the shade, threw him a block of hay, loosened the cinch and entered the house.

Melissa looked at him and said, "Something's wrong, what is it? I deserve to know." Laughlin said, "You're right. I didn't want to scare you so I held back part of the telegram. Shorty and two men are on their way to Uvalde and Shorty is saying he's going to kill me. Don't worry; Jim and Glen Ray are in pursuit; I'm just being cautious and ready." Melissa tried not to show it, but she was very afraid and concerned.

Meanwhile in Laredo, the Rangers met for breakfast and tried to figure out where Shorty and his two cousins were going. Jim said, "We don't know if what he told the girl about going to kill Laughlin was a fact or just a drunk bragging." Shorty and his men had painted themselves into a corner. In Mexico, the banditos were after them for cutting up one of their women, the sister of the head bandito and, on the American side, the Rangers were looking for them along with every marshal, sheriff, and bounty hunter. Glen Ray spouted, "Once this group sobers up they'll forget about killing Laughlin and think about their own survival. Jim said, "Yea, but we can't disregard the threat."

Nathan said the outlaws didn't have provisions for the trail but on the way they would probably hit a ranch up for money or supplies. Jim told Marshal Luke Starrett about how Nathan had responded in Mexico and saved them from the banditos. Luke smiled and said, "I thought he would do well. I'm proud to have him as a deputy." Nathan said, "I want to be a part of this chase. Ranger Laughlin treated me with respect when no one else did, I owe him. I know where all the ranch houses are between here and Uvalde. I think we should ride from ranch to ranch alerting the ranchers. Shorty's gang will try not to be seen; they'll kill a young calf for food and stay out of sight. Our best chance is for them to break into a ranch or bunk house and get whiskey. When drunk they get brave and stupid."

They all agreed and after getting supplies and a pack horse, they started on the ride. Jim said, "Nathan you're still just a Deputy Ranger and we're going to see Laughlin. Luke may never get you back." Nathan beamed, he couldn't wait to see Laughlin and thank him.

The two Rangers and their appointed deputy Nathan started toward Uvalde. Nathan was to take them to each ranch along the way. They would ask the ranchers about Shorty and gather any available information.

On the second day they came to the Circle W Ranch and were told one of the drovers out looking for strays saw three men at a distance riding toward the west. Jim asked if the drover could take them to the area where the riders were seen. He had hopes of picking up a trail. Three horses leave a good trail for several days.

They picked up the trail and with the information supplied by the drover they were two days behind Shorty. The important thing, they were on the trail, the bad thing was the men were going towards Uvalde.

Jim told Glen Ray and Nathan, "With Shorty going after Laughlin, rather than fleeing you can tell what kind of person we're after. The two cousins are probably looking for a way to impress and Shorty is probably staying half drunk. He's letting revenge overrule good thinking." They didn't need to ride into Uvalde and tell Laughlin the men were coming. With his experience they knew he was already prepared.

The Rangers lost the trail as they neared Uvalde. The outlaws had merged with the Stage Trail and it was impossible to follow their tracks so the Rangers rode into town, checked the saloons and livery stables; anyplace the outlaws might be hiding.

After they were satisfied the men weren't in town they rode toward

Melissa's ranch. As Jim, Glen Ray and Nathan rode up to the gate, Candido and six riders rode up on them with pistols drawn. The Rangers identified themselves but were asked to surrender their pistols until Laughlin identified them. They did and rode on toward the ranch. Laughlin came out on the front porch and told his men, "Good job. These men are all Rangers." Nathan was about to burst with pride, his idol and savior had just called him a Ranger.

Laughlin said, "Dismount. Candido get someone to take care of their horses. Give them special care; they've been on the trail several days. Come on in the house; don't want somebody trying to pick us off with his rifle." Once inside Laughlin looked at Nathan and said, "Melissa, come meet our newest Ranger, Nathan. This is the man I told you about; he's really made me proud. By the way, what is your last name?" Nathan grinned and said, "You ain't gonna believe me, it's Law. Nathan Law." Laughlin grinned, shook Nathan's' hand and said, "How about that, the name fits. I am proud of you Nathan Law."

They all spent the night at the ranch and early the next morning a young boy was stopped at the gate. He told Candido he had a note for Ranger Laughlin. They took him to Laughlin and he said a man gave it to him last night, but told him to deliver it this morning and paid him a dollar to be sure he handed it to Laughlin. Laughlin put his hand on the boys shoulder and said, "Thank you. Maria get this boy some breakfast and pack him a lunch for his trip back to town."

The Rangers were all gathered around Laughlin waiting on him to read the note. Laughlin read the note out loud to everyone. It said, 'Meet me at Flat Rock Mountain on Rocky Creek tomorrow at twelve noon. Laughlin said, "Flat Rock is a perfect place for an ambush. It's been used in the past when Indians attacked the cattle drives. The drovers would get on top of the rock and hold the Indians off for days. Shorty is trying to set up an ambush; he'll never face off with me in a showdown. He could also be trying to draw us away from the ranch leaving Melissa unprotected." "You couldn't get enough whiskey in him to face me, I'm sure of that. I think he has a plan to get us to Flat Rock, shoot our horses out from under us putting us on foot. Shorty won't be with them, he'll be coming this way passing thru Grey Rock Pass and then to the ranch thinking he can get Melissa as a hostage then by using her, get me in the open for a kill shot."

"Jim, you and Glen Ray go to my corral in the morning and get two horses. I don't want you taking the chance that yours could be shot out from under you. Nathan, you'll stay in the house with Melissa, Candido and his men will guard outside and around the house. Glen Ray, you'll ride out of sight behind Flat Rock, dismount, get in rifle range and wait. Jim, you'll do the same, get in position and wait, don't expose yourself so they can get a shot. Wait on them, when Shorty doesn't return they'll panic and try to leave. Bring them in alive if possible. If Shorty is with them and they get away it'll be easy to trail them. With them on the rock they have the advantage; we must always turn the advantage around in our favor."

Laughlin sat with Melissa and said he was taking extra precaution and she would be safe. Her reply was, "I'm not worried about me, I'm worried about you."

The next morning the men prepared for the twelve o'clock meeting. Laughlin told Candido to put one man with a rifle in every room of the ranch house and told Nathan not to let Melissa out of his sight. As they started to leave the ranch Glen Ray saw that Laughlin was on Sam and said, "Thought you would be leaving Sam here today." "No, there may be a chase today." Then Laughlin smiled and said, "When Sam saw the other horses leaving the stalls and I came in, he almost kicked the wall down. The son of a gun knew we were going out today." Laughlin said he would wait for two hours at
Grey Rock Pass then if Shorty doesn't show up, he'd ride to Flat Rock and they'd regroup.

Jim got in place, as directed, in front of the giant rock; Glen Ray rode out wide and circled to the rear of the rock. He dismounted and was getting in place when he saw two horses tied up in brush with hopes they were concealed. Glen Ray grinned and thought about how Laughlin had figured out what Shorty would try to do.

Glen Ray took out his rifle, fired a shot that would hit the rock and he hollered, "Might as well give up. We've got your horses and you're surrounded. Jim, fire a shot out front so the boys can see they are." Jim sent a shot glancing off the rock. "It's all over, you boys didn't kill anyone and we'll have Shorty soon. Give it up, don't be fools. We can starve you out, you're gonna get thirsty, you can try to shoot it out till you run out of ammo or you can come down and surrender. You'll go to jail but you won't hang." One of the men hollered down, "We're coming down, don't shoot." "Leave your rifles and pistols on the mountain, put your hands on your head and come to your horses," shouted Glen Ray.

In about twenty minutes they were down at the horses. The Rangers tied their feet in the stirrups, hands behind their backs and tied the horses to each other. They headed back to the ranch through Grey Rock Pass.

Chapter 9

Laughlin had placed himself directly in the middle of the pass; there was only about thirty yards on either side of the rock he was hiding behind. Laughlin heard Shorty's horse coming and when he was within twenty yards Laughlin stepped out holding his rifle and said, "Hello Shorty, what a surprise to see you here." Shorty was liquored up but his face registered surprise and shock. Laughlin said, "Ease off your horse but keep your hands high." Once on the ground Laughlin put down his rifle and said, "Shorty, you never had any intention of facing me at Flat Rock. You thought I would go there and you could go to the ranch and get Melissa as a hostage or you would try to shoot her at long range with your rifle. You were easy to figure, the only way you want to face me is in an ambush. Now prove me wrong, here I stand, you've got your pistol holstered and so is mine.

Come on Shorty, you're real bad, cut up women, back shoot people, bragging about killing Ranger Beasley, telling how you're going to kill me. Come on Shorty, here's your chance, just you and me. Come on Shorty, draw, it will probably be better if I do shoot you. Come on, come on, here I am." Laughlin was walking toward Shorty as he talked. Shorty said, "Don't kill me, let me live, give me a chance." "You've had your chance to draw on me," with that said Laughlin pistol whipped Shorty's face from one side to the other. Each blow sent blood flying. "Unbuckle your belt, get your knife, and let's see if you can cut a man." Laughlin pitched his pistol out of the way and went to his boot for his knife. Shorty slashed at him, missing. Laughlin gave two quick slashes; one to each side of Shorty's face, the next two went across his chest, just like the girl in Mexico was cut. With that Shorty dropped his knife and said, "Mercy, no more." Laughlin put his knife away, picked up his pistol, put it in his holster and looked at Shorty. He said, "Shorty killing is too good for you, you are going to hang, it will be in Uvalde and I'll be there to see it happen."

BANG! A pistol shot rang out, the bullet caught Laughlin in the back of his left shoulder. It spun him around and he saw an image. He pulled his pistol and fired twice. The man fell backwards and was dead before he hit the ground. Shorty had seen this, grabbed his pistol from the ground and was trying to shoot when one of Laughlin's shots hit him in the chest. He fell dead.

Laughlin was lucky the pistol shot had caught him in the fleshy part of his shoulder and the angle of the shot allowed the bullet to pass thru without striking any bones. He walked over to the man that shot him and immediately recognized him as Bucky Buchanan; better known as the 'Widowmaker', a well known bounty hunter.

Laughlin removed his shirt and tied his bandana over the wound on his shoulder. It was easy to figure what happened. Bucky was trailing Shorty for the reward, Laughlin found him first. Bucky heard the gun fire, rode up and saw Laughlin arresting Shorty. He shot Laughlin and was going to shoot Shorty. He would then take both bodies to town, claim Shorty shot Laughlin and he shot Shorty. He could collect the reward for Shorty and be a hero by killing Laughlin's killer.

Jim and Glen Ray had heard the shots and came riding up at a gallop. Laughlin assured them he was alright and explained what had happened. They told him about their capture and after loading the two bodies over their horses, they headed to Uvalde. Laughlin went to the doctor for treatment. The wound was cleaned, bandaged and Dr. Milles told him to go home and let Melissa give him a lot of tender loving care.

Buck and Ben Blackwell were locked up in jail with no bail. Shorty and the 'Widowmaker' were laid out, in open coffins, in front of the undertakers.

Laughlin, Jim and Glen Ray rode out to the ranch and made everyone aware of the happenings. Melissa hadn't been told about Laughlin being wounded. When she saw him she almost went into shock. Laughlin assured her it was only a flesh wound and he would be good as new in a few weeks. She remained upset and concerned.

Candido and Maria prepared and served barbecue outside that evening in celebration of having all the people involved in Captain Beasley's death accounted for. The case was now closed.

Laughlin told the Rangers to follow him. They walked to the bunk-house and sat in front of it. Laughlin said, "I wanted to get away from everyone so we could talk. Boy's, I'm very proud of all of y'all. Jim you are seasoned and solid as a rock. Glen Ray, you can ride with the best, and you are just starting your career. Nathan, I have faith in you. It takes courage to come back from the grave the way you did. Men like you are what make the Rangers a very special group. I have tried to totally give up being a Ranger, but I can't. The Rangers are going to be set up in Districts and I am going to be working Captain Beasley's old District out of my ranch in Uvalde. This will allow me to be with Melissa most of the time. Only on special assignments will I be going out in the field. Nathan, I would like for you to move here and work as my assistant. Jim, Glen Ray will ya'll consent to working the District answering and taking directions from me?" Jim said, "I think I can answer for the group. It would be our pleasure." "Then consider it done," said Laughlin.

"Jim, Glen Ray your first job is to see Candido and take that good looking black filly to Mr. Fox in Abilene. Tell him to breed her to Fred's stallion then you bring her back here. I want to see what kind of colt they will produce. Y'all take some time, have fun in Abilene. Wire me and keep me aware of what's happening. Let the telegraph operator know where you'll be in case you're needed."

Laughlin went back to the house, into the bedroom, undressed and laid down on the bed. Melissa saw him go to the room and knew he was tired and hurting from the wound. She walked over to the bed, sat down, looked at him and said, "Laughlin you don't have to worry about telling me of your decision. I know how you feel about the Rangers and I told you, I'll take you any way I can get you. I have no life without you. Working out of Uvalde and not going out in the field will be fine.

You can be involved with growing and developing the Rangers and still be involved with the ranch and be with me. Go to sleep, I love you." Laughlin felt very relieved, he was afraid Melissa was going to be upset.

Next morning, Glen Ray and Jim went to the corral. Jim cut the little filly out and Glen Ray roped her. They put a lead halter on her and prepared for their trip to Abilene. As they rode Glen Ray talked about the race Whiskey and Diablo were eventually going to have. He knew Fred would accept the challenge. Jim's thoughts drifted toward Linda, he was looking forward to seeing her.

As the Rangers rode toward Abilene Glen Ray trying to get the ever silent Jim involved in conversation, said, "Jim, how did you get started with the Rangers?" "Not much of a story," said Jim, "Just liked what the Rangers did and wanted to be part of the organization." "Come on Jim," prodded Glen Ray," tell me about your life, were you a hell-raiser converted to a Ranger? Talk to me, it's a long way to Abilene." "Alright," said Jim "but its boring."

"I was born in Bowie, TX, north of Ft. Worth. My parents were from Oklahoma, but moved to Texas in hopes of starting a Baptist Church. I was born in a little house in town and grew up in church. I like to read, taught myself Spanish while going to school. My mother and father are still alive, one brother, one sister and one sister still born. I worked on ranches during roundups, then the Civil War started. I joined the Confederacy and was part of a group that rounded up mustangs, broke them and made them saddle ready for the Calvary. Did some blacksmith work and worked with the gunsmith. I practiced whenever possible on my quick-draw and marksmanship with a rifle and pistol. Figured if I could get thru the war without being killed I would try and join the Rangers. I served under Captain Beasley when he was a colonel in the Confederacy. Never married, didn't have time for it. Besides all that I ain't much for looks, the ladies all like desperados like you." Glen Ray looked at Jim and said, "I don't buy that, I think you are just shy around the ladies."

Jim was thirty-two years old, six feet tall, broad shoulders, narrow waist, brown eyes, very muscular with short brown hair, always clean shaven and seemed to be clean and neat appearing all the time. Glen Ray had grown to respect Jim as a Ranger and as a man.

The days were getting shorter and cooler and the nights were chilly, cold if the north wind was blowing. It was less than a month till the wedding was to take place in Uvalde. They needed everything in Abilene to be good, no problems. They could relax a little and then return with the filly and attend the wedding. Melissa's mother and father would be present and now that Captain Beasley was dead, they wondered who the best man would be.

Up ahead, Glen Ray and Jim could see the stage coming; it had left Abilene going east and was about ten miles out. The stage driver was an older fellow named Crazy Red Slocum. His nickname was given to him by the Indians. He was captured during a raid and he acted crazy, ate dirt, talked to himself, pulled off his clothes and ran around naked. The Indians would not kill a crazy man because of their beliefs. His act saved his life and earned him his nickname.

Red told the Rangers they were going to Abilene at the right time. "There was going to be a dance and cookout in two days sponsored by the local cattlemen. Be lots of fun, dancing, drinking, cock fights and horse racing. Be seeing you boys, losing time, can't be late." The stage disappeared in the dust. Glen Ray looked at Jim and said while grinning, "I bet Diablo will be in the race, prize money and side bet with Fred. Hear that Whiskey got to get you in town for some rest and get your legs fresh again. Jim, are you a dancer?" "No, not really," blurted Jim, "I'll probably eat and just stand around and watch." "Jim Weaver, you ain't as sly as you think," spouted Glen Ray, "I noticed how you looked at Linda last time we were here." Jim blushed and said, "Hush up boy or I'll throw you in the jail and not let you out till the party's over."

It was Saturday; the party had started around noon. Glen Ray had decided to leave Whiskey and the filly in the livery stable, then, he would ride back out to Mr. Fox's ranch with Fred. The horse race was to take place at four o'clock in the afternoon. The race would be one half mile long, thru town to a marked turnaround outside of town and then back down Main Street. The rules were simple, anyone could ride, saddle or bareback, no restrictions.

Fred came to town riding another horse and leading Diablo with Mr. Fox riding in his buggy. In the back of the buggy was a racing saddle weighing less than fifteen pounds. Also in the buggy were a Mexican woman and a young girl around twenty years old that was the most beautiful girl Glen Ray had ever seen.

He rode over to the buggy, dismounted, greeted Mr. Fox, punched Fred on the shoulder and asked, "Who, and where did those two beautiful girls come from; and where did you find that mule you're leading?" Fred said, "This is my mother Rosa, this is my little sister Angelina and that mule is going to outrun Whiskey by five lengths."

Glen Ray had never seen Diablo without a saddle. He was magnificent, broad across the rump, long bodied, high withers, and long legs; black as the blackest night. Whiskey is going to have his hands full and then some.

Glen Ray turned his attention back to Angelina. He could not help but stare in efforts to absorb her beauty in his mind. She had hair so brown that it had a black sheen and it hung to her waist line. Her eyes were the darkest prettiest brown possible and they enlarged as she talked and were bright with happiness. She had on a red blouse open at the top and hanging on the shoulders, it was trimmed with white lace blousy half sleeves and tapering down to a very petite waist. She completed the outfit with a full length skirt decorated to a Mexican flavor and tiny little leather shoes. Everything she said was in English and she said it with vocal and body expressions.

Fred could see how taken Glen Ray was and he said, "Amigo, you stay away from my sister, her boyfriend is the son of Pancho Villa and has killed seven men over her, four of them were Rangers." Mr. Fox overheard and he burst out laughing and said, "Glen Ray, don't pay Fred no mind. I want to see you and Angel dancing tonight." Glen Ray thought, Angel, how well that describes her, he was excited.

Jim sat down at a table with Linda in the Bent Elbow Saloon. They had a drink and began talking. He told Linda everything that had happened in Laughlin's life including his upcoming marriage. Linda listened without interruptions and once Jim had finished she said, "Thanks for telling me Jim, as you know he's, was; a very special person to me, more than I let him know."

Jim looked at her eyes and to his surprise she wasn't crying. He said, "Linda, I've had feelings for you since the first time we met. Because of the relationship between you and Laughlin I never exposed my feelings. Hopefully, after a while you'll give me an opportunity to be in your life. I don't want to rush you, would just like to know if there's a chance." Linda placed her hand on Jim's hand on the table and said, "Ranger Weaver, would you take me to the dance tonight?"

There were eleven horses entered in the race. It was very evident that Whiskey and Diablo were the horses to beat. The purse was for one hundred dollars, considering a Ranger made a dollar a day; it was worth the $10 entry fee. Fred had the racing saddle on Diablo and Glen Ray was forced to ride with his trail saddle, a much heavier rig. The two men made a side bet of ten dollars and then mounted. They lined up in the street from one side to the other. The starting gun was fired and they were off and running. Down the straight away of Main Street, after about an eighth of a mile Whiskey, Diablo and two other horses were leading the pack.

Chapter 10

They were outside of town and a group of boys were sitting beside the road to see them race by. As the horses came by the boys, the two barking dogs they were holding broke loose and charged into the side of the horses. One of the dogs ran under Whiskey causing him to stumble and almost fall. Glen Ray was experienced and pulled hard to keep Whiskey's head up and his actions prevented them from falling. The stumble had cost them about twelve lengths and the way Diablo was running it would be very difficult for Whiskey to catch up. They did the turnaround and Whiskey had gained three lengths. Glen Rays' only hope was that Whiskey's stamina over a half mile would be greater than Diablo's. Whiskey was strong, ridden every day and never seemed to tire.

It was now Diablo by six lengths with a quarter mile to go. Fred was glancing back over his shoulder and applying the whip hard to Diablo. Glen Ray was leaning forward in the saddle talking to Whiskey, urging him on, faster boy faster. With only an eighth of a mile left Diablo was leading by three lengths, but he was tiring. Fred continued to urge Diablo on. You could see by his stride and rhythm he was tiring. Whiskey was smooth, head stretched out and giving Glen Ray everything he had. He had never lost a race before and he didn't like a horse running ahead of him. The lead was down to two lengths and Glen Ray could see the finish line. One length, a hundred yards left, come on Whiskey; stretch it out whispered Glen Ray. The two horses crossed the finish line side by side; it appeared to be a dead heat. There was no signal; the three judges were huddled and talking. Glen Ray was walking Whiskey, cooling him down when the judges called for them to gather at the starting line. "Gentlemen, you both have fine horses and you gave us an exciting race. We have discussed the finish and we all agree it's a dead heat – a tie."

Fred turned to Glen Ray and said, "Like hell it was a tie. Your horse fell down and still caught me, what a finish. He's got great stamina; never seen a horse finish that strong. Money is yours Amigo; your horse is faster than mine." Glen Ray said, "We appreciate your compliments, but I'm not taking your half of the money. Let's walk'em out some more, cool'em down and then I'll show you my talent on that dance floor."

Mr. Fox walked over to Glen Ray and said, "Son I'll give you fifteen hundred dollars for that horse right now, cash money." Glen Ray said, "Sorry sir, money can't buy my horse; but if you would like to use him as a stud while I'm here, you can." Glen Ray paused then continued, "Did you see the filly I brought to leave for Diablo to service?" "Sure did," said Fox," I'll take you up on the offer to use Whiskey with some of my mares. Come on out tomorrow, spend a few days, relax. Angel has just about worn me out talking about you. I know she would like to see you hanging around the ranch.

The group filled their plates with steak, beans, corn on the cob, squash, potato salad and anything else you could fit on your plate. They all sat at tables pulled together under a large tree. Mr. Fox blessed the food and they ate and enjoyed fellowship. Glen Ray admired Angel; Jim admired Linda, Glen Ray gave Jim an 'attaboy wink' and Jim blushed.

The evening cooled down, the lanterns were lit and they went to the dance floor. The dance floor was dirt scraped clean, wet, swept, wet, swept until the surface was like a rock. It was a trick learned from the Indians in their tepees. The band was good, a mixture of cowboys, bankers and anyone that had an instrument they could play. They brought the piano out of the saloon and the music was good. The first song was a polka and everyone danced, including Jim and Linda.

Fred was an excellent dancer and the first dance was with his mother. Glen Ray danced with Angel and they did well. The next song was a waltz, Glen Ray looked at Jim and he was gliding around, definitely he and Linda were the best couple on the floor. Glen Ray and Angel danced over next to Jim and Linda. He said to Jim, "How did the son of a Baptist Minister ever learn to dance? You're good. I'm proud of you." Jim grinned and said, "I learned it in Ranger training, read the manual."

The night was coming to an end and everyone was exhausted. Mr. Fox probably danced more than any of the men, Jim was second. When Jim and Glen Ray went to their room, Jim told Glen Ray, "Go on to Mr. Fox's by yourself. Take the filly and I'll be out in three or four days. By the way, Angel is beautiful and very nice. She talked to me about you when we were dancing. She is very interested. I helped you out. I told her you didn't love your wife." Glen Ray said, "I liked you a whole lot better when you didn't talk all the time."

Glen Ray was up early, skipped breakfast, went to the stable, saddled up, put the lead rope on the filly and mounted up. It was a chilly overcast morning with a brisk north wind blowing in his face. He thought back to the shooting in Laredo, being in jail and how his life has changed. Today he's a Texas Ranger, well respected and loves being one. He spoke out loud, 'Thank you God, I won't let you down.' When he rode thru the gate at the Ranch, Mr. Fox met him. They greeted each other with big smiles and a firm handshake. Mr. Fox said, "Where's the dancer? Couldn't he get up this morning?" Glen Ray was laughing as they walked into the house. Mr. Fox said, "Sit down at the table, drink some coffee, breakfast will be served shortly." Glen Ray removed his hat, brushed his hair back and sat down. The kitchen door swung open and there carrying coffee and cups was Angel. When she looked at Glen Ray her eyes lit up, her smile overpowered and dominated the room. Glen Ray got up, helped her set the coffee down, told her she was beautiful and gave her a hug.

Fred and Manuel had seen the horses tied up in front of the ranch house and joined Glen Ray and Mr. Fox. Fred told Manuel to take the horses to the corral, keep them in stalls away from the other horses. Mr. Fox said, "I've never seen a horse finish the half mile the way Whiskey did. I really want to try and get a stallion out of him to breed my mares."

Fred said, "He's the fastest horse I have ever seen, and that includes race horses. I've got work to do. I'll leave you two guys alone. Remember, my sisters' boyfriend is the son of Pancho Villa, very jealous, has killed seven men, four of them Rangers." Angel heard what Fred said and threatened to throw hot coffee on him. Fred danced out the room with an invisible partner and a big smile.

Angel served eggs, biscuits covered with gravy, bits of sausage and pancakes with butter and syrup. She kept their coffee hot and her eyes on Glen Ray.

Glen Ray said, "Mr. Fox tell me about being a rancher." Fox said, "Son, this is a prime time for the ranchers, beef is needed back east. They are building railroads, stockyards and slaughter houses. Everything I worked for is now starting to pay off. Beef and ranching is big business. A young man can make a lot of money in the next fifty years. The country is growing and growing fast. You could become a good rancher; maybe do what Laughlin's getting ready to do, raise horses and cattle."

Mr. Fox leaned back in his chair and said, "I've always admired the Rangers, and at one time I was a Ranger. This year 1874, Governor Richard Coke will organize six companies of Texas Rangers, 75 to a company. They will be stationed in districts at strategic points over the state in order to be on hand when ranchers are raided. You boys will now be seen as Peace Officers, before you were semi military. As you know, Laughlin is part of the new districts. This is a fine time to be a Ranger. The organization has changed from fighting Mexicans and Indians to capturing outlaws and train robbers with Rangers now acting as Peace Officers."

"You see son, I grew up with all this happening. You're a young Ranger and I just wanted to educate you a little about the Rangers." Glen Ray was in awe of Mr. Fox's knowledge and he thanked him for all the information. Unknown to Glen Ray, Fox was one of the first original Texas Rangers.

Mr. Fox said, "Let's talk about horses. You leave that filly here with me; we'll keep her 'til she has a quality colt that's the stallion and stud Laughlin wants. Son, I really am impressed with your horse Whiskey. Hopefully you can hang around here for a few days while he breeds some of my mares. I'm going to let Angelina off from her chores here at the ranch house; you kids have fun for a few days. You can count on the Rangers calling you into action soon."

Mr. Fox gave Glen Ray and Angelina the use of his buggy and they rode into Abilene. Jim and Linda greeted them and they all went to dinner. It was a fun time; they enjoyed re-living the dance and planned a picnic for the following day. After dinner Angelina went with Linda and Glen Ray stayed in Jim's room.

Jim said he had received a wire from Laughlin directing him to be in Austin in ten days to testify as the arresting Ranger in the trial of Buck and Ben Blackwell. It said for you to come back to Uvalde and he would brief you on a problem over in Laredo.

The next morning the foursome had breakfast and the girls were made aware that duty called and they would be leaving. Jim would leave after breakfast and Glen Ray would return to the ranch and leave the following day. Glen Ray and Angelina were riding in the buggy returning to the ranch when he noticed Angelina was very quite and sad, not her normal happy self. He asked, "Angelina, what's wrong? Why ain't you talking; you look so sad?" She said, "Glen Ray, it's not fair for me to allow myself to have feelings for you. I am Mexican; our relationship would not be accepted. Your people would not accept me or my people; especially the men would not like it." Glen Ray said, "We've barely established a relationship; who knows where it might go. I enjoy being with you and with your permission, every time I'm in the area I'd like to see you." She smiled and they continued their ride to the ranch.

Glen Ray told Mr. Fox he would be leaving and returning to Uvalde, then to Laredo. Mr. Fox said, "I would like to send five mares over to Laughlin for Sam to breed. I'll send Fred with you to bring back five mares for Diablo to breed. I want you to take one of my best bulls and two cows. Tell Laughlin it's my wedding present and to fence off a couple of sections of land and start a herd. There's going to be a big demand for beef."

The next morning Fred and Glen Ray left the ranch driving a bull, two cows and five horses toward Uvalde. They drove the mini herd all day then bedded down by water and grass. It was chilly and a nice fire for coffee and heat was started. They ate some beans, jerky, drank some coffee and relaxed.

Glen Ray said, "I need to ask you something. With me being white and Angelina being Mexican is that a problem? I know we just met, I enjoy her company but I don't want to create any situations for her." Fred said, "It is preferred that races don't mix. You and she would be accepted by your people easier than you by the Mexican men. They would resent you taking their women." "Can you accept me and her having a relationship?" asked Glen Ray. Fred responded, "I am responsible for my family now that my Papa is dead. I want Angelina to be happy and treated right. The two of you just met, but if it continues and develops, you have my blessings." "I plan on continuing a casual relationship with her whenever I'm in Abilene," said Glen Ray. Then continuing, with a grin, barked "By the way, this 'son of Pancho Villa crap', can I take him?" "Amigo, if he existed I would bet on you." said Fred. When they reached the ranch in Uvalde they drove their little herd thru the front gate and to the ranch house. Melissa was in the house and Laughlin was at the corral. They saw the unusual sight and all met in the yard.

Laughlin said, "What's this, what's going on?" Glen Ray and Fred laughed and Glen Ray said, "Mr. Fox sent Sam five girlfriends to be returned and sent you and Melissa your wedding present. You are now in the cattle business and Fox wants to be responsible for starting your herd. He says lots of money will be coming in the cattle business and you're to fence off two sections for a new herd. Says the Army needs horses, the country needs beef and you can do both." Laughlin grinned and said, "Well I guess he just made a cattleman out of me." Then he turned to the big Santa Gertrudis and said, "Mr. Bull, your name is JJ Jr."

Candido saw the group in the yard and rode up. They explained what was happening and Candido said, after meeting Fred, they would take care of the animals. Glen Ray dismounted and sat on the porch with Laughlin and told him what all happened in Abilene including Mr. Fox's talk about the Rangers. Laughlin said, rather abruptly, damn, if Fred hears about adding on more Rangers, he will want to join, don't tell him, Mr. Fox needs him." Then Laughlin told Glen Ray a story Fox had related to him about a Cougar hunt Fred had been on.

He said, "It seems that Fred was on his belly crawling very slowly. He had heard the squeal of a deer fawn early that morning and had seen a big cat drag the deer to a group of trees. It was probably six hundred yards to the tree line where the cat entered and Fred could not see the cat. He knew the mountain lion would be in the tree lying on a limb and eating his prey. He continued to crawl, stop, look and crawl some more. He had his 45.70 across his arms in front of his face and all he wanted was a shot. He had been tracking the cat for six days. It all started when the cat killed one of Mr. Fox's thorough-bred colts. He had paid for stud service to his mare and the colt was going to be his stud. Fred was about three hundred yards from the tree he thought the cat might be in. He lay for at least thirty minutes staring at this one tree for movement. Nothing, he focused on another tree and started the same process.

After about ten minutes a tree branch moved unnaturally. Fred knew the cat was there. It had finished its meal, was lying on a limb digesting the food and had shifted its weight just enough to move the limb. Fred continued to stare and then he saw the tail hanging down. This let him know which way the lion was facing. He could not see enough to get a shot so he decided to move to his right several yards. A twig snapped. The cat had heard him; its' head came up off the limb giving Fred a shot. It didn't run because it had only used one of its senses, hearing.

The wind was in Fred's favor as planned and he had not been seen. He eased the rifle in front of him, set the rear sight for three hundred yards, and eased it up to his shoulder while lying flat on the ground. He put the sight on the cat's head, looked thru the rear peep, started pulling on the trigger slowly, slowly, must not panic or hurry, slowly – BOOM – the barrel jumped up and back from the recoil.

Fred saw the cat had been turned side ways from the broadside head shot; it fell lifeless to the ground. He looked at the cat and said, "No coyote is too far, no rustler can ride away and no cat can hide." Then he made a travois out of some limbs, attached it to his "D-ring" on the saddle, loaded the cat and started back to the ranch; he wanted Mr. Fox to see the cat. Then, as Fred rode down the ranch road; Mr. Fox was in the yard waiting on him. The mountain lion was on the travois and in full display for Mr. Fox to see. Fred swung out of Diablo's' saddle and onto the ground. Mr. Fox firmly shook his hand, embraced him and told him he had done a great job." Manuel, one of Fred's brothers was admiring the cat. Mr. Fox told him to get the lion prepared and take it to town. Manual was to tell old man Johnson to do a good job on him, full creep mount and to patch up that head. He would know who shot it. Fred is a head shot man." Mr. Johnson made saddles, bridles, anything to do with leather and had done many mounts for Mr. Fox.

Fox told Fred to come in and tell him about the hunt. They went to the living room and sat down, enjoyed a drink while Fred told his story of the hunt. After telling the story and answering all of Mr. Fox's questions, he told about the rock where he fired his pistol with ya'll and how well he had faired compared to you two. Then Fred told Fox how he really admired the Rangers. I'm sure he felt a little hurt that I hadn't asked him to join us and Fox had never told him that I wanted him. He had no idea that one day the ranch could be his, so out of respect for Mr. Fox, I hadn't asked.

Glen Ray assured Laughlin he wouldn't mention the Ranger expansion plans to Fred. Then Laughlin said, "Marshall Luke Starrett in Laredo needs help.

There's a ranch east of Laredo owned by Will Guthrie and his four sons: Barney, Charlie, Alvin and Frank. The ranch has a number of cowboys that claim to be drovers but in reality are outlaws and gunmen. They are suspected of stealing cattle and horses from local ranchers, changing brands and then when the herd is large enough, they drive them to Ft Worth to be sold. They're coming into Laredo shooting up the town, attacking the locals, harassing and beating up anyone that gets in their way. They take over the saloon, stay crazy drunk for about three days and then leave town. Ranches in the area around Laredo are reporting loss of cattle and drovers shot. Marshall Starrett can't get any deputies; they're too scared of the 'Hell Raisers' as they call themselves. When Jim gets through testifying in Austin he'll join you and Nathan in Laredo. Jim will be joined in Austin by Billy Joe Smith, a seasoned Ranger. First priority is law and order in Laredo. Set up in the town and don't go out after anyone till we get their attention. Oh, guess what they are calling you now, 'Baby Ranger'." Glen Ray said with a stern face, "I can assure you I am no baby." Laughlin laughed.

That night Glen Ray told Fred about Laredo. He said he would be leaving at daylight, ride into Uvalde, get Nathan and then head toward Laredo. True to his word, he didn't mention the Ranger's need for new recruits.

The next morning Laughlin helped saddle them up, they said good-bye, Glen Ray rode toward Laredo and Fred toward Abilene. When Glen Ray arrived in Uvalde, Nathan was ready. He had been briefed by Laughlin and they rode out quickly together. About five miles outside Uvalde Nathan said, "Rider coming up behind us." Glen Ray didn't have to look twice, he recognized the horse. It was Fred. He laughed and said, "Amigos, I must have taken a wrong turn, I am lost." Glen Ray grinned and said, "Come on, I can't make you a temporary Deputy Ranger, only Laughlin can. I'll wire him from Laredo."

They arrived in Laredo and met with Marshall Starrett who said, "The 'Hell Raisers' hadn't been in town for about a week. This was a normal procedure, be gone for a week, come in town for three or four days, stay drunk and wreck the town. The Mayor is the one who wired Laughlin asking for help. He's all over me but I can't get deputies and one man can't stand up against fifteen or twenty drunken men."

They took care of the horses then went to the restaurant for dinner. While eating they heard several riders galloping down the street. The Rangers, including Fred, walked out on the sidewalk and saw the riders going into the saloon. Glen Ray said, "Let's start now, we need to make it known the Rangers are in town. Nathan you go in the front door with me. Fred, you and Luke go in the back door."

Chapter 11

Glen Ray and Nathan walked in; the riders were the banditos they had faced in Mexico. All six of them were lined up at the bar. Nathan had the hammers back on the shotgun. Fred and Luke came in the back door and were standing behind the bar. The leader turned around, faced Glen Ray and Nathan and said, "Amigo, it's you the 'Baby Ranger' and 'Shotgun'. We no do nothing over here in your town. We just come in for tequila and see some new ladies, we no cause problems. We heard you got Loco Shorty and his two compadres. We no fight, lets celebrate, pour some tequila for me and my friends, no cause problems." Glen Ray said, "Fred, you and Nathan take their guns and put them behind the bar on the floor. Luke you stay where you are, keep them in front of you." "Ok, El Capitan Bandito, now you, only you join me at a table for a drink. Fred come join us, I may need an interpreter." Glen Ray said, "I want the truth why are you here in Laredo. The bandito said, "My name is Rene. Three of my men were in Laredo and the 'Hell Raisers' said they didn't like Mexicans. They dragged my men behind horses till they were dead. Then they hung them by their feet in trees by the river for us to find. We want to find them. One of the dead men was my brother."

Glen Ray said, "We will take care of this like we did the men who hurt your sister. Let us do our job. You and your boys go back to Mexico. The Rangers don't have a problem with you and your men, let's keep it that way." "What's your name Ranger?" asked Rene. My men named you 'Baby Ranger'." Glen Ray smiled and said, "Call me whatever you like, my name is Glen Ray and 'Shotgun' is Nathan Law." "Senor Glen Ray, we hear you pretty fast with you peestoll. Me, I pretty fast also, we make a good team, no? We can be amigos or we can kill each other, we no wanna do that. We amigos, you have my word." Rene got up from the table, walked out of the saloon, mounted and rode toward Mexico.

Marshall Starrett said, "The banditos name is Rene Alvarez, a killer, thief, Indian fighter and a hero in his country. Border life along the river is based on survival. Here he is an outlaw, there he is a hero. I have never had trouble with him or his men. I don't confront or challenge them, their livelihood depends on their reputation, very macho and if challenged it will lead to trouble. This makes two confrontations you've had with him and not a shot fired, amazing." All the men retired for the night and the remainder of the night and the next day until about five o'clock was uneventful.

Then suddenly, while they were all in Marshall Starrett's office, they heard what sounded like a herd of cattle coming down the street. It was the 'Hell Raisers', Glen Ray counted eighteen men. They pulled up in front of the saloon. Some went in and some remained mounted shooting their pistols in the air and under horses' feet causing runaways. A couple of the men rode their horses into the saloon and began firing into the ceiling. The saloon quickly vacated except for the 'Hell Raisers', bartender and the girls.

Luke said, "The leader, Alvin, is the oldest brother. Frank is next to the oldest, then Charlie with Barney being the youngest. Alvin is mean and Frank likes his pistols; Charlie just follows and Barney gets drunk then likes to show off. Glen Ray said, "They know you and Nathan so Fred and I will go in the saloon like customers. Give us ten minutes then one of you go in the front door and the other in the back. Have your scatter guns cocked and ready."

"If a gun fight starts, we get the brothers, after that, it's over. Fred, are you sure you want in on this?" Fred nodded his head, touched the tip of his brim and said, "Amigo, let's go to the fiesta."

They casually walked into the saloon and toward the bar. It had calmed down inside, the only customers were the 'Hell Raisers'. They were drinking, playing poker, playing with the girls and acting like drunks act. The Rangers' badges were hidden and by the time they reached the bar you could have heard a pin drop.

Glen Ray said to the bartender, "Give us whiskey and leave the bottle." Alvin walked over to the bar with all eyes on him and said, "This is our saloon, no one drinks here when the 'Hell Raisers' are in town." Before Glen Ray could respond, Barney, pistol in hand staggered to the bar, got in Fred's' face and said, "Let's do this Mexican like we did the other ones." Alvin snapped back, "Shut up Barney, keep your mouth closed."

Glen Ray said, "Alvin, we know who you are, we're Texas Rangers, we've been sent here to bring law and order back to the streets of Laredo. We're going to take you and your brothers to jail for the murders of those three Mexicans you hung at the river."

As planned Luke and Nathan came thru the doors. Fred grabbed Barneys arm and slammed it onto the bar causing Barneys pistol to come out of his hand. Fred grabbed Barney's pistol, hit him over the head, knocking him out. He caught Barney's body and pulled it up against him like a shield then pointed the pistol at Alvin's face. Glen Ray told Luke, "Get Barney, Nathan, help take him to jail." Then he walked over and took Alvin's gun. With Fred's pistol still pointed at Alvin's face, Glen Ray said, "None of you boys want to get Alvin killed so don't move a muscle. Now hear me, violence is going to stop beginning right now. Sure you boys number close to twenty; I can have twenty Rangers here in two days. Now the next time you come to town, go by and check your guns in to the Marshall. There's going to be a temporary ban on carrying firearms in town."

Luke and Nathan had left with Barney; Frank had seen Alvin put down in front of the 'Gang'. He decided to be brave with only two Rangers holding them. He said, "Alvin, I can take this kid." Alvin said, "No you drunk fool, this Mexican will kill me. All of y'all, get out the door and get on your horses." "That's right," said Glen Ray. "Then we'll let him go but Barney stays in jail." They all eased out of the door leaving Alvin alone with the Rangers. Glen Ray told Alvin, "I will get proof you were rustling and hung those three Mexicans. When I do, you and the ones responsible will hang."

Frank burst through the door with gun in hand and said, "I got 'em Alvin. They're dead men." Before Frank could point and aim Glen Ray had drawn and fired a shot to the middle of Frank's chest. As he was falling he fired a harmless shot in the floor. Fred shoved Alvin to the swinging front door of the saloon. Glen Ray said, "Now you're going to jail. Holler to your men that Frank is dead and to ride, now, before I kill you." Alvin hollered, "Don't try him. He's too fast. Frank had his pistol out of the holster and he still beat him. Go, get out of town. Tell my ol' man to come get us, get us out of jail." The remainder of the 'Gang' rode back to the ranch. Charlie hated to tell his Paw what happened because, if he was drunk, there would be trouble, lots of trouble.

Their Father, Will Guthrie, was a big man, in his late forties with a bulldog face, big thick lips, bushy eyebrows and nasal hair sticking out of his nose. He had a scar from an Indian fight on his forehead and cheek. He was big shouldered, broad chested, dirty, smelled of whiskey and tobacco. Long bushy hair, out on the sides, yellow teeth, stubble beard and body odor that would knock a buffalo to his knees. Alvin was clean but was a mean looking man, medium build, harsh eyes, gruff voice, beard and long hair. Charlie looked out of place with light hair, fair complexion, slight build and quiet. Rumor has it he was the fastest brother with a gun.

Charlie and the gang rode up to the ranch house and told Will that Frank was dead and Barney and Alvin were in jail. "Who killed Frank? Did they back shoot 'em? What happened?" "No sir," said Charlie, "Frank had his pistol out of the holster at his waist; the Ranger drew and shot him in the chest. The Ranger is fast, fastest I've ever seen and he looks like a baby, real young. Fast, fastest I've ever seen," he repeated, still in shock.

"What are Alvin and Barney in jail for?" growled Will. "Barney was drunk and mouthed off about those Mexicans we hung. After Frank tried to kill the baby-faced Ranger they locked Alvin up with Barney", replied Charlie. At hearing this, Will instructed his boys, "Have the men ready at sun up, we're going to town. If the lawyers can't get them out we'll bust them out."

Meanwhile back in town, Glen Ray and Marshall Starrett talked about the charges to file against Barney and Alvin. Finally they agreed to file disturbing the peace, drunk and disorderly conduct; that was all they could legally do. Glen Ray heard Barney's remark about the Mexicans, and it was said that he had witnessed it.

The next morning the 'Gang' saddled up with Will on the lead horse. They rode directly to the jail. Luke and the Rangers stood on the porch and the riders stayed mounted. "Turn my boys loose!" shouted Will, who was already drunk. "Can't do that," said Luke. "You got money to pay their fines?" "Charlie, pay them whatever the amount is," said Will. "Its fifty dollars apiece," said Luke. "Pay 'em Charlie" growled Will. Charlie followed Nathan to the cell and they were released. Their gun belts had been robbed of ammunition and their pistols were empty. When they were on their horses Nathan threw their belts and pistols at them.

Will said, "Who killed my boy?" looking at the Rangers. Before Glen Ray could answer Alvin said, "It was the young one, the one the banditos call 'Baby Ranger'. "Baby Boy' or whatever you name is you had no cause to kill my boy," muttered Will. He was just having fun and celebrating like all hard working cowboys. I will make you pay. We're going to bury my boy, be ready; I'm going to kill you Ranger Boy." Alvin and Barney started cussing and threatening as they rode off. One of the riders handed them a bottle. Suddenly Alvin swung his horse around and rode up to Glen Ray. He said, "Just you and me 'Baby Boy', just you and me, I will be back then it'll be just you and me." His horse reared, turned sharply and Alvin was still hollering, 'just you and me' as he rode out of town.

Luke said, "You can't go out in the street for a gunfight. He knows he can't beat you no matter how much he drinks, he's not stupid." Nathan said, "He's just trying to get you out in the open so one of his men can shoot you from a roof top."

Glen Ray said, "The quickest way to dissolve the gang is to take away its leaders. We've got to deal with Will and Alvin; Barney is just a young kid that gets his bravery out of a bottle. I don't think Charlie really wants to be part of 'em, he's just being pressured by his father and brothers. I'll go in the saloon and wait; if Alvin wants to challenge me he can come inside. That way I'll have protection from a man on a roof."

Glen Ray went to the saloon with Fred. He sat at a chair with his back to the wall with a clear view for a silhouette shot in the doorway. All lanterns were turned off. Fred's job was to watch the back door while sitting with Glen Ray. After a few moments, Glen Ray said, "How you like being a Ranger. Exciting enough for you?" Fred grinned and said, "Better than any mountain lion hunt I've been on." "Yea," said Glen Ray, "but the cat can't shoot back."

Luke and Nathan were to stay in the jail, rifles ready and not to come out. About three o'clock in the afternoon, Glen Ray heard horses; it was the 'Hell Raisers'. They reigned up in front of the jail and Alvin hollered for Glen Ray to come out, "Just you and me 'Baby Boy'!"

Luke hollered out the window, "He's having a drink in the saloon, told us to tell you to go on down, he would like to see you." Nathan said, "Mr. Guthrie, I suggest you don't move, both barrels of this shotgun are pointed at you and my finger is shaking. Any of your boys makes a move you go down – let Alvin go visit 'Baby Ranger', just him and the baby, just like he wanted it."

Alvin looked up on the two roofs for his bush whackers, they were in place but the Ranger was inside the saloon. "Come on boys, let's all go to the saloon and hang a Ranger." Nobody moved. Mr. Guthrie was drunk and he said, "Go get him boy, no son of mine is afraid, go in that saloon, drag him out dead. We'll prop him up on the porch and take target practice. Go on, go get 'em."

Alvin got off his horse, walked out in the middle of the street till he reached the saloon. Glen Ray could see him thru the swinging doors standing in the street. "Come on out Ranger, just you and me. Come on out 'Baby Boy', just you and me." "Come on in," said Glen Ray. "I've got your last drink poured and sitting on the bar." Alvin was still hollering, "Come on out", he had his ambush set up. He glanced at the roof tops and his men were gone, instead he saw where each man had been standing, a bandito with a rifle. Now he was on his own, the ambush was gone; he knew he couldn't take the Ranger in a fair gunfight. Glen Ray heard a familiar voice, it was Alvarez, "Hey, 'Baby Ranger', you stay in there. I have some business to take care of out here in the street."

Chapter 12

One of Rene's friends in Laredo must have ridden across the river and told him what was happening. He had slipped down the alley and stepped out in the street facing Alvin. Glen Ray hollered, "Watch out, he's got men on the roof." Rene answered, "No mas amigo, my men took their places. His men are lying in the alley, they don't feel pretty good." "Hey Senor 'Hell Raiser' man, how you say, just you and me. Maybe you like to hang me like you did my brother? Come on Senor Wildman, just you and me. My name is Rene Alvarez, my brother's name was Jesus Alvarez. The last words you are going to hear are his name, JESUS ALVAREZ." **BOOM! BOOM!** Two shots before he fell, **BOOM! BOOM! BOOM! BOOM!** Four more pumped into his body when Alvin hit the ground.

Will Guthrie jumped off his horse and ran to his fallen boy's body. Glen Ray walked out on the porch of the saloon. Rene was reloading his pistol. Mr. Guthrie had been kneeling beside his boy's body. All at once he jumped up, turned toward Glen Ray and said, "This is your fault, all this is your fault." He reached for his pistol; it barely cleared his holster when Glen Ray's two bullets hit him. He fell back across his boys' body.

Rene said, "'Ranger Babee', all my men are on the roofs, why you no go and arrest who you want. We make sure the 'Hell Raisers' don't get lost." "Gracias, Rene. We are amigos." "Hey," said Rene, "maybe someday me and you might fight, you are mucho rapido. Maybe Rene would have to cheet." Glen Ray grinned, nodded his head, touched the front brim, just like Laughlin, and then he turned and walked to the marshals' office.

Luke and Nathan were in the process of locking up Charlie and Barney. When the 'Gang' saw there was no double barrel shotgun sticking out the window they rode away quickly. Rene and his men fired a few shots over their heads as a parting gesture. Somehow you got the feeling the gang known as the 'Hell Raisers' was no mas.

Luke said he would wire Laughlin and tell him that, due to the Rangers, the Streets of Laredo were once again safe. He said, "You boys go on up to your rooms, relax, and I'll see you about seven for a mesquite cooked sirloin." They said thanks and started walking. Fred said, "Hey amigo, you know that son of Pancho Villa?" "Yea, what about him?" asked Glen Ray. "I don't think his daddy could handle you. Fastest two draws I've ever seen," answered Fred.

At dinner Luke looked across the table and into Glen Ray's eyes and said, "Son, you're fast, fast as I have ever seen, you've got nerves of steel, nothing scares you. Just want to give you a little advice. Don't get over-confident and careless. You've picked up a nickname 'Baby Ranger' and you will be well known and stories will be told about you. The majority of the people will fear you; others will be trying to make a name off you. Gunfighters won't know how fast you are, they think they are fast and won't be reluctant to try you. Always keep the advantage in your favor, you're smart. You have already demonstrated that to me. I am very impressed, especially since you are so young."

"Why did they give me the 'Baby Ranger' nickname?" wondered Glen Ray. "Son, take a look in the mirror," suggested Luke, "long blond curly hair, blue eyes, dimples, pearly white teeth and a mama's boy smile – accept it, you're the 'Baby Ranger' and easily identified. Take it as a compliment, look how well Billy the Kid is known." Fred said, "My sister calls him baby and he don't mind." Glen Ray shoved Fred on the shoulder and said, "Shut up amigo. By the way, is there a woman in your life?" Fred said, "A woman in my life, you mean women in my life. Every woman in every cantina is my woman. Remember, 'No coyote is too far, no rustler can ride away, no woman can steal my heart.'" "Yea, yea amigo," said Glen Ray, "your time will come."

Nathan, who had no knowledge of Laughlin's reluctance to make Fred a Ranger, was with them at dinner and asked Fred, "hey, are you going back to the ranch in Abilene or have you decided to become a full time Ranger?" Fred looked at Nathan, directly in his eyes, and said, "I am a man of integrity and I promised my Papa I would take care of Mr. Fox"; He glanced at Glen Ray and continued "that I will do." Glen Ray nodded and winked. "Boys I want you to know you put on a show out there today," said Luke. "Stories will be told about the Streets of Laredo."

The next morning they all met at the Marshals' office. Luke said that Jim Weaver and Billy Joe Smith were on the way and should arrive tomorrow; they couldn't be reached in time to be stopped. He said, "I'm going to bring our prisoners out one at a time and see if we can get a confession out of them for the murders of those three vaqueros."

Nathan went to the cell and brought out Barney. Luke sat Barney down at the table with the group then he walked around the room for a minute, stopped, looked at Barney and said in a calm voice, "Did you ever see a man hang? It's not a pretty sight. Sometimes an eye will pop out of its socket, sometimes your neck doesn't break and you're hanging and choking to death. When that happens' men hold onto your legs and lift their bodies off the ground so that the extra weight breaks your neck. If the hangman wants to, he purposely miss-figures your weight to watch you do the dance of death till you suffocate." Barney was no longer drunk and brave from whiskey. He was scared, very scared. Luke said, "Everybody knows you boys killed 'em. You said you did in the saloon. Tell us what happened, give me a confession and I will get you life instead of death by hanging." Barney said, "I don't want to hang. We did it, me, my dad, Alvin and Frank. Charlie wasn't there; he had gone to Beeville to see his girlfriend."

Charlie could hear what was being said from his cell. Luke said, "Charlie is that right, were you in Beeville?" "Yes sir," he answered, "I was with my girlfriend Wynona Brown, she will tell you I was there for three days." "Well Charlie, here's what I'm going to do, you were not involved, but you were involved in the threat of a Rangers life. I'm going to recommend to the judge that you get five years probation, under the stipulation that you return to that ranch and make it a working cattle ranch. No 'Hell Raiser', just a good hard working rancher. You don't have to follow anyone any more; you can be your own man.

Don't come to town with your gun. You think you're fast, that man right there," pointing to Glen Ray, "is fast. Had you faced him they would be reading over your grave. You've got a chance for a new start, screw it up and me or the Rangers will come after you. I don't think you are like your paw and your brothers, don't prove me wrong, do we have an understanding?" "Yes sir,", said Charlie," yes sir, thank you sir. I won't let you down, thank you sir." The two of them would remain in jail waiting on the circuit judge.

Glen Ray said, "Come on Fred, let's make our walk thru the streets, we need for the townspeople to feel safe. Nathan, lock the door when Luke leaves and don't let anyone in, we'll be back shortly." Fred said, "Glen Ray, I've never had to face someone and draw against them. The only men I've killed were rustlers at Abe Silas' ranch and that was long range rifle shots. What's it like knowing the loser will die?"

"Laughlin taught me it's all mental," replied Glen Ray," You must relax your muscles, don't hurry, be smooth and make your shot count. It's no good to get the first shot off and miss; you may be killed by a slower gun. Relax, take your time, and be sure the advantage is yours." Fred grinned and said, "You mean to tell me you were taking your time. Just how fast are you amigo?" Glen Ray smiled.

They walked and when they came to the saloon where Glen Ray had shot the gambler, he said, "My life changed right here, thought I would be hanged for killing a gambling man. Nathan saved my life by testifying, Laughlin gave me an opportunity to be someone, a Ranger. My life changed, I am blessed."

Having completed their rounds, they knocked on the jail door and Nathan let them inside. Glen Ray and Fred had stopped by the restaurant and asked that three meals be sent to the jail. In a short while the lunches were delivered and they sat at a table in the jail eating and talking.

Glen Ray said to Nathan, "Did you see how Luke used your method to get a confession? Hanging gets anyone's attention, maybe you taught old Luke something. Nathan, tell us about yourself, we know very little about you." Nathan said, "Well, there was a time I couldn't talk about it, but here goes. I was born in Tennessee; married with two children. We owned a farm and the future looked bright. Then came the war; I was a captain for the South. Then came Shiloh and a cannon ball tore my leg off at the knee. When I returned home, my farm was gone; my house burned to the ground and my family missing. That's when I turned to alcohol; partially for the pain but mainly because of the grief and trying to forget. I slowly made my way to Texas to hide from my memories. Then Laughlin inspired me by showing he cared. He told me my family wouldn't want me to ruin myself grieving over them. They would want me to carry on with my life and be the person I was before the war. He said men are measured by how they deal with adversities. Thanks to Laughlin, I'm back and now living my life as a Texas Ranger; my wife and boys would be proud of me. No one knows what happened to my family; probably killed by soldiers or carpetbaggers. I believe the only family I still have is my sister. She had been living in Atlanta but we got separated during the war. Now I don't know where she is."

Luke had walked in and heard part of Nathan's story. He asked, "Nathan, what was your sisters' name?" Nathan replied, "Bonnie Churchill, she was married to a confederate soldier named Seth and they lived in Atlanta when the war started."

Luke thought about Nathan's conversation and decided he was going to wire the war office and see if Seth Churchill could be located. Luke would keep it quiet; he didn't want to give Nathan any false hopes.

The Rangers finished their lunch and decided to visit the gunsmith.

Glen Ray was having a different grip and some trigger work done on a handgun then he was going to teach Nathan how to quick draw.

Jim Weaver and Billy Joe Smith rode in to Laredo late that evening. They had orders from Laughlin to stay in there with Luke to be certain the 'Hell Raisers' didn't regroup. They were to tell Glen Ray, Nathan and Fred to return to Uvalde. Laughlin also warned that small parties of Indians or commancheros were raiding ranches and farms around the Eagle Pass area. Small ranches were being burned, their horses stolen, and victims mutilated. The women were being used and then killed which meant the group did not want to be slowed down with captives or they would have taken all the women.

Jim told Glen Ray that Laughlin would probably send them out when they reached Uvalde. The location of the raids would be studied and a group of Rangers would be dispatched to try and make contact.

Back at Fox's ranch in Abilene, Angel was setting a plate of eggs, bacon, biscuits and gravy in front of Mr. Fox at the breakfast table. She warmed his coffee and asked, "Senor Fox, have you heard from Glen Ray and Fred?" He said, "Sweetie sit down and have a cup of coffee with me. Now don't you worry about them two boys, they can take care of themselves." "Senor Fox, when you met your wife did your heart hurt when she wasn't with you? Did you think about her all the time?" asked Angel. "Yes honey and I still think that way and she's been gone seventeen years," answered Fox. "I am assuming that's the way you feel about Glen Ray," "Yes, yes", Angel responded, "don't you think he's beautiful?" "Well I don't know if I would
say he's beautiful," Fox replied, "but if you say so I will agree. I will say this, Glen Ray and your brother are two 'damn good men'."

Later on that evening, about an hour before sunset, Mr. Fox was sitting on the front porch. He enjoyed watching the sun set and remembering things from the past, especially about his wife. Angel came out of the house and asked, "Can I get you some coffee?" "Sure," he answered, "and get yourself a cup then come join me; I need some company."

She returned with the coffee, sat down in the swing with Mr. Fox and asked, "Have you heard from Fred and Glen Ray?" Fox replied, "Now I wonder how I knew that would be the first question you would ask." Continuing he said, "Sheriff Cletus Meeks sent word they had done their job in Laredo and I could expect Fred to be showing up in a couple of weeks. Who knows about Glen Ray, wherever he's needed he has to answer the call. You miss him don't you?" "Yes sir", said Angel, "all the time and I try not to think about him. Mr. Fox, tell me about your wife, I know you loved her very much."

"You are right, so very right. I did and still do love her very much. I met my wife when I was twenty-two years old. I was a Ranger and our job was to range all of Texas. I met Maude while I was on a patrol. We got married and I remained a Ranger fighting Indians while Sam Houston was defeating Santa Anna in 1836. At that time I left the Rangers to be a rancher. Maude and I started this ranch, slept in tents till we could build a house and start a herd. During the Civil War we kept expanding the ranch and growing the herd. Maude couldn't have children so it was just me and her – she was beautiful and I wanted to give her everything. All she ever wanted was me. She would ask me to walk over there," and he pointed to Knob Hill. "From there you can see for miles; she would thank God for all the beauty he put in the world. When she died I buried her up there." He paused for a moment, then, with a tear in his eye, he continued, "someday I'll be buried there with her."

Angel said, "I wish I could have known her. Did you give up the Rangers for her?" "Not just for her," he said, "for both of us so we could be together all the time. I don't say much about me being a Ranger. I don't want Fred to know. But that's wrong, the thrill is there and it's his choice. They would love to have him."

By now the trio, Nathan, Glen Ray & Fred were on their second day of the journey to Uvalde when they noticed smoke to the south towards Eagle Pass. It was a lot of smoke, like you would expect from a burning house.

As they rode hard toward the fire, it was evident they were too late. The ranch had been attacked and burned. It was a small place used for farming, probably had a couple of mules, jersey cow and a couple of horses. The barn was burned to the ground. In the yard lay a young man maybe twenty-five, he had been scalped and mutilated. Beside him lay a boy not more than five years old. He had been scalped and his stomach ripped open exposing his intestines. The family pigs were taking advantage of the two bodies. Inside the half burned house was a naked woman tied spread eagle to the four-poster bed. She had been violated and then parts of her body had been removed, mercifully her throat had been cut. Nathan lost all control and went into a fit of rage. He was thinking, 'This is what happened to my wife and children.'

After a while all three men found their composure, buried the bodies, and Nathan said a prayer. They mounted up and started trailing. It was estimated at least six horses, probably the group Laughlin referred to in his telegram. The trail led directly to another small ranch. As they rode closer to the ranch and could see clearly, it appeared to be undamaged. When they were within a hundred yards the family ran out of the house to greet them. "Rangers, Rangers, oh thank God," said the father while he was holding a two year old girl in his arms. The wife was holding a very young baby and a young man about sixteen was holding a black powder rifle. The fathers name was Lester McKenzie. He and his family owned a section of land, six hundred and forty acres with a few horses and cows. They farmed primarily and tried to raise some cattle; anything to survive.

Lester told them he was going to milk the jersey cow at daybreak when six Indians rode up in front of the corral. He said, "Their horses were painted up and they had on war paint. I had a shotgun in the barn and prayed to God for help as I ran to get it."

"There's been a big white owl staying in our barn so when I opened the door it flew out directly over the Indians. They pointed up in the air at the owl; started whooping and hollering then rode off at full gallop. I don't know what happened, but that owl saved them and our lives."

Fred said, "Amigo, I can tell you what happened. The Mexicans and Indians believe that a white owl is really a brown owl turned white when a spirit leaves a body but instead of going to heaven, it enters the owl. The brown owl then has the ghost in it causing it to turn white. It is extremely bad luck to see one, it usually means death. The CURANDEROS, witch doctors, preach this and it is accepted as fact. The Indians won't come back to your ranch.

Glen Ray told the family they should load up in the wagon and go to Laredo until the Indians are caught. They refused, said they had worked too hard to leave their ranch unprotected. An attitude you would expect from God fearing, honest, hard working people like the McKenzie's'.

The Rangers said goodbye and continued on their search. As they rode on Glen Ray said, "Hey Fred, is all that stuff true, what you told them about the owl?" "Amigo, it's true," said Fred, "I'm glad I didn't see the owl, it would concern me." Nathan laughed and said, "It's true. I've heard it before; for sure the Indians believe it."

Chapter 13

Back in Laredo, a telegram came in for Marshal Starrett. It was from the war office in reference to his inquiry about Seth Churchill. The telegram said he was in Atlanta and gave his last known address. Luke sat down and wrote a letter informing Seth that Nathan Law was a former deputy of his and now a Texas Ranger. Any information on his family would be appreciated. It was mailed and once again he decided to keep all the information to himself.

Meanwhile, the Rangers continued to trail the Indians, it was easy and they weren't trying to hide their trail so they rode all day, camped with no fire and ate jerky. They agreed there was a good chance of catching up with them the next day. If the Indians knew they were being followed they would try an ambush. The Rangers' best bet was to catch them camped, then after dark, take 'em by surprise. That night they set up shifts for guard duty, two sleeping and one watching.

The night passed without incident and they were in their saddles at sun-up. It was a cool, overcast day with an occasional light shower, a good day for tracking. Around ten o'clock they heard gunfire. Being careful not to ride into an ambush they rode toward the shots. Soon they were able to see a small ranch, the roof was on fire and the Indians were attacking. Three of the Indians were on horseback circling the ranch house while three more had dismounted and were making their way toward it.

Glen Ray said, "We are about one hundred yards out; dismount and secure your horses then get your rifles and get on your bellies. We'll all fire at once. Our first shots will be the three horses standing without mounts. Nathan, take the one on the left, I'll take the center one; Fred, take the one on the right. Our second shots will be for the mounted rider's horses. I don't like shooting horses, but we have to put them on foot. Everybody ready. On three – one, two, three." Three rifles went off together; three horses fell. They directed the next shots to the remaining three horses, down they went with riders tumbling.

One of the Indians was on his knees trying to get up when a shot was fired from the house. Down the Indian went. Fred was squeezing off one. The rifle went off and the Indian turned a flip. Another Indian that had been on horseback was limping bad and trying to run past the house. BOOM! Down went the third Indian from the rifle in the house. The three remaining Indians ran for the corral to get on ranch horses. Glen Ray fired his rifle and the fourth Indian fell. One of the Indians was inside the corral and firing back, the other Indian was trying to catch a horse. The horses were scared from the gunfire and were racing around in the corral trying to get out.

All of a sudden a horse went by Glen Ray and Fred, it was Nathan. He had mounted up, had his sawed off shotgun in his hand and was riding hard for the corral. The Indian inside the corral got a shot off, but missed. Nathan's horse jumped the corral fence knocking the top railing off. When the horse landed, Nathan fired one barrel at the Indian with the rifle. The double ought shot hit him in the chest and knocked him into the railing on the corral. He slid down onto the ground with half his chest blown away. The other Indian came running at Nathan probably in hopes of getting his horse. From about ten feet away the shotgun roared again. The Indian was hit flush in the face; the velocity of the shotgun flipped him backwards.

Nathan was reloading the shotgun while still sitting on his horse when Glen Ray and Fred reached him. Fred held the horses bridle while Glen Ray helped Nathan off his horse. With excitement in his voice, Glen Ray said, "Nathan, good job, but you're crazy. We could have taken them without you risking your life. You rode right into them, you were fearless, you could have been killed." Nathan had a blank look on his face as he answered, "I saw what they did to that family, didn't want any of them getting away. What they did could have happened to my family. I don't have anything to lose, my life ended when I lost my family." Then he continued, "Did we get 'em all? Let's go check; make sure they're all dead then I'll finish off any horses that are still alive." Glen Ray looked at Fred and said, "Maybe something to that owl story, they are all dead after seeing it." Fred nodded, "Si, amigo, it is the truth."

The fire on the roof had gone out; it was a sod roof, not very combustible. A young man about sixteen stepped out of the house holding a 45.70 Springfield. Behind him stood his mother, a younger brother and a sister; they were unharmed. The boy introduced himself as Johnny, 'John Bridges'. He was very calm considering what all had just happened. Fred said, "Good shooting, you got two of them." Johnny laughed and said, "Those were my last two bullets. If you guys hadn't showed up we were gonna be dead." Then he continued," It's just us; my dad died a year ago. Got kicked in the head while he was bucking out some young horses." Johnny looked at Nathan and said, "That was really something what you did. You must not be afraid to die." As they turned their horses toward Uvalde, Glen Ray thought; how right you are young man, how right you are.

At the Rocking Horse Ranch, back in Uvalde, Melissa and Laughlin were making wedding plans and had agreed to have the wedding on January 1st instead of in December. They wanted Jim, Glen Ray, Fred, Mr. Fox, Angel and her mother at the wedding. After the new date was set Melissa asked a question she had been avoiding. "Laughlin, who is going to be your best man" she asked? Laughlin gritted his teeth; you could tell he was thinking about Captain Beasley, he didn't answer.

The next morning Melissa was in the backyard crying. Laughlin stepped out of the kitchen dressed in pants and boots, no shirt. Earlier, when he woke up; Melissa wasn't in the house and it scared him. When he found her in the backyard he could see that she had been crying. "What's wrong?" he asked. "Nothing", she answered. Again he asked, "What's wrong Melissa?" "Nothing", she insisted. That's when he noticed she was holding something in her hand. His first thought was a telegram with bad news. He pulled the paper from her hand, opened it and read the note. It was the note from Linda he had placed in his wallet. 'Oh my God', he thought. 'How could I have been so stupid; I had forgotten that I had it? Why didn't I throw it away?' He got himself together and reverted back to one of the standards he had set for himself, always tell the truth.

"Melissa," he said, "I'm so sorry that you had to see that note. Linda is someone from the past that was in love with me, but I was not in love with her. You are my first love. I had no reason to keep the note; hell I forgot I had it and I'm sorry for hurting you." "You didn't love her?" she blurted. "NO!" he shouted. Then, more like a statement than a question, she said, "I am your first love." "YES!" said Laughlin, then he continued, "Well, I don't know, sure thought a lot of Sam before I met you. "Oh Laughlin, if I was big enough I would beat you to death." said Melissa with a sigh of relief. Laughlin ended the exchange with a sly, "Yea, well come on in the house and you can love me to death."

When they awoke the next morning, it was a good brisk autumn day, a great day for a horse ride. Laughlin had Sam and Princess saddled up and ready for a ride around the ranch and then on to town. Laughlin's wound was healing rapidly and he was ready to ride.

They rode to an area he had selected to start stretching fence. It was time to honor Mr. Fox's request and get started being a cattle rancher. He showed Melissa the area and explained that there was good grazing and water would come from the creek. With proper rotation of the cattle, they could fatten the herd, drive them the short distance to Abilene and get a good price. Then the railroad, not drovers, would take them up north.

Melissa pretended to be listening but her mind was elsewhere, whatever Laughlin wanted to do was fine with her. She said, "Ranger man, if you didn't have an injured shoulder Princess and I would embarrass you again with a race." Both of the horses had not been out in a while, it was cool and they wanted to run. Laughlin exercised good judgment and held back; "next time Sam and I'll let you show off your speed", he snorted.

They rode into Uvalde with plans of having dinner in the restaurant and staying overnight, returning to the ranch on the following day. The horses were put in the livery stable. Melissa went to the restaurant and Laughlin to the telegraph office. There was a telegram from Luke in Laredo; all was quiet – no more 'Hell Raisers'. Laughlin left the telegraph office and went over to Sheriff Oral Fox's office just to talk.

Oral was the brother of J.J. Fox and was sixty-nine years old. He should have retired some time ago but he was in good shape and had been a lawman during some rough times. He had a reputation of being firm, but fair and could still perform when necessary. He was about six feet tall, bald headed, red complexion and kept an unlit cigar in his mouth. He was someone Laughlin enjoyed; he could tell lots of stories. He had been a Ranger with his brother J.J. but decided to be a sheriff so he could have a home and family.

Laughlin pulled up a chair in the jail and the two men started talking. Oral said, "There's a gunfighter in the saloon. It's Wes Lockhart, he ain't done nothin', not making any threats, but he was a friend of Bucky Buchanan, the 'Widowmaker'. Before you killed Bucky they would sometimes work together when bounty hunting." "Is he over there now?" asked Laughlin.

"Yes," I'm sure he is" said Oral, "he always has a meal at the restaurant about four, then he goes to the saloon, sips whiskey and enjoys the girls."

Laughlin pulled his pistol, opened the cylinder, checked the load, closed the cylinder and spun it. "Let's go over and see why he's in town", he growled.

Oral and Laughlin walked into the saloon and went directly to the table where Wes was sitting. Laughlin said, "Hello Wes, we're going to sit and visit with you for a spell." Wes looked at Laughlin and said, "I know who you are, you're McFarland, Ranger McFarland." Laughlin said, "That's right. Let's get straight to the point. Why are you here?

What do you want?" "Ranger, I don't want any trouble", said Wes, "I'm just here to visit my old friend the 'Widowmakers' grave and pay my respects." Laughlin replied, "You've been here three days, you've had plenty of time. I don't want you here in the morning when the sun comes up." "Why Ranger, that's downright unfriendly of you," uttered Lockhart. Then he added, "Sheriff Fox, this is your town, do you want me out? Can't you take care of the town any longer, have to get the Rangers in here to hold you hand?" Wes snickered and lifted his whiskey glass up to his mouth to take a drink. When the glass touched his lips Oral hit the bottom of the glass with a hard right hand. The glass broke when it hit his teeth breaking off two of his lower front teeth and one upper front tooth. The broken glass cut his lip. His tongue and the inside of his mouth had a deep gash. Blood was pouring out of his mouth. Laughlin slammed Wes' head to the table and held it down while Oral took away his gun. Blood was still flowing when Wes was allowed to raise his head. McFarland looked into his eyes and said, "Mister don't get cute with a Texas Ranger and don't you ever show disrespect to this man." Then with a stern look, Laughlin continued, "He can devour you, you are nothing compared to what he's faced. Be glad he's older and has mellowed some because if he hadn't we would be taking you to visit your friend alright, in a box. Make your arrest Oral; lock him up. I'll go get Doctor Milles. Doc may not want to sew him up." Then he chuckled and added, "Hell, he might let him bleed to death."

Laughlin went to the restaurant and sat down at the table Melissa had set for them. She asked, "How is Oral? Did you enjoy your visit?" "Oh yea", he answered, "Oral's a good man, a lot of fun to be around, keeps you entertained."

While they were having dinner and wine, Laughlin said, "Now I'll answer your question about my best man. I have decided it will be Captain Beasley with Mr. Fox representing him. Mr. Fox doesn't make a habit of telling people that he was a Ranger. When the organization was formed he was one of the first Rangers, he and Captain Beasley served together till Fox retired and became a rancher." "I think that's a wonderful idea", said Melissa, "does Mr. Fox know?" Laughlin said he was sending a telegram inviting him and that he could stay at the ranch with them. Then he added, "Having our wedding at the local church will allow the rest of our out-of-town guests to stay in the hotel." "Oh, I'm so excited I can't wait," said Melissa, "wish it was tomorrow." Then, with excitement still in her voice, she added, "Oh my goodness, I've got to start making plans for my mother. Laughlin, we've got so much to do, I want it to be perfect. It's only eighteen days before January the first." With Melissa so excited Laughlin hoped his area would remain quite, at least till after the wedding and honeymoon.

The next morning Laughlin and Melissa prepared for their horseback ride back to the ranch. They were in front of the livery stable, getting ready to mount up when they saw three riders at the east end of the town, it was Glen Ray, Fred and Nathan. Laughlin told Melissa to go back to the restaurant and wait. He would be along shortly, had to fill out reports and meet with the men. The men all went to Oral's office and sat down. Nathan told Laughlin about Laredo, the Banditos and the Hell Raisers. Laughlin complimented them on working with the banditos. He said, "We've got all we can handle here on our side, maybe this will discourage some of the border violence."

Glen Ray told them the details of the Indian fight, especially Nathan's efforts. Laughlin swelled with pride and said, "Excellent job Rangers. I'm proud of all of you." Then he looked at Nathan and said, "Nathan, we're finding out more and more things about you lately, all good. You're becoming a damn good Ranger."

Nathan was sitting at the table with his arms on top of the table and hands interlocked. He leaned back, reached in his left pocket and pulled out a silver dollar. "I was sitting in the saloon with you in Laredo; you gave me this silver dollar. You said, 'Thanks for the information, consider yourself my deputy and keep me informed of anything you hear.' Calling me your deputy sounded good, it made me feel like somebody. I decided, no more booze, get my life together and work toward being a Ranger. Every time I started shaking and wanting a drink, I would pull out this silver dollar, look at it and regain my strength. Thank you Laughlin, you gave me renewed courage and the Lord is now in control of my life."

Laughlin said, "Thank you men, y'all come to the ranch tonight, we'll burn a few steaks. Glen Ray, don't leave, I need to speak with you." Glen Ray tensed, had he done something wrong, was Laughlin mad at him? They both sat back down at the table. Laughlin looked very stern when he looked into Glen Ray's eyes. "Luke Starrett wired me that when the newspaper reported the 'Hell Raisers' story you were referred to as 'The Baby Ranger' and Nathan was called 'Shotgun'." Laughlin tried to keep a stern face but failed, he grinned and said, "Talk to me."

Glen Ray said, "The banditos gave us the names. I guess because I look so young, they call me baby. Shotgun is a good name for Nathan though; you should see him in action. He has nerves of steel, ain't afraid of nothing and he's deadly with that shotgun. Loads it with double ought buck, it cuts people in half." Then, with sincerity in his voice, he added, "Laughlin, I want you to know, I trust this man with my life, don't let the peg leg mislead you, he can take care of himself and then some."

Later they all met at the ranch for the cookout and drinks. After supper Laughlin told Nathan to go back to Uvalde and help Oral. He told him about Wes Lockhart and to be careful when Oral released him. Then he told Glen Ray and Fred to return to Abilene, spend some time relaxing and wait on orders. They were reminded of the wedding on January 1st and Laughlin gave Glen Ray a note for Mr. Fox.

The Rangers were up at daylight with Glen Ray and Fred preparing for the Abilene trip. Nathan said goodbye and headed back to town. The other two shook hands with Laughlin, told him to tell Melissa thanks for everything and they would see her at the wedding then they mounted up and headed west.

The sun was peeking up over the horizon. It was an overcast day, the north wind had come in during the night and the temperature was dropping. They put on their ponchos and tied their bandanas over their head, and under their chins, covering their ears. Put on their hats, pulled the brim down, slipped on their cowhide gloves and rode directly into a twenty five mile wind coming out of the northwest. Around noon it started sleeting and getting colder, they were experiencing a Blue Norther.

They were on the stage road and heard the stage coming from behind. "Whoa, whoa; hello Rangers, tie your horses on the back of the stage, get in; get out of this weather. I'm empty all the way to Abilene, I was just carrying mail, now, hell I'll be hauling celebrities." It was Bob Bell; they climbed on top with Bob so they could talk a while. The sleet had turned to light snow and the wind was blowing harder. Bob said, "Been hearing some stories about you boys. That was a mess in Laredo till y'all got there. Newspaper is telling all about it, Baby Ranger. That's what they call you, right? Glen Ray nodded as Bob continued. "Nathan is being called Shotgun Law – Baby Ranger and Shotgun Law. Fred, you're clean, they ain't named you. Heard about the Indian fight. Seems you boys been staying really busy." With that being said the men alternated driving while two stayed inside the stage out of the wind. They stopped in Menard for the night. Menard was very small but it had all they needed, lodging, food and a livery stable.

The next day was cold, with bright sunshine, no wind and three inches of snow on the ground; a beautiful scene. They rode till the first switch station was reached. The stage got fresh horses, while Glen Ray and Fred left the stage so they could maintain a proper pace for their horses; otherwise, fresh horses for the stage every so often would soon run their horses to death.

A couple of days later they reached Abilene late in the evening, deciding to get a room, clean-up, eat and get a good nights sleep before leaving for Mr. Fox's ranch the following day. Linda, who was in the saloon when she was told the Rangers were in town getting a room at her place, quickly went to the hotel and checked the register to see who they were. She sent word to their room that steaks were on her and they were to meet her in the hotel restaurant at seven.

When they entered the restaurant; it was dimly lit with candles and lamps. Linda had purchased a player piano so customers could enjoy music while dining. It reflected a sense of female ownership with a romantic atmosphere. Linda greeted them and led them to a very nice table complete with candles and wine. They sat down and Glen Ray wondered who Linda would ask about first, Laughlin or Jim. She said, "I have heard about Laredo and the Indian raid, I'm so glad you all are safe. How is Jim? I tell you, that man nearly danced my legs off at the street dance." Glen Ray told her Jim was on patrol in Laredo and would be there until Laughlin's wedding. "Oh, how is Laughlin?" she asked. Glen Ray answered, "Well, a back shooter got him. He was shot in the shoulder but has recovered. Linda's bottom lip trembled as she stammered, "But he's alright now, he's recovered, right?" "Yea", said Glen Ray, "everything is fine, just busy getting ready for the wedding."

Linda changed the subject and told Fred she had someone for him to meet. Then she said, "Her name is LaQuita; she came in on the stage from San Antone about three weeks ago and asked for a job. I gave her a job in the kitchen. When I have an opening I will use her as a waitress. She is a hard worker, won't work in the saloon, very nice girl."

Linda got up and went to the kitchen. A few minutes later she returned with LaQuita. LaQuita had dark brown hair hanging to her waist, brown eyes, olive complexion, big lush lips, and a beautiful enticing smile. She stood five foot four and was very well built. When Linda introduced her to Fred; they stood and stared at each other, then sat down. Linda said she had to go to the saloon. Glen Ray said he was tired and was going to his room. This left Fred and LaQuita alone. They were still looking at each other and communicating in Spanish until about 2:00 AM. Fred said his goodnights and tried to slip back into his hotel room without waking Glen Ray; it didn't happen.

Glen Ray looked up and said, "Amigo, how did you like LaQuita, she is very beautiful." "Amigo, amigo, amigo, I'm in love, no mas leaving Abilene," shouted Fred. "What about all your women in the cantinas?" queried Glen Ray. "No mas," said Fred, then he sheepishly added, "well, maybe a little bit." Glen Ray threw a pillow at Fred and said, "Go to bed amigo, I don't want to hear about it."

Linda and LaQuita had breakfast the next morning with both Rangers. It was entertaining; Fred and LaQuita were knocking over salt shakers and spilling their coffee, Fred was showing off all his manners. He was trying very hard to impress LaQuita by standing up when she approached or left the table and pulling out a chair when she sat. Saying please when asking for the syrup or chewing with his mouth closed and daintily wiping gravy or syrup from the corners of his mouth. Glen Ray couldn't eat; he was watching the show that 'Don Juan' was putting on for them. When the meal was finished they said their goodbyes and walked out to their horses. The snow had melted and the street was muddy. Glen Ray said in a feminine voice, "Freddie, do you think you could carry me across this mud to my horse and then help me get my foot in the stirrups? Oh, Freddie you're so sweet and soooo handsome." "Shut up amigo," said Fred," from now on you have to get my permission to see my sister."

As they rode toward the ranch the temperature was around fifty, the snow had melted and there wasn't any wind. The air was fresh and crisp; it was a beautiful day to be alive. Glen Ray looked toward the heavens and said, "Thank you Lord for this day: and Fred said, "Si, gracias Dios por un buen dia." As they continued, their conversation turned to Nathan. Fred said, "I am really impressed with Nathan, can you believe he was living out of a bottle and sleeping in alleys?" Glen Ray said, "Nathan is a man, a very strong man. You see, after what happened to him, had he been a weak man he would have drank himself to death. A guy like Nathan can be knocked to his knees, shake it off and get up again. You can't knock a man of his caliber to the ground and count him out." "Well said amigo," said Fred then added, "I agree, he can ride with me anytime."

Fred said, "Let's talk about horses, your horse. I have a sorrel filly at the ranch, she's due to be in season for the second time. Purposely didn't breed her the first time; wanted her to be a little older. Diablo was going to be my stud, but since seeing your horse, I've changed my mind. Whiskey and that filly will throw an outstanding colt. You should see her, looks just like Whiskey. Let's breed them and I'll take care of the colt here at the ranch, but he'll be yours." "Naw, Fred," said Glen Ray, "let's breed, but you can have the colt; that way you can finally say you have a fast horse. Fred playfully pulled his sidearm and pointed it at Glen Ray who threw his hands up in the air and said, "Put your pistola away amigo, only teasing," then he added, "Laughlin says Melissa's filly is pretty fast too. I'll bet Diablo and Princess would throw a mighty fine colt."

Sometime after lunch they arrived at the Fox ranch. They rode up to the yard gate and Manuel came running to say hello to his brother and take the horses. Mr. Fox greeted them, told Fred to go see his mother so she could see he was alive then come back to the house for sandwiches. Glen Ray and Mr. Fox headed for the ranch house.

When they entered, Angel ran out of the kitchen, threw her arms around Glen Ray and said, "Ola, I'm so happy to see you." "I'm happy you're back too," said Fox, "first time she's smiled since you left." "I'll go and make you lunch," said Angel. "Is Fred coming?" she asked. "Yes, after he kisses and hugs his mother, if he don't I won't let him eat," uttered Fox.

In a few minutes Fred came up and Fox sent him back to get his mother. When she arrived they sat around the table, Angel included. Fox blessed the food and thanked the Lord for the boys' safe return. They ate while carrying on a long conversation. Of course Glen Ray teased Fred about LaQuita. Everyone was excited hearing about her and Mr. Fox demanded Fred bring her for Sunday dinner. Then Fox said he would like to spend some private time with the boys. They went to the living room, sat down and Fox said, "Tell me about Laredo and the Indian fight." They told Mr. Fox all about Laredo, the banditos and

Fred told about Glen Ray's fast draw. Fred talked about the owl, the Indians and Nathan. Mr. Fox listened intently; you would think he was visualizing riding with them.

Then he said, "Good job boys, you're all good Rangers." Fred said, "Mr. Fox, I'm just plain Fred, not a Ranger only a temporary deputy and I'm back at the ranch to stay." Fox responded, "I need to level with you Fred; I haven't been dishonest, just didn't present all the facts. I was one of the original Rangers and remained a Ranger until I gave it up so Maude and I could start this ranch and be together."

"I loved being a Ranger. It's a thrilling, dangerous life, and once you get Ranger blood in your veins, you will always want to be one. I served with Captain Beasley and told Laughlin lots of stories about him. The Captain was a hell of a man. Fred, if you desire to be a Ranger then you have my blessings." "My job is here on the ranch, with you" replied Fred. It's like you are my grandfather. My father told me you were the finest man he ever knew. My job is to take care of you." "Fred you are the son I never had," said Fox," your daddy was so very proud and you were a good son to him. I love you and your family very much." The two men got up and embraced, repeating their affection for each other.

They sat back down and Mr. Fox looked at Glen Ray, focused his steely eyes and said, "Son, you are fast becoming a top notch Ranger. Hell, you're just barely twenty-one and stories are circulating all over the state about the 'Baby Ranger and his lightening fast gun. You'll draw lots of attention, just like Laughlin. Drunks and gunslingers will want to try you head on, then, later it'll be back shooters you'll have to worry about."

"Times are changing; the Rangers are going from Indian fighter to peace officers. The states' becoming more populated, which means more violence, outlaws, rustlers and range wars. Texas is growing and changing daily and the demand for more Rangers is growing. Enough said, hell, if I was a young man I would join the Rangers" then he laughed heartily.

Glen Ray said, "I have a note here for you from Laughlin," and handed it to Mr. Fox. Fox put on his reading glasses sliding them to the end of his nose, opened the envelope, pulled out the paper, leaned his head back and read the note. His face lit up, he lowered his head, looked at Fred and said with excitement, "We're going to a wedding, Laughlin and Melissa's. Tell your mother she and Angel are going along with you, Glen Ray and all the other Rangers. I'll be representing Captain Beasley and acting as Best Man. How 'bout that – we're going to the wedding," Fox was excited.

Chapter 14

At the Rocking Horse ranch back in Uvalde, Laughlin was up early. It was a pretty day as he rode in to town. It was like old times, just him and Sam. He had a couple of things he wanted to get done. Send some telegrams, go to the jail and work with Nathan on the use of his pistol.

He went to the telegraph office to wire Luke Starrett and his two Rangers in Laredo. They had sent a wire saying everything was quite and peaceful, almost boring. He grinned and walked out toward the jail. When he reached the jail, he knocked on the door and Nathan let him inside.

Oral was doing some paper work and posting the wanted posters while Nathan was cleaning his shotgun and adjusting a cartridge belt that fit over his left shoulder and hung on the right side of his waist. It had been custom made for him and was to be used for shotgun shells. Laughlin walked over to the cell holding Wes Lockhart. Wes was sitting on his cot; he looked up exposing a swollen jaw, three missing teeth and swollen blue lips. Laughlin grasped one of the bars of the cell and asked, "Wes, how you doing today? Have you had a change of attitude since our last meeting?" Wes tried to mumble something but his tongue was swollen from the cut and it made understanding him difficult. "Oral, your guest has been here three days, you want to put him on the road or keep him here a while longer?" Oral said, "Might as well get rid of him, he ain't no company, can't understand a word he says." "Oral is that his gun belt and saddle bags hanging up on the rack?" asked Laughlin. Oral nodded yes and Laughlin walked over to the rack, removed the pistol from the holster and ejected every bullet including those from the gun belt. He threw the saddle bags to Nathan and said, "Remove any cartridges in the bags; he's leaving here without any ammo."

Laughlin continued, "Wes, here's the deal, I had your horse saddled, he's tied out in front. We're going to let you out, you get on that horse, spur hard and keep spurring. You ride out of town, don't look back and don't ever come back. If I ever see you here in the vicinity, we won't talk with our hands like we did this time, next time my gun will do the talking. Now, do we have an understanding, have I made myself perfectly clear?" Wes was shaking his head yes and trying to mumble something. Laughlin stuck his gun belt and gun in his saddle bags, walked out and tied them on his horse. He said, "Let him out, I want him running to the horse and I want the horse running when he hits the saddle. Oral opened the cell door; Wes ran out the door, got on his horse and spurred him hard. The horse lit out with clods of dirt flying from his hooves. When last seen he was running full out.

Laughlin said, "Nathan, now that we don't have to baby sit, Oral and I are going to give you some tips on how to use a pistol. You don't need any help on that scattergun, let's go over to the gunsmith and let the Rangers buy you a pistol and a rifle."

The gunsmith shop was an interesting place. It had a wide variety of used rifles, pistols, and holsters on display along with all kinds of ammunition. The owner was an old timer and could do it all but his specialty was trigger work. His name was Bester Neugent. He was approximately sixty years old, had gray hair hanging to the middle of his back and wore a big black Stetson with one crease in front of the crown. He had on a long sleeve shirt with a leather vest. His britches were tucked in to ankle top boots and he wore a hand tooled oak leaf holster and belt sporting a classic peacemaker 45 complete with pearl grips. He was well liked and everyone called him Uncle Bester.

Uncle Bester knew everybody, greeted them loudly due to a hearing loss from all the years shooting. Laughlin said, "I want that holster and belt hanging right there," while pointing to a number of holsters. "Give me that Colt 45 peacemaker with cutaway trigger guard and that Winchester 44-40 rifle with the adjustable rear sight. I want six boxes of cartridges for each. Set up an account for the Rangers and send an invoice for what I bought today. Ammunition is to be signed for by me or Nathan. Has the trigger on the pistol been worked on?" "Yes, it's a hair trigger", said Bester. "Thank you Uncle Bester," said Laughlin, "we'll be coming back soon for more ammo."

The three men rode out of town to an area that had a wash creating a bank they could safely shoot into. Laughlin helped Nathan adjust the belt and holster to his liking. Then he checked the pistol to make sure it was unloaded and stuck it in Nathan's holster. Laughlin turned toward the wash and said, "This is what I am going to teach you to do." He drew and fired. If you were holding your extended arms in front of you with hands eighteen inches apart and ready to clap when he drew, you could not have done it before he fired. "My God," said Nathan, "I thought Glen Ray was fast." Laughlin and Oral gave Nathan mental and physical training and after six boxes of shells Nathan was really getting the hang of it. He didn't want to quit when they left. Laughlin told him, "Unload your pistol at night in your room, stand in front of the mirror; look into your eyes, draw and dry fire at least one hundred times per night. I will come back in a week and see how you're doing. Oral, you old rascal, you're invited to my wedding; you better be there to keep all them young Rangers under control." Oral grinned and said, "You couldn't keep me away. I'm gonna kiss the bride."

Laughlin, Oral and Nathan rode back to the jail and went inside. As they sat down Laughlin said, "Oral, I want you to know how I respect men like you, your brothers and Captain Beasley. Y'all tamed this country. You fought Indians, Mexicans, commancheros and established law and order. That's why I got upset when Wes was trying to put you down. Oral, I hope that I am as much a man as you are when I'm sixty-nine." Oral acknowledged Laughlin's praise with a simple nod.

Laughlin continued, "Nathan, I like what I saw today but remember, no bullets, dry fire, one hundred draws a day for a week. Next lesson, we'll work on accuracy, no good if you're fast but can't hit anything. You gotta learn to draw and fire the same way you practice. Most men are nice and loose when practicing, but when they have to face someone down they get tense, lose their rhythm and the gunfight. You've already demonstrated no fear so just relax and be smooth. Glen Ray learned to relax, that's why the swiftness of his pistol is talked about today."

When Laughlin left the jail he went to the general store, bought Melissa a sack of candy and some material he thought she would like for a dress. Melissa loved to sew and he knew she would be pleased with his gift. It made him feel good to buy her something. Caring for her was nice; he was learning to enjoy it. He walked out of the general store with his purchases in hand, looked at Sam and said, "Now don't be jealous, I bought you something," then he reached into a bag and handed Sam a great big apple.

Back in Laredo, Luke went to the telegraph office; he had a wire from Atlanta. Luke's hand shook as he held the paper and started reading the message. It was from Seth, it read, '**Got your letter. Claudia died two years ago – pneumonia. Sterling and Boots here with us. Claudia was notified by the war office that Nathan was dead, she came here to live with us.**' Luke paused and wondered what he should do next. He decided to send a wire to Laughlin in Uvalde, marked personal hand deliver.

The telegraph office in Uvalde received the wire and the operator sent it to Laughlin at the ranch. Laughlin and Melissa saw the rider coming and they both feared orders for the Rangers, trouble somewhere. "Telegram for Ranger McFarland," said a beaming young man, you couldn't help seeing his admiration for Laughlin. Laughlin gave him two bits, told Melissa to take him to the kitchen and get him a piece of her pecan pie.

Melissa quickly took care of the young man and returned to the front yard. Laughlin was sitting in the swing, his hands in his lap holding the telegraph. He was gazing out towards the barn, but you could see he wasn't looking, he was in deep thought. "What is it Laughlin, is it bad news?" asked Melissa. Laughlin turned, looked her in the eyes and said, "It's about Nathan's family." "Have they found them, are they alright?" she wondered. "Yes and no," said Laughlin, "the boys are ok but Nathan's wife, Claudia, passed away 2 years ago. "I've got to go to town in the morning; Nathan will be staying with us for a while."

Early the next day, Laughlin rode to Uvalde, reigned up in front of the sheriffs' office, dismounted, and tied Sam's reins to the hitching post. Nathan and Oral stepped outside on the porch, "Hello Laughlin," said Nathan, "it ain't been a week but I'm ready for another lesson." Laughlin said, "You boys got any coffee?" "Yea, yea come on in, I'll make a fresh pot," said Oral.

They sat at the table, stirred and cooled their coffee. Laughlin took a sip and said "Oral, nobody makes coffee like you." Laughlin took another sip, set his cup down, looked sternly at Nathan and said, "I've got something to tell you." Nathan stared into Laughlin's eyes and nodded as Laughlin continued, "Luke Starrett contacted the war office; you were reported dead, not wounded in action. He asked about Seth Churchill and his whereabouts. Seth's home was lost, burned to the ground by Sherman and the Yankees. After the war, Seth and your sister rebuilt in another part of Atlanta. Your wife and boys, thinking you were dead, moved to Atlanta and lived with Seth and your sister." Nathan's expression had never changed; he was still starring into Laughlin's eyes. "Nathan, I'm sorry, your wife died from pneumonia two years ago, but your boys are alive and well. They don't know anything about your being alive, and still think you're dead. It's your choice as to what you should do."

Nathan stood up still looking at Laughlin paused and said, "Thank you Laughlin for telling me. It's time for me to make my rounds." He picked up his shotgun and started walking through the town, up one side of the street and down the other.

Oral said, "Laughlin don't worry, he'll never go back to the bottle. Let him grieve and get over it." Laughlin said, "I agree, better make another pot of coffee, make it strong."

Nathan completed his rounds in the town and returned to the sheriffs' office. He placed the double barrel shotgun in its rack and said, "Town's quite, had a nice relaxing walk, practicing what you told me about relaxing." He turned toward the empty cell and drew his pistol. Laughlin was impressed; he was already faster than some of the men he had faced. Nathan put his pistol in his holster, walked over, sat down at the table and said, "I loved my wife with all my heart and soul. Now she's gone, I can't do anything about the past, I'm a Ranger and Laughlin you've given my life back to me. You taught me how to deal with adversity. Had I not learned this, I would be back sucking on a bottle. Don't worry about me, I'm solid. I have my pride back and nothing will take it away from me. I'm a Ranger and would like to bring my boys here, let them grow and hope they'll want to be Rangers. I can't wait to see them." Laughlin said, "Get'em out here, they can work on the ranch. We're going to need more help now that we're starting a herd."

Nathan said, "Thank you Laughlin, thank you." Laughlin thought to himself, he handled it like a man, but a man's heart hurts just like everyone else's, some just don't show it. He knew Nathan was hurting for his wife.

Back on the Fox ranch in Abilene, Fred was told to take the buggy to town Saturday night and bring LaQuita to the ranch Sunday for a bar-b-que. He was to tell Linda to come with her and he would take them back to town Monday morning.

Fred was all excited about bringing LaQuita to the ranch and then he panicked and thought to himself; what if she turns me down and won't come back with me. How embarrassing that would be – oh, Glen Ray wouldn't let me live it down, would probably have to shoot that 'Baby Ranger'. No, can't do that, he's faster than me. I could tell my sister she couldn't see him anymore. No, then she would kill me – please LaQuita say yes.

Saturday night came with the temperature in the sixties and dropping to the low fifties, so Fred threw a couple of blankets in the buggy for Linda and LaQuita. Riding in the open air buggy, the girls could get chilled, especially if the wind was blowing. Fred said a little prayer, praying that LaQuita liked him and would come to the cookout. Upon arriving in Abilene, he went to the livery stable where he left the horse and buggy then went to the water trough, threw some water on his face in hopes of removing the trail dust and ran his wet hands thru his hair. Clifton, the livery stable owner, saw what Fred was doing and smiled. Clifton was an elderly man, moustache, beard, worn out Stetson, thin and dressed for work. His biggest asset was his sense of humor, everyone in town loved Clifton.

When Clifton saw Fred, he said, "Hey, compadre, never seen you spruce up like this before when you come to town. For two bits you can strip down and bathe in that horse trough. What's the occasion?" he said with a grin. "Not going over to the hotel restaurant are you?" Clifton slapped his leg, did a little dance and laughed heartily. He knew what was going on and was enjoying razzing Fred. "Ain't you got some work to do? My horse needs to be rubbed down and fed." said Fred, then he continued, "Yea, I'm going to the restaurant, but only to eat," "What's over there?" questioned Clifton, then he broke out in a grin.

Fred walked over to the hotel porch, brushed himself off, re-arranged his hat, and entered. When he walked into the restaurant Linda saw him and showed him to a seat. "How is Mr. Fox, how you doing, and what are you doing in town?" she asked; all the questions you would expect.

"Mr. Fox sent me in to invite you and LaQuita to the ranch for a bar-b-que tomorrow. He wants to meet LaQuita and really wants you to come." Linda said, "Count me in, I don't care how busy we are, I don't miss a party at Mr. Fox's." "Linda" asked Fred, "do you think LaQuita will go with me, does she even like me. "Well now, I don't know, why don't you ask her? Linda replied. I will tell you this much, Glen Ray said she had been seeing Pancho Villa's son. You be careful, that guy is a bandito. I'll send her out to see you." Fred was still laughing when LaQuita came to the table. Hearing the laughter, she asked, "Ola! what

are you laughing about? Do I look funny?" "No, no, just thinking about something Linda said." Then he commented,
"You look beautiful, I like your hair the way you have it pulled back. Listen," Fred stammered nervously, "uh, Mr. Fox wants you and Linda to come to the ranch for a cookout & fiesta tomorrow. Will you go?"

Realizing that Fred was struggling to ask her to go with him, LaQuita said mischievously "Fred, I like Mr. Fox, but he's too old for me, how about you, do you want me to go?" "Don't be loco; sure I want you to be there" said Fred, sheepishly. "Then ask me?" she growled. "LaQuita, will you go to the party with me?" he asked. "I would love to go with you," smiled LaQuita, 'we'll have fun and I'll be with the most handsome man at the party." Fred blushed, pulled his shoulders back and thought to himself, 'I knew it; I knew there wasn't a doubt in my mind, I wasn't worried, I knew she would go. Wait till I see that big mouth lying 'Baby Ranger', telling Linda that bit about Pancho Villa. A man shouldn't say things if they aren't true. He smiled then started to enjoy his dinner.'

The next morning Fred had the buggy ready and waiting on the girls in front of the hotel. They came out carrying things from the restaurant: bread, cake, jelly, covered dishes of beans and potato salad. They carefully loaded the items in the buggy and were on their way to the fiesta. It was a clear, sunny day with no wind and sixty degree temperature. A day that was custom made for a party. After arriving at the ranch, everyone started getting ready for the celebration.

Glen Ray and Angel were both busy helping with the set up and preparation. They were both aware of the other one's whereabouts at all times. Glen Ray really enjoyed spending time with Angel. She always looked beautiful and
had a way of expressing herself. Very Happy, smiling, teasing and tantalizing; if she was happy, he was happy.

Mr. Fox was sitting on the porch swing when he called out to Glen Ray, "Come on over here, and pull up a chair, let's talk." When Glen Ray sat down, Fox continued, "You know Fred Thinks a lot of you. Talks about you all the time, says he thinks you soon will be the top Ranger in the field. I agree, there ain't anything I don't like about you and Fred. If I had son's I would be happy if they were like you boys. Let me ask you a question. Where do you want to be in twenty years when you are forty-one years old? Do you want to still be dodging bullets or do you want a family? Don't get me wrong, the Ranger organization is just starting to grow. There will always be a place fer a man of your caliber. The hardest thing I ever did was hang up my guns. Being a Ranger builds pride like no other organization. Only a select few can qualify and live the life demanded of a Ranger. Laughlin is the best at the present time; he is attempting to make a major decision in his life. Personally I hope he can give it all up and become a fulltime rancher.

Glen Ray thought for a few moments then responded, "You asked me about my future and I'll try to tell you how I'm thinking. At the present time I am twenty-one years old, a free spirit, and no obligations except the Rangers. I enjoy being a Ranger and I want to be a good Ranger, eventually the best. Later in life I want to Have a family and be a rancher raising cows and breeding horses. A place like the one Abe Silas has. But right now, I want to ride the Ranger winds and wherever they take me, that's where I'll go.

"Mr. Fox, I know you are concerned about my relationship with Angel. Hopefully she can accept a casual long range relationship. Our relationship has just started; we'll see where it goes from here. You have my word; I will always treat her with respect and try not to hurt her. I won't make any commitments, she's free to do as she pleases, see whoever she likes and live her own life."

Mr. Fox, with his dark piercing eyes staring into Glen Ray's, said, "Son, I will honor what you just said. Treat her with respect and don't hurt her; otherwise, I think you know you will answer to me.

Just before lunch, Mr. Fox greeted a buggy being driven by a stranger. It was John Van Slyke, a cattle buyer. He was a tall slender business man, well dressed in a suit, vest and tie, wearing a Stetson. He sported a moustache with no beard. He appeared to be about forty years old. Mr. Fox introduced him to everyone and when he got to Linda it was obvious Mr. Van Slyke was interested. When everyone sat down to eat, he sat next to Linda. During dinner, Glen Ray noticed Fred observing Van Slyke. It was evident he didn't like all the attention the stranger was giving Linda. After they finished the meal, Fred got Glen Ray by the arm, pulled him out of hearing distance and asked, "Amigo, you see how that dude is trying to impress Linda? I don't like it." "Yea, I agree," said Glen Ray, "wish Jim was here to stand his ground." Since there were no improper advances, He and Fred just made a mental note of the stranger should he become a problem.

Saturday at the cookout, some of the drovers that could play instruments and sing provided the music for dancing. Everyone danced and had a great time. As usual Mr. Fox was king of the dance floor; he wore out Linda and LaQuita. When LaQuita wasn't dancing with Mr. Fox she was dancing with Fred. When they danced it was evident that something special was going on. Glen Ray and Angel danced when Mr. Fox didn't have her.

As the evening was coming to an end Mr. Fox told Fred he was impressed with LaQuita and wished them well. As they were cleaning and putting things away, Fred said, "Come on Glen Ray let's go talk to Linda about that dude." Linda saw them coming, grinned and said, "Hi boys, did y'all have a good time? Never mind, I saw you two 'old mother hens' watching me all night. No, I wasn't impressed with Mr. Slyke and yes, I would rather have been with Jim." They looked at each other, grinned, nodded to Linda, touched the brim of their hats and walked away smiling.

Chapter 15

In Uvalde Nathan, Still grieving for his wife, sat down at the table in his room with pencil and paper. His hands were trembling as he wrote: 'Hello boys, I love you and I loved your mother very much. Hopefully we can bury all the pain from the past and with Gods' blessing be reunited. I am a Texas Ranger and would love for you boys to come to Texas. You have a job waiting on a ranch soon to be owned by my Ranger Captain. You can work on the ranch and when you're old enough, a Ranger career is waiting for both of you if you want it. I love you both and will be anxiously awaiting a return letter. Your loving father.' Nathan folded the letter, put it in an envelope, sealed it, and took it to the post office. He told the postmaster to take special care with this letter; his family had been found and he was to send someone to the jail if any mail came for him. He left the post office feeling good.

Oral was making his walk thru town when he saw Nathan come out of the post office. He hollered across the street and motioned for Nathan to come join him. They walked along talking and Oral asked about the boys. Nathan said, "Sterling is eighteen and Boots is sixteen. Sterling is smart, loved school, likes to read and has lots of integrity. Boots is wound up tight, very active and into everything. He loves horses, riding, hunting, and isn't afraid of anything." "How did he get the name Boots?" asked Oral. "His real name is Joel, Joel Dean Law" said Nathan. "When he was five years old we bought him a pair of boots for his birthday. He loved his boots and one day while he was sleeping his brother hid them. The next morning he couldn't find them. Somehow he sensed it was his brother's doing. Didn't make any difference that his brother was older and bigger, he lit into him anyway throwing fists and hollering, 'Where are my boots!' he demanded. His brother gave him back his boots and for a long time after that he wouldn't take his boots off at night, he slept in them, thus the nickname Boots; probably won't answer to Joel anymore."

When Nathan returned to the ranch, it was around eight-thirty in the morning, a bright sun shiny day in the mid-fifties. Laughlin told Nathan to get his pistol and some ammo then follow him to the barn. They saddled two horses and rode out on the range into a box canyon. After dismounting, Laughlin marked a target on the sandstone and placed Nathan approximately ten yards in front telling him to draw and fire.

Nathan made a fairly fast draw and somewhat accurate shot. Laughlin told Nathan to unload the gun and draw again. This time when he did it was fast and smooth. Laughlin said, "I just wanted to prove a point to you; it's all mental. With no bullet you're fast and smooth. Live round, rough, slower and loss of accuracy – results dead man – not him – you. You must shoot the way you practice, relaxed and smooth." They practiced for about half an hour; Nathan improved with each draw. They called it a good day and as they were riding back to the corral Laughlin asked Nathan if he was excited about finding the boys. He answered, "Very excited, hopefully they will come to Texas."

Meanwhile, back at Fox's ranch, the group was loading up for the return trip to Abilene. It had been decided that in one week, Glen Ray, Fred, Rosa, Angel, Linda and Mr. Fox would leave for Uvalde. They would be there in time to celebrate Christmas, the wedding and New Year's together. On the trip back to town Slyke asked Linda to ride back with him, she declined. Fred, with LaQuita sitting next to him, got a big grin on his face when Linda slid in beside LaQuita. "Awright" he said, "let's go to Abilene."

When Fred returned to the Fox ranch, he and Glen Ray rode up to the ranch house where Mr. Fox was sitting in the swing enjoying the cool crisp day. He said, "Come on up and set a spell. Let's talk a while." They sat down and Mr. Fox brought up the owl and the Indian story.

He said, "You know boys the Indians were superstitious. They believed in the Great Spirit. He rewarded the faithful and punished the wicked. The medicine man was looked upon with respect and they listened to his sayings. The happy hunting ground was home in the great beyond and often things were buried with warriors for them to use when they arrived there. Revenge was their goal; sympathy or regret was considered a weakness. They were cunning and treacherous. To meet you in the open was not to their liking. They wanted to lie in wait and spring upon you like the mighty puma. They delighted in torturing captives. When you told me about the owl I was reminded of the moonlight and dog stories. It was believed that the fiercest dog would not molest an Indian, nor would it even bark if a large band of Indians were surrounding a house on a moonlit night. They believed it was a moon charm cast over the dog by the moon God."

"The Indians could steal a horse that, after a long day's ride, the white man considered tired and worn out; mount the same horse and by some unknown means cause him to travel like a fresh mount. Whenever tracking with the Rangers we would get up on a high place and look over the surrounding country to see if the Indians were near. This process was repeated often as we rode. The Indians were crafty but at times, seemed to be dumb. One time up by Bowie at Queens Peak, a couple of men had moved into the area but hadn't had time to build a house. Living in tents and covered wagons, they would turn their horses out to graze at night. One night a horse with a rope on it was staked out with two hobbled mares and colts. The Indians stole the horse on the lariat, but, although they were too dumb to figure out how to remove the hobbles on the other horses; they were cunning enough to cut their legs off to deny their use by the white man. Trouble with the Indians was they couldn't get along with themselves, fought each other all the time. Aw, listen to me, sitting up here reminiscing and boring you boys to death."

Back in town a telegraph had been delivered to Linda at the restaurant; it read 'Can't wait to see you at the wedding. I arrive on the twenty-third so we can celebrate Christmas. Love, Jim'. Linda smiled and thought how nice of Jim to send her a wire. She was happy about going to the wedding, but was concerned about meeting Melissa. Mr. Fox was trying to get her and Jim together and insisted she go. He didn't know about her and Laughlin, this was going to be interesting.

Only five days until Christmas Eve. Jim was on his way from Laredo, Billy Joe was to stay and help patrol Laredo and the area – Jim, was going to the wedding and was sure to see Linda.

Meanwhile Melissa was sitting at the kitchen table in Uvalde planning and preparing for the wedding. She came across Linda's name and paused, hmm, this will be difficult.

Mr. Fox and his Abilene group were preparing for their trip to Uvalde. They were loading up and getting ready for the trip. It looked like a wagon train. Fox, Linda and Rosa rode in the first buggy; Fred, Angel and LaQuita were in the second buggy with Glen Ray riding along on horseback.

In Laredo, it appeared the weather would be good for traveling and everyone was excited. Before leaving Luke warned Jim about the recent Indian raids. Luke and Jim agreed there could well be more Indian parties working the area along the Rio Grande. Ranches dependent on the river water were easy pickings for small bands. They could rob, burn and kill days before being discovered. Jim decided to stay on the stage road and every so often ride to a high vantage point to see what was ahead and around him.

On the second day he had ridden to a view point and spotted a lone rider coming toward him riding full out. Jim rode to the side of the stage road and, when he heard the riders hoof beats, he rode out blocking the trail. "Pull up fellow, pull up" Jim shouted as he held up his open palm. It was a young man about sixteen years old. His horse was lathered badly and breathing hard. He was obviously shaken and out of breath as he said, "Indians, Indians attacked our farm! I was out looking for our cow and they burned down the house and barn. Killed my maw and paw, took my sister with them." "How old is she?" asked Jim. Still breathing hard and excited, the youngster replied, "Seven years old," replied the boy, "can we go try and get her back? Do you have an extra gun?" Jim waved his outstretched hands and in a soothing voice said, "Calm down son, calm down. Here get yourself a drink from my canteen, try to calm down."

Jim succeeded in getting the boy calmed down. "I am sixteen years old" said the kid in a much steadier voice, "my name is Jerry Jack Tennyson, and my sister's name is Samantha." Then tears flooded his eyes once again at the mention of his sister. Jim told him they would go on to Uvalde, leave him there and get a posse to pursue the Indians. Jerry Jack said, "You ain't leaving me, I'm goin' with y'all when ya head out after 'em."

It was Jim's plan to take the boy to Uvalde, have Sheriff Fox try to locate his kin then send a burial detail to the farm. He knew the Indians would kill the girl or take her to their camp to be raised with their children. To rescue the girl would require that the Rangers steal the girl back. A very risky business since under attack Jim knew they would kill her immediately. When Jerry Jack told Jim his parents had been dismembered, he prayed the little girl hadn't witnessed their actions.

Meanwhile, the telegraph operator in Uvalde had ridden out to the ranch, found Nathan and gave him a telegram. Nathan was excited, he was sure it was a reply from his boys. He said a prayer before reading the reply 'God, please let the boys come here and live with me.' Then he opened the telegram and it read: 'Boys will be leaving soon headed for Uvalde, TX – by train then by stage.' It was signed, Seth. Nathan shouted, "My boys are coming, my boys are coming!" Laughlin heard him celebrating and said, "Congratulations! Get 'em out here, I'll put 'em to work, maybe make Rangers out of 'em." Nathan was beaming with happiness and pride – he knew all this was because of Laughlin and Sheriff Starrett.

It was now the twenty-third of December. The mini buggy train from Abilene had arrived at the Rocking Horse Ranch in Uvalde just in time for the next day's Christmas Eve celebrations. The entire group would be staying at the ranch thru Christmas; then they would move to the hotel in town for the wedding and reception.

Laughlin and Melissa greeted everyone in the yard as the buggies arrived. Mr. Fox introduced Angel, Rosa, LaQuita and Linda to Melissa. All eyes were on Melissa and Linda as they were introduced, it was uneventful; they conducted themselves very ladylike. Questions were asked about Jim and his arrival time, they had expected him to be at the ranch before they got there from Abilene. At sunset Jim and Jerry Jack rode through the gate at the ranch. Jim informed them what had happened and said, "Let's get this boy some food, a bath and a place to sleep, he's been through a lot."

Laughlin and Jim went to the bunk house for privacy. Laughlin said, "Jim, as you know, when there's a hostage involved it makes things difficult. It's probably a raiding party of seven or eight; burning, stealing and killing. We don't know where they came from, maybe Mexico, maybe just a raiding party on a killing spree. We've got to do some research, wire Eagle Pass and Del Rio to see if anything's been reported. We can't just take off riding; we've got to determine which direction they're traveling. As for the girl, she's either dead by now or they'll keep her alive and return to camp. Jim, get some rest. Then he continued, "The morning after Christmas you, Glen Ray, Nathan and Fred will go out and try to find them. I'll tell Mr. Fox there's a little girl involved, he'll understand. We'll take Fred, he's an excellent tracker."

The young man, Jerry Jack, that survived the Indian raid, felt guilty. He kept saying he should have been there to help fight the Indians. Everyone prayed for him and his sisters' safe return. He was a fine looking boy, brown curly hair, well built, muscular, intelligent eyes and very courteous with good manners.

Christmas day was special, everyone gathered in the living room around the Christmas tree and Mr. Fox said a special Christmas prayer. It was a prayer of thanks for the birth of Jesus, the Savior. Then there were presents to be opened. Melissa had made sure there were some for Jerry Jack.

It was a great Christmas dinner with a menu of turkey, dressing, roast beef, sweet potatoes, vegetables, salads, pies, cakes, cornbread and fresh baked bread. Everything you could possibly want in a buffet style lay-out. Everyone overfilled their plate, sat down, and enjoyed good food and fellowship.

After dinner Melissa was in the kitchen getting organized and leaving things out for sandwiches and snacks. She poured herself a cup of cof-fee and sat down at the table to relax for a moment. Linda walked into the kitchen and said "May I sit down?" "Sure, get yourself a cup of cof-fee and join me." Linda poured herself a cup, sat down and said, "You agree we need to talk, right?" "Yes," replied Melissa, "I'm glad you came to me, otherwise I would have come to you." There was a short pause then Linda said, "Laughlin is a wonderful man. I loved him, but he refused my advances and said he didn't love me." She took a small sip of coffee and continued, "Then he told me all about you and said you were his first love. Melissa, you are a very lucky woman and I wish the best for both of you. Linda's mood seemed to change as she said, "Jim and I are seeing each other now and I feel very strongly about him. He and Laughlin are good friends and I want it to remain that way. There will be other functions like this in the future and Melissa, I want to be viewed as your friend, I want us both to be friends."

Melissa had never stopped looking in Linda's eyes as she said, "Thank you Linda, I appreciate and accept what you said. Yes Laughlin is a wonderful man and I love him more than life itself. Who knows Linda," Melissa said with a smile, "we might both be married to Rangers some-day and need each others' support." They stood up, gave each other a hug and departed as friends.

Chapter 16

Oral rode out early on the morning after Christmas to meet with Laughlin and the other Rangers. He said, "Boys, I've got bad news. Burial party went out to the Tennyson place, saw buzzards circling 'bout half mile from the cabin, it was Samantha. Don't have to tell you what the savages did to her." Oral paused, got a hardened look on his face before continuing, "I got a wire from Del Rio. Another ranch with a family of five was hit about forty miles east of Del Rio, all dead.

Laughlin said, "I was afraid of this. Raiding parties don't take hostages. The quickest way to stop these raids is to kill them like you boys did that last bunch. When a couple of parties don't come home and they know the Rangers are riding, they back off." Oral said, "There are two posses' being organized now, one in Eagle Pass and one in Del Rio. They'll ride toward each other making the Indians aware they are being pursued and force them toward the river and Mexico." Laughlin replied, "We're going to give the posses' time to make contact before we get involved." Then he turned to his rangers and said, "After the wedding, I'll send you boys out after that raiding party if the posses have located the area they're in. I'm not sending you out to chase ghosts. Hell, they may be in Mexico by now."

Laughlin and Oral gave Jerry Jack the bad news and he took it like a full grown man. He had grown up a lot in the past few days. Laughlin told Jerry Jack that he wanted him to stay on at the ranch and work as a ranch hand. Jerry Jack said he would love to and appreciated the offer.

The day before the wedding, Melissa's father and mother arrived from San Antonio. They were late; one of the switch stations had been attacked by a small party of Indians. Ben Miles and his three boys fought them off with rifles but lost the barn and horses. Without fresh horses, the stage lost time and was responsible for Melissa's parents' late arrival in San Antonio.

Laughlin told the Rangers, "This must be the same ones that hit the Tennyson place. We need to be looking for two groups of Indians; one close to Del Rio and the other around Eagle Pass. After the wedding go to the switch station and ride toward the river. When you make contact, shoot the horses, that'll put 'em on foot."

Finally the day arrived; it was time for the wedding. Everyone was dressed in their finest clothes. Mr. Fox was excited to be representing Captain Beasley as Laughlin's best man. Melissa's mother and father, Clarissa and Benjamin, were also excited and most certainly approved of Laughlin. Melissa looked a lot like her mother while her father was a rugged, manly looking handsome man.

As the church filled, people spilled out into the yard. Some were busy setting up tables with food and dinner for the reception. The piano from the hotel/restaurant had been placed under a shade tree while musical instruments were being tuned and made ready for the dance.

Inside, at the front of the church, stood Mr. Fox, Laughlin and the Preacher, James Morgan. As Melissa entered the church all eyes turned to her. She was escorted by her father who led her to Laughlin. As the ceremony began Laughlin and Melissa never took their eyes off each other. They repeated the vows, kissed one another and the preacher said, "I now present Mr. & Mrs. Laughlin McFarland." Mr. Fox kissed the bride, Glen Ray, Fred, Nathan, Oral and Jim also kissed Melissa – then Laughlin took her by the arm and started walking down the aisle toward the doorway. Once outside she turned backwards and threw the bouquet of flowers. They went up in the air and landed in LaQuita's arms. Fred saw her make the catch and said to himself, 'Am I ready for this?'

The reception started at six in the evening and was scheduled until midnight. Everyone ate, danced, drank and danced some more. Laughlin and Melissa were on the dance floor dancing to a slow song. He was holding her very tight when she looked up with tears in her eyes and said, "Laughlin, there is no way I could be happier than I am today,

I love you with all my heart." The honeymoon night was spent in the hotel which was full of people who had attended the wedding.

The next day Glen Ray, Jim, Fred and Nathan made plans for a lengthy chase. They took the usual provisions: jerky, beans, hard tac, corn-dodgers, coffee and lots of cartridges. As they were mounting up a rider came down Main Street, it was Jerry Jack. He rode up to the Rangers and said, "Give me a rifle, I'm going with you. They killed my family." Jim said, "Son, we
can't take you along, it's too dangerous and you're too young." Jerry Jack said, "Mister, I'm sixteen years old, boys twelve and fourteen fought for the South against the Yankees. If you don't let me ride with you, I will just drop back and follow you." Laughlin had walked out of the hotel, heard the conversation and said, "Let 'em go, rather he was with y'all than running around out there by himself. I probably couldn't keep him here anyway." "You're right Mr. McFarland, can I have a rifle?" "Nathan, go get him one from Oral" spouted Laughlin.

Everyone except the Rangers started their trip home. Laughlin sent six drovers with Mr. Fox for safety. He didn't want four women and a man of Fox's age trying to protect themselves on the return trip to Abilene.

On the second day the Rangers reached the switch station that had been attacked and were told by Ben Miles, the switch station operator, that it was a raiding party of seven. He told them the leader wore a confederate jacket and a large gentlemen's top-hat. Ben said that they rode off to the south towards Eagle Pass and the Rio Grande after they burned the barn and stole the horses. Showing an unusual sense of awareness, the Indians seemed reluctant to waste themselves against three rifles barricaded in the house.

Jim told the boys this was a typical raiding party, killing, torturing, stealing and burning. When aware they are being chased, this party will not run, they are out for the excitement of killing. We will have to be on guard against an ambush and night attacks. The stage stop is about as far from the border as they'll go. They like to stay close to an escape route across the river into the Davis Mountains on the Mexican side of the border..

Jerry Jack asked, "Mr. Weaver, why do the Indians steal the horses, what do they do with them?" Jim said, "Son, the horse is used in a number of ways. When the Indians are camped and in groups, the amount of horses a brave has determines his value, he buys his wife with horses. A raiding party like the one we're chasing takes the horses for food. The horses taken from the switch stations will run with the Indians while they are moving. You don't see saddle bags on the Indians ponies do you? Indians carry nothing but their weapons, a few good luck charms and trinkets. When they're hungry a stolen horse is slaughtered for food. If pursued, they abandon the horses and simply steal some more. Out in the Davis Mountains, there are large herds of wild burros which the Indian has survived on for years. The number of burros however has diminished recently with trappers taking and selling 'em to the Army."

By now Sterling and Boots were on the stage leaving San Antonio. They had been in route to Texas for over a week. It was very difficult leaving Uncle Seth and Aunt Bonnie. They had raised the boys along with their natural children and loved them as if they were their own.

Claudia had never recovered from the war. Losing Nathan, their home and lifestyle, had affected her mentally. She grieved over the loss of Nathan and became violently ill with depression, going for days without eating. She became so weak that her body couldn't fight the pneumonia and she died. In actuality, she grieved herself to death over the loss of Nathan.

Sterling was the oldest, he was only eighteen but a brilliant boy. He was a big and strong boy with short curly brown hair combed back and parted. He also had a nice smile with an intelligent look in his eyes. Sterling loved to read and was very interested in law. Boots was sixteen; he was a strong well built boy, rather big for his age. Though he was still a boy in many ways, he was a man when he had to be; developing that trait since the loss of his father. Boots had shoulder length hair, a dark complexion with blue eyes a boyish grin and dimples. Boys his age would call him pretty boy. A sissy he was not. He would fight at the drop of a hat. The boy was afraid of nothing and seemed to enjoy fist fights. He would laugh about them win or lose. This fearless, never give up attitude, gave him an infectious personality.

Luckily Mr. Fox and his "wagon train" had arrived back at his ranch in Abilene without any incidents on the trail. The threat of Indians always existed, but Laughlin had provided them with an escort of drovers for protection.

One of the drovers was a young man about twenty five, his name was Sandy. Sandy was an average looking cowboy, medium build with a cocky personality that liked attention. During the trip, it was evident he had tried to showcase himself to the girls, particularly LaQuita.

Sandy was in charge of the group so they took their orders from him as designated by Candido, Melissa's foreman. Mr. Fox told Manuel to cut out twenty-five cows, no bulls, for Sandy and the drovers to take back to Laughlin. Although Fox had already sent Laughlin a bull and two cows, he wanted to be sure Laughlin got into the cattle business so he was helping to speed things along. As the drovers were leaving for Uvalde, Mr. Fox rode up to Sandy, stopped his horse in front of Sandy's horse so now the men were facing each other. Mr. Fox said, "Sandy, out here in this country the quickest way to Boot Hill is to try to take another man's woman. Don't try to deny it, I don't even want a reply just hear what I'm telling you. It's for your own good. I watched you trying to impress LaQuita all the way out here. She's Fred's woman, fool with her and Fred will kill you. If he don't, I will. Do you hear what I'm telling you? When Sandy didn't respond, Fox nudged the two horses together and said sternly, "Say 'yes, sir' damn you, and get them cattle moving for Uvalde." "Yes, sir," said Sandy, but he resented Mr. Fox telling him what to do.

Later, before Laughlin and Melissa returned to the ranch from their honeymoon in Uvalde, he had news from the telegraph office that everyone was back in Abilene safe and sound. There was no news of the Rangers and their pursuit of the Indians. Laughlin knew it could be a long chase, but, as he had warned the Rangers, the Indians were on a killing spree. They hate all white men and love to make war.

By now, the Rangers had left the switch station and were heading south toward Eagle Pass and the border. It appears there were three groups of raiding parties. The Rangers had taken care of the first group while the second group was raiding near Del Rio and now we have this new group at the switch station. Jim thought the raiding parties would head back toward Eagle Pass and work the farms along the river from there to Del Rio. They would have easy pickings attacking the helpless farmers; then, if necessary, they could high-tail it across the river into the mountains of Mexico. They are probably feeling secure by now figuring that both posses had lost the trail and given up. Jim decided they would head south; going to every farm or ranch and every water hole. There were Indian and Mexican trails in the area that had been used for years. If the raiding parties felt secure, Jim was sure they would follow familiar trails. Fred took point and looked for fresh horse tracks while riding to all the high vantage points scanning for Indians. If clear, he signaled the Rangers and they continued riding. Everything was being done to avoid an ambush.

On the second day they spotted buzzards circling a short distance ahead. The Rangers hoped it was a dead horse that had been used for food, not a human. As they neared the buzzards, Fred said, "It's a horse." The Indians had killed and ate it raw. They knew a cook fire would have given away their location. Jim looked at the horse and said, "Comanche's, we're after a Comanche raiding party." Jerry Jack asked, "How do you know its Comanche's?" Jim said, "Indians have a way of branding their horses, each tribe has its own way. Comanche's split both ears of the horse; Kiowa's split one ear and crop the other." He held the ears up for Jerry Jack to see; both ears had been split.

They had a trail to follow now. Although it was old and tracking was slow, Fred, an excellent tracker, was able to follow. Late in the day Fred rode to a vantage point and saw a wagon. It was at a spring about a half mile ahead. Buzzards were circling and, as they rode up, several flew off.

They discovered a partially scalped man next to the burned wagon. Only a small circular piece of scalp from the top of his head had been removed. The wagon had been pulled by steers. They were dead but still hitched to the yoke. The wagon hadn't been burned, which meant the Indians didn't want smoke to be seen and compromise their position. Nathan rode out about a hundred yards and found the body of another man. He had been tortured, mutilated and fully scalped. Jim told Jerry Jack that this man must have run and did not show bravery. That's why he was fully scalped, the other man had died brave and only a small circle of his hair was removed.

They dug holes, buried the two men, said a prayer and decided to spend the night at the water hole. Being a very dark night it was not one the Indians liked for fighting. They prefer moonlit nights. Although the Rangers believed the Indians would not attack, they posted guards then tried to get some sleep.

Chapter 17

The next morning they continued toward the border west of Eagle Pass. About mid-day Fred signaled from a vantage point to hold up, evidently he had seen something. When he rode down from high ground he said, "The Indians are about a half mile ahead." He didn't get a good count but they had several stolen horses with them. Jim said, "If we charge them they'll make a break for Mexico. Aware that we're Rangers, they'll know we have them outgunned. Indians don't like fighting out in the open, especially against Rangers with rifles." Glen Ray said, "Why don't I try to draw them out. Get back up on that knoll, hide behind some rocks and be ready. I'll ride up on 'em, shoot at 'em, then turn and ride back leading them into your rifles. They can't catch Whiskey and can't shoot accurately enough off a running horse so I should be alright." "Ok," Jim said, "Let's try it. I think they will follow you; probably thinking you're by yourself." "Everyone get in place for a good shot," said Glen Ray. Jerry Jack led the horses out of sight. His job was to take care of the horses and prevent them from getting loose. Nathan, knowing his shotgun would be useless at long range, handed it to Jerry Jack giving him extra fire power if the Indians approached the horses.

From the knoll the Indians were visible. Glen Ray rode toward the Indians as if he was some crazed relative trying to pay back the Indians. He fired his pistol at them several times then turned and raced toward the knoll with the Indians in hot pursuit. The Indian ponies were no match for Whiskey. Glen Ray stayed well ahead but the Indians had taken the bait. He rode past the knoll, stopped and pulled Whiskey down to the ground then slid his rifle from its' scabbard, took aim and fired. The Indians were even with the knoll so it was about a hundred yard shot for the Rangers. Glen Ray's first shot knocked the horse from under one of the Indians. The Indian got up to run when Glen Ray heard Fred's rifle 'BOOM'. The big 45-70 spoke and the Indian was knocked backwards as the 500 grain slug hit him in the chest.

The Indians, realizing they had ridden into an ambush, turned in an attempt to ride out of rifle range. Just then another Indian was knocked off his horse, leaving five. Glen Ray elevated his rear sight and took careful aim at one of the braves riding off. 'BOOM', the big gun bucked and another brave fell from his horse, lifeless. The other four were riding hard and were about 300 yards away when, Fred's' 45-70 roared again with the same results. The Indian was knocked from his horse. The other three were beating their horses, trying for more speed.

When they were about 375 yards out, 'BOOM', there were only two left. It seemed all the rifles were going off at the same time as both horses fell throwing the Indians to the ground. Glen Ray jumped on Whiskey and took off in pursuit of one of the Indians. He looked to his right and there was Jerry Jack on his horse, holding Nathan's shotgun in one hand and riding hard after the last Indian. Glen Ray decided he could catch his man later; he had better help the kid. Didn't have to. Jerry Jack caught the Indian, ran over him with his horse and as the Indian tried to get up he received the load from both barrels. "Let's go get yours, Glen Ray, he's getting away", said Jerry Jack. The Indian running was wearing a confederate jacket and had a top hat in his hand. Glen Ray untied his lariat from the saddle, made a loop while riding, caught the Indian, and threw the loop around him. Whiskey stopped and it threw the Indian to the ground as the rope tightened. Glen Ray drug the Indian for about a quarter of a mile to where the other Rangers were waiting. Nathan, with pistol in hand, was riding to each downed Indian shooting them in the head. When Jerry Jack saw him going to his Indian, he rode over to Nathan and said, "Let me borrow your pistol." Nathan handed him the pistol and without hesitation Jerry Jack fired a shot into the Indian. He handed Nathan his pistol, then he reached in his pocket, pulled out his knife, bent down and scalped the brave. Nathan looked at Glen Ray, Fred, and Jim and said, "He'll do."

They left the Indian bodies for the buzzards, coyotes and wild hogs then rode toward Uvalde with their captive. His legs were tied to the stirrups with his hands behind him and a noose around his neck.

As they rode, Jerry Jack rode up beside Jim and said, "Thanks for letting me ride with y'all." Jim said, "Young man, you did the job of a man, we were impressed." "Thank you, sir", said Jerry Jack, "I feel better now knowing that, except for him," pointing at the captive, "the ones who killed my family are dead. Jerry Jack looked at the Indian and, without emotion, said, "Ranger Weaver, can I shoot him and then take his scalp like he did my family." "You know," said Jim, "under the circumstances I'm tempted to let you do it, but I tell you what I'll do, here's my pistol, we're going to ride on up a ways and scout the area. You guard him while we're gone but don't let him get away."

The group had ridden off only a short distance when they heard a pistol fired six times. They waited. Jerry Jack rode up to where they were waiting and handed Jim his pistol. Jim asked, "What happened?" "He tried to get away" replied Jerry Jack. They looked at his belt; it had a second scalp hanging from it.

By this time, Sandy and the drovers had arrived at the Rocking Horse ranch with the twenty-five cows. Laughlin looked at the cows and said, "It appears Mr. Fox wants JJ Jr. to be busy. Put them in the pasture and let JJ loose for a couple of days then put him back in the bull pen."

When Candido rode up and saw the cows Laughlin said, "Come on up to the ranch house, I need to talk with you about some things. Laughlin poured two cups of coffee as they sat on the sunny side of the porch. It was mid January and the sun felt good, a beautiful 'Thank God I'm alive' day!

"Now, here's what my plan is for the cattle," spouted Laughlin," I want you to send cowboys out after mavericks, don't let them return empty handed. If there are any herds nearby, I'll make an offer of horses or blacksmith work for calves. I'm gonna stretch wire and practice pasture rotation to preserve grass as well as getting involved in windmills. We'll build our fences so the four corners meet in the center of a watering tank. That way one water hole can supply four fenced pastures. As long as the Army wants horses we'll stay in the horse business. I have some interest in breeding fine, high dollar thoroughbred horses."

Then Laughlin paused and added, "Nathan's two boys will be arriving soon and Jerry Jack will be coming when the Rangers return. I'll be spending some time with all three of 'em so I can turn them into cowboys, good cowboys. I want 'em to know about horses, like Fred and Glen Ray. I'll get Glen Ray involved when he's not out patrolling his territory."

Ironically, Sterling and Boots had just left San Antonio heading west when the boys asked if they could ride on top with Bob Bell, the stage driver. Bob enjoyed the company and you could bet by the time they got to Uvalde they would know lots of stories. They were accustomed to hills, mountains and tall pine trees but now they were in the southwest Texas badlands. Bob had them watching for Indians. He Had given Sterling a shotgun and Boots a rifle then told the boys if the stage was attacked to fill the air with lead. Inside the stage was a young attorney on his way to set up practice in Abilene. His name was Stewart Coffee. Coincidently, he and Sterling had become acquainted while waiting on the stage in San Antonio. They enjoyed a mutual interest in law and politics. Boots had excused himself from the two of them and was trying to see all of the San Antonio area.

When they left the next switch station, Sterling sat inside while Boots remained on top with Bob. Stewart asked Sterling if he would like to read some of his law books as they were traveling. Sterling was delighted; it was as if he was craving knowledge, like a horse craves water after a long ride.

At about this same time, the boy's father, Nathan and the Rangers were riding into Uvalde from the south. Nathan wished they were on the stage road but it ran east – west from San Antonio. He knew the stage was due to arrive today and you could see he was excited. The timing was just about right for the boys to arrive.

Jim said, "Nathan, are you excited about seeing the boys?" Nathan replied, "Can't hardly wait, a month ago I thought they were dead." Glen Ray said, "With Jerry Jack and your two boys out on the ranch, Laughlin may have his hands full. Then he paused, looked at Jerry Jack and said, "Jerry Jack, you think you'll like ranch work compared to farming?" "Yes sir, I love horses and I used to think about cattle drives and being a drover or cowboy all the time", he answered. Nathan spoke up and asked, "You ever think about being a Ranger?" "No sir," said Jerry Jack, "but now, that's what I'm going to be." The Rangers looked at each other and grinned; they wished he could join them right now.

The stage with Boots and Sterling pulled into Uvalde. Laughlin and Melissa were there in hopes the boys were on board. They were. Laughlin, looked at Boots grinned and said, "Bob who's your new shot-gun guard?" "Name's Boots. Says his daddy's a Ranger," then he winked at Laughlin and continued, "know anything about that." Without answering, Laughlin said, "Hello Boots, I'm Ranger McFarland and this is my wife Melissa. Welcome to Uvalde and a new life. Is that your brother in the stage?" "Yes sir," said Boots, "another passenger is giving him some books to read, he loves to read." The stage door swung open, Sterling stepped out and said, "I
overheard you Mr. McFarland, my name is Sterling, very glad to meet you and your wife."

Melissa spoke up, "The name's Melissa and I'm very glad to meet you boys. Your dad has told us a lot about you and, as Laughlin said, wel-come to a new life."

Laughlin suggested they go to the restaurant. He figured these two big old boys must be really hungry. Then to be sure the restaurant could handle it, he asked, "Melissa, you got enough food to fill these boys up?" She nodded yes as they began to head in that direction.

The boys only had one old worn out suitcase and, what little the two of them owned, didn't even fill that up. Melissa had it delivered to the hotel and they went in the restaurant to eat. They ate like you would expect two trail weary young men to eat, ravenous! After gorging themselves with food and beverage, the boys and Laughlin headed for the livery stable to get the buggy. At the end of Main Street, five horses rounded the corner, it was the Rangers. Laughlin said, "Boys look down at the end of the street. You're about to meet your paw. They've been out chasing an Indian raiding party. He wanted to be here but duty called." The boys stood erect, military style, threw back their shoulders, head high and tears flowing. You could see the pride in their eyes, their dad, a Texas Ranger.

Nathan saw Laughlin and the boys as he continued to walk his horse, looked up toward heaven and said 'Thank you Lord', then spurred his horse as he galloped toward the boys. He dismounted, ran to the boys with peg leg and embraced them. Tears were flowing all around. After many hand shakes and pats on the backs, they told him how much their mother loved him and had never stopped talking about him. He said, "Boys, I got lots to tell you and I want you to hear it from me, but not now, let's celebrate." Sterling said, "Paw" as he removed his hat, "Can I pray?" "Certainly, please do." "Oh gracious heavenly Father, thank you for hearing our prayers and reuniting this family once again. In Jesus' name we pray. Amen."

Laughlin said, "Nathan you drive the buggy, get Melissa and your boys and go to the ranch. We have some reports to fill out. When finished I'll ride your horse back to the ranch. Jerry Jack you ride out with me and the boys." Before leaving for the ranch Melissa had meals sent over to the jail. They sat at the table in the jail and gave their report. When Laughlin heard about Jerry Jack he was extremely impressed. He said, "Jerry Jack, the only way I can show you how impressed I am with you and your bravery is to tell you that when you become of age the Rangers want you." Jerry Jack couldn't hide his excitement as he said, "Thank you sir, I can't wait. Maybe I can still go on some patrols."

Laughlin grinned and said, "We'll see, all of us in this room salute you, good job, well done."

After the boys finished their meals and all the reports were completed they rode out to the ranch. They talked as they rode; Jerry Jack listened, spoke only when asked a question and showed he had intelligence and common sense. Laughlin thought to himself, 'This kid could pass himself off as Jim's boy,' he liked Jerry Jack.

Laughlin took Jerry Jack under his wing for the next three days allowing Nathan to get reacquainted with his boys. Now it was time to get back to normal. Laughlin had breakfast with the boys and told them today was going to be the first day of their ranch life.

He took the boys along with Candido to the bunkhouse to start their tour. He started by explaining the bunk house had fifteen individual bunk beds. Each cowboy had his own little area for his bed, rifle on the wall, trunk and under bed storage. In the middle of the room was a large pot bellied stove for heating in the winter. In the summer, beds were moved to the porch to avoid the heat. Outhouses were out back away from the bunkhouse and were rotated from time to time.

The kitchen was a large area with a fireplace in each end of it. It had a stove-oven used for cooking and the eating area had large wooden tables and benches. The cook occupied a room built on to the kitchen. A good cook was a valuable person; men would quit other ranches to work for you if you had good food and a good cook.

Outside was the blacksmith shop. He made shoes and repaired wagon wheels; in fact, anything made of steel was his specialty. Then of course there was the barn, corrals and smoke house.

Laughlin said, "You don't need as many men for a horse ranch as you do for cattle. Eventually, we'll have about thirty cowboys when we get the herd built up."

They joined the crew in the bunkhouse for supper and Laughlin introduced the boys to the men. He told them he wanted the boys to learn horses, horsemanship and all the traits of being a cowboy.

A cocky remark was made by Sandy when he said, "Cowboys don't baby-sit, they'll need to learn and learn fast." Laughlin walked over to Sandy, stared him in the eyes and said, "I understand the cowboy code, these boys had better be treated fairly, and given a chance to learn. I have a feeling they'll surprise you, don't take them lightly." Laughlin had found out Sterling and Boots had been on the battlefield for the South when Sterling was twelve and Boots was ten. It had gotten to the point if you could hold and fire a weapon, the south needed you, age didn't matter. He already knew what Jerry Jack was capable of, Sandy didn't.

At five in the morning the cook was hollering "rise and shine, you're burning daylight!" A cowboy's day started at daybreak and ended at sunset. The cooks name was Flap Jack since his specialty was flap jacks, butter and syrup. He was a short man, maybe fifty years old, medium build, reddish brown beard, full head of hair and a twenty year old Stetson. It had a high crown with the brim turned up in the front and down in the back. He was wearing an apron that probably hadn't been washed in twenty years and constantly grumbled under his breath. The food was good but the wranglers wouldn't dare compliment him. Called it hog food, slop for the pigs. Which was just a ritual; most of them went back for seconds.

After eating, Sterling, Boots and Jerry Jack picked up their tin plate, walked over to the sink, set it down and said, "Thank you Mr. Flap Jack, the food was good." Flap Jack turned to the regular cowboys and snorted, "There now, you heathens hear that, these boys got some manners, know good food when they eat it." The wranglers laughed then said mockingly, "Thank you Mr. Flap Jack – come on farm boys let's go break some horses."

They went to the corral that was holding seven or eight horses. Sandy gave Jerry Jack a rope and told him to lasso a horse." When that was done he told Boots, "'Ear' him down while Sterling puts a bridal and saddle on him."

They did as they were told; the horse was rearing, snorting, and tossing his head from side to side. After several efforts Sterling was able to mount him. He didn't last, was bucked off and hit the ground hard. Sandy laughed and called him a farm boy. Sterling tried again, same thing, down he went. Sterling got up and brushed himself off. Sandy was hollering "You ride like a girl; my mother could ride that horse." Sterling glared at Sandy and remounted. Same thing only this time he landed on his back and it knocked the wind out of him. Jerry Jack helped him to the fence then returned to the horse and Boots. "Hold his nose under your arm; bite him hard on the ear" said Jerry Jack. Boots did as told. Jerry Jack tied the reins together to get a short rein, jumped on the horse and said, "Let him go!" He pulled hard, as hard as he could on the short reins preventing the horse from lowering his head. He bucked around the arena about twice and then started trotting. Jerry Jack rode him out the gate, around the bunkhouse and barn before returning him to the corral. Sterling said, "Good ride. How did you do that?" Jerry Jack said, "Got to keep his head up, if he gets his head down you're in trouble."

They spent the rest of the day breaking horses. Boots caught on and before long he looked like a pro. He was strong and determined showing good rhythm with the horse. Jerry Jack also improved with each ride. Sterling didn't ride anymore he just helped catch and ear down. Sandy continued to harass Sterling and told him he had a rocking horse he could try. At the end of the day Sandy rode up to Sterling and said, "Take my horse, unsaddle him, cool 'em out, rub him down, put him in his stall, and give him some hay and oats."

As Sterling led Sandy's horse to the barn, Boots walked with him and asked, "You okay, Bubba?" "Yea, don't worry, I can handle it," he replied. Then Boots asked, "What do you think about paw being a Texas Ranger?" "I'm really proud. Wonder what he wants to talk to us about tonight." "I don't know," answered Sterling, "said he would be out after supper to see us; probably wants to talk about mom."

Sterling and Boots left the barn and went to the water pump. They removed their shirts, pumped water for each other and prepared themselves for supper. They went to the bunkhouse before going to the kitchen where there was a bouquet of wild flowers lying on Sterling's bunk, placed there by Sandy. Then they went into the kitchen where the other wranglers were sitting down eating. Sandy said, "Sterling I've been hard on you today, let's make up. I've set you a bowl of beans and coffee at your place, sit down, let's eat." Sterling took a bite of beans and tears came to his eyes. They were hot beans. The bowl was full of crushed jalapenos. Though his eyes were filled with tears, Sterling showed no reaction. He ate the beans while beads of sweat popped out on his forehead then he took a sip of his coffee in hopes it would quench the burning; it was full of salt. He drank it down as if nothing was wrong, picked up his plate and started toward the sink. Sandy stuck his foot out and tripped him. Boots had seen Sterling in action many times and had never seen him beaten in a fist fight. He knew it was just a matter of time before Sandy paid the price for his actions. He didn't have long to wait.

Chapter 18

Sterling got up off the floor, looked into Sandy's eyes and said, "Sandy, you've had your fun." With that said, Sandy jumped up from the table swinging at the same time. He missed but Sterling didn't landing a straight right that split Sandy's right eyebrow; blood started flowing. The wranglers grabbed them as Flap Jack, with cast iron skillet in hand, said, "Take it outside, or I'll bust your skulls with this skillet." The wranglers pushed them out in the yard. Sandy grabbed Sterling and they went to the ground rolling and throwing punches.

Nathan had ridden up to the ranch and was walking to the bunkhouse with Laughlin. They could both see the men fighting. Laughlin started forward to break it up but Nathan grabbed his arm and shook his head no.

Sandy and Sterling were still on the ground; they rolled up under the hitchin' post and tried to get up. Sandy was on top and got up before Sterling. He kicked Sterling in the private parts and continued to kick him. Sterling managed to get up, but was bent over from the kick to the groin. Sandy landed four or five unanswered blows to the back of Sterling's head. Suddenly Sterling, while bent over, charged Sandy and drove him into the wall of the bunkhouse. Sterling put his left hand in Sandy's face pushing his head against the wall. With his right hand he threw five hard blows to the stomach and rib cage. He let Sandy go with his left hand and as Sandy bent over from the blows, he hit him with a left uppercut that straightened him up. Then Sterling threw the final blow, a hard straight right that knocked a tooth out and broke Sandy's nose. Sandy collapsed to the ground, semi-conscious; the wrangler's drug him to the water trough and dunked his head it.

Laughlin and Nathan looked at each other, nodded their heads and smiled. They walked over to where Sterling and Boots were standing. Nathan, as if he hadn't seen a thing, asked, "What's up boys, did we miss something?" Sterling said, "Everything's fine, no problems. Sandy was giving me some riding tips." Laughlin said to the boys, "Come on up to the porch. I want to talk to you and then your paw wants to spend some time with you."

When they reached the porch the boys and Nathan sat down as Laughlin continued, "Boys, I want to say something about your paw. Your paw has demonstrated to me all the things needed to be a Texas Ranger. The Rangers are proud to have men like him and you boys should be proud to call him your paw." With that said, Laughlin walked away.

"Boys" said Nathan, "I wanted to talk to you and make you aware of some things before you heard it from someone else. During the war a Yankee cannon ball took off half my leg. The doctors cut the remains off at the knee, put some bandages on it and sent me home. When I finally made my way back to our home in Tennessee, it was gone, burned to the ground. Someone else was living on our land and saying it was theirs. No one seemed to know what had happened to you boys or your mother. Some said soldiers killed ya'll, some said ya'll burned up in the fire. The same thing had happened to your Uncle Seth's place. His house was also burned and no one knew what happened to him or his family either. To get away from the memories I moved here to Texas. The pain in my leg and the hurt in my heart started me drinking. I crawled up in a bottle and was hiding from the world. I had become a hopeless drunk, a street person living in alleys. I had completely lost all my self respect; my soul was dead. Then that man, Laughlin McFarland, found me and brought me back from the grave, giving me new life. He gave me back my self respect and offered me a reason to live. For that, I will be forever grateful.

"I found out later that instead of being listed as missing in action, I had been listed as dead. All the time your mother thought I was dead and I thought y'all were dead. Due to God's grace we are now reunited, you have your lives in front of you and I have you and the Texas Rangers. I love you boys and will always love and miss your mother." "Paw," said Sterling as he and Boots got up to embrace their paw, "we love you and mother loved you, the last thing she said before dying was your name."

The next morning at breakfast Sandy came to the table, he was a mess. His eye brow was cut open, his eye was swollen shut, his nose was swollen, he was purple under his eyes, a tooth was broken and he had trouble breathing. Sterling approached him, stuck out his hand and said, "I would like to shake hands and be friends." Sandy looked at him through his swollen eye lids and said, "You can go to hell, I'm not going to be friends with you. I'm going to
get you." Sterling said, "Sorry you feel that way, I would like to be friends, violence doesn't solve anything, it just breeds tragedy."

Meanwhile, near Del Rio, Rene and his banditos were within a quarter mile of the Indian camp on the Mexican side of the Rio Grande. A small raiding party was taking scalps along the river. Rene had heard the Rangers had eliminated two raiding parties, and the third party they had heard about was working around Del Rio. The Indians had been getting liquored up, running wild along the river and thrill killing.

Rene and his banditos had been on the trail for a couple of weeks. The Indians had crossed into Mexico and were hiding in the mountains. The Banditos had lost the trail; the raiding party was back and ready to start killing again.

It was almost dusk; Rene and his men had found the track again and were hiding in the brush where they could see the camp. The Indians had built a fire and were cooking horse meat. Rene could see the dead horse on the ground. The braves had several bottles of liquor and were passing them around, whooping, hollering and displaying scalps on a lance.

Rene told his men to mount up; they would make a charge and get the Indians before they could mount up. Some of the Indians were staggering drunk already and probably couldn't mount a horse.

The banditos charged at full speed. Firing their pistols they stampeded the horses. The Indians were now on foot and virtually helpless to the mounted Mexicans. There were five Indians and six banditos. All five Indians never made it out of camp. Rene said, "Don't kill any of the wounded." Two were still alive. Rene laid the wounded Indians on their backs, spread eagle. He tied each arm and each leg separately to stakes driven in the ground. They were scalped and then their stomachs were opened up exposing their innards. On each Indian still alive, they cut into a gut creating a smell that would attract hogs, javelinas and cougars. When darkness came, they would still be alive watching their intestines being eaten and pulled out of them. The dead ones were all scalped, beheaded and dismembered. Two of the banditos tied their lariat to one leg each, got on horse back and rode away pulling their legs off and splitting the lower part of their body. Then they were left lying. Night was only an hour away, the hogs and coyotes would soon be feasting. The Banditos had done exactly what the Indians would have done to them had the roles been reversed. By doing so, Rene knew that any Indians that may see this battle ground, for some time to come would be less likely to continue their deadly raids in this area.

Back at the ranch, Sterling and Boots had taken a couple of weeks to establish their pecking order and settle in among the rest of the wranglers. Sandy, unable to live with the beating Sterling gave him, had disappeared.

Laughlin told the boys he wanted them to select a horse, break him, train him and make him into a cowpony. Once that was done he would give them the horse for their own. Sterling selected a bay mare. He knew mares were usually easier to ride and, in most cases, were even tempered. Jerry Jack selected a big buckskin gelding and Boots picked a big paint stallion that stood sixteen hands tall, with high withers. He was long bodied, had a wide rump, held his head high and was extremely spirited.

Candido said, "I can go along with you two boys, but Boots, that's War Paint, he's never been ridden and no one has tried him more than once. He could easily become a killer horse, I've been thinking about doing away with him." "That's the one I want. War Paint, I like that" replied

Boots as he flashed his boyish grin. Sterling had improved and after five or six trips to the ground he rode his horse out of the arena and out to pasture. Jerry Jack got on and never hit the ground, he literally wore his horse out; he was one heck of a cowboy.

Glen Ray was at the ranch visiting with Laughlin when Candido ran to the house. "Boss, boss, Boots wants War Paint. Do I let him try?" Laughlin said, "Come on Glen Ray, let's go down there and talk him out of it." Too late, the boys were in the corral, a rope was around War Paint's neck and wrapped to the pole in the center of the corral. Sterling was pulling on the rope. Jerry Jack had War Paints nose under his arm while biting his ear, and was being lifted four feet off the ground while Boots was chasing him with a saddle and bridal. War Paint would rear, shake his head and Jerry Jack would go flying across the corral. Then he'd buck and get all four feet off the ground at the same time. This went on for half an hour with Laughlin and Glen Ray enjoying the show knowing full well the boys would give up. It wouldn't last long. War Paint was lathered and frothing at the mouth. Sterling was strong and he finally gained some ground. He had pulled and wrapped the rope around the pole till it settled War Paint slightly. Jerry Jack bit the horse's ear and blood began to flow as he applied a head lock.

Boots managed to get the saddle on War Paint's back but he bucked wildly sending it five feet straight up. Boots was laughing; he was having fun. Jerry Jack said, "Boots pick another one, this one's killing us." "Nope, this one's mine" Said Boots, then added as he retrieved the saddle, "I helped y'all, now y'all help me." Luckily War Paint had tired a little; this had been going on for almost an hour. Finally Boots slipped the saddle over the paint's back, quickly cinched it down and went for the bridle. War Paint realized the saddle was on his back and started again, rearing and bucking with all feet off the ground at once; Jerry Jack went flying again. He came down hard and said, "Dam it Boots, get another one." "Nope, I'm gonna ride 'em", said Boots defiantly. Glen Ray said, "At first I was betting on the horse, but damned if I don't believe those boys are going to do it."

War Paint stopped, stood still, his body was trembling, he was tiring. Boots eased up to his head and slipped on the bridle; he reared and Jerry Jack went flying. "Dammit, I'll give you my horse, I'll buy you one; this horse is killing me" blurted Jerry Jack. "Shut up Jerry Jack, get back on that ear," shouted Boots who was grinning from ear to ear. He was ready to try it again. Glen Ray and Laughlin moved closer and crawled up on the top rail so they could be ready if needed. Laughlin whispered to Glen Ray, "If anything goes wrong, shoot the horse."

Boots put a foot in the stirrup and pulled himself up and in the saddle. "Let 'em loose, let 'em loose," he screamed as Jerry Jack disconnected the snap from the halter. Boots pulled with everything he had trying to get War Paint's head up. He was loose, the rodeo was on and it lasted three jumps. Boots went straight up in the air and landed on the seat of his britches. He bounced up laughing and said, "Let's do it again." "Damn it Boots, you can't ride that horse," said Sterling. He realized he had just said the wrong thing, now he knew Boots wouldn't give up.

Once he and Boots got in a fight. Being the older brother, he whipped Boots. Boots threw some water in his face, rested, then came back for more. Sterling whipped him again, same thing, he was back again. Sterling whipped him the third time. Same thing, rest and he was back again. Sterling was completely worn out and this time Boots whipped him. That's the way Boots was wired. Sterling loved his brother.

The trio went after War Paint again, after ten minutes Boots was back in the saddle, rodeo time. He made half a dozen jumps and landed face first in the dirt. This happened two more times, with the same results. Boots was taking a beating, but War Paint stood there trembling, he was tiring. Jerry Jack said, "Boots, ride that damn horse, I've spent more time riding his head than you have in the saddle." Boots laughed and said, "Let's do it again, this time he's mine."

Glen Ray said, "I've never seen such desire and ability to withstand pain. He'll be black and blue all over in the morning, probably won't be able to get out of his bunk; that is if he don't get killed today." Laughlin said, "I bet he rides 'em this time." "I'll take that bet for a dollar," said Glen Ray.

"Let 'em loose, let 'em loose" barked Boots and the Rodeo was on again. War Paint had all four feet off the ground. His rump was in the air and he was running around the corral, bucking and kicking. Glen Ray said, "I've never seen a horse buck like that. Pull his head up Boots, pull, he's tiring," shouted Glen Ray. "Wait a minute, I bet on Boots, you didn't" said Laughlin. "Aw, you can have that dollar" said Glen Ray then he continued, "Pull, pull, keep his head up, attaboy, ride 'em cowboy." War Paint finally stopped bucking for about five steps; then it was as if he had gotten his second wind. Away they went again, rodeo time, Boots was laughing and hollering, "Is that all you got, come on War Paint, give me some more."

Finally War Paint was exhausted, just like the fight with his brother, Boots had worn him down. He and War Paint rode out the gate and into the pasture, Boots spurred and kicked him out. What a burst of speed and he was worn out. "Did you see that?" said Glen Ray. "That horse can run."

Boots rode War Paint back into the corral. Sterling and Jerry Jack were on the ground stretched out; they were exhausted. Boots rode over to them and said, "Y'all go catch that big roan horse with the blaze face, War Paint don't have enough spirit, I don't want him." Then Boots laughed, spun War Paint and they went back through the gate into the pasture. Boots ran him flat out for about a quarter of a mile. Then he turned around and rode back to the corral where Laughlin and Glen Ray were sitting on the fence. With a big grin Boots said, "How y'all like my horse?" Glen Ray said, "They ain't no Indian pony gonna catch that horse; you've got yourself something there."

Laughlin said, "Boys, y'all put on a show today. Candido had asked to put War Paint down, nobody could ride 'em, called him a killer horse. I came down here to stop y'all, but you had already started. By the way, Glen Ray didn't believe you could ride 'em – give my dollar to the boys."

Laughlin and Glen Ray walked back to the ranch and sat down on the porch to talk. Laughlin said, "What do you think about those boys?" Glen Ray thought carefully then replied, "They are all three good boys. I would take Jerry Jack and Boots on the trail now; they'd both make good Rangers. Now Sterling is a brilliant boy, tough as nails and I heard what he did to Sandy, but I see him in law or politics."

Upon hearing this, Laughlin said, "Glen Ray, I want you to take Jerry Jack and Boots with you on some of your Indian patrols. The Rangers have some extra pistols and rifles up at Oral's office. Start teaching them to shoot; I think they are mature enough. Don't want 'em in any gunfights in the streets of Laredo. Teach them all you know about horses, breeding, care and riding. I want them to learn to be good wranglers, start them in Ranger training; they are too good to lose." Laughlin paused for a moment then continued, "

"I'm going to see what I can do about getting Sterling some help with schooling – I want to see him in the Capitol someday."

Then, as if by some miracle, Stewart Coffee, who had been in Abilene for less than six months, had set up his law office and already his business had outgrown a one person law firm. He was amazed at how much his service was needed and was in real need of someone he could train as his assistant. Stewart remembered Sterling, recalling his interest in law and what a nice, intelligent person he was decided to invite him for an interview. After mailing the letter, Stewart anxiously awaited a reply.

Chapter 19

Back in Laredo Luke Starrett had gotten wind of a lone gunman in Cotulla who tried to hold up the bank. The teller scared him away with a gun he had hidden under the counter. Apparently shots were fired but, as far as Luke knew, no one was hurt. Still Starrett was concerned. Billy Joe had gone to Cotulla four days ago and, since he hadn't returned nor been heard from, Luke decided to wire Laughlin informing him of the situation.

In Abilene, at Linda's restaurant, LaQuita, now working as a waitress, had developed a promising relationship with Fred. They had been spending all their available time together. When she approached a table which was occupied by a lone cowboy, she recognized the customer. It was Sandy from Laughlin's ranch.

In her usual pleasant manner, she said, ""Hello Sandy, what brings you to Abilene? Are you still working for Laughlin?" "Naw baby" he said, "that ranch life was too boring for me." LaQuita could tell he had been drinking, he was cocky and arrogant. She said, "What can I get you?" He took a sip of whiskey and slurred, "You baby, you're what I want, how about it?" "Sandy" she said, "I'm involved in a relationship with Fred and even if I wasn't, I wouldn't be seeing you." "What the hell do you mean, ain't I good enough for you?" he shouted. LaQuita told him he was drunk and he should place his order or get out. He was having none of it and said, "I told you, I want you baby." She turned to walk away and he grabbed her arm and pulled her back. "Don't walk away from me when I'm talking" he slurred.

About that time, Cletus Meeks, the sheriff, just happened to walk in for dinner. He had seen Sandy grab LaQuita's arm so he walked over to the table with his hat in hand and asked, "Do we have a problem here?" "No, no problem that I can't handle," said LaQuita. Cletus nodded then gave a hard stare at Sandy and said, "Bring him a cup of coffee on me. Cowboy when you finish that coffee, get out of here and stay out of my sight. You better be glad it was me and not Fred that walked in." Meeks then walked to a table and ordered his dinner.

Sandy thought to himself, well that's two of 'em out here I don't like, old man Fox and that part time Ranger. LaQuita was hoping that Fred might be coming to town soon with Manuel who was due to pick up supplies. Then she wished he wouldn't because this incident might get someone killed.

The next morning as Fred drove the wagon into town for the much needed supplies, he laughed, remembering how Mr. Fox had asked him to go. Normally it would have been Manuel going alone. Fox had said with a big grin, "Fred, I hope you don't mind going into town after supplies." "Oh no, no I don't mind," Fred had answered to which Fox replied, "By the way, if you happen to see LaQuita, tell her hello." Then Fox, with a huge smile on his face, gave Fred a wink.

Fred stopped the wagon in front of the general store, went inside and gave Charlie Perkins, the owner, his list provided by Mr. Fox. He walked back outside while his order was being filled and saw Cletus Meeks crossing the street coming toward him.

"Hello Cletus, how's the law man business, boring?" he said with a grin. Cletus laughed and said, "You know better than that, been on any good hunts lately?" "No, it's been real quite," said Fred, "I like it like that." "You remember that wrangler that worked for Laughlin, Sandy," Said Cletus. "Yea, I do," answered Fred, "seems he disappeared after Nathan's boy whipped him in a fight." "Well, he didn't disappear," said Cletus, "he's here in Abilene. Then he continued, "I don't like him, bad feeling about that guy. He was in the restaurant a couple of days ago and I walked in while he was giving LaQuita problems." Fred's smile disappeared. His jaw squared and his eyes flashed as he said, "Where is he, I'll take care of him." Cletus answered, "Haven't seen him since that night, probably long gone by now; he's a drifter."

Fred went up to the restaurant to eat, see LaQuita and find out what happened. When they met Fred asked about the incident and she replied, "Fred, it's alright, he was just drunk, no harm done." She laughed, looked at Fred, batted her eyes and said, "Is my baby jealous? You know you are my man." He said, "You damn right I'm jealous." "Oh hush, I don't like you when you are mad. Give me that smile, the one only you have." The tension on his faced eased, then he smiled that broad smile she was accustomed to.

It had only been a few hours since Sheriff Starrett had wired Laughlin with his concerns when a drover came riding into Laredo leading a horse with a body draped over it. He stopped in front of the marshal's office where a large crowd was already gathering to see who the dead man was.

Luke came out of the office and gasped, "It's Billy Joe. Where did you find him?" The cowboy said, "I work for the Dos W Rancho up north of Cotulla and his horse came up to our corral with a bloody saddle. We back tracked and found the Ranger back shot." Luke was glad that Jim and Glen Ray were expected back the next day.

In Uvalde, Laughlin was on his way to see Oral, when he met the young man that always delivers telegrams. As usual the young man smiled and said, "Mr. McFarland, how much longer before I can become a Ranger?" "Not much, you're getting there" said Laughlin. The boy went on, "Here, you have a telegram from Sheriff Starrett and a letter for Mr. Sterling Law." "Thanks, I'll take 'em both" replied Laughlin as he gave the boy a coin, turned around and headed back toward the ranch.

Suspecting bad news, Laughlin was hoping that Glen Ray, Jerry Jack and Boots, who were out rounding up mavericks, would return soon. When Laughlin entered the gate and headed toward the blacksmiths, Sterling was there getting his horse shoed. Laughlin hurried along anxious to see why Sterling would be getting a letter from Abilene. Sterling saw him coming up, waved and met him while he was still mounted. He looked at Laughlin's horse and said, "Hello Sam, did you give the boss a good ride? then continued, "Hi sir, how are you?" "I'm doing fine

Sterling" replied Laughlin, I've got a letter for you, it's from Abilene." "Abilene?" said Sterling a bit surprised, "I don't know anybody, wait a minute, let me see it. Laughlin handed over the letter. Sterling looked at it and said, "Yea, it's from Stewart Coffee, the attorney." He hurriedly opened the letter, proceeded to read it.

A big smile covered his face, then he looked at Laughlin and dropped his head. "What is it Sterling", asked Laughlin, "Is it bad news?" "No sir" said Sterling, "Stewart wants me to come to Abilene for an interview, he needs an assistant." "Well that's wonderful, when does he want you?" inquired Laughlin. Without hesitation Sterling answered, "Sir, I can't leave you, you gave me a job and with everything you've done for my paw." "Hold on,
hold on. What do you want to do?" asked Laughlin. Sterling heisted then responded, "Well sir, I always dreamed of being a lawyer and being in politics." "Then that's what you are gonna be, you go for that interview and you get that job" was Laughlin's staunch reply. Sterling thanked him several times. He was beaming with happiness. Laughlin grinned and said, "Sterling, we can always get more cowboys, lawyers are hard to fine. I am proud of you boy, congratulations."

Sterling waited till after supper to tell Boots and Jerry Jack about his interview. They both were happy for him and wished him well. Tears started rolling down Sterling's cheeks. "What's wrong?" said Boots, "why are you crying, this is your chance to be somebody." Sterling said, "Bubba, we ain't never been separated, I don't know if I can leave you." Now they were both crying. Boots knew Sterling would be taking the morning stage to Abilene.

Stewart met the stage when it pulled up in Abilene. Laughlin and Melissa had bought Sterling some nice presentable clothes so he wouldn't look like a wrangler. Stewart was always well groomed and in control. He was quite handsome and had impeccable manners. He led Sterling to the restaurant for what Sterling thought would be a casual lunch prior to his interview. They ate lunch and remained at the table for about forty-five minutes talking.

Sterling said, "I'm so sorry, I know your time is valuable and I have taken up too much already. When do you want me for the interview?" Stewart laughed and said, "We just had it. You have a job if you want it."

Meanwhile, when the Rangers returned from gathering mavericks, Laughlin told Glen Ray, "Pick up Jim tomorrow in Uvalde and press on to Laredo." Then with that stern stare that only Laughlin has, he continued, "I got a telegram from Luke Starrett, a Ranger's been killed, back shot."

It was early morning on the second day of their ride when Jim and Glen Ray arrived in Laredo. It had rained on them most of the way, unusual for South Texas, even if it was April. It was still raining hard when they went to Luke's office.

Luke said he had some more information about the robbery and the murder of Billy Joe. The robber's mask had slipped off the gunman's' face during the shootout and the teller got a brief look. He said the man didn't look like a wrangler. He had three missing teeth and scars on both his upper and lower lip.

Jim thought for a moment then said, "Sounds like you just described Wes Lockhart, the man Oral and Laughlin ran out of Uvalde. Question is, was Billy Joe trailing him as the bank robber or, did he just happen up on Billy Joe and back shoot him simply because he represented law and order?"

Jim answered, "I believe Billy Joe was trailing the robber when he was bushwhacked. When it quits raining and dries up, I think Wes Lockhart will show up and start running the saloons. The rain's coming from the north and I'm sure there're some creeks that can't be crossed. When it dries, he'll show up."

In Uvalde, Melissa told Laughlin she wanted to speak with Boots and

Jerry Jack. He walked down to the bunkhouse where they were pitching horse shoes. "I don't know what you boys have done, but the boss lady wants to see both of ya at the ranch house." They went to the water pump, washed their faces, combed their hair back with their fingers, swallowed hard and walked to the main house.

Laughlin was on the porch swing with Melissa at his side. The boys stood in front of her with their hats held waist high. "Hello boys, my y'all look handsome tonight" said Melissa. They looked at each other and blushed. She continued, "Tomorrow is Sunday, Laughlin and I are going to church and you boys are invited. It would just break my heart if y'all didn't accompany us to church, so be in the buggy at six in the morning; it takes a while to get to church from here." She wished the boys a goodnight then went inside with Laughlin.

Early the next morning the buggy pulled up in front of the church with time to spare. Melissa looked beautiful in her church dress; Laughlin was handsome in his suit while Jerry Jack and Boots looked nervous. Melissa looked at them and said, "My, my, you boys do clean up good. I bet there's some girls in there going to be interested in y'all." As they entered the church and sat down about three rows from the front, Brother James Baker Morgan began delivering his sermon. If the devil had been in the house he couldn't have survived; Brother Morgan was an impressive preacher.

After church, they had a covered dish lunch and, as you might expect, the girls had discovered Jerry Jack and Boots. All through the sermon, Boots had caught one of the girls looking at him. He didn't mind, she was very pretty. They were going around the tables filling their plates when Jerry Jack said, "See that girl in the blue dress." "Yea," said Boots. Jerry Jack continued, with a sly grin on his face, "Did you ever see anything that pretty?" "Yea," said Boots, "that one over there in the white dress. Let's go meet 'em." "Are you kidding me," said Jerry Jack, "I ain't going over there." "What," barked Boots, "here you are an Indian fighter and you're scared of a girl, watch me, I'll go get her for you." "No, no fool, come back here," urged Jerry Jack. Then with an "Oh my", it was too late. Boots had walked up to the girl and said something, pointing to Jerry Jack. She smiled and they came walking over. Boots said, "This is my friend Jerry Jack." "Hi," said Jerry Jack. The girl started laughing; it scared him, "What did I do wrong." he asked. "Nothing," said the girl. Then she continued, "He said you were a deaf mute and wanted to meet me." "I'll kill 'em," growled Jerry Jack. "I mean yes, I did want to meet you." They both chuckled then introduced themselves. Her name was Cindy Morgan, the preacher's daughter. The girl Boots was keen on was Audrey Fox, granddaughter of Oral Fox. When Boots heard this he crushed his hat in his hands, which he had been holding at his waist and swallowed real hard. He wondered where this relationship would lead, if anywhere.

Later in the afternoon the group, Laughlin, Melissa, Jerry Jack and Boots, loaded up in the buggy. The boys were in the back with Laughlin and Melissa up front as they headed back to the ranch. Jerry Jack said to Boots, "You know this church thing ain't so bad after all." Melissa and Laughlin, having overheard the comment, glanced at each other and smiled.

The next morning Jerry Jack and Boots were way down on the south end of the ranch looking for mavericks. The horses were walking slowly and the boys were engaged in casual talk. Boots said, "I heard you killed and scalped two Indians." "Yea," said Jerry Jack, "they were part of the band that killed my family." "Did it bother you?" asked Boots. "Not at all, it was justified" said Jerry Jack, then he continued, "You ever kill anybody?" "Yea, when me and my brother were on the battle-field," said Boots. "Bother you?" asked Jerry Jack. "At the time it didn't 'cause I knew they were trying to kill me. Now I know they didn't want to be on that battlefield either" replied Boots.

Jerry Jack asked, "How did you like going to church?" "I loved it, met Audrey; I can't wait to go back" said Boots. "That's not what I meant", snorted Jerry Jack, then he continued, "How did you like **church**? Did you hear what the Reverend Morgan said about how God controls our lives? Both of us have been through some bad times, but look where we are now. What do you think God has planned for us?" Boots replied, with a big smile on his face, "I don't know about me, but I think maybe you are going to be a preacher; let's race."

After a half mile run they reigned up and Boots said, "Do you know how to dance?" "No, do you" asked Jerry Jack. "No," said Boots, "how are we going to learn." Jerry Jack replied simply, "I don't know but I ain't practicing with you, let's race. After another short run they stopped again and Jerry Jack said, "Your brother's tough, smart too." "Yea, someday he will be a State Politician just like my mother wanted" said Boots. "What do you think we will be Boots?" asked Jerry Jack. "Without a job if we don't find some mavericks" answered Boots.

They knew the first load of wire would be coming in about a week. Laughlin had told them there might be trouble. Word was out he had ordered the wire and there was already grumbling going on. Things were changing. Open range and mavericks would soon be a thing of the past. He knew barbed wire would have the biggest impact ranching had ever seen.

Chapter 20

By this time the weather in Laredo had cleared, the sun was shining and there was a new man in town; it was Wes Lockhart. Having heard there was a high stakes poker game going on, Jim, Glen Ray and Luke decided to walk down to the saloon and check it out. Lockhart was at the poker table and he was playing with lots of money. Luke walked over to the table, stood to the side of Wes and said, "Fold up your cards, let's go over to the jail and talk." "What fer," responded Lockhart, "talk about what, I ain't done nothing." Luke drew his pistol, stuck the barrel against Wes' right ear and said, "You had your chance, now you're under arrest. Luke lifted Wes' pistol out of his holster while Glen Ray and Jim each grabbed an arm as they headed to the jail; they weren't gentle. This man was a suspect in the death of a Ranger and they needed a confession.

Once in the jail they made him aware that the bank teller had described him as the robber. Since Billy Joe had been trailing the robber when he was killed, Lockhart was the prime murder suspect. "We're locking you up 'til we get the teller down here from Cotulla to identify you," spouted Glen Ray.

"I want a lawyer, I know my rights, get me an attorney. There's one across the street, I saw his shingle, I want a lawyer" growled Lockhart. "Lock him up, you're charged with suspicion of robbery and murder," said Luke. "Jim will you go across the street to the telegraph office and get that teller down here. Tell Clem, the lawyer, that Wes has requested his services" continued Luke.

When the lawyer arrived he told Luke, "You've got to let Wes go, you don't have a choice. He hasn't done anything you can prove. Hell, I know there's a dead ranger but all you can do is get that teller down here as a witness. If the teller identifies him, you can put him in jail. But right now, you don't have anything linking him to Billy Joe's death.

Wes was in his cell and could hear the conversation. He said, "Hear that, let me out, you ain't got nothing on me. You Rangers think you're so high and mighty, y'all ain't nothing to me. Let me out, tell 'em Clem, tell 'em to let me out." "He's right gentlemen," retorted Clem, "you've got to release him, there's nothing to hold him on." When they were forced to let him out of the Laredo jail, Lockhart immediately rode out of town and disappeared.

Jim and Glen Ray rode up to the Cotulla Bank about a two day ride from Laredo. They wanted to talk to the teller about the robbery and shootout but after hearing about the Rangers death, he got scared and was now refusing to testify; said he couldn't be sure what the robber looked like. It was very evident he feared for his life leaving the Rangers with nothing.

Jim and Glen Ray were riding and talking as they returned to Laredo. Jim said, "We know who robbed the bank, Billy Joe was tracking him and got ambushed. My bet is Wes is in Mexico laying low." Glen Ray said, "He's in trouble if Rene and his banditos find him. I don't think they'll like a bounty hunter among them."

While Jim and Glen Ray were returning to Laredo, Nathan was riding out to the Rocking Horse in hopes Laughlin would work with him some more on his drawing speed and accuracy. Luck was on his side, Laughlin was at the blacksmith shop talking with Tom Gibbons, about the upcoming fencing project.

Jerry Jack and Boots, out searching for mavericks, had found five and were in the corral branding them. Laughlin hollered at Jerry Jack and Boots. He told them to get their rifles and join him and Nathan behind the barn. The boys soon returned, they wanted to learn how to shoot. Laughlin found an old rusty bucket and some wire. He walked out to a small tree with an overhanging limb, put the wire around the bucket handle and wrapped the wire around the branch. The bucket was dangling about four feet off the ground. He told Nathan to stand ten yards in front of the bucket, draw and fire.

The boys and Laughlin were watching as Nathan lined himself up, took a deep breath, drew and fired. The bucket kicked, it had been hit. "Put two in it this time," said Laughlin. Same thing, Nathan squared himself, took a deep breath, relaxed, drew and fired. The bucket kicked twice.

Jerry Jack said, "Wow, Mr. Law that was fast." Boots, beaming with pride, said, "That's my paw." Laughlin gave Nathan a few more tips on pointing as he aimed and adjusted his holster, both height and angle. "Do it again," said Laughlin, "this time three shots." Nathan went thru his routine, drew, BOOM – BOOM – BOOM, the bucket kicked after each shot. Jerry Jack said, "Mr. Law, you were faster that time. Mr. McFarland, show us how you draw." Laughlin didn't have his pistol on so he asked Nathan if he could borrow his. "My pleasure," said Nathan, "I want to see you draw myself." Laughlin buckled up the belt, adjusted the holster slightly, removed the pistol, spun it to get the feel and holstered it. He squared up to the bucket, almost faster than you could see and certainly faster than you could count, he emptied the revolver. The bucket had six new holes in it. Jerry Jack and Boots eyes were wide as saucers, their mouths were hanging open and they were speechless. Nathan smiled at them both and said "Now boys, that's fast!"

Laughlin said, "Get your rifles, a Ranger uses his rifle more than his pistol. Indians fear Rangers because of our long range rifles and marksmanship." Then Laughlin set up some targets at one hundred, two hundred and three hundred steps. He helped all three set their sights at one hundred yards, the approximate distance of his hundred steps. After letting them fire a number of rounds at that distance, he showed them how to elevate the rear sight for longer distances. They all did very well, especially Boots whose smile was contagious and his accuracy deadly. Although he had learned to shoot on the battlefield, Boots approached everything with a sense of humor and an ear to ear smile.

That night, Nathan and Oral were finishing their walk thru town. They returned to the jail, sat down at the table and shuffled the dominoes.

Oral said, "Nathan, you still practicing on your draw." "Just this after-noon and again every night," said Nathan, "just like Laughlin told me. If he says do it, I will do it." "Let me see how you're doing," said Oral. "Give me a demonstration." Nathan stood up, faced the empty jail cell, made ready, relaxed, drew and BOOM!, the gun fired. Oral 'bout fell out of the chair, it scared him so bad. "Oral, I'm sorry", said Nathan with a sheepish look on his face, "at night I practice with an empty gun in the room, I forgot it was loaded." Oral laughed and said, "Good thing we didn't have a prisoner, be hard to explain why you shot 'em in the cell. Get out there on the porch and tell everybody we're alright. Oh, by the way, that was fast, real fast."

It was a brisk morning on the Fox Ranch when he and Fred hooked up the buggy and headed into Abilene. As they arrived and were tying the horse and buggy to the hitching post, Fox told Fred to go visit with Linda and LaQuita while he spent some time with the lawyer that had just come to town. Fox had seen the sign on the building, which read: **Stewart Coffee – Attorney At Law. A**s Fred was happily heading towards the restaurant and LaQuita, Fox entered the lawyer's office and was greeted by a nice young man who introduced himself as Sterling Law. "Sterling Law, I know a Ranger named Law, any kin?" asked Fox. "Yes sir, that's my paw" said Sterling. "What!!!" exclaimed Fox, "boy I know about you and your brother. Know your paw well. Your paw's a fine Ranger, fine man, glad you boys found each other. How did you get over here working for an attorney?"

Sterling replied, "I met Mr. Coffee on the stage coming to Uvalde, we talked, told him someday I would like to go to law school. Several months later he sent me a letter and here I am. I'm saving my money in hopes of one day going to Austin and attend law school." "Outstanding young man, outstanding. Have a dream, work for it and one day it will be a reality" said Fox. "Oh, Mr. Fox, this is Stewart Coffee, my boss" said Sterling. Stewart had heard the conversation from his office and stepped out to meet Mr. Fox.

"Mr. Fox, my pleasure to meet you," said Coffee, "I've heard so much about you; it seems you are a living legend. How can I be of service to you today?" "I need to update a will, a man my age better make plans," Fox said, while smiling. "Come on in my office and sit down" said Stewart as he closed the door behind them.

They both sat down and Mr. Fox told Stewart he only had two relatives, his brothers, Oral, a lawman in Uvalde and Herman, a rancher. Then he said, "I want my brothers to each have one fourth of the ranch; that's land only. I want Fred Ramirez to have the remaining half with all my money to be paid out to him over a period of thirty years. I want Ranger Laughlin McFarland to be my executor of the will." Then, referring to Sterling, Fox asked, "How long before that boy will be ready for law school?" "A year", replied Stewart, "but he won't be financially able. He has started a savings account for his education." Fox rubbed his chin in thought and said, "Here's what I want you to do, unbeknownst to him, at the end of a year if he's still working for you and you agree he's worthy, I'll pay for his schooling."

Hearing this Stewart said, "Mr. Fox, that's the nicest thing I have ever heard of, you are truly a legend." "Son I'm in my seventies and I've got the biggest cattle ranch in West Texas. I take great pleasure in seeing my money benefit someone who is worthy" replied Fox.

Mr. Fox left Stewart's office and was walking across the street to the restaurant. Sterling was looking out the window at Mr. Fox as he thought out loud, "I heard he is very wealthy." Stewart looked out the window and watched Mr. Fox enter the restaurant and said, "My daddy always told me 'A man's wealth is not measured by the amount of his money, but by the sum of his deeds.'" I think I understand what he meant now that I've met Mr. Fox."

Stewart asked, "Sterling, how are you enjoying Abilene and working in the law office?" "I love it," said Sterling, "I'm learning from listening to you and your clients." "Sterling," said Stewart, "feel free to take any of the law books you like home with you to study. I'm very impressed with you, you're intelligent, crave knowledge, especially law, and you have good work habits. I am extremely pleased with you and your efforts. Keep up the excellent work and good things will come to you." "Thank you," said Sterling, "As you know it's always been my dream to someday be in law or politics, so I greatly do appreciate the opportunity you've given me."

At the restaurant, Fox, Fred, Linda and LaQuita were finishing their lunch. Cletus had received a wire from Laughlin telling him about the Ranger being killed in Laredo. When he told Linda, she knew Jim and Glen Ray would be investigating. With the weather threatening, Mr. Fox said they needed to start back and avoid the storm.

When Mr. Fox and Fred were about five miles out of town, talking and enjoying the ride, a rifle shot rang out! The bullet blew a hole in the leather backrest, not six inches from Mr. Fox's back. Fred put his arm on Mr. Fox, pulled him down almost to the floorboard, grabbed the whip and put the horse in a hard run. When they reached cover, he pulled up to survey what was behind them and saw nothing. They weren't being pursued. Mr. Fox said, "Turn around, let's go after 'em." "No sir," said Fred, "I don't have my rifle; I'm taking you to the ranch. I'll come back and track him. Believe me, nobody shoots at you and gets away with it. I'll get this hombre."

When they returned to the ranch, Fred saddled up Diablo; made provisions to stay out several days, and told Mr. Fox he was heading out to find the bush whackers trail. When he arrived back where the shot was fired, he rode up in the rocks and immediately found a trail. It was easy to follow; the horse was missing a shoe. He followed the tracks all the way to Abilene but in town, the trail was lost among all the other horse traffic. Fred decided to ride to Blackie Beasley's blacksmith shop and make him aware of what had happened. Blackie agreed to let Fred know should anyone ask him to shoe a horse. Feeling certain that Blackie would follow up on his request, he went to see Cletus Meeks and told him he didn't know for sure who the shot was meant for, him or Mr. Fox. Afterwards he stopped at Linda's restaurant to inform Linda and LaQuita, then rode hurriedly back to the ranch.

As he rode he was trying to figure out why someone would shoot at them. It appeared the motive might be grudge related, not a robbery attempt. Who could possibly not like Mr. Fox? When he reached the ranch, he went inside, sat and discussed what he had found, nothing just a horse with a shoe missing.

Fox thought carefully before he spoke, then said, "Abe Silas still hate's me for the death of his brother, but that was so long ago I don't think he would still be trying to have me killed. I know that drover Sandy dislikes me, I could see that when I warned him to stay away from LaQuita." "Yea," said Fred, "LaQuita told me he was bothering her in the restaurant and how Cletus ran him out." After a moment of silence, Fred continued, "I'm going to ride over to the Silas ranch and ask some questions." Mr. Fox said, "That'll be fine but be careful, the shooter could have been after you not me. Think I'll get my exercise, I'm going to walk over to Knob Hill and visit with Maude for awhile," added Fox.

Fred spun Diablo around and headed back to town where he asked Cletus to ride with him to the Silas ranch. When they arrived there, it was just like the last time he was at the ranch, barking dogs and a run down house. Abe was on the porch filthy and foul mouthed, holding his shotgun in his hands. Cletus said, "Abe put that shotgun away before it gets you in trouble." He lowered the shotgun, leaned it next to the wall and said, "What do you want? Then he motioned towards Fred and continued, "I want that Mexican out of here." "Somebody took a shot at Mr. Fox, know anything about it?" asked Fred. "Did they hit 'em? I hope they killed him" snorted Abe.

Just then a rider was approaching the corral; Fred knew who it was, Sandy. The horse was giving in to its right rear hoof, usually the sign that a shoe was missing.

Cletus looked at Abe and asked, "That man at the corral work for you?" Abe glanced at the corral then responded, "Yea, that's right, just started." "Get him up here" ordered Cletus, "I want to talk with him." Abe hollered toward the barn for Sandy. He came walking up in his usual cocky way and mumbled. "Yea boss, you need me?" Cletus asked, "Where were you two days ago about two o'clock?" "I was out on the ranch doing my job, rounding up mavericks" replied Sandy. Then he turned towards Abe and said, "Tell 'em Abe, you know where I was." "Yea that's right, rounding up mavericks," said Abe. Cletus said, "Somebody took a shot at Mr. Fox. If you hear anything about that we would appreciate any information you could give us." Cletus began to turn his mount around and leave when he stopped suddenly and looked sharply at Sandy and said, "Oh, by the way, your horse is limping on his right rear leg." "Yea I know, he threw a shoe, got to put a new one on him" said Sandy. As they rode off Cletus said, "Well, looks like we got our man, now we got to get some evidence."

When they returned to the ranch, Fred and Cletus met with Mr. Fox and filled him in with all the details about Sandy. They all agreed he was the shooter, just didn't have any proof. Fred said, "Let me go over there to the Silas ranch by myself. I'll get a confession, I'll beat it out of him." "No!" said Mr. Fox. "You're not going to do that." Cletus said, "I agree, stay away from him. Keep Mr. Fox safe till this is settled."

Mr. Fox said, "I made him mad when I told him to stay away from LaQuita. He is jealous of Fred. He drinks too much and has a cocky, better than everybody attitude. I understand Nathan's boy whipped him pretty good in a fist fight before he left Laughlin's ranch. I'm safe here on the ranch; just don't want Fred to get bushwhacked."

Although Fred and Mr. Fox were safe on the ranch, it was a different story for LaQuita who was now getting off of work. She had finished her shift and was heading for the boarding house.

It was a dark night without a shimmer of moonlight. Sandy was drunk. He had been drinking all day with Abe Silas and still had a bottle hidden under his coat. He watched as LaQuita came out of the restaurant and started walking toward the boarding house which was located at the end of the street. To get there she had to pass the livery stable, which except for the horses, was unoccupied. Sandy quickly ran to the livery stable and hid outside behind a tree. When LaQuita came walking by, he grabbed her, muffled her mouth with his hand and drug her into the stable. It appeared the town had retired early; the rain had stopped but no one was on the streets.

Sandy drug LaQuita to an empty stall at the back of the stable. She was fighting desperately and trying to scream. He hit her in the face with his fist, "Think you're too good for me," he said, "I'll show you." He hit her five more times, she was unconscious. As she lay in the hay on the floor of the stall he kept repeating, "To good for me; Fred will kill me; Fox will kill me, I'll show y'all. Too good for me, I'll show you not to make Sandy mad." Then, like a mad man, he ripped her blouse away and tore off her dress. He had knocked her unconscious and she was bleeding badly from her mouth and nose. Sandy slid down to the floor and raped her. After it was over he knew he was in bad trouble. In a moment of panic, he pulled his pistol to shoot her so she couldn't tell anyone who did it. He couldn't pull the trigger; people would hear the shot. Getting away was all he could think of. I've got to run, he thought; Fred will be after me. He paused a moment longer, took one more look at LaQuita, then ran out the door and into the alley where his horse was tied. Hurriedly he mounted his horse and rode off toward the Silas ranch. He continued to drink from the bottle in his coat, was in a panic and mumbling out loud. "Abe will tell 'em I was with him, that I didn't go to town. Maybe she will bleed to death during the night." He rode back to the Silas ranch and up to the bunk house to get his duffle bag, saddle bags and some food. He planned to leave and hide out but he didn't know where; he was too drunk and couldn't think straight. He fell across the bunk and passed out.

The next morning, Clifton, the livery stable owner, arrived at five o'clock. He was going from stall to stall throwing blocks of hay for the horses when he heard someone groan. He found LaQuita in the stall and ran for help. Cletus was in his office when he got the news. He sent someone to get Doc Jameson, who lived about a half mile outside of town, and then on to the ranch for Fred.

When Sandy finally awoke, the sun was shining in his face through the bunk house window. He realized where he was and what he had done. Once again he panicked knowing he had to get away before anyone found him. His horse was wandering around outside trying to get at the hay inside the corral. Sandy caught his horse, mounted and rode out past the ranch house. Abe saw him and hollered as he rode by. Sandy paid him no mind; his only thoughts were to get away.

While Sandy was making his get-away, Mr. Fox was heading toward his corral where Fred was saddling Diablo. As he approached Fred, Fox in a loud shaky voice said, "Fred, a rider just came from town, you're needed there, LaQuita's been hurt. Then he continued, "I'll have Manuel bring me in soon as we can get the buggy hitched up." After a momentary pause, Fox added nervously, "You'd better hurry, she's asking for you. All I know is she was attacked by someone and she's been taken to Doc Jameson's place."

Fred rode Diablo flat out all the way to the doctors' house. When he rushed in, they were still attending to her, cleaning up her face and stitching her cuts. She was conscious but just barely able to talk.

Cletus stopped Fred before he could get in the room and said, "She's going to be okay but she has a bad concussion. There are cuts on her lips and eye brows, her face is swollen badly and she can barely see. Doc says she will make it, but Fred," he hesitated, then with his head down continued, "she was raped." "Who did it?" demanded Fred. "She said it was Sandy, he attacked her when she was walking home after work, happened in the livery stable," answered Cletus. "I'm going in to see her and then I am going after that bastard. I'll send him to hell" promised Fred.

As he entered her room, his voice softened as he said, "Hi baby, it's Fred. You're gonna be alright, I'm here." She turned, attempted to talk but it was hard to understand her. Finally she managed to say, "He raped me Fred. I am so sorry, now you won't love me" she cried. "Baby, baby, baby, don't you worry about nothing, everything's gonna be fine" said Fred as he gently squeezed her hand. "Fred," said the doctor, "no more, don't want her to exert herself, we need to get her some rest." "Bye baby, I love you", uttered Fred as he headed for the door.

Cletus grabbed Fred by the arm as he rushed out of the room, and said, "Fred, just you hold on, I'll get a posse together to ride with us, we'll catch him." Fred looked hard at Cletus and barked, "Ain't got time for no posse gathering, I'm riding." Then he jumped on Diablo and rode 'hell bent for leather' towards the Silas Ranch. When he rode up, Abe came out on the porch just as Fred said, "Sandy raped my woman and beat her, has he been here." "Yes, he left about an hour ago, riding south", said Abe. "Don't know exactly what happened, but if it's true, I hope you get 'em and kill'em. I don't hold to no woman raping." Fred knew he could pick up Sandy's trail since he only had an hour head start.

About an hour and a half into his ride, Fred could see Sandy and his horse about a quarter mile ahead. He was riding full out straight towards Eagle Pass and the Mexican border. Apparently, he was staying on the road to avoid loss time and trying to beat any would be posse across the border. Diablo quickly closed the gap. Sandy, after looking back and seeing Fred, wildly emptied his pistol at him.

Chapter 21

As Fred drew nearer, he took his rope from the saddle, made a loop, swung it over his head and threw it. The rope caught Sandy down around his waist as Fred pulled hard on his reigns. Diablo set down, like a good roping horse does with a calf, jerking Sandy backwards off his horse. He hit the ground hard. Fred said, "Get up, get up and look at me." Sandy was barely able to get up and he looked at Fred and said "I ain't done nothing, what's this all about." "I'll tell you what it's about", raged Fred, "you tried to kill my best friend, Mr. Fox; you raped and nearly killed the girl I love, that's what it's all about. Then Fred continued, the rage still on his lips, "You'll never rape another woman." Fred drew his pistol and shot Sandy in the testicles. The blood gushed from his loins. Sandy screamed as he held himself and fell to his knees pleading, "Don't shoot me, don't kill me! I'm sorry I shot at Mr. Fox, don't kill me! I'm sorry for what I did to LaQuita, I was drunk."

Fred, still mounted on Diablo, brought Sandy's horse to him and growled, "Unbuckle your gun belt, let if fall to the ground, slide the rope from around your waist and put it around your neck." "No, no!" Sandy was pleading and crying. "Is that what LaQuita was saying when you beat and raped her? snarled Fred, "do it now or I'll shoot off one of your knees." Sandy put the loop around his neck and continued to beg. Fred was having none of it as he continued, "Get on your horse." "I can't, I'm hurt and bleeding bad; I need a doctor" cried Sandy. BOOM! Fred's pistol fired and the bullet struck Sandy in the right foot. He spun and fell screaming even louder. "Get on the horse!!" commanded Fred. Sandy barely managed to get in the saddle when Fred said, "Start riding, I'll tell you when to stop." By now Sandy was crying profusely as he sobbed, "You're gonna kill me, I'm sorry, please don't kill me."

They rode for about a mile until they reached a secluded area down in a deep draw. There was a tree with a limb extending out, a perfect hangman's limb. As they rode under it, Fred threw his end of the rope over the limb and tied it to his saddle horn. He backed up Diablo tightening the rope till Sandy was standing in his stirrups. Fred circled Diablo around the trunk wrapping and securing the rope then he said, "Sandy, I could let the posse take you for trial, the hanging judge would hang you. Hell, the posse may hang you if they get you and I may hang you right now myself. No matter what happens, you're gonna hang. I didn't tie your hands for a reason; I don't want to break your neck when I hang you. I want you to try and pull yourself up when I run the horse out from under you. Don't want you to die fast; I want to watch you strangle and dance before you die."

Sandy had both hands on the noose around his neck, screaming and begging for mercy. Fred said, "Vaya con Dios amigo," and slapped the horses' rump. Sandy was kicking, chocking and gasping as he performed the dance of death. His face turned purple, his eyes bugged out and his arms fell to his side; he was dead. Fred rode over and shot him six times in the crotch. Then he took hold of Sandy's' horse and removed the bridle and cinch. The saddle fell to the ground and Sandy's' horse was free to roam. This was the way of the west.

Fred turned and started walking his horse back toward the road. He reloaded his pistol, holstered it and started praying. When he reached the road he turned and headed toward Abilene at a slow walk. About five miles down the road he met Cletus and the posse.

Cletus pulled up, looked at Fred and said, "Did Sandy ride all night and make it to Mexico?" "Yea, guess he did," said Fred. "Alright boys", said Cletus, "let's turn around, he's in Mexico. We'll never get 'em now." They all rode in to Abilene; Cletus said, "Go on Fred, I'll take care of the reports, go see LaQuita." Fred nodded and started to turn Diablo when Cletus said, "Looks like you lost your rope, might want to stop and get one before you go to the ranch." "Yea, I'll do that" replied Fred as he nodded, touched the tip of his hat with his fingers and rode toward the doctors' office.

When he arrived there, he tied up Diablo, dismounted and went inside. Doc Jameson was at his desk when he saw Fred come through the door. He said, "Fred come over here, we need to talk. She's gonna be alright. She'll recover physically, but she will have some mental scars that you must help her with. She's gonna believe she didn't fight hard enough; she'll feel guilty, unclean and think you won't love her anymore." Jameson looked Fred straight in the eyes and continued, "Her mental health and how fast she recovers will depend on you. Mr. Fox has already been here. He wants her moved to his house so you two can be together and she can be tended to properly. I agree. In a couple of days bring the buggy and take her home.

Now, we have one more big thing to worry about, pregnancy." Fred said, "Thank you doctor, now can I go see her?" "Yes you may," he answered, "Fred, she's a fine girl and has been asking for you all the time she's been here."

Fred entered the room, kissed her on the lips, squeezed her hand and said, "How's my pretty girl?" "I'm alright," she said weakly, "are you okay?" Fred answered softly, "Yea baby, I'm fine. I'm here to spend time with you. You go back to sleep, I'll be here when you wake up." Fred sat in the chair and held her hand all night.

When LaQuita woke up she saw Fred slumped over in the chair. He had his head on her bed and was holding her hand. She smiled and then tears came to her eyes when she thought about what had happened. Fred woke up just as Linda was bringing breakfast from the restaurant. Fred fed LaQuita and remained with her until midday; she was much improved. He told her he was going to the ranch to get the buggy, then he would come back, spend the night and take her home the next day. The doctor had approved the plan.

Fred rode back to the ranch on Diablo and stopped at the picket fence where Mr. Fox was standing. "How's LaQuita, is she gonna be alright?" asked Fox. Fred pushed his hat back on his head, wiped the sweat from his brow and answered, "Yes sir, I came to get the buggy, doc says I can bring her here tomorrow." "That's wonderful, wonderful, go on get the buggy and get back to her." replied a relieved Mr. Fox. Fred had turned

Diablo toward the barn when Mr. Fox called his name. He stopped Diablo and looked back over his shoulder. "Fred," asked Fox, "did you find him?" Fred responded sternly," Yea, I found him. Mr. Fox, with a knowing grin, rode off to get the buggy.

The next day Fred brought LaQuita back to the big house. Mr. Fox put her in a guest bedroom, made her comfortable and told Rosa and Angel not to leave her side. Fred and Mr. Fox walked out on the porch and sat down to relax and ponder the situation. Coming through the front gate was an old buggy in bad shape being pulled by a mule. As it came closer they recognized the driver. It was Abe Silas. Abe pulled the buggy up to the gate and stopped. He was clean shaven, had on clean clothes and was sober; he looked totally different.

"JJ, is that you?" shouted Silas. "Yes it is," said Mr. Fox. Abe asked if he could talk to him. Fox nodded yes, then he and Fred walked to the fence but stayed on the inside. "How can I help you Abe?" asked Mr. Fox. "JJ", said Abe, "I don't hold to what that hand of mine done to that girl. Didn't know he was that kind. I'm sorry and hope she gets well soon. JJ, I've been a fool, ruined my life hating you for something you done to my brother. Hell, he was stealing. He was no good and deserved to be hung. I've been wrong and just wanted to come tell you face to face that I'm sorry." Mr. Fox said, "There's always something good that comes from something bad. LaQuita's tragedies ended you're feud with me. I never had ill feelings for you. Abe, come on in, let's have something to eat and you can meet LaQuita." They met, had lunch, exchanged some pleasantries then Abe left for his return trip.

On the Rocking Horse Ranch in Uvalde, Melissa was having supper with Laughlin when, suddenly she mumbled, "It's so sad what caused Boots, Jerry Jack and Sterling to be here, but I am really enjoying them. I am so proud for Sterling, but still I miss him." She paused, then continued," What a wonderful person Nathan is, Laughlin, I'm so proud of you and what you did to help him." Without taking a breath, she went on, "mention the boys to Nathan and you can see his eyes light up with pride and love. Jerry Jack and Boots act like brothers you know, they are always together. Are they learning about ranching? Melissa paused, then in a disgusting tone uttered, "Laughlin you haven't said a word, talk to me." Laughlin chuckled and said, "Is it my turn?" "Yes, I want to hear about the boys", Melissa said sheepishly.

Laughlin said, "Sterling is very intelligent, has lots of common sense, always in control, tough, very tough, no one in the bunkhouse will try him. He will eventually be a man of importance. On the other hand, Boots is carefree, fun loving, very smart, determined, has tremendous physical ability and a never say die attitude." He hesitated, then, as if in awe, said, "His horse is War Paint; nobody had ever been able to ride that bronco. He put on a show of determination in breaking that horse like I've never seen." Now Jerry Jack has more courage than most men I've known," continued Laughlin, "he's a thirty year old man in a sixteen year old body. He could be a ranger right now but he needs to learn how to use a pistol." Laughlin took a breath and, as an afterthought, said "I'll take care of that." He thought for a moment, then continued, "It's kinda like these are my boys, I love all of 'em." "Laughlin, do you think Nathan will ever get over the loss of his wife?" queried Melissa. "Not completely, but the greatest healer of all is time" said Laughlin.

The next day five wagon loads of wire were delivered to the ranch. It was time to start the fencing project. With Laughlin being a Ranger, it would keep some of the trouble away. Times were changing, railroads were laying new track every day, stock yards were being built along with more and more windmills. Breeding was being more selective to produce heavier beef. Fifteen hundred mile cattle drives would soon be a thing of the past; herds would soon be going by rail. Surveyors had completed their job; the real work would be the many miles of fencing that had to be stretched.

Jerry Jack and Boots had given Laughlin a count, he had approximately one hundred and fifty head of cattle; he wanted five thousand. He told Melissa 'ole JJ Jr. has lots of work to do. So did the boys and his wranglers. The Army wanted a hundred and fifty head of horses delivered to

Ft. Davis, pronto. It would be good experience for the boys. Candido would also be going, he had made the trip before, but Laughlin's plan in the future was for the boys to make all the drives themselves.

He told Candido to get started picking the horses, take only stallions and geldings. He estimated, after the order was filled, he would still have about five hundred horses; presently he had a little over six hundred and fifty. The boys were excited when they heard the news; it would be their first drive. Their excitement spilled over into the bunkhouse where, after supper, they asked Candido to educate them about the drive. Candido said he would be glad to tell them what he knew and that he wished more wranglers would ask. He said most of them thought they knew it all.

Candido started off by telling them a horse and cattle drive differ in the fact that it takes more men for cattle than horses. Cattle drives are very slow; the cattle have to travel slowly because they eat as they walk then bed down at night. Horses, on the other hand, can be moved faster; they don't bed down and eat all night. You can usually control a herd of horses by putting hobbles on the lead mares thereby causing the others to stay with them. "Laughlin told us, 'No mares'," suggested Boots. "He understands I need three or four lead mares," said Candido, "it just makes it easier to keep them bunched." Then he continued, "You boys take your rifles, Laughlin told me to give you a couple of six guns. We're going into Iron Eagles territory and horses are attractive to the Indians. We could have trouble even though they stay away from the fort while troopers are patrolling the surrounding area. Candido added soberly, "As a matter of fact, if the Indians are active, troopers will probably meet us halfway. We need to get the horses to the fort and return as quickly as possible, there's fence to be built. Y'all pay attention; Laughlin said in the future he wants you boys to be capable of overseeing the herd and the drovers. He has a lot of confidence in ya'll and thinks you boys have the ability. Know what? I do too, we leave in three days." With that, Candido began overseeing preparations for the drive.

Meanwhile, hoping to find Rene, Glen Ray and Jim had ridden across the river into Mexico. Rene would know if Wes was in the area. They returned to the old missions that were now being used as a cantina and brothel. As they walked in they saw a girl with scars on her face. She came over to them immediately; it was Rene's sister. She stopped, looked at Glen Ray and said, "Gracias, Senor Baby Ranger, you kill loco Shorty, gracias." Jim asked about Rene's whereabouts. She said he was in Eagle Pass chasing Indians but was due back soon.

The Rangers slept on the ground outside the cantina that night. They arose early and were on the trail toward Eagle Pass without so much as a cup of coffee. They would stay on the Mexican side of the river where they expected to bump into Rene and his banditos.

As anticipated, about noon they met Rene and his band riding toward them. "Ola! It's you amigo, Baby Ranger, my compadre, Ola" shouted Rene. As they closed the gap between them Glen Ray asked, "Rene, you remember Jim?" Rene glanced at Jim and answered, "Si, how you do amigo?" "Senor, we're looking for a man that robbed a bank and back shot a Ranger" barked Jim.

"Si, we know this hombre, we see him in Eagle Pass" replied Rene. "How do you know who I am talking about," said Glen Ray. "I haven't described him yet." Rene shot back, "No, amigo, you no tell us, he tell us he keel a Ranger. We think maybe eet's you or your amigo. Where is Shotgun Shorty? He eez plenty good weeth dat shoot gun. Hombre call heemself Wes, broke teeth, mucho grande scar on leeps – we know he eez bounty hunter, he no know we know – he brag about keeling a Ranger and wanted to ride weeth us. We tell heem it eez okay, come ride weeth us to Mexico." "Where is he now?" asked Glen Ray.

"Amigo, we no like bounty hunters and we theenk maybe he keel our Baby Ranger. Maybe he eez hanging in a tree across the river from Eagle Pass. Maybe we take heez money and heez horse, he no need no more." "He told you he killed a Ranger?" asked Jim. "Si amigo, robbed a bank and back shoot the Ranger, said all Rangers no good, that not true, you pretty good Ranger." Said Rene. Glen Ray smiled at him and said, "Gracias amigo, you pretty good bandito." Having no further business in Mexico, Glen Ray and Jim left for Laredo. They had to report to Marshall Starrett and wire Captain McFarland of their results.

Nathan, still in Uvalde, rode out from town and delivered a telegram to Laughlin. "Got a wire for you Captain from Jim," said Nathan. "Nathan, you don't have to call me Captain, Laughlin's just fine" said McFarland. "No sir, need to show my respect, you're my Captain" replied Nathan. After reading the telegram Laughlin shouted, "Good news, good news, Billy Joe's killer has been found. It was Wes Lockhart and banditos hung him in Mexico." "Glen Ray and Jim get along good with the banditos," he added, "and I wanna keep it that way."

At the Rocking Horse Ranch, while Candido was preparing for the trip to Fort Davis, Boots and Jerry Jack were anxiously awaiting the drive when Boots said, "We need to make trail maps, that way, if necessary, we can return without getting lost." Then he continued, "Jerry Jack you think 'ole Iron Eagle might try to take our horses?" "Sure do," said Jerry Jack, "if he sees us he'll try to get the horses and take them to his hidden camp. When 'ole Iron Eagle sees War Paint, Boots, you're gonna be a dead man. That's an Indians favorite, a big ole fast paint horse." "He'll never get War Paint," said Boots, "and I'll take a bunch of 'em with my rifle." "You are getting pretty good with that Winchester, I believe you can kill an Indian at three hundred yards" remarked Jerry Jack. "Four hundred," said Boots as he grinned and continued, "Laughlin said there's a buffalo gun hanging above Mr. Fox's mantle. It's a 50 caliber Sharps." Jerry Jack chimed in, "If that rifle could talk I bet we would hear some stories. Oral Fox told me that in he and his brother's younger days there was no law. His brother was the law, said he had hung lots of Indians and rustlers. Don't seem possible, he's such a kind person now," said Boots, "In fact, my brother wrote me a letter telling me he met Mr. Fox and what a fine man he was." Then, as though tiring of the story said, "Come on Jerry Jack, let's go down behind the barn and shoot at that bucket with our pistols. Hell, let's practice with both our rifles and our pistols." Jerry Jack remarked, then continued, "Candido told me Iron Eagle stole a herd and captured the drovers. Then they tied some of 'em to an ant hill, sliced their eye lids and left 'em to die. Others were gut shot and left stranded. Said it takes three hard weeks for a man to die after being gut shot." "Shut up, let's go practice with our rifles," said Boots, with a grin.

It was now the second day of the drive; Candido had said they were making good progress. The first day they had ridden drag with Candido on point; Will and Jesse were the outriders. Flap Jack and his chuck wagon was a welcome site at the end of a long day. It didn't take them long to find out that riding drag was for the green horns. They had eaten trail dust all that first day but today they were the outriders. Even though outriding was hard work, you had to keep the horses bunched and go get strays, it was fun. They just hoped 'ole Iron Eagle wasn't around.

That night in camp Jerry Jack said, "Boots, do you think there really is an Iron Eagle? I'll bet Candido made it up just to scare us." Boots replied, "maybe so, maybe not, but in my sights he'd be a dead eagle."

Going toward the Davis Mountains they had ridden through a hail storm and were gaining altitude. That night was cold with temperatures in the low 20's. Candido hobbled the three lead mares they had brought and let the horses graze. They were close to Alpine and the land was flat and bare, easy to keep up with the horses. It was cold and getting colder. The high altitude and night air made the camp fire feel good. Candido said "We are close to the Fort, a day and a half ride. Now we can just follow the stage road all the way in. The troopers haven't come to meet us so things must be quiet with the Indians. Tomorrow I want both of you boys riding point and remain there till we get to the Fort then we'll bring 'em in." With that said, Candido turned his attention to Boots and barked, "Boots, you've got the first four hour watch then it's your turn Jerry Jack." It was all new and exciting for the boys. Boots' smile kept getting bigger and bigger; he was enjoying it more and more.

The boys could see Ft. Davis in the distance. Jerry Jack and Boots had taken point and were bringing in the horses.

Ft. Davis was named after Jefferson Davis prior to him becoming President of the Confederate States. Originally the site of the Fort was an Indian camp. A stage stop was set up in 1850 for the mail route between El Paso and San Antonio. The Fort was formed in 1854 with troops to patrol and protect the area from Apaches. During the Civil War the Fort was attacked by Apaches and abandoned until 1867. The Ninth Calvary reoccupied the Fort in 1867 and that was who needed the horses they were delivering. The Davis Mountains surrounded the Army Post where most Indian bands passed through undetected. The Mescalero Apaches made their seasonal camp in the area of the Fort. As West Texas settlements increased, raids into Mexico and along the San Antonio-El Paso trail became a way of life for the Apache, Kiowa and Comanche alike. Few Americans had seen the Davis Mountains prior to 1846. After the war with Mexico a wave of gold seekers, settlers and traders came through the area needing the protection of the military post.

Boots and Jerry Jack, along with Candido and his vaqueros brought the herd inside the fort and into the corrals. They beamed with pride when an Army officer looked at the horses and said, "Fine looking horses, good job boys." Then the officer in charge said to Boots, "Son, that paint horse you're riding, is highly valued by the Indians. You better hope 'ole Iron Eagle don't lay his eyes on him." Boots gave the officer a nod of thanks and proceeded to prepare for the night.

Candido had collected payment and put it in the bank; it was by far too much money to be traveling with. He then joined the rest of the group as they explored the city. The area surrounding the Fort was a pretty place with mesas and flats, providing snow in the winter and heat in the summer. Boots told Jerry Jack that, except for the absence of pine trees, the area reminded him of Georgia. They returned to the barracks at the fort and lay down on their cots. Boots said, "I guess this

Iron Eagle is real, but he ain't getting War Paint. If I can't whip 'em, War Paint and I will out run 'em." There was no response from Jerry Jack, he was sound asleep. Before starting back they all rested and got a good nights sleep.

The next morning they were up with the troops, breakfast in the mess hall and then to the corral to get their horses. Boots was saddling up when four young Indian scouts walked up. They were dressed in Army uniforms complete with hats and had long braided hair hanging down past their shoulders. They were talking about War Paint. Boots could hear them but didn't understand what they were saying. Jerry Jack was leading his horse toward Boots when he saw the Indians. Not liking Indians, Jerry Jack pulled his Winchester from its' scabbard and walked over with rifle in hand and said, "What's going on Boots? Raiding party got you pinned down?" "I think they like War Paint", said Boots, "but I can't understand them." One of the Indians spoke, "We wantum you horse." "Yea, well Chief you no getum......my horse." As Boots said that, Jerry Jack worked the lever action on his rifle.

Chapter 22

The Indian said, "Me tradeum plenty good squaws for horse." Jerry Jack started laughing and said, "Chief, plenty good horse, run like wind, he need more squaws, maybe five," and he held up five fingers." "Ug, we tradeum, me go getum", mumbled the Indian. "Damn you Jerry Jack, shut up", spouted Boots, "I don't need you making things worse." Then Boots turned and addressed the Indian, "Chief, chief, come back, he loco, my horse, no tradeum, vamoose, go away or whatever the word is." The Indian frowned, walked away saying, "Plenty good horse, me want um."

Jerry Jack was still chuckling when he said, "Boots, as long as I've known you, you've been smiling. I made a good trade for you; got you five wives and you quit smiling. Five wives, man I had you fixed up. Wait till I tell Audrey you were trying to trade War Paint for five squaws." Boots smiled again and said, "Let's get started home, I'm ready to go to church."

Back in Uvalde, Laughlin was beginning to show concern over Boots and Jerry Jack when Melissa asked him to sit down and eat his breakfast. She inquired, "What's making you so nervous? Then added, "As If I didn't know. Laughlin grinned and said, "I wish I was with those boys. Candido should get them there today. I'll ride into town and see if I have a telegram. Melissa gave Laughlin that knowing glance and said, "Laughlin, you know that nice little runner will bring it when it comes in." Laughlin didn't know she hadn't slept all night. She had been thinking what it would be like if they had children of their own.

The boys were now on the second day going back when Boots saw five Indians riding even with them but staying well out of rifle range. Counting the cook, there was eight Laughlin men carrying rifles. The terrain was flat and, hopefully, the risk was too much for the Indians who feared the rifle. The Indians rode in full view until dark. Candido said they probably would attack during the night so they all stayed up and ready but the attack never came. Evidently the Indians didn't like the odds of going up against the long rifles. Most likely they were afraid of the 45-70 Springfields. They called them "'Fire Stick' with a whole lot of lead, little bit of powder, shoot far and kill 'm dead." Since the night met without any incident, they were up early and continued their return trip.

It was Saturday evening when Boots and Jerry Jack arrived at the ranch. They walked up knocked on the door and nervously nudged it open. There stood Laughlin and Melissa, in the kitchen, making pecan pies for church. Boots shuffled his feet, ran his fingers around the hat he was holding in his hand and said, "Uh, uh, well, we was just wondering, do you think we could ride in with y'all when you go to church tomorrow?" Laughlin looked uncertainly at the boys and spouted, "Melissa, the boys are here and they were wondering if they could go to church with us tomorrow, what do you think? will we have room in the buggy?" Melissa came to the door, stood next to Laughlin and said, "Yes, yes they may. I never dreamed you boys liked Brother Morgan's sermons enough to come back." "Oh yes ma'am, he's good," said Boots. Melissa looked at them both and knowingly said, "I know why you two want to go, not because of Brother Morgan's sermons", chuckled Melissa; "But that's okay, any way to get you into church is okay with us."

The next morning they loaded the buggy and went to church. As usual, third row from the front. Boots and Jerry Jack found Cindy and Audrey, they all smiled then church began. After a couple of songs, Brother Morgan read from the Bible. Boots saw Jerry Jack reach in his shirt and pull out a small Bible, open it, and begin reading along with Brother Morgan.

During the after church buffet Boots said, "Where did you get that Bible?" "My maw gave it to me," said Jerry Jack, "she would read to me from her Bible as 'sis' and I followed along in my Bible." Boots said, "I don't read too good, maybe you could read some of it to me sometime." Cindy and Audrey had sat down with them while they had lunch. They told the girls about the trail drive and of course Jerry Jack told the story about the squaws. Everyone laughed and a good time was had by all.

The fence project at the Rocking Horse Ranch was progressing at a record pace. Laughlin had hired extra people and they were stringing wire about as fast as he could get it delivered. It was midday; Laughlin was with the fence building crew when he saw riders coming toward him. When they got closer he counted twenty three riders. They were led by Ned Barlow and Jim Driskol, owners of separate ranches north of Laughlin's spread. They rode up quite and solemn. Laughlin knew what the visit was about, fence, so he asked, "You boys part of a posse?"

"No, we just came by to talk to you", said Driskol. "Does it take twenty three men to talk, you must have a lot to say" snorted Laughlin. As Driskol and Barlow started to dismount, Laughlin said, "Hold on, don't ever step down on another mans property until you're asked." They looked at Laughlin and, knowing who he was, stayed in the saddle. Laughlin was upset that they had come over in a show of force rather than asking for a meeting to discuss his plans for fencing. Having been shown no respect, Laughlin said, "You're here, uninvited, about my fencing. Now, Mr. Barlow, Mr. Driskol, turn around and ride out of here. If you two men want to talk to me, be at my house at seven this evening but don't you ever come back on this ranch trying to show strength with your riders. Now ride!"

At 7:00 P.M., when Driskol and Barlow showed up at the ranch, Laughlin invited them in, served them coffee and said, "How can I help you?" "Well, uh, well, uh. We don't like you putting up fences," said Barlow. "Go ahead" said Laughlin, "I'm listening." Barlow continued nervously, "Well, uh, it's always been open range, we don't need fences. Horses will tangle up in fences, riders will get hurt and cut up; fences are no good. Drives can't be made with fences." Laughlin said, "Gentlemen, times are changing, the day of the fifteen hundred mile cattle drive through open range is over. Beef will go to market by rail. We'll breed heavier stock by controlled grazing and rotation of pastures to allow grass re-growth as necessary. Windmills will be built when there are no rivers or creeks in your pasture. Don't fight progress, join in, be part of it. What you boys are saying is you want your herd to be able to roam, eat my grass and drink my water. You resent me, fencing property that I own. Well I'm sorry gentlemen but you can do the same thing I'm doing on your ranches. Can I warm up your coffee?" There was a slight pause then Laughlin continued, "I want to be your friend and I'll work with you in a drought, but if you over graze that's your problem. Move your cattle to better grazing; only difference now is you can't put them on my grass; it's behind fences. I hope we can leave here as friends tonight, but don't try to tell me what I can and can't do on my ranch. Are all your questions answered?" Without comment, Driskol and Barlow left, Laughlin could tell they weren't happy with the results of the meeting but riding up on him with a show of force was not the way to approach Laughlin.

The boys were back from the drive, Jim and Glen Ray were in Laredo and the fencing was ahead of schedule. Nathan and Oral were taking care of Uvalde while Sterling was learning law and saving his money for law school. Everything was fine except for the pending tragedy in Abilene. LaQuita was physically recovered, although, just as the doctor said, she was having some mental problems dealing with the situation. Mr. Fox, Fred, Angel and Rosa were being a tremendous help. They all wondered what would happen when she returned to Abilene and reality. It was not mentioned but silently, everyone was concerned about a possible pregnancy.

Fred and LaQuita were at the ranch walking in the yard after supper when she stopped suddenly, looked into Fred's' eyes and said, "Fred, I'm afraid Sandy may come back and hurt me again, he's never been found and no one knows his whereabouts. When you went after him, you caught him, didn't you? I know you did. If not, you would still be out there after him. I know you Fred, you caught him didn't you" she pleaded. Fred stepped in front of her, a hand on each of her shoulders, looked into her eyes and said, "Don't worry; He won't be bothering anyone."

That afternoon Fred and Mr. Fox helped LaQuita get in the buggy for the trip back to Abilene. The doctor had checked her and said she was ready to resume her normal activities. Arrangements had been made with Linda for her to stay at the hotel for about a week. The doctor told Fred and Mr. Fox that when she returns to Abilene, she could have flashbacks when she is on her way home at night and sees the livery stable. He recommended that she be escorted home for a few weeks. He said, "Fred, show her lots of attention and love, and remember, 'time is the greatest healer'." As they neared town you could see the expression on her face was turning into fear.

When they entered the restaurant, LaQuita told Linda she wanted to go back to work. Linda, like everyone else, told her she needed to take it easy, but she said she wanted to start right now. Thinking work may take her mind off the incident; Linda agreed and immediately put her to work.

Sterling came in to have his evening meal. When he saw Mr. Fox and Fred, he went to their table to say hello. They were glad to see Sterling and invited him to eat with them. He accepted, sat down and they all ordered. LaQuita took their order and Fred was closely watching her, she was doing fine. Mr. Fox and Fred would be spending the night and returning to the ranch the next day.

After the meal was finished they ordered wine, sat and talked. Mr. Fox asked Sterling about his job and ambitions and was thoroughly impressed with him. When it was time to close the restaurant; Fox invited Sterling out to the ranch for Sunday dinner and a tour. Sterling was excited and accepted the invitation.

The next morning Fred and Mr. Fox were in the buggy returning home when Fox said, "Fred, whatever time you need to help LaQuita, you take it. The ranch will run itself." "Thank you sir, I appreciate it" said Fred as Fox continued, "Fred, son, I know you're concerned just like we all are, praying that she's not pregnant. As you know, you're like a son to me and I'll support and help you. No matter what happens, I'm here for you."

It was Saturday. Fred had ridden to town with plans on staying until Sunday evening. He was anxious to see LaQuita, but he took time to visit with Doc Jameson and discuss her progress. Doc Jameson told Fred, "She's feeling quite ashamed and afraid that you won't want her anymore. All the other things I have mentioned," He said, "are to be expected. It will take time to heal."

Linda let LaQuita off at noon on Saturday and all day Sunday so she could have time with Fred. Fred had the buggy so they rode out of town, talking as they rode. LaQuita said, "All the people in town are talking about me. I can't bear to walk in front of the livery stable so I cross the street. I feel dirty; I bathe three or four times a day and I can't eat or sleep. I have nightmares and I somehow feel guilty, thinking I should have fought harder or screamed louder; anything to get away from him." Fred said, "Baby, baby, everything will be alright, I love you and you're safe; it's going to be fine." LaQuita was beginning to cry as she sobbed, "Fred, you won't love me any more, I just know it, you won't want me." "Baby, none of this is your fault", said Fred lovingly. Then, as he took her hand in his, he continued. "You've never told me about your mother, is she in San Antonio, we could get her out here you know." "I don't want to talk about my mother," said LaQuita as she continued to tremble and cry. "I'm so ashamed, you won't love me any more, you won't want me," she kept repeating the words over and over again.

Fred held her tight, kissed her, told her he loved her and said, "What's happened has not and will not change my feelings for you." LaQuita stopped crying, looked at Fred and said, "I was due to start my monthly cycle a week after the incident; It didn't happen. Now I've missed my second monthly cycle. Fred, I'm pregnant!!! What am I going to do?"

The worst possible thing had happened, Fred was stunned but unshaken. He said, "I told you, everything will be fine, I'm here for you, no matter what happens, we'll get thru it together." They were both quiet as Fred drove back to the doctors' house. When they arrived there, the doctor gave LaQuita some laudanum; it would help her sleep.

Linda was making LaQuita stay with her. That way she could watch her at work, be a good friend and try to help her get thru her depression. Linda was in the room when Fred and LaQuita arrived. They all sat and talked for a while and it appeared that LaQuita was feeling better; Linda was good for her. Fred excused himself and went to his room.

Sunday they left the ranch and went to church. After the usual lunch, Fred readied the buggy for the return trip. He told them he would be back the following Saturday. Just as he was leaving, he told LaQuita he loved her then he drove off while both girls waved goodbye.

When Fred reached the ranch Mr. Fox was on the front porch waiting for him. He sat down on the porch as Mr. Fox asked, "How is she?" "I've got bad news," said Fred, "she's pregnant," and then he cupped his hands to his face, started sobbing and repeating," Why, why, why did all this happen?" Oh my God," said Fox, "I don't know, I prayed so hard." They talked quietly for about an hour; then retired for the night.

Back in Uvalde, Laughlin rode into town and went to Orals' office. "Got any coffee left?" he asked. "Sure, sure, if we don't I can durn sure make a pot. How you doing Laughlin?" asked Oral. "It's been pretty quite all over. Guess I'm the hottest topic in town, me and my fences" said Laughlin. "Yea, there's been some grumbling, it'll go away" mouthed Oral as Laughlin went on, "Candido and the boys are back from Ft. Davis. Delivered all the horses, didn't lose a one of 'em."

"Hello, Captain," said Nathan as he opened the door and entered the jail office." "Hello Nathan, getting any faster?" replied Laughlin. "Hope so", answered Nathan, "bout wore my holster out practicing." They all laughed, then Oral said, "I wouldn't want to pull on him; he's pretty fast." "Good,

good, keep practicing," Laughlin said proudly then turned to Nathan and asked, "Heard from Sterling, we sure miss him out at the ranch." "Yes sir", answered Nathan, "he's happy and doing real good; met Mr. Fox, when he went to make a will." "That was bad about LaQuita," said Oral. "Wonder how Fred's doing, they were a really good couple, hope she's okay." Nathan asked, "Did they ever catch Sandy?" Laughlin said, "I don't think he'll be coming around anymore."

Laughlin looked at Nathan, then at Oral and said, "You know Boots is kinda sweet on your granddaughter, don't you Oral." "That's just fine with me", said Oral, "I'll take him for a grandson any day but I don't know about Nathan being an in-law," they all laughed. Laughlin said, "I tell you, I wish all three of them boys were mine. Damn, I like those boys. Melissa worries about them like they were her children. Jerry Jack sees Boots as his brother and jokingly tried to trade War Paint to some Indians over at Ft. Davis. Had a deal made for five squaws but Boots wouldn't take it." Oral laughed heartily and said, "I'm going to tell Audrey."

Oral said, "Laughlin, I got a wire from Sheriff Elick up in Ft. Worth yesterday. There have been a couple of train robberies around Dallas. It seems that when a train stops to take on water is when they're attacked. Trains have a lot more money than a stagecoach. They robbed one a while back up in Nebraska and got away with $60,000 dollars. Elick thinks it's a fellow named Bass and he's believed to be heading for Texas." "Yea, just what we need, train robberies", spouted Laughlin. "By the way, you can remove that John Wesley Hardin poster. Rangers got him after three years; he was in Pensacola", he added. He'll be down in Huntsville soon if they don't hang 'em." Nathan said, "That's the guy that shot a man for snoring, ain't it?" "Yea, that's right", said Laughlin, "he's a cold blooded killer"

In Abilene, about noon, Cletus Meeks rode up to the Fox ranch. As he stepped up on the front porch Mr. Fox opened the door and said, "Cletus, come on in." Cletus removed his hat, stepped inside and said, "I've got bad news. LaQuita's dead." "Oh my God, no!" said Mr. Fox as he tried to sit down. "What happened? Fred was with her all day yesterday."

Cletus was wringing his hat in his hands as he said, nervously, "Linda woke up early this morning and LaQuita was still in bed. She had taken some laudanum to help her sleep. Linda was bringing her coffee for when she woke up, but when she entered the room, she saw LaQuita hanging from the closet door. She had taken a bed sheet, tied a knot in it, opened the closet door, threw the knotted part of the sheet over the top then closed the door. Then, apparently, she stood on a chair, tied the sheet around her neck, kicked the chair out from under her and hanged herself." Cletus paused for a moment then continued, "Linda's not doing well; Doc's got her at his office and Mr. Underwood has LaQuita's body at his funeral home. I thought we might tell Fred together. I'm sure not looking forward to it."

Chapter 23

Fred had seen Cletus' horse tied in front of the ranch house and suspected something was wrong. He quickly rode to the ranch house, burst thru the front door and asked, "What's wrong? Is LaQuita alright, what's wrong?" Mr. Fox walked over to Fred, put his arms around him and said slowly, "Son, she's dead."

The funeral services took place in church and then the casket was loaded in a wagon and driven to Mr. Fox's ranch. No one knew anything about LaQuita's family, so Mr. Fox had her brought to the ranch for burial on Knob Hill. As everyone gathered on top of the hill for the burial service, Linda and Angel sang a hymn. The preacher spoke his piece then Linda and Angel sang another hymn. They were all walking away as the casket was lowered into the ground and back-filled.

Under the circumstances, Fred and Mr. Fox had held up about as long as possible. It was very hard on Fox; the burial on Knob Hill had brought back memories of his wife Maude, and he knew his tears would come later, behind closed doors. He was worried about Fred who had grown very silent. Fox could see he was deeply depressed and nursing a broken heart.

After the service was over there was a covered dish buffet laid out at the ranch house. Linda would be staying overnight. Mr. Fox would not allow her to return until the next day. Sometime during the night Fox got out of bed, walked out on the front porch and looked toward Knob Hill. He saw Diablo on the hill and he knew Fred was telling LaQuita goodbye.

A week had passed since LaQuita was buried. Mr. Fox had ordered a headstone for her grave and was expecting it soon. Late that evening Fred came in from a hard days work on the ranch. He rode directly to her grave. Mr. Fox saw him holding Diablo's rein and standing at the metal fence protecting the graves. It was about a quarter mile from the ranch house to Knob Hill. Fox's horse was saddled and tied to the hitching post so he mounted up and rode to the cemetery. Fred was standing there looking at the grave with tears in his eyes. While still mounted, Mr. Fox said, "Mind if I dismount and join you." Fred said, "No sir, please do, I need some company." Mr. Fox slid out of the saddle, tied his reigns to the D-ring on his saddle, walked over, put his hand on Fred's' shoulder and asked, "You doing alright, are you okay?" "Yes sir", replied Fred, "just don't understand why it had to happen, she was a good girl."

Fox thought carefully and said softly, "When I lost Maude I was mad, mad at God, just like you're mad now. God controls our lives; we are his children, all of us. He can take us home anytime; the reward is in Heaven not here on earth. We must be prepared to go and those of us who remain have the right to grieve the loss of our loved ones and then carry on with our lives. I miss Maude terribly, but I know she's in Heaven and I know when God calls me, we will be reunited. Everything happens for a reason son, God has a plan. God gives everyone a free will, but doesn't cause bad things to happen; that's our doing."

Fred gathered his thoughts before answering, then said, "Mr. Fox, I'm lost, hurting and confused. At times I want to get on Diablo and ride off away from memories. I think about becoming a full time Ranger, throw caution to the wind and if I get killed, so be it but I know LaQuita would want me here with you. This is where I belong. Now I know how you felt when you lost Maude."

"Fred", said Fox, "with your permission, I'm going to have Cletus wire Sheriff Cobb in San Antonio. Maybe he can help find LaQuita's kin. You know, she never mentioned anyone?" Fred replied, "No, she refused to talk about it, always changed the subject. The only thing I ever knew was her last name, Benavides."

A few days later Mr. Fox received a letter from Sheriff Cobb in San Antonio. It was a reply to his letter about LaQuita. The sheriff said he had found out LaQuita had worked at a place called Fatal Corner. It had dancing girls, girls with short skirts serving drinks and a gambling room on the second floor. LaQuita's mother was a prostitute. LaQuita refused to follow in her mother's footsteps, but she did work serving drinks. It was a rough place with murders, suicide and jealousy killings. LaQuita was exceptionally pretty and had been assaulted a couple of times before she disappeared. No one knew where she went. Mr. Fox read the letter again, threw it in the fireplace and watched it burn. Only he would ever know the contents of the letter.

In Ft. Stockton, a telegram had been sent from the 9th Calvary requesting that 100 horses be delivered in 30 days. Laughlin was aware of what was happening and why they, along with Fr. Davis, needed horses.

The Fort had four regiments; one of them was the Buffalo Soldiers. They were the black soldiers. The Indians had named them Buffalo soldiers due to their dark, kinky hair which was similar to the buffalo. The Indians felt like the buffalo fought ferociously till death and so did the Buffalo Soldier. To the Indian, the name of Buffalo was a sign of respect.

The Buffalo Soldiers were sometimes given sickly and crippled mounts left over from the Civil War. It hadn't taken long for the Buffalo Soldier to learn that your horse could be the difference between life and death. A Fact that was especially true in this harsh, arid and mountainous country. As a result, they soon became excellent riders and learned how to care for their horses, almost better than themselves.

Laughlin had heard from Rangers that the Buffalo Soldiers of Ft. Stockton were badly in need of new mounts. The Rangers said they fought bravely but were given the worst of everything, including uniforms. He was fairly certain that his horses would become white trooper mounts and the Buffalo Soldiers would get the replaced horses. He told Candido to get organized, cut out the horses, and take the same men as last time except use Wylie as his cook. With all the extra help building the fence, Flap Jack was needed at the ranch; besides, Laughlin knew that Wylie liked to cook.

The sale of the horses was coming at a good time; it helped with the fencing expenses. After gathering up the horses and stocking up on supplies, Boots, Jerry Jack, Wylie and the other wranglers headed for Fort Stockton.

The horse drive was in its third day and they were passing thru Indian country. They were several days away riding south-southeast of the fort when Candido, who was riding point, saw seven riders at a distance. He was sure they were Indians. Acting as though nothing was wrong, they continued on their drive.

As night fell, they set up camp, hobbled three lead mares and posted double guards. Jerry Jack sat down by the fire with a cup of coffee, looked up at Boots and said, "I'm uneasy, feel like Indians are watching us; I can feel 'em." Will and Jesse were riding guard, watching the herd. It was well after midnight. Boots and Jerry Jack couldn't sleep so they moved their bedrolls next to where the horses were grazing. Boots had hobbled War Paint, allowing him to graze freely.

It was a moonlit night, just what the Indians preferred. Boots saw a crouched figure trying to remove War Paints' hobbles. With pistol in hand he ran toward War Paint. It was an Indian brave; he saw Boots and tried to run. Boots dropped him with a single shot. Jesse was riding hard and firing at the Indians on horse back. They had stolen about twenty five horses and were riding off with them.

Jerry Jack and Boots quickly saddled their horses and started trying to get the rest of the herd settled down and under control. Jesse found Will, his skull had been split with a tomahawk and he was scalped. Boots and Jerry Jack found the Indian Boots had shot, he was still breathing. Jerry Jack said, "He's still alive Boots, finish him." Boots drew his pistol, aimed at the Indians head and fired. Jerry Jack said sternly, "Scalp him." "No!" said Boots, You can." Jerry Jack dismounted, pulled out his knife and scalped him. They spent the rest of the night rounding up the herd and giving Will as decent a burial as possible. Jerry Jack said a prayer as they covered up the shallow grave, then bedded down for the night.

The rest of the night went without incident. At sun-up Candido told them, "We have to drive the horses hard and get to the fort before we're hit again. It appears we lost less than twenty head." They drove the horses so hard the chuck wagon could barely keep up.

Late in the afternoon they saw riders approaching from the direction of the fort. It was troopers, a welcome sight. When they rode up you could see they were black; it was a patrol of Buffalo Soldiers. Due to recent Indian trouble throughout the area it was routine for a patrol to be dispatched to escort the herd. The sergeant said there was a party of seven that had been raiding, burning and stealing. When the soldiers were made aware the Indians had stolen some horses, the sergeant in command quickly called out seven names and told them to, "get those horses back, we need 'em."

Boots rode over beside Jerry Jack and said, "Laughlin was right, look at the horses they're on." Jerry Jack agreed, "Old and worn out, but look at the men, their good riders, good horsemen."

The remaining troopers quickly joined in driving the herd. At the end of the day, camp was set-up, guards were posted and there was a much better feeling of security than the previous night.

The sergeant in command was Bill Hackett. He was a big man, well over six feet and at least two hundred fifty pounds. He had a booming voice and was fairly handsome with strong facial features. It was evident that when he gave a command the troopers responded, immediately. Sgt Hackett sat down close to the fire with coffee in hand and said to Boots, "Mr. Boots, you don't talk like a Texan, where's yore home place." "I was born in Tennessee", said Boots. "Yassuh", said Hackett, "I thought so, I's from Memphis." Boots asked, "How did you get to Texas and out here fighting Indians?" Hackett responded, "Well suh, after we's freed, we didn't know what to do, it was worse than bein' a slave. I joined up wif da Army and they sends me to Texas. I's down at Ft. Clark in Brackettville fer a spell, know where dat is? It's nice big spring, fresh water all the time. Sherman he burned Atlanta down, was y'all in da war?" "Yea, me, my brother and my paw," said Boots. Hackett gave Boots a side look and said, "How old you was, ain't more'n sixteen now." "I was ten", said Boots, "my brother was twelve." Hackett thought for a moment then said, "Uh huh, I knowed it was getting bad, South woulda won if it hadn't been for railroad and factories supplying dem Yanks. South ain't had no way to get supplies. Did you ever kill any a dem Yankee Blue Bellies?" "Yea, guess so, ain't proud of it though", muttered Boots.

"You boys sho nuff brought some good hosses", said Hackett, "sho wish we'd get'em." "Why won't you get'em? Yours are in bad shape", said Boots. "These hosses go to the white troopers", said Hackett. After arriving at the fort, Candido and the wranglers decided to hang around until the Buffalo Soldiers returned to see if they recovered the stolen horses.

On the third day the soldiers returned with all the horses plus six Indian ponies. Boots and Jerry Jack watched as they drove the horses in to the corral. They hoped the new horses would go to the Buffalo Soldiers, they deserved them.

The horses were sold at Ft. Stockton. Thanks to the Buffalo Soldiers, all the horses they started with were delivered. Boots had spent time with Sgt Hackett and was impressed with him. They spent time talking about Tennessee, but both agreed they preferred Texas. Boots told him if possible to select the big bay stallion; he had spirit and was fast. Sgt Hackett told him he didn't have any family, unless some of them escaped after the war. He said during the re-construction it was bad for the slaves. Said slaves were freed but the KKK was hanging the blacks. Since they couldn't get jobs, they didn't know how to survive. That's why he joined the Army. Said it gave him protection, besides, he'd rather fight Indians than be hung by the Klan. When Boots told

Jerry Jack what the Sgt had said, Jerry Jack responded with, "I don't understand all this, why is there so much hate in the world."

The horses had been delivered to Ft. Stockton, again money was put in the bank and they were heading back to the ranch. This trip had been a real learning experience for the boys. They had met the Buffalo Soldiers, lost one of their men and Boots had killed his first Indian. Boots remembered back to when he finished off the wounded Indian with his pistol and how Jerry Jack had scalped the Indian. It didn't seem to bother Jerry Jack; but Indians had killed his family so Boots assumed that was the difference.

On the third day after leaving the fort Jerry Jack saw nine Indians in the distance, they were holding back, trailing and staying out of rifle range. Candido said, "They're after horses and guns. They won't try us out here on flat land during the day, they'll hit us tonight." That night the horses were tied to the chuck wagon, fully saddled with their cinches loosened. They hadn't made a camp fire and had placed three men under the wagon with two men in it.

They got in place, rifles in hand and waited. Candido said, "Watch your horses, they'll tell you when the Indians are coming and from which direction. Watch the ears, when they stand up straight and the head is fixed and staring out in the dark, the Indians are coming from that direction."

About two hours after sunset War Paint turned and looked toward some brush about thirty yards from the wagon. He pointed his ears, raised his head, arched his neck and continued to look toward the brush.

Boots and Jerry Jack were in the wagon. Boots nudged him and pointed toward the brush, Jerry Jack nodded back. Two Indians crawling on their bellies appeared. They were headed toward the horses. Boots figured they would untie the horses, run them off, round them up later and ride away. He didn't think they wanted to battle the rifles. It was likely that some of the braves had bow and arrows. Boots shouldered his rifle and whispered to Jerry Jack, "I'll get the one on the left, you take the right." They aimed and fired. Fire shot out the barrels as the bullets struck the Indians almost simultaneously. Boots' Indian tried to get up but he quickly worked the lever of the 44-40 and it roared again. The Indian was dead before he hit the ground. A flaming arrow came through the air and struck the sideboards of the wagon. Candido slid out from under the wagon and was trying to smother the flame when an arrow struck him high in the back. Three more Indians came running into camp toward the horses. The combination of fire and gunfire spooked the horses. They were rearing and pulling on their rope, trying to break free.

Wylie had a 12 gauge scatter gun that he kept in the wagon. BOOM!! Both barrels erupted from under the wagon. One Indian was cut down and another was hit. Boots and Jerry Jack finished the wounded one with their rifles and Jerry Jack shot the third as he retreated toward the brush. If it was the group seen earlier, then there should only be four more. They quickly reloaded, put out the fire and secured the horses while Wylie and Jesse tended to Candido. You could hear the other Indian ponies as they rode off in the dark.

Boots was walking toward Candido to see how bad he was wounded when he heard a pistol shot. It was Jerry Jack; he was going to each Indian, putting a bullet in their head and scalping them.

They put Candido in the wagon and made him as comfortable as possible. The arrow had hit shoulder bone but did not puncture a lung. They managed to remove it and stop the bleeding. The Indians were not seen anymore. They had lost five of their braves and weren't fools, the odds were not in their favor. At sunup, Boots, Jerry Jack and the rest of them started toward Uvalde with Candido in the wagon. They knew he would need doctorin' so they moved at a rapid pace.

When they arrived in Uvalde Candido was taken to Doc Milles for treatment. He said Candido would be fine in four to six weeks but would probably have a stiff shoulder for awhile. Laughlin had sent a wire to Glen Ray and Jim instructing them to go to San Antonio. From there they were to go to Austin and then over to Comanche. This itinerary pleased Glen Ray because Austin had horse racing once a month during the trades' day festivities. At a trades day you could race your horse, bet on cock fights; trade your horse, dog, or mule, anything of value. It was a big event with people coming from miles around just to participate

So far their patrol had been uneventful in each town, just the usual saloon fights, drunks and rowdy cowboys, nothing the sheriff couldn't handle. Glen Ray however, had entered Whiskey in a race in Comanche and won with ease. Now they were headed for Abilene. There would be a big race there that he believed he could win, however, he had heard about a horse from Lubbock named Shooting Star and wasn't sure that Whiskey could take him.

Jim was anxious to see Linda and they both wanted to see Fred. While in Comanche, they had been informed about LaQuita. They were sad and very concerned about Fred. The trip would take a while since they would be riding to Brownwood and then on up to Abilene.

When Jim and Glen Ray rode into Brownwood they went to see Sheriff Brady James. Brownwood served as part of a wagon train route, stagecoach and freight wagon stops. On occasion, drovers would take their herds off the Chisholm Trail and, due to the water and grass, detour thru Brownwood. When they did this, it made for an exciting day. The herd would be driven down Main Street creating a need for all the merchants to close their doors until the herd passed through. When the drovers took the herd outside of town to the grasslands, they would hold the herd several days, while they went to town and got drunk.

The Brownwood jail was a two story sandstone building. Court house records were kept on the second floor while the jail and sheriffs' office were on the first. Wagons going to Austin, Ft. Worth or Waco were easy prey for Indians and outlaws. The railroad hadn't made it to

Brownwood yet, and all supplies were by wagon trains called freighters. They found Sheriff James in his office. He said he was glad to see the Rangers; he needed their help.

There was a large herd outside of town and drovers were coming in every night raising hell. There were shootings in the streets, horses being ridden
into the saloon, merchant windows shot out and women being harassed on the street. Brady said he didn't have any deputies, just himself and he couldn't handle the problems alone. One cowboy in particular, named Red Stinson, was the leader. He was mean sober and really got mean when he was drunk. Sheriff James asked if the rangers would accompany him to their camp so the drovers would know what was expected of them.

On the way out Jim said to Glen Ray, "It's the same ole story every cattle drive has; bad boy shows off in town when he's drunk and gets killed by a lawman or gunslinger before he's twenty-five." As they rode into the cow camp, several drovers were around the campfire by the chuck wagon so they moseyed over to it counting the men in camp and noting their whereabouts. Jim asked the group gathered around the fire, "Who's your ramrod?" A tall, thin, weather beaten man about thirty years old stood and said, "That'd be me, Claude Davenport. I'm the ramrod." Jim said, "Claude, I'm Ranger Weaver and this is Ranger Porter, you already know the sheriff. Looks like you boys have been creating some problems in town; there'll be no more; you've had your fun. You boys git the herd moving at daylight and don't come to town tonight. Comprende?" While Jim was talking a cowboy rode up, dismounted, walked over to Claude and stood beside him, staring at the Rangers.

The man was in his early twenties. He was a very large, robust man, around six feet tall, weighing two sixty or more. He had red hair and a red beard with snuff stains at the corners of his mouth. His belly hung over the buckle on his gun belt. He was a dirty man showing no respect in his appearance and probably had little respect for anyone or anything else. Then he looked around, taking in the scene and belted, "What the hell's going on Claude, who are these guys?" Claude said, "Red, calm down, these men are Rangers and we've been asked to leave in the morning and stay out of town tonight." "The hell I'm staying out of town", growled Red, "I've got money to win back and a woman to see tonight. Ain't nobody gonna tell me to stay out of town, and that includes Rangers." Then he stared at the Rangers defiantly and said, "I'll be in town tonight along with the boys."

Chapter 24

With a stern calmness Jim, said, "Mr. Davenport, keep 'em here or you won't have any cowboys left in the morning; they'll either be dead or in jail." "Me and the boys ain't afraid of you Rangers; you'll be seeing us tonight," said Red. Sheriff James said, "Boys don't be foolish, you can stay in camp tonight and ride in the morning or be in a lot of trouble, the Rangers meant what they said." He paused to let his words sink in, then added, "Good bye gentlemen, I don't want to see you again!!!" The three lawmen turned and rode toward town as Jim said to Glen Ray, "Do you think they will come to town?" Glen Ray answered, "If Red gets a bottle, yes. I don't think the ramrod wants trouble, but, he won't be able to control Red if he's drunk." Jim said, "I agree, Reds' no gunfighter, just a big bully that gets drunk and mean. If he should come in tonight, we'll have to try to arrest him, but, if he tries to draw, kill him, don't take any chances."

When they arrived back in town, Glen Ray and Jim checked into the hotel, bathed and were having supper at the restaurant with Sheriff James when one of the drovers entered the restaurant. He spotted the lawmen, quickly ran to them and said, "Red and Claude argued, Red shot and killed Mr. Davenport and has taken over." Then he added, "I don't want any part of what they are going to do. They're going to drive the herd down Main Street and shoot up the town."

Brady said, "I don't have enough men to ride out and try to turn the herd. We'll just get the street cleared and warn everyone the herds coming." The drover, with urgency in his voice, said, "The herd is no more than twenty minutes behind me." Jim told Brady to have some wagons turned over at the end of town blocking the entrance to Main Street. The herd was close, you could hear them coming. The wagons were torn apart as the herd burst through and rumbled down main-street, destroying everything in their path. As they ran on the boardwalk they knocked down the posts that were holding up the porch roofs causing them to collapse. It was a disaster; everything in the path of the herd was destroyed. When the herd finally passed through, the three law-men mounted up and rode in pursuit of Red and the drovers. About a quarter of a mile outside town they met Red and eight men. The two groups rode up and stopped, ten yards apart, face to face.

Sheriff James said, "Red, you're under arrest for the murder of Claude Davenport, disturbing the peace and destroying property." Red said, "You ain't arresting no one, me and my men will run over you like our cattle did the town." Jim said, "You boys need to turn around, get the herd and go. Red, you can drop your gun and go to jail sitting in the saddle, or laying across it on the way to the undertaker. It's your choice." "You Rangers talk big", said Red, "you're looking at nine guns against three, and y'all are all dead." Jim said, "Red, all you've got is an audience, eight of your men are going to watch you die. I'm finished talking." Jim squared up in his saddle, sat up tall and said, "Drop your gun or prepare to die, that goes for every one of you men." One of the drovers said, "Do what he says, boys we're not gunfighters, lets drop our guns," they did. Red looked around and said, "All of y'all are gutless and yeller, not me," and he reached for his gun. His pistol never cleared his holster when a bullet from Jims' 44 pistol ended his life. Jim looked at the remaining drovers and said, "This didn't have to happen, he could still be alive. You boys start that herd moving, don't wait till morning and drive 'em tonight." Jim said, "Take Red with you. Don't bury him close to this town; bury him on the trail." The drovers retrieved their guns, tied Red across his horse and started moving the herd away from Brownwood.

Glen Ray, Jim and Brady turned and walked their horses slowly toward Brownwood. Jim took a deep breath and said, "Killing a man is easy; living with it is the hard part."

The next morning the Rangers had breakfast with Sheriff James, filled out reports, wired Laughlin with an update and then rode toward Abilene. Jim had decided to ask for time off to spend with Linda; he had things to discuss with her.

Back at the Rockin' Horse Ranch, Laughlin told Melissa that he was going to fence an area for a horse pasture. He wanted to get some pure blood Morgan mares and a Morgan stud. He wanted to breed quality horses. He said, "Our herd has Mustangs that we captured. They're okay to sell to the Army but what I want to do is raise some good Saddle and Quarter Horses." Then he added, I would also like to raise some Morgans; fine race and trotting horses. They are the most beautiful of all horses."

"The Army would want them for their officers. We could get large sums of money for the Morgans if we fence a separate pasture and tend to them properly; not just let them graze. We could also take them to a race, win it and then sell the horse at the track to people who have just seen him run. There is plenty money to be made with quality Morgans."

Although it had already been a few months, Laughlin was pleased with his fence building project, it was ahead of schedule. The bull pen had been completed and JJ was doing his job. He was a Santa Gertrudis bull and was producing larger and heavier stock.

The horse lot was also completed and waiting on a good Morgan stud. Laughlin had located a breeder around Montague that had the best race horses in Texas. He was trying to acquire a Morgan mare and get her bred or buy his own Morgan stud. By now he had a pretty good horse herd and was meeting the Army's request.

It had been eighteen months since Boots, Sterling and Jerry Jack came to the ranch. The year is 1879 and things are changing, some for the good and some for the bad.

When the Civil War ended a large number of men returned to nothing and some of them became outlaws. With the railroads reaching more and more places, drovers aren't needed for long, lengthy cattle drives so many of them have turned to a life of crime. The Indian is no longer the biggest threat; it is now the outlaws; men with no other way to support themselves. Violence and crime is spreading all over the west with train robberies, rustlings, bank and stage holdups. Because of its size, Texas was in need of more law enforcement, including more Rangers.

Jerry Jack and Boots had become top notch cowboys and Laughlin knew he would miss them when they became Rangers. Because of the need for more Rangers, younger men were being recruited. The country was being overrun with Civil War veterans and drovers, put out of work by the railroads, were turning to the outlaw way of life. Town marshals were losing control, especially in northern locations like Kansas, the Dakotas and even out west in Tombstone. Known gunfighters were becoming lawmen and taking advantage of the lawlessness in some of the towns. Laughlin knew the same thing would be moving into Texas and he dreaded it.

It had been a while since the boys had delivered the horses. Since returning from Ft. Stockton they had been involved with all the things necessary to build fences and operate a ranch. Jerry Jack and Boots would be eighteen on their next birthday; time was passing fast. When work permitted, the boys were still attending church while continuing to see Audrey and Cindy on Sundays. Boots had shown a lot of interest in the Bible and wanted to know more so Jerry Jack read stories to him about King David.

When it was time for church, Laughlin told the boys they could ride in on their horses and take the rest of the day off if they wanted to spend some time with the girls. As usual, Laughlin, Melissa and the boys sat in the third row from the front. When the singing stopped, Reverend Morgan stood up, walked to the pulpit and said, "Today we are going to talk about King David." Boots nudged Jerry Jack and said, "You told him didn't you." Jerry Jack didn't say anything, he just grinned.

Reverend Morgan told about how David had killed Goliath with a sling shot, became the King, sinned with Bathsheba, and then was forgiven for his sins. Boots listened to the message, not once did he drift off and smile at the girls during the sermon. Afterwards, when they were singing, Reverend Morgan stepped up and said, "Is there anyone here today who would like to come forward and accept Jesus Christ as their savior?" Jerry Jack got up from his seat, stepped in the aisle and walked up to Reverend Morgan. Boots thought to himself, 'I believe that Jesus died for our sins and the only way to heaven is through Jesus; I'm going down there.' He walked down the aisle to join Jerry Jack, who by now had tears in his eyes. When he looked at Laughlin he could hear Melissa crying. Boots became misty eyed, then he cried full out and it felt good.

After church they gathered for the buffet lunch. As they finished eating, Reverend Morgan came over to where the boys were sitting with the girls and said, "I'm real proud of you boys. Boots, I understand you like to hear about King David." "Yes sir", answered Boots, "he's my favorite, a great warrior chosen by God to be King." "Well, you keep reading that bible; there are lots of things I think you will like," said Morgan. The Reverend turned his attention to Jerry Jack and continued, "By the way Jerry Jack, we need a youth minister. If you're interested, come see me." "Thank you sir, but I don't know enough to teach", replied Jerry Jack. Reverend Morgan pointed at Boots and remarked, "You've been teaching ole Boots here, haven't you? Remember, God has a plan."

The boys spent the remainder of the day with the girls before starting back to the ranch. They were riding side by side with their horses at a walk when Boots asked, "Did you see and hear all those people congratulating and blessing us today?" "Yea, I did", answered Jerry Jack, "wasn't that great?" Then Boots asked, "Hey, you gonna be the youth minister?" Jerry Jack said he was gonna think about it; especially since Reverend Morgan thought he could do it. Then he stopped, thought about it for a minute, and said, "Yea, yea I'm gonna try it." Boots said, "I thought me and you were gonna be Rangers." "I'm gonna be a Ranger, nothings changed", replied Jerry Jack. Boots laughed and said, "I guess you'll preach to 'em before you arrest'em, I'm gonna call you the 'Preaching Ranger'."

In Stewart Coffee's office in Abilene, Sterling had been asked to come in and sit. As he was taking his chair, Stewart said, "Sterling you've been with me for a year, what are your thoughts about your future after a year of exposure to law?" "I love it", said Sterling, "even more now than I did before you hired me but my goal is the same, save money and go to school. Then, hopefully, pass the test as an attorney and go into politics. I'm thinking in five years I'll have saved enough money for school. In the mean time I'll keep reading, observe you and ask a lot of questions." "Sterling", said Stewart, "I've been watching you since you were hired. You study all the time; I truly believe you could pass the test now. Your ability exceeds some of the students I was exposed to when I was in school." "Thank you," said Sterling, "I have been blessed this past year. I am so thankful for what you have done for me." Stewart smiled and said, "Thanks I appreciate that. Now, I want to tell you something. When you complete your schooling and have your license to practice law, if you want to return to Abilene, I will make you my partner. How about it? 'Coffee and Law'" "Oh my god", said Sterling, "Stewart, you can't be serious! This must be a dream!" "It's no dream", Stewart replied, "Now, I've really got good news for you." Sterling already had tears in his eyes, tears of joy as he said, "More good news, nothing could be better than what you just told me!"

Stewart leaned back in his chair and said, "Your schooling is paid for. Mr. Fox is going to pay all expenses." "Mr. Fox is paying for my education! Cried out Sterling, "I can't believe it!" Stewart chuckled and said, "Well believe it; he has been monitoring you since I hired you. He wants to help because you are trying so hard to help yourself. Remember what I said to you once: 'A man is not measured by his wealth.'"

It wasn't long before Sterling was accepted to attend law school in Austin. Stewart told him to make plans to go, then said, "Don't worry about me and the business, I'll make do until you return."

Clifton, owner of the livery stable, loaned Sterling a horse and saddle to ride out to the Fox ranch. When he arrived, Mr. Fox was thrilled to see him and greeted him with, "How you doing, come on in, tell me about your plans." They sat at a table to talk where Fox had set out some fresh milk and pecan pie. As Fox poured the milk and cut the pie, Sterling said, "Mr. Fox, a short time ago I was in Atlanta, had no future, my maw was dead, and I thought my paw was dead. That left just me and Boots with nothing to look forward to. Now look at me! I'm here in Texas, my paw's alive, my brother and I have a job and I'm getting ready to go to law school. God has really blessed me. Now why you volunteered to pay for my schooling I don't know, but I can't tell you how much I appreciate your blessing. It's the nicest thing I have ever heard of and I promise I won't let you down. Someday I'm gonna be a Senator for the State of Texas." "Son', said Fox, "you can thank me by doing just what you told me. You see, when I was a young man, I fought to tame Texas with my six-shooter and rifle." Fox took a sip of milk and a bite of pie then continued, "There will always be law enforcement with sheriffs, marshals and Rangers fighting to enforce the law. But it's equally important that we have someone in the Capital who's fighting just as hard for Texas. We need someone promoting our great state; going to Washington and representing us and bringing in more railroads. With goods being shipped to Galveston Port as well as going all over Texas and the rest of the state, we're gonna need 'em." At this point Fox paused, looked Sterling right in the eye, and spoke firmly, "I think you have the qualities for what we need, men of vision and integrity. What I did for you, I also did for Texas."

In Uvalde it was Saturday night, Laughlin had been out all day with the fence crew. When he came in, he bathed, ate supper with Melissa then went to bed. Later, when she came to bed, she snuggled up next to him and said, "Laughlin, I've really enjoyed the boys here on the ranch," then, without even taking a breath she continued, "Can we talk about having a child?" Laughlin said, "I agree about the boys. I've really gotten attached to them. They still want to be Rangers and they're almost old enough. Lots of trouble coming at a bad time; trouble coming up from the north: gunslingers and outlaws. But to answer your question, I must ask a question. Do you still love me?" "Yes," she answered, "you know I do." "Alright," said Laughlin, "but only three, no more than three. The first born has to be named Sam if it's a boy, Samantha if it's a girl." "Oh Laughlin, you still love that horse more than me," she smirked.

In town Sheriff Oral Fox had gone home and Nathan was making his mid-night rounds before going back to the jail to retire for the night. As usual he was carrying his shotgun which earned him the title of 'Shotgun Law'.

As he passed the bank, he saw a flicker of light coming from the back-room where the safe was kept. He carefully entered the passageway between the buildings leading to the back door. When he got to the side window, where he had seen the light, he was able to see thru a tear in the curtain. There were two men with candles trying to open the safe. Sterling eased around the corner, stood next to the back door and shouted, "Come out with your hands up, you're under arrest." A shot rang out from across the alley as a bullet hit the wall next to Nathan's head. He turned and saw an image of a man holding three horses.

Chapter 25

Nathan heard a second shot coming from across the alley. He saw the flame from the barrel just as the bullet struck the wall and answered with a blast from a single barrel of his shot gun. He heard a scream and then the sound of lungs gurgling blood. Just then the door burst open. A man ran out shooting wildly as he came thru the door. The second barrel of Nathan's shot gun ended the man's life. Some of the flesh and blood had hit the open door to Nathan's left. The man had taken the full load from one barrel at about ten feet. Nathan's' shotgun was empty. As he was in the process of re-loading, the last man ran out the door with a pistol in his hand. He saw Nathan and turned to shoot. Instinctively Nathan drew his pistol, just like he had practiced, fired and killed the man before he could get off a shot. A crowd had gathered. Nathan assured them he wasn't hurt then went over to the jail and sat down at the table. He put both hands on the table, bent over, bowed his head and said out loud, 'Thank you Laughlin, without your help I would have been standing there with an empty shotgun. What you taught me saved my life; I knew how to use my pistol.'

Word about the shooting was sent to Laughlin at the ranch. He told Jerry Jack and Boots to get mounted; they were going to town with him. When they rode past the undertakers in Uvalde, they saw the three bodies propped up and displayed on planks. They had been placed outside by the boardwalk for the benefit of picture seekers.

The Rangers proceeded on to the jail where they found Nathan and Oral. Laughlin immediately asked, "Nathan, are you alright? Did you get hit?" "No sir, I'm fine" replied Nathan, "your training with the pistol saved my life. My shotgun was empty and the feller had me dead to rights with pistol in hand but I was still able to beat him."

"Good job Nathan, you handled yourself well" said Laughlin. Boots was filled with pride at hearing the praise laid on his father as McFarland continued, "I want to talk to all of you about what's coming. The outlaws, rustlers and gunfighters are getting ready to take over the country. Too many men out of work stealing and killing with their guns for hire. It's gonna get tough for lawmen and we need to be aware it's coming. Every Ranger sector is enlisting young men because of the need for law enforcement." He paused for a second, looked at Boots and said, "Boots, when you and Jerry Jack are eighteen, I can sign you on as Rangers. Question is do you want to be a Ranger and battle gunfighters? Turning his attention to Nathan and Jerry Jack he went on, "Nathan, do you want your boy Boots to be a Ranger and face death everyday? Jerry Jack, do you want to be a cowboy or do you want to be a Ranger?"

"Captain McFarland," said Nathan, "Thanks to you I'm now a Ranger and will be as long as they'll let me. Boots has my blessings, he's more man now then plenty I've seen." Boots looked at Laughlin and said, "I love the ranch and what we do, but my desire is to be a Ranger like you sir. I've heard so much about you since I've been here; I want you as my teacher. You're the best."

Jerry Jack said, "Sir I owe you for giving me a new life. I consider you, Melissa, Boots and Sterling as family, but, I want to be a Ranger and I hope Boots and I can ride together when it happens."

After hearing their replies, Laughlin said, "Melissa's gonna cry when y'all are both eighteen and start riding as Rangers. By the way I appreciate all the compliments, but there's another Ranger in this room." Laughlin nodded towards Nathan and continued, "A hell of a man – he can ride with me any time."

By this time Jim and Glen Ray had ridden into Abilene where there was a banner stretched across the street reading 'Pioneer Days Horse Race, $1000 for three day winner'. Glen Ray said, "Look at that, – winner gets one thousand dollars. This will be my chance to see Shooting Star; for sure they'll bring him here for that kind of money. The race was scheduled for the next weekend and Glen Ray knew he had to get

Whiskey rested up if they were going to win. He felt reassured however, since Whiskey had never been beaten."

They went to the livery stable before stopping to see Linda at the restaurant. Linda was happy to see Jim, said she had been worried about him since he had been gone so long. Then she told them about LaQuita's death and how Fred was suffering from severe depression.

Jim stayed with Linda and said he would come out to the ranch in three or four days. At sunup Glen Ray was in the saddle riding to the ranch. He was anxious to see Angel, Fred and Mr. Fox. He also wanted to put Whiskey in their corral so the big stallion could rest.

When Fred saw Glen Ray ride thru the main gate, he rode out to meet him. As he reined up beside Glen Ray he said, "Ola amigo, I've missed you. It's good to see you." Glen Ray said, "Compadre, are you alright, how you doing?" Fred answered, "Some bad days, some good days. The hurt in my heart won't go away." "I see you're still riding that mule, Diablo," said Glen Ray. "If that thing you're riding will make it, follow me to the ranch house," mocked Fred. They both had a little chuckle as Fred continued, "Mr. Fox has been waiting on you." Then with his sly grin he went on, "Angels not here, Pancho Villa's son came and got her. They're probably honeymooning in Mexico by now." Fred laughed then said "Come on mule, let's show this Baby Ranger the way to the house." He spurred Diablo and was gone like a roping horse after a calf. "See that Whiskey," said Glen Ray, "we got that to beat for sure and who knows how fast this Shooting Star is."

Mr. Fox was on the porch with Angel at his side. You could smell dinner all the way out in the yard. "Howdy Glen Ray," said Fox, "somebody here wants to see you." Angel came off the porch, ran down the stairs and hugged Glen Ray. After a little kissing and hugging, they went inside, sat down and had Sunday dinner.

After the meal Mr. Fox asked, "How long you staying Glen Ray?" "Jim and I are supposed to stay here until Laughlin wires us where and when to go," he answered. "Good," said Fox, "then we can get rooms at Linda's and take in the horse race and street dancing next weekend." "Yes sir," squawked Glen Ray, "I'm gonna enter Whiskey but I gotta get him some rest and plenty of oats. I'll exercise him sparingly till the race. There's gonna be some good horses to run against, including Diablo." Mr. Fox said, "I want to show you something tomorrow. It don't seem like it's been that long but Whiskey's got a son. That big blaze faced sorrel Morgan mare of mine had his colt, fine looking, gonna make a good stud."

Glen Ray spent the afternoon with Angel. He knew that Fred wanted to talk but they could do that the next day.

After breakfast Mr. Fox, Angel, Fred and Glen Ray walked up Knob Hill to LaQuita's grave. Fred said, "I don't know why it had to happen, everything was so good. After a while we would've been married and lived here on the ranch. She loved Mr. Fox as much as he loved her. We could have been happy here raising kids and taking care of Mr. Fox." "I'm so sorry compadre. Things happen that we can't control or even understand," said Glen Ray. Then he paused and added," Amigo," referring to Sandy, "is he in hell now?" "Yea amigo, he's in hell," replied Fred, "let's go down and exercise our horses."

They walked to the corral where Mr. Fox had Whiskeys' colt running loose. The young stallion was with his mother, a large well defined Morgan mare. The colt was a beautiful sorrel with a blaze face and three white stockings. Mr. Fox said, "Gentlemen, meet Three Paws, ain't he a beauty." The colt was frisky and broke into a run. "Look at that," said Glen Ray, "look how he runs." His head was up and he hit the dirt like a feather falling to the ground. You could see he was going to be fast. He ran over to where the men were looking over the rail of the corral, stopped, looked, lowered his head, bucked and ran away.

"What a show off," said Fred, "he's gonna be something when he's a three year old. I Heard Whiskey won up in Comanche," Fred added. Glen Ray answered, rather humbly, "Yea, didn't have much competition."

"I don't know about that amigo," said Fred, "Whiskey can make the others look slow." Then he added, "What do you know about Shooting Star?" "Well," said Glen Ray, "he's supposed to be the fastest Morgan in Texas. He's from up around Lubbock and he's beating all the horses in the area including the ones from Oklahoma. I think Laughlin is buying a Morgan marc that's been bred to him and a stud out of 'em."

"Laughlin wants to continue to sell horses to the Army," said Fred, "but he's really interested in the Morgans for racing – thoroughbreds, that's what he wants. He's not only a good Ranger, but he's a good business-man. He's got two boys, Boots and Jerry Jack that can ride anything they get on." Then Fred gestured towards the two of them and asked, "Mr. Fox, are you and Glen Ray gonna watch me in the rodeo? I'm gonna ride saddle bronc' then Manuel and I are going to team rope." "Sure we're gonna be there," said
Mr. Fox. Then he asked, "Hey, how they gonna set up the horse race?" "First five horses on Saturday, first five on Sunday to qualify for the finals on Monday when the top ten horses run in the finals for one thousand dollars," said Fred.

They started walking toward the ranch house when Mr. Fox said, "Manuel, hitch up the buggy, Glen Ray's gonna take Angel on a ride and a picnic down by the creek, ain't you Glen Ray?" "Yes sir, yes sir," said Glen Ray rather excitedly, "I certainly am gonna do that." Then he added rather humbly, "Glad I thought of it."

Jim and Linda, having slept in, were in the restaurant having coffee and a late breakfast when Jim said, "Linda, I know we haven't seen much of each other, but I think about you, a lot. If I ask you a question will you give me a straight answer?" "Yes, certainly," she said, "ask me." Having been given the green light, Jim said, "How do you feel about me, is there a chance for you and I to be together?" "Jim," she said, "as you know, I thought I was in love with Laughlin but maybe it was just infatuation. You know, him being a Ranger and all. However, I've recently discovered qualities in you that I want in a man. You're kind and understanding. Linda paused for a moment, then continued, "I can talk to you, you're honest and not selfish. I may own a saloon but I believe in the Good Book and so do you. Yes, there's a really good chance for us, quite frankly, I didn't know how you felt about me since I own a saloon." There was a real serious look on Jim's face as he said, "Linda, I had to kill a man last week, it wasn't my first nor will it be my last. Someday it could be me, troubles coming: killers, outlaws and gunslingers. I could be back shot or outdrawn at any time but that's not the real problem. My concerns are, it's getting harder for me to get over killing a man. I haven't told you, but I'm going inactive for a month and with your permission I'd like to spend some time with you." "Jim, that would be wonderful," said Linda, "I told Melissa that one day we might both be married to Rangers." Jim smiled and said, "That would be nice, I'll do my part to try and make it happen." Everyone was in town for the activities: rodeo, horse racing, chicken fights, mule pull and other festivities.

Glen Ray drew a bye and didn't have to race until Sunday. Fred was in the first race and was scheduled to ride then rope after the horse race. The horses were brought to the starting line for the usual half mile run down main-street. They would continue on outside of town, around a barrel and back to the start/finish line. Fred had been looking at 'Shooting Star' being led down the street from the livery stable. He was magnificent, probably a three year old Morgan Stallion, strawberry roan in color with a blaze face. He was the strongest looking horse Fred had ever seen. Diablo and Shooting Star rode up to the starting line and waited for the gun.

The whole clan was there, Mr. Fox, Glen Ray, Manuel, Angel, Jim and Linda. They were trying to find a vantage point to watch the race. BANG, the gun went off and the race was on with Diablo and Shooting Star in the lead. For the first leg they were side by side at least four lengths ahead of the other horses. They were neck and neck as they approached the barrel at the half-way mark. Fred knew he had to get to the inside as they went around the barrel. It would give him a length if he could get in position but Shooting Star had the inside and Fred couldn't cut him off. As they started the leg home, Shooting Star had gained a length. Back down the straight away toward Main Street and the finish line, Diablo never gained a step. Shooting Star maintained his lead and won by one length.

Glen Ray joined Fred who was walking out Diablo to cool him down. After walking a few steps, Glen Ray asked, "Were you full out?" "Yea," replied Fred, "Diablo gave it all he had." "Was he holding Shooting Star back," wondered Glen Ray. "Don't think so," said Fred, "you can take him in the finals. Whiskey's faster than him. Then Fred took his hat off, slapped his side with it and said, "Hell, I could've beaten him if I had just gotten on the inside of the turn."

Next to come were the rodeo events. Fred had to hurry to be on time for his first event, saddle bronc' riding. He checked his draw; he was third man up and had drawn a horse called 'Nightmare'. Each cowboy would get one ride a day for two days, then whoever was left would ride in the finals on Monday. High score on the final day would determine the winner. Fred had participated in several rodeos and he knew the cowboy to beat was J.D. Kirster from Amarillo. J.D. was the first man up. He had drawn 'High Pockets', a great big tall, strong horse that was hard to ride. J.D. rode him with ease and scored a respectable 79. Fred crawled up on the rails of the chute as Glen Ray helped him ease down on Nightmare who immediately started bucking and rearing in the chute. He slammed Fred against the gate, bruising his knee. Glen Ray was trying to get Nightmare back in position. Finally Fred was situated and hollered "Let 'em loose, let 'em loose." The big bronc' came out of the chute and jumped straight up with all four feet off the ground. When he landed he put his head down and his rump in the air but Fred had gained position and was spurring in rhythm. Nightmare hit the fence hard but Fred stayed on. He made the eight seconds. The pick up men helped him dismount and he waited in the arena for his score. The announcer shouted out, "We have a new leader, an 82 for that young cowboy, let's give him a hand."

Fred walked to the chutes where Glen Ray was and said, "How 'bout that, amigo. I'm in first place." Glen Ray said, "Hell of a ride, your leg okay?" "Yea," said Fred, "I'm ready for tomorrow. I've drawn 'Sidewinder'.

Next would be the 'team roping' event with Fred and his brother Manuel teamed together. Fred roped the head but Manual missed the heels. They received 'no time' for their efforts but Fred's little brother, who was only fifteen, was becoming a good cowboy. After the rodeo it was party time, street dancing, chicken fights, mule pulls and lots to eat and drink.

Mr. Fox congratulated Fred on his ride and asked if Whiskey could beat Shooting Star. Glen Ray said, "I don't know, we'll find out tomorrow." Fred said, "I've qualified for the finals; amigo, why don't you finish second or third tomorrow which will qualify you for Monday. They will be thinking about Diablo in the finals. If you stay close after the turn, Whiskey will out run him to the finish line. Whiskeys too strong at the end, no horse can run with him the last half of a one mile race. I'm gonna bet on you." "Me too," said Mr. Fox.

Glen Ray had danced with Angel several times when Mr. Fox came by, snatched her like a coyote stealing chickens, grabbed her arm and literally ran to the dance floor. Just then a tall well dressed, affluent looking man about fifty walked up to Glen Ray and said, "My name is J.D. Blackwood, I own 'Shooting Star'." "Glad to meet you," said Glen Ray, "Just call me Glen Ray," he didn't say Ranger Porter. "I hear that blazed face sorrel of yours is fast," said Blackwood. "Well," replied Glen Ray, "he's out run a few Indian ponies; don't know how fast that makes him. At that Blackwood said, rather surly, "Tell you what I'm gonna do Glen Ray, I'm gonna give you a chance to make a hundred dollars." "That sounds like good money," said Glen Ray coyly, "but I've already got a job." J.D. responded matter-of-factly, "Naw kid, I ain't talking about a job. I'll bet you a hundred dollars my horse out runs yours Monday." "I ain't got that kind of money," said Glen Ray, "the Rangers don't pay but a dollar a day." "Rangers? Are you a ranger," asked Blackwood, rather surprisingly. Glen Ray looked him in the eye and said, "Yep, that's me. Hearing that Glen Ray was a Ranger, Blackwood asked if he was the

'Baby Ranger'. Glen Ray answered in the affirmative then said, "I'll see if I can find a hundred dollars. They say a fool and his money are soon parted. One of us will be a fool come Monday."

When Glen Ray told Fred about Mr. Blackwood wanting to bet him a hundred dollars, Fred said, "Bet him amigo, I know horses, Whiskey can take him. How much money you got?" Glen Ray counted his money in all his pockets and said sadly, "I've got forty-five dollars, that ain't enough." "Here amigo," said Fred, "I've got enough." Then he continued, "We'll split the winnings. Give me your money and I'll take it to Blackwood tomorrow. Okay, amigo," said Glen Ray, "but if we lose, you've got to let me eat at the bunk house."

Glen Ray laid down to sleep and thought about his strategy for the race. He decided he would hold Whiskey back and just qualify for the finals, then he could surprise them on Monday.

The night passed swiftly. Sunday morning after breakfast it was time to get ready. Soon afterwards all riders would be called to the starting line. Everyone was there to see who the winners would be. Money was being bet, lots of money. Glen Ray's plan was to let Shooting Star have the inside. Then Monday he would surprise them by quickly forcing Whiskey to the inside. There were five horses lined up and ready when BANG, they were off.

Chapter 26

Whiskey was strong, he had been rested a week and he felt fast. Down the street they ran with Whiskey and Shooting Star dead even. Shooting Star's rider looked at Glen Ray, surprised that they were side by side. As they made the turn, Shooting Star was on the inside and came around the barrel leading by a length. Whiskey felt really smooth, he was running well. Glen Ray almost hated to hold him back. They were going toward Main Street with about an eighth of a mile remaining. When Whiskey quit responding and Glen Ray couldn't hold him, he said, "Okay big boy, show'em what you got." Having been given his head, Whiskey took his cue and flew by Shooting Star. In desperation Shooting Star's rider was whipping him hard but Whiskey continued to pull away, getting stronger the farther he ran. When they crossed the finish line Whiskey had pulled five lengths ahead of Shooting Star. Mr. Blackwood ran over to his horse and rider trying to find out what had happened. Glen Ray dismounted and started walking Whiskey to cool him out when Fred ran over to them and said, "What a race, what a horse, I thought you might hold him back today and let him loose tomorrow." Glen Ray said, "Tried, couldn't hold him back, he can't take it when a horse gets in front of him." "I just love 'em," said Glen Ray with a big grin. "Were they holding Shooting Star back," asked Fred?" "? "Naw," replied Glen Ray, "his rider was about to beat him to death with his quirt as we went by 'em."

Mr. Fox was over talking to Blackwood. Afterwards, he came over to Fred and Glen Ray with five hundred dollars in his hand and said, "Here boys, this is your money." Fred looked at the money, got a surprised look on his face and questioned, "Our money, what do you mean, our money? We only bet a hundred dollars on tomorrow's race." Fox replied, with a sly grin on his face, "Oh, you know, I guess I'm getting old, don't hear so good anymore. I gave 'em your money for tomorrow, then I told him you wanted to bet five hundred on today's race. Here, take your money." "No sir, that's your money," spouted Glen Ray. "Like I said," repeated Fox, "I'm gettin' old." Then he reached in his pocket and pulled out five more hundred dollar bills. He grinned real big and said, "I must have bet twice, once for y'all and once for me," then he slapped his leg and laughed loudly. Glen Ray said, "I can't believe you took such a gamble." "Son," said Fox as he cocked his head to one side and winked, "I didn't gamble, I know horses. Have you forgotten, I offered you fifteen hundred dollars for Whiskey? Boy, you've got a horse there; fastest horse these ole eyes have ever seen."

"Oh, by the way," he added, "it's between you two boys tomorrow; Shooting Star's going home. Come on Fred," said Glen Ray, "it's rodeo time. I've already checked, you're fourth man up and you're on Sidewinder." Glen Ray hesitated for a moment then continued, "Don't want to pressure you none, but I'm gonna put a hundred on your ride today."

Then, as he was walking Whiskey to the livery stable, Mr. Blackwood approached him and said, "Ranger Porter, do you always ride that horse when you're out on patrol?" "Yes sir," said Glen Ray, "I sure do, he's my buddy." Blackwood scratched his head, looked puzzled and said, "I just can't believe it, a working horse. Tell you what, I'm willing to do, I'll give you fifteen one hundred dollar bills now and write you a check for fifteen hundred more, is that a deal?" Glen Ray laughed and said, "Thank you, that's a lot of money, but Whiskeys not for sale." Almost pleadingly, Blackwood went on, "Son that horse could be shot out from under you any day out there on patrol. Let me buy that horse, I'll give you four thousand dollars, hell you can buy a small ranch with that kind of money." "No sir, he's not for sale," insisted Glen Ray, "but if you have a Morgan mare send her out here, it's a thousand dollar stud service." "I'm going back to my ranch today," said Blackwood, "there'll be one on the way tomorrow." If you like," responded Glen Ray, "You can go out to Mr. Fox's Tuesday and see what kind of colt he sired, a mare foaled a few days ago. Fine looking colt out of a Morgan; he's gonna make Mr. Fox a fine stud." By this time they had reached the livery stable. Glen Ray, still leading Whiskey, stopped, looked at Blackwood and said, "Sorry I got to go, my buddies coming up in saddle bronco, gotta go help him."

When Glen Ray walked over to the holding pen, Fred, who was standing there checking out sidewinder, looked up and said, "Hey amigo, now that me and you have some money, this horse will probably kill me. Look how big and strong he is, looks like a big mule." Offering encouragement, Glen Ray said, "You can handle him amigo, lay back on him, spur over his shoulders, get your timing and he's all yours." "Yea," said Fred, "I've got to ride 'em, Mr. Fox bet on me." "You can do it amigo," urged Glen Ray, "but don't just ride for Mr. Fox, hell I bet a hundred on you myself." "Damn," said Fred, "look at 'em, he's about to kick the chute apart now." "Naw, he'll be worn out by the time you get on," hoped Glen Ray. "Yea, right," said Fred half-heartedly, then added, "If I ride 'em, half what y'all bet is mine." "Okay," said Glen Ray, "that's a deal.

Up on the chute, Glen Ray was trying to hold Sidewinder's head so Fred could get on. The big bronc reared, stood up and tried to jump out of the chute. He managed to get his head and feet up over the top railing before they got him back in the chute. They couldn't get him situated in time, so they let another cowboy go ahead of Fred. Finally they got settled down enough for Fred to ease on, slip his boots into the stirrups, lean back, and pull hard on the reins. Both Fred and Sidewinder were wide eyed with anticipation when Fred nodded his head and shouted, "Let 'em loose." Fred was sitting on the horses withers and leaning back. He continued to spur while pulling hard to keep Cyclone's head up. Fred was making a beautiful ride. Sidewinder was bucking hard with his head down and snorting like a bull. Dirt was flying from his rear hoofs and it looked like his butt went ten feet in the air when he bucked. Fred was beautiful, never out of position and in perfect rhythm with each jump. He made the eight seconds as the pick up men helped him off and the crowd cheered. When the announcer barked out a score of ninety-two, Fred threw his hat in the air and let out a victory yell.

When Fred got back to the chute area, a grinning Glen Ray started congratulating him and said, "You made that horse look tame, hell of a ride." Then, about half serious, he added, "You're making us rich, let's quit our jobs, go to all the rodeos, you ride and I'll bet." "Amigo," growled Fred, "this ain't my first rodeo, but it could be my last. When that big son of a gun bucked, he jarred every bone in my body. But you're right," he added, "I'm one hell of a rider ain't I, and pretty, too," he continued laughingly, as he pulled his Stetson all the way down over his ears. He grinned at Glen Ray and repeated, "I'm pretty and I'm rich," as he clowned around with his hat pulled down.

Glen Ray thought this is great; it's taking his mind off LaQuita. Mr. Fox was in the stands and had turned so he could see Fred and Glen Ray behind the chutes. Glen Ray looked at him and gave a thumbs up; Fox was probably thinking the same thing. When the team roping came up, Fred and Manuel participated. Today they caught and tied the calf in twenty-four seconds but, with them not scoring on the first calf, they were out of the competition. It didn't matter to Manuel; he was having a good time and begging to ride broncos in the next rodeo.

With the day's events over and the anticipation of tomorrow's race, another big night of celebration was in store complete with eating, drinking and dancing. It was an eventful night. There was a shooting when two drovers got drunk and fought each other. One of them was wounded, but luckily, it wasn't a killing. Sheriff Meeks and his deputies made the arrest without further incident.

Glen Ray spent some time with Whiskey, fed him, rubbed him down and admired him. He looked at Whiskey, remembering past races and Indian chases as he thought about the money he had been offered by Mr. Blackwood. Rolling the numbers in his mind, he walked in front of the big stud and placed his hand under the horse's chin. Glen Ray looked in Whiskey's eyes and said, "Don't worry Whiskey, you and I will always be together, and that's a promise."

Glen Ray was up early and had breakfast with Fred and Angel while Mr. Fox slept in; he had partied too hard. After breakfast, Angel joined

Linda as they went to Fox's room to wake him and offer him a cup of coffee.

The day's race was scheduled to start at ten; Fred and Glen Ray were preparing their horses. A record first place prize of one thousand dollars was being offered. This was the biggest race ever in Texas. There were thirty-two horses entered with an entry fee of one hundred dollars each. The riders were waiting for their horses to be called to the starting line. Glen Ray said, "Good luck amigo." Fred responded with, "Yea, good luck to you too amigo." Then he added, "Remember I'm riding a mule, take it easy on me." They grinned at each other, shook hands, mounted up and rode to the starting line. BANG, the starting shot was fired. Whiskey got a good start and had two lengths on Diablo at the turn. Glen Ray went to the inside at the turn and let Whiskey run on his own. Whiskey's tail was up and his head was extended; he was flying. Glen Ray grinned and said, "Go ahead big boy, you love to run, give it all you've got." They crossed the finish line ten lengths ahead of Diablo and the rest of the pack.

Mr. Fox and spectators walked with Glen Ray as he cooled Whiskey down. With amazement in his voice, Fox said, "Son, let me tell you again, I ain't never seen a horse finer than Whiskey, Hell, I've never seen a horse get stronger as he runs." Glen Ray smiled and said, "I think a lot of him myself, he just made me more money than I make in two years as a Ranger." "Son, when you want to go in the horse business, let me know, we got our stud in Whiskey," promised Fox.

When Fred walked over to where Glen Ray and Mr. Fox were, he said, "I guess I can say I've got the second fastest horse in Texas, right amigo." They all laughed and Fred said, "Come on, its rodeo time." Fred was in first place with total points in saddle bronc and, with a decent ride, he could win. He had drawn a big buckskin gelding named 'Undertaker' who had a habit of pushing riders into the fence. Rumor had it that one cowboy had been killed while riding him and several others had been seriously hurt. Fred knew he would have his hands full.

Fred was fifth up – J.D. had ridden his horse and it was now up to Fred. He needed a score of 87 to win and take home the two hundred and fifty dollars in prize money. When Fred was called up, Glen Ray crawled up on the chute to assist. Undertaker was snorting, rearing and trying to kick down the chute. Glen Ray grabbed his ears and pulled hard, trying to hold his head still. Fred eased down in the chute and onto the saddle, pulled his hat down around his ears, adjusted his hands and hollered, "Let 'em go." As the chute opened, Undertaker came out bucking hard and, as expected, turned into the chutes. Fred held on and was looking good. It looked like Fred had glue on his britches, he wanted that prize money. Undertaker was bucking so high it looked as though he was standing on his head. Fred was a hell of a cowboy and was putting on a hell of a show. He made the buzzer. The pick up men got him off and onto the ground. Fred's' hat went thirty feet in the air; he was jumping and dancing around the arena. The score was announced: eighty-nine, Fred was the winner. The crowd applauded with an uproar as Glen Ray jumped off the chute and ran out to congratulate him. Mr. Fox was cheering, clapping and celebrating so hard he nearly 'bout fell out of the stands.

When Glen Ray reached Fred he grabbed his hand and shook it hard, slapped him on the back and said, "Great ride, you're one hell of a bronco rider." Fred looked at Glen Ray and said, "I rode today for LaQuita, I know she was looking down and watching."

The three days had been fun and profitable. To this day, no one knows how much Mr. Fox had won but he was extremely happy. After spending the night in Abilene, they all returned to the ranch, except for Jim.

In Uvalde Laughlin said he would be monitoring Boots and Jerry Jacks progress and when Glen Ray returned from Abilene, he might let them go on patrol with him. One more month and Boots would be eighteen. Jerry Jack, since he was a month older, had already turned eighteen. Laughlin had told them they could become Rangers when they were both eighteen, but he was now asking them to wait. Riding in groups and chasing Indians was a lot different than going in a saloon and facing a gunslinger. He told them to do the same thing he had instructed Nathan to do while learning to use his pistol.

In the meantime, they continued going to Church and seeing the girls whenever possible. Jerry Jack would read the Bible to the youth class and, whenever Boots requested, he read it to him at night in the bunkhouse.

Laughlin told 'em he was buying four Morgan mares from a man in Montague. Two were to be bred to Shooting Star with the other two being bread to Whiskey. The horses would be sent to Austin by rail, then meet a train taking them back to Uvalde. He told them he had received a wire from Glen Ray telling him that Whiskey outran Shooting Star at the Pioneer Days race in Abilene. Then Laughlin went to the bunkhouse and had supper with the boys. After finishing their meal he asked Candido, Jerry Jack and Boots to meet with him at the kitchen table.

"How's your shoulder?" he asked Candido. "Fine, fine, a little stiff in the morning, but its fine," answered Candido. Then, matter-of-factly, he added, "It takes more than one arrow to put down a good Mexican vaquero." They all laughed then Laughlin said, "I'm meeting with y'all to tell you what my plans are for raising horses, fine horses. Candido, I want the horse lots set up inside good fencing with one lot for mares and fillies and one for our studs. We'll need separate stalls for the studs to keep them from fighting. I'm sending Jerry Jack and Boots to San Antonio to pick up four Morgan mares that were sent by rail from Bowie, Texas. As you recall, I told you Whiskey outran Shooting Star over in Abilene, so my stud just may wind up being Whiskey. Jerry Jack, you and Boots get on the trail in the morning. Take hobbles to shackle the horses at night. These are high dollar horses and I want you to guard them with your life." The next morning the boys were up early, saddle bags packed and on the trail to San Antonio.

Jerry Jack had picked himself a new horse. Boots had helped break the horse and it was proving to be a fine mount, big, strong and solid white in color. Jerry Jack named him Pistol. He was a two and a half year old and, from what Boots could see, he could probably give War Paint a good race. With its cool days, November was a good time for traveling. They made good distance the first day before camping that evening at a place with thick grass for the horses and a nearby creek. When the sun had set for the day, they built a nice comforting fire. As they sat around the fire chewing on turkey jerky and talking, Boots said, "Jerry Jack, are we ready to be Rangers? You know chasing Indians is different than going in a saloon after a gunslinger." "Yea, we're ready," said Jerry Jack, "our practice drawing and shooting has paid off. We're both fast; your dad told me so. We just have to stay disciplined and make every shot count." Then, with a grin, he added, "As Laughlin says, 'Take your time fast'.

Boots said, "I agree, Laughlin has trained us well. Now we need experience. I keep hearing what he says, 'When you shoot, shoot to kill.'" Jerry Jack looked at Boots and said, "Your paw impressed Laughlin. He was praising him to Oral after the shoot out the other night and I overheard them talking. Oral said your paw was fearless and damn fast with his pistol." Boots said, "Jerry Jack, I consider you my brother, when we become Rangers we will always ride together. I want you to know I will always have your back." Jerry Jack said, "Boots, I don't have any blood family, I also consider you my brother. I would lay down my life for you and yes, I will always have your back as well."

They rode into San Antonio about an hour before the train arrived with the horses. Jerry Jack was impressed. Living on the farm he had never seen any of the cities in Texas. Boots told him Sterling would soon be going to Austin to study law. Then he looked at Jerry Jack and said, "How 'bout that, my brothers gonna be a lawyer and I'm gonna be a Ranger. Who would have thought it, two years ago we were in Georgia with no future." Boots paused for a moment, looked at Jerry Jack and said, "God has blessed all of us, me, you, my brother and my paw. He truly does hear and answer our prayers. Thank you Lord."

An off ramp was being laid out to the car the horses were in as the sliding door was opened. The horses were tied so Boots and Jerry Jack went in with their lead ropes and got the horses. People appreciate fine horses and a number of folks were standing around admiring them, they were beautiful. Boots nudged Jerry Jack and said, "Look at those three guys standing over by the depot. See how they're looking at the horses. Looks like trouble to me."

Chapter 27

One of the three men was extremely thin. In fact he looked so thin I doubted he would even cast a shadow. He was tall and dirty with a cigarette hanging out of his mouth. His eyes were those of a drunk. They were red, sunk in and bloodshot. The other two appeared to be drifters. They had a shifty look and evil eyes.

The boys tied two horses in line, holding the lead horse as they rode. Jerry Jack was leading the two mares that had already been bred while Boots lead the two young fillies. They led the horses out of town and back on the trail to Uvalde. The horses led well and, but, since it would soon be nightfall, they set up camp, hobbled all the horses allowing them to graze then sat down and lit a fire. Jerry Jack said, "Boy, that train was something, first time I ever seen one. How does it pull all those cars?" Then like a wide eyed youngster, belted out, "I sure would like to ride one someday. You know what the Indians call a train, don't you?" "Yea," said Boots, "an Iron Horse. Jerry Jack piped in, "I can see 'em now; riding along side that big locomotive and shooting it with arrows."

Boots held up an open hand and said, "Something's bothering the horses, listen, someone's riding in." Three riders rode into camp. It was the three men they had seen in town looking at the horses. "Howdy boys," said the skinny one. "Can y'all spare some of that coffee you're drinking?" They all three started to dismount, when Boots said, "Hold it fellas, don't get down until you're asked." The skinny one roared, "Ha, ha, hear that boys, this kids giving us orders." Boots said, "Mister, I said stay in your saddles. Now what is it you want?" In a calmer voice, one of the drifters said, "We just want to be friendly and have a cup of coffee." He looked over towards the horses and continued, "Y'all sure got some fine looking horses. What's two kids like y'all doing with good horses like those." Boots said, "We're takin' 'em to a Ranger over in Uvalde." "A Ranger," chimed in the skinny one." Then he mocked them with, "Hear that men? These boys know a Ranger. Ha, ha." His manner showed contempt for the Rangers.

Boots looked at Jerry Jack, reading his eyes; he was ready. He knew if they had to draw now, he was to take the man in front of him but, if he was on Boots' left side, he would take the man on the right. Laughlin had told them you don't want to be shooting the same man while another one kills you.

The slim rider seemed to be the leader of the bunch and, after a few seconds of intense silence, he said, "Tell you what; we're experienced drovers so why don't you boys go back to San Antonio and play with the girls. We'll take these horses over to Uvalde and give 'em to your Ranger friends, right boys?" One of the other men said, "Hell Slim, 'nuf talk, lets shoot'em and take the horses." One side of the man's face was a solid scar. It looked as if someone had held his face to a campfire. The third man was drunk and had a bottle in his hand. Slim said, "Boys, we're gonna take these horses and we're gonna kill y'all." Jerry Jack spoke for the first time and said, "Slim, I hope you boys are right with the Lord, 'cause if you go for your gun, we're gonna send all of ya straight to hell. So it's best you ride out of here alive rather than draped over your saddle dead."

"Hear that boys," said slim, "these kids think they can take us." "Hell Slim, I told you to kill'em," said Scarface as he reached for his gun and the other two followed suit.

Boots and Jerry Jack made their draws with Boots putting a hole in Slims chest. Jerry Jack made a heart shot on Scarface and they both put a hole in the third man. The trio had failed to get off a shot. All three fell from their saddles and hit the ground dead as a sack of cow patties. Boots looked at Jerry Jack and said, "Well I guess now we know what it's like to face a man and kill'em." "Yea," said Jerry Jack, "were you scared?" "Yea," said Boots," I was scared, were you?" "Yea, but it was us or them," said Jerry Jack. "What are we gonna do with the bodies," asked Boots. "In the morning we'll wrap 'em in their blankets and lie 'em across their horses," said Jerry Jack. Then he said, "It's a two day ride to Uvalde, we'll take 'em in to Sheriff Fox."

The rest of the two day trip was uneventful and the boys rode into Uvalde just before sunset. They were leading seven horses, four unsaddled and three with bodies tied over their saddles. A crowd followed them down the street to the sheriffs' office. Oral and Nathan came out and asked what had happened. The boys explained briefly; then Nathan led the horses with the bodies to the undertakers while the boys took the mares and fillies to the livery stable before returning to the jail. Sheriff Fox had purposely waited for Nathan to return before speaking to the boys.

When Nathan joined them, Fox said, "Well boys, you've been in your first gunfight; still want to be Rangers?" They both answered, "Yes sir," as the sheriff continued, "How do feel about killing a man?" Boots said, "Sir, Jerry Jack and I have talked about it. They pulled on us, we had no choice." "Then you could do it again, without any hesitation?" inquired Oral. "Yes sir," said Jerry Jack, "we could and, as Laughlin taught us, we shoot to kill when we pull leather." Nathan spoke up and said, "Why don't you boys stay in town tonight, then I'll ride out to the ranch with you in the morning." They agreed and the next morning they delivered the four horses from the train plus the three they got from the attempted rustling. While Nathan was in the house with Laughlin and Melissa, he removed his gun belt and put it in his saddle bags. His shotgun remained in its' scabbard on his saddle. It was common for him not to wear his pistol when at the ranch.

It was late in the evening when Nathan returned to Uvalde. As he rode by the saloon he heard a shot from inside. He turned his horse, rode up to the saloon and tied up to the hitch rail. A young gunslinger stepped out of the saloon with a gun in one hand and a bottle of whiskey in the other. The young shootist looked at Nathan and his peg leg, laughed and said," can you dance with a peg leg?" Nathan's star was hidden by his jacket when he looked at the gunslinger and said, "Yea, I can dance a little, when I have to." Nathan realized he had forgotten to put his gun belt back on before leaving the ranch, but he still had his shotgun.

A crowd had gathered as the gunslinger grinned and said, "Well peg leg, you're gonna dance now," and started shooting at Nathan's foot and peg leg. Nathan, in order not to get a toe blown off, began hopping around while everyone started laughing. When the last bullet had been fired, the young gunslinger, still laughing, holstered his gun and turned around to go back into the saloon. Nathan turned to his horse, pulled out his double barreled shotgun, and cocked both hammers back. The loud audible double clicks' carried clearly throughout the Uvalde air. Suddenly the crowd stopped laughing. The young gunslinger also heard the sounds as he turned around very slowly.

The silence was almost deafening. The crowd watched as the young gunman stared at Nathan and the large gaping holes of those twin barrels. The young man found it hard to swallow. The barrels of the shotgun were unwavering in Nathan's hands as he said, "Son, did you ever dance?" The young man swallowed hard and said, "Yes sir I have." "Have you ever danced without your britches?" asked Nathan. With a quiver in his voice, the young man answered, "No sir, but I've always wanted to." "Well you're fixin' to," growled Nathan, "Pull off your boots, gun belt and britches." The young man did as told. Nathan said, "Son, I'm a Texas Ranger," as he pulled back his coat exposing his badge he went on, "See that jail house down there about two blocks away." "Ye uh yes sir, ah, ah see it," stuttered the youngster. "Good," said Nathan as he ordered, "Now get out here in the middle of the street and start dancing toward that jail house. You're under arrest and don't stop dancing 'til you get to the jail."

You could hear the crowd laughing at the young gunslinger all the way to the jail. Oral had heard the shots and was standing out on the front porch of the jail watching a half naked man dancing down the street. Nathan danced him by Oral and into the jail. Put 'em in a cell and hang up the keys," said Nathan. Oral came back inside the jail and with a grin said, "I'm sure there's an explanation for this." "Oh yea, yea," said Nathan, "the man likes dancing and he was just showing me some steps." "Where are his britches?" asked Oral. "Ah, he danced plumb out of 'em," joked Nathan. Oral laughed and said, "Come on let's go get some supper."

Back in Abilene Mr. Fox, Stewart, Fred, Glen Ray and Sterling were waiting for the stage to arrive. Sterling would be going to Austin to start school and Mr. Fox, along with the others were there to wish him well and see him off.

The stage pulled up and stopped, horses were changed quickly and the stage was ready to roll. Sterling shook Stewarts hand, hugged Mr. Fox, tried to say "Thank you" and broke down crying. Mr. Fox said, "Here now, no need to cry, be happy, go up there and show 'em who you are." Sterling loaded up then Bob Bell got 'em rolling and he was off to Austin. Mr. Fox looked at the stage as it disappeared down the old dusty road and said, "There goes a fine boy; he will come back a fine man."

The trip was uneventful, no Indians, no highway men, just dust and bumps. After arriving in Austin Sterling found his boarding house and checked in; it was a place mainly used by students. After getting things in order, he decided to walk around and see the Capital Building, locate the library and try to get familiar with the surroundings. His classes would start the next day, he was excited. He found the library, surveyed the law books, found one on criminal law and took it to a table to read. After awhile he closed the book, sat back in the chair and looked across the room at a girl who was also reading at a table. She had beautiful long blond curly hair a great complexion, green eyes, and large well defined lips. She was also dressed very nice with expensive looking clothes. Looking up she caught Sterling staring. They smiled at each other and she went back to her reading.

Sterling had been ready to leave but now he didn't want to go so he opened his book and acted as if he was reading. In reality he was try-ing to get up enough courage to introduce himself. Finally he said to himself, 'Well here goes nothing,' got up and returned the book to its proper place. After putting the book on the shelf, he turned to walk away and ran right into the girl he had been looking at. She had been putting her book up in the same area where Sterling had found his and was standing behind him when he turned around. Surprised, and rather awkwardly, He said, "Oh, I'm so sorry. I apologize for being so clumsy." She grinned and said, "No, it's not your fault, no harm done."

Sterling thought, 'Well, do something you idiot. You've already run over her.' Then, drumming up the courage, he said, "My name is Sterling, Sterling Law." She said, "My name is Emily Henderson and I am happy to meet you, Mr. Law." He said, "Oh please, call me Sterling. I was just leaving but maybe I'll see you here again." Emily said, "I was also leaving, will you walk me outside." "Certainly," said Sterling, a little surprised, "it will be my honor." "Are you from Austin?" she asked. "No," he said, "originally from Tennessee but now I'm living in Abilene. I moved here to attend law school," "Law school!" she remarked, "How interesting. Do you like law?" "Yea, law and politics" answered Sterling thinking 'man this is better than I expected'. They sat down on a bench and continued to talk. He asked where she was from. She told him she had been in Austin for about twenty years and was also in school studying to be a teacher. Sterling couldn't help but stare at her; she was so beautiful with eyes so soft they made you feel warm when you looked into them. After a little more small talk she said, "I really must be going, lots to do before tomorrow when school starts." "Yea I know me too," said Sterling, "listen, do you think we could have dinner tomorrow evening?" "Yes," she responded, "that would be nice. They agreed to meet at the Statesman Restaurant the next evening at seven thirty. She smiled and he said, "I really have enjoyed our time together. I'll see you tomorrow evening." Sterling watched as she walked away, she was gorgeous.

It had been three days since Jerry Jack and Boots had returned from San Antonio with the horses. They were riding the area north of the ranch house and looking for mavericks. Riding side by side, Boots said, "Still feel the same after the shootout." "Yea, like I said, it was us or them, better them than us," was Jerry Jacks answer. Boots said, "I do feel better now about going into saloons and facing down gunslingers. I think that's why Laughlin was reluctant to send us on patrol." "Yea, me too," agreed Jerry Jack as he continued, "By the way Boots, you're pretty fast, not as fast as me, but, maybe with some practice." "I admit you're fast," exclaimed Boots, "now let's see how fast Pistol is; let's go War Paint." Off they went side by side and running hard. After about a mile they pulled up, walked the horses again and resumed talking.

Boots asked Jerry Jack how he and Cindy were getting along. Jerry Jack said they were doing fine and she really was pleased that he was teaching the youth class at church. Jerry Jack wondered how Boots and Audrey were doing. After assuring him they were doing fine, Boots said, "She doesn't much like me becoming a Ranger. Says it's too dangerous, thinks I'll be gone all the time." Then turning his attention to Jerry Jack asked, "What's your plan, you still gonna be a Ranger?" "You know I am," said Jerry Jack. "Wish you would hurry up and turn eighteen so Laughlin can sign us up." Then, out of nowhere, Boots said, "Hey, I'm impressed with Pistol, he runs good. I think you should rename him." "Yea, like what?" asked Jerry Jack. "Caboose," snickered Boots, "he's always gonna be following War Paint." Yeehaw yelled Boots, spurred War Paint and out across the pasture he went. Jerry Jack just shook his head and grinned.

Chapter 28

In Austin, the first day of school had come and gone for Sterling. It had been a wonderful day, studying law and going to dinner with a beautiful girl. After school Sterling hurried back to his room and prepared to meet Emily at seven-thirty. The restaurant was close to the Capital and easy to find, he was early. It was an expensive looking place. Sterling knew his budget wouldn't allow many dates such as this. He was waiting inside the restaurant when Emily came thru the doors. She looked so beautiful that it overwhelmed him. He was nervous, clumsy and infatuated; he had never seen beauty such as hers.

They were shown to a table and Sterling, exercising all his manners, was trying very hard to impress Emily. They complimented each other on how beautiful and handsome each looked, then exchanged comments about the first day of school. Sterling told her he had been working for an attorney and reading law books for over a year. Then he laughed and said, "Everything we read today I've already read back in Abilene. Enough about me; tell me about you and your family." Emily grinned, looked at Sterling and said, "My father's an attorney here in Austin." "Wow, that's great," said Sterling with excitement, "hopefully I can meet him." "Don't worry, you will, he's joining us for dinner," she said, "His treat."

In a short time a well dressed man in a suit, vest and top hat approached the table. He was exactly what you would think an attorney should look like. He had dark hair, masculine eyebrows, was smooth shaven, and well groomed. He sported a perfectly trimmed moustache, had a pleasant smile with very alert intelligent eyes, a near perfect male specimen which probably contributed significantly to his daughter's beauty. When Emily introduced her father as Lloyd Henderson, he said, "Very glad to meet you young man. Emily, you described him perfectly: he is a handsome young man. Sterling Law, a good name for an attorney," he continued as he sat down and ordered wine. "Tell me about yourself young man." Sterling told about the war, his lost family, how he got to Abilene, his paw the Ranger, Stewart's practice and Mr. Fox. Mr. Henderson exclaimed, "Mr. Fox is paying for your schooling you say?" "Yes sir he is," said Sterling then proudly added, "I am so very lucky to know him." "Fox, Fox from Abilene? Is this JJ Fox, the retired Ranger?" queried Mr. Henderson. "Yes sir, you know him?" asked a surprised Sterling.

"Know of him, heard many stories here in Austin about him." Lloyd replied as he paused then continued, "What a great Ranger; could have been Governor of this state if he wanted it. You have a very interesting background young man. What are your goals?" Sterling said, "I want to graduate from law school and then go into politics. Mr. Fox said I had to return to Abilene as a State Senator and I'm certainly going to try." "Outstanding," approved Henderson, "daughter, you have my permission to see this young man anytime you want." He looked at Sterling and, like a father giving advice to a son, said, "Don't give her all your time, I want to show you around, got some people I want you to meet, including the Governor." After dinner he picked up the check much to Sterling's delight, excused himself and left the two of them alone. It was a pleasant fall evening in Austin. Sterling and Emily walked around a while then sat on a bench and talked. It was very evident they enjoyed each others company.

On the ranch back in Abilene, Mr. Fox and Glen Ray were sitting in the living room discussing horses when Fox said, "Son, Whiskeys' too good a horse for you to be riding out on the range with Indians shooting at you and trying to steal him. It'd be a shame if you or that horse got shot, but he's a great stud horse, a gold mine for you. Mr. Blackwood, Shooting Stars' owner, came out here and offered me two thousand dollars for Three Paws. I wouldn't take it. Now maybe I'm crazy, but I don't need the money, just want to see what you and Fred can do about making him a racehorse. Why don't you leave Whiskey here; I'll use him for a stud with my Morgan mares and split the money with you when we sell his foals. People all over are going to hear about Whiskey beating Shooting Star."

Fox thought for a moment and in a much stronger voice said, "Beat 'em Hell, Whiskey demolished him, sent him home early. Whiskey's going to be a popular boy with lots of stud fees coming in." Then, almost in desperation, Fox urged, "Hell, take my horse, Billy Jack, he can run with Diablo, he's fast." Glen Ray had listened intently to Mr. Fox and nodded as he spoke, "You know, Mr. Fox, I'm gonna do what you say, we're partners, right?" "Yes sir," said Fox, "Glen Ray, we're in the quality horse business, partner," and they shook hands as Fox continued, "By the way, where did you get Whiskey? I know he's got a lot of Morgan blood in him." Glen Ray replied, "Yes sir he does. I don't go around telling this but I won him in a card game up in Denton. Fella that raises horses had lost some money to me playing poker. He paid me part of my money and gave me a beautiful Morgan colt in trade for the rest. That was the best deal I ever made. I named him Whiskey because the guy that lost to me was making whiskey bets playing five card stud. I really love Whiskey. We've traveled lots of miles together and we're pals but, you're right, he'll be better served as a standing stud." The two men shook hands and Glen Ray went outside to make his peace with Whiskey before taking possession of Billy Jack.

Laughlin sent a wire asking Glen Ray to come to Uvalde. After receiving the wire, Glen Ray saddled up Billy Jack, a big strong Morgan, strawberry roan in color. Glen Ray said goodbye to Fred, Angel and Mr. Fox; he had already said his goodbyes to Whiskey the night before.

They were all standing in the yard when Glen Ray mounted Billy Jack and looked toward the corral. Whiskey was standing with his head over the top rail looking back at him. Glen Ray tipped his hat as he rode off, and once again looked at the corral. Whiskey was running up and down the fence, neighing at Glen Ray and bucking. He knew he was supposed to be carrying Glen Ray. 'Don't worry old pal, I'll be back," said Glen Ray as tears filled his eyes and rolled down his face.

Once again it was Sunday in Uvalde. Melissa was beginning to show her pregnancy just a little and Laughlin was beaming with pride. Jerry Jack and Boots were sitting with the girls. Boots had joined the youth class to listen and learn, not to teach. When church started, Brother Morgan spoke about when Jesus baptized John the Baptist, then how and why he was thrown into prison and beheaded. After the service as they gathered for the usual lunch, Brother Morgan sat down at the table with Jerry Jack, Boots, Audrey and Cindy. He said, "I heard you boys are almost ready to join the Rangers." "Yes sir," said Boots. "We're ready now, just not old enough." "Well boys," said Morgan, "I'm sure you've been told about the dangers involved, just remember this; God is riding with you, don't ever abandon him, he won't abandon you. Ask for his help, pray and worship him. He answers prayers and helps those who help themselves." "Brother Morgan," said Boots, "I would like to be baptized." "Me to," said Jerry Jack, "we do everything together, baptize us together." Brother Morgan was excited as he blurted out, "Certainly, certainly, next Sunday during the service, praise to God. Jerry Jack, I would like to speak with you in private before you leave." "Let's do that now," said Jerry Jack, "I'm anxious to hear anything you have to say." They excused themselves from the group and went to Brother Morgan's' study.

"Sit down and make yourself comfortable," said Morgan, "this is all good, I'm not going to tell you to stop seeing Cindy. Jerry Jack, you are a special person, the Lord is in you. You are a godly person, a leader and very much an instrument of God. Son, you could be a preacher, and a good one. You're learning the Bible very fast and you understand what you're reading. Then Brother Morgan got real serious and continued with, "I know you're getting ready to be a Ranger, but son your calling is that of a preacher. Maybe not today, maybe not tomorrow, but sometime in the near future you will be a preacher." "Thank you sir, thank you," uttered Jerry Jack, "I admit sometimes I do hear the calling and I want to know more about Jesus' time here on Earth but I must ask something; Can I be a Ranger, take lives and still be accepted by God?" Morgan reminded him of David, the greatest warrior of all men who was chosen by God to be the King. Upon hearing this reminder, Jerry Jack said, "Thank you sir, will you pray for the men Boots and I killed, it'll make me feel better."

Over in the jail Nathan and Oral were playing dominoes and passing time. Nathan's' dancing gunslinger was still in jail waiting on the arrival of the circuit judge. The prisoner's name was JoJo White. He was twenty-two years old with no wanted posters but he had been arrested several times for disturbing the peace or being drunk and disorderly. He was a well built good looking kid; clean shaven and stood about five foot ten at one hundred-eighty pounds with dark long hair and brown eyes. Oral looked at JoJo sitting in the cell and said, "Young man, do you realize that you're fortunate to be alive? That was a Texas Ranger you were shooting at, you're damned lucky he didn't give you both barrels of that shotgun." "Yes sir, I know it," said JoJo, "I was drunk. I can't handle whiskey; it gets me in trouble every time." Oral pointed to Nathan and said, "It was Ranger Law here who made the arrest; it's up to him what happens to you. If you go before the circuit judge, he'll probably give you five years hard labor."

Oral turned to Nathan and continued, "Nathan, what do you want to do with him, he's your prisoner." Nathan said, "Son, if you apologize to me and make me believe it, I'll turn you loose. Couple of restrictions though. One, you go out to Ranger McFarland's' ranch and help build fences for thirty days and two, be in that church down the street every Sunday." JoJo sighed a breath of relief and almost shouted, "Sir, that's a deal, I don't want to go to prison. I apologize, sir; I'm sorry, thank you for not killing me." "JoJo," said Nathan sternly, "if you screw up and don't keep your promise, I'll come get you and you'll go to the Huntsville Penitentiary, understand." "Yes sir, Yes sir, I promise," said a relieved JoJo.

Oral released JoJo from his cell then, he and Nathan left the jail and rode out to the McFarland ranch to meet Laughlin and Candido who were working with the fence crew. They put their horses in the corral and walked out behind the barn where Boots and Jerry Jack just happened to be practicing their marksmanship. The boys had two buckets hanging separately from a tree and were drawing and firing one shot only, this continued till one missed. Nathan and JoJo stood at the edge of the barn door and watched as the boys practiced. Each of them had drawn and fired six times without missing.

They were reloading when Nathan and JoJo approached them. Nathan turned, and said, "Hello boys, how you doin'? This is JoJo White. JoJo I want you to meet my boys, Jerry Jack and Boots. The boys and JoJo nodded at each other then Boots said, "Alright paw, I saw you watching us, now let's see what you can do." Nathan smiled, walked over to the buckets, made a lightening fast draw, and fired two accurate shots, one in each bucket. "That's my paw," said Boots and they all laughed as Boots went on, "JoJo you're wearing a gun, show us what you got." "No, no, think I'll pass," said JoJo, "maybe some other day." With that being said, the action was over. Nathan told JoJo to get his gear and he would show him the bunkhouse.

After they walked out of hearing distance, Jerry Jack said, "Boots, did you hear what your paw said when he introduced us." "Yep, sure did," said Boots, "if your my brother, then I guess you're his son. Come on brother, six shots rapid fire." Boots was flashing his big ole smile as they took their positions to continue their practice. Nathan was in the bunkhouse when JoJo asked, "Mr. Law, are your boys Rangers?" "Naw, but they will be in twelve days," said Nathan. "Mr. Law, you're fast with that six gun," stated JoJo, "now I know who you are. You're 'Shotgun Law' aren't you?" Nathan nodded his head as JoJo continued, "Thank God I'm still alive. Your boys are fast, faster than anybody I've ever seen." "Well," said Nathan, "the man you'll meet this evening, Laughlin, is faster than any of us. There isn't any man I know that would stand a chance against him.

Several days had passed when Glen Ray came riding through the gate at Laughlin's' ranch. He was saddle weary from the long ride and was ready for a soaking bath. Everyone was glad to see him and quickly asked about Whiskey; no one had ever seen him on any other horse. He got a real sad look on his face and said, "A rattlesnake bit Whiskey and I had to put him down." He couldn't keep from laughing and everyone knew he was lying. After the laughing subsided, he told them all about the race, his winnings and why he wasn't riding Whiskey.

Laughlin told him that he had two Morgan fillies and hoped to get Whiskey's colts from them. Then, after saying their usual hello's, Laughlin said excitedly, "Hey, I hear Whiskeys' the fastest horse in a mile race in Texas. Wish I could have seen the race." How about Diablo?" he added. Glen Ray said, "Hell, Laughlin, Diablo can run with Shooting Star anytime." "What about you," said Laughlin, "are you gonna stay in the Rangers or become a rancher." Glen Ray replied, "A rancher has to have land, I don't have any, no I'm a Ranger." He shifted his hat a little and added, "Mr. Fox is going to raise and sell horses then split the profits with me. I'll put money in the bank then maybe, when I'm old and all shot up, I'll buy me a ranch."

A week had passed since JoJo arrived on the ranch taking up with Jerry Jack and Boots. They liked him; he was beginning to loosen up and talk more. One evening, after supper all three of them were sitting on the bunkhouse porch when Boots asked JoJo about his life.

JoJo said he was from Fort Worth. Said he had been on several cattle drives, and lived a drover's life herding cows, drinking and raising hell. On his last cattle drive he got in a fight with one of the other drovers. They drew on each other and he killed the drover. It was a fair fight and there were witnesses so he didn't serve any jail time. After killing a man in a gunfight he thought, he was a gunslinger. He started hanging out in saloons, learned to play cards and was barely surviving when he came to Uvalde. "I had been thinking about being a gunslinger and an outlaw until the incident in town, I'm lucky to be alive. After seeing y'all behind the barn the other day I realized I'm not fast, all I did was outdraw a drover. I was just wondering; since I like it here working on the ranch, do y'all think Mr. McFarland would let me stay and work for him." "Ain't but one way to find out," said Boots, "and that's to ask him."

Just then Boots looked up, saw Laughlin and said, "Here's your chance,

I see him coming this way from the ranch house." "Hello boys," said Laughlin, "how do you like building fences?" "I like it, matter of fact I want to see if you will give me a full time job," said JoJo. "Well," said Laughlin, "Candido says you work good and I'm getting ready to lose two men, so the answer is yes." "Thank you sir," said a happy JoJo, "I'll make you a good hand." Then, since Boots would be eighteen the next day, Laughlin said, "Boys tomorrow I'll send the paperwork through and you'll both be Texas Rangers. I'll swear y'all in at Orals', want your paw to be there, he'll be proud, hell, we'll all be proud." Boots and Jerry Jack were all smiles as Laughlin turned to JoJo and remarked, "Who knows young man, maybe someday you'll be taking the oath."

Back in Abilene, Jim went to the post office and dropped off a letter to Uvalde in care of Ranger Laughlin McFarland. It read:

Laughlin, I have asked Linda to marry me and I am requesting a six month leave of absence from active duty. We are engaged and after six months, if we still feel the same about each other, we will be married. At that time I will resign from the Rangers and help Linda manage the saloon and the hotel/restaurant. Congratulations on starting your family, maybe someday I too will be a father. Sincerely, Jim Weaver

Up in Fort Worth, Indian Jack and his gang of five men were on the south end of town drinking in a saloon called 'Hells Half Acre'. Indian Jack was a half-breed. He was twenty-six years old, five feet ten at approximately one hundred and eighty pounds. He had long black braided hair hanging on each side of his ears. He always wore a tall crowned businessman's hat, deerskin vest, blousy shirt, necklace, pistol and knife. He was a fairly nice looking man with high cheek bones, typical of his heritage, and the dark skin of an Indian with bright white teeth. He spoke broken English and, when sober, was fairly intelligent. However, most of his escapades had happened while drinking. And he had spent five years in Huntsville for stealing.

He had assembled a gang and they were making plans to rob a train. The plan was to hit the train as it stopped to take on water near San

Marcos just south of Austin. Trains consistently carried more money that stages and, if you knew when large sums were being carried, fifty thousand dollars or more could be stolen. The money was usually carried in an enclosed mail car with deputies inside protecting the safe. The plan was, when the train stopped for water, kill the deputies as they come out for fresh air or to relieve themselves. Once the deputies were eliminated they would drag the safe out of the boxcar, blow it up with dynamite and make off with the money. The final leg of Indian Jack's plan was to complete the robbery then ride west toward Llano and hide out for about six weeks in a cave. He figured by then the posse would have given up and they could head south for Mexico. They completed their plans and determined they had to be in place in one week which was an easy ride from Fort Worth. They made the trip and camped about a half a mile out from where the train would make its water stop.

Chapter 29

The next day they hid in the nearby trees and brush but still within rifle range. The train was on schedule. It stopped, the water spout was lowered, and the mail car door slid open. Two deputies jumped to the ground while one, with rifle in hand, stood guard. A single rifle shot from the trees dropped the deputy at the door. Two more shots dropped the remaining two standing outside the car. One of the gang members jumped on the engine and tied up the engineer. A rope was thrown in the mail car and the safe was dragged to the ground by one of the outlaws on horseback. Dynamite was quickly attached to the door and lit. It exploded. The charge was perfect and it blew the safe door open. The money was put in saddle bags then every one mounted up. Indian Jack shot the wire down on the telegraph pole as they rode away toward the south. They would go about a mile then turn west toward Llano.

Back at the Rocking Horse Ranch in Uvalde, It was late in the evening when Laughlin was in the bunkhouse talking with Glen Ray, Jerry Jack and Boots. He said he had received a wire from Steve Ballard, the sheriff in Waco, informing him about a train robbery. Three guards had been killed and the bandits rode off with about fifty thousand dollars. Five men were involved, they all wore masks but Ballard suspected it was Indian Jack and his gang. They had been hanging out in Hell's Half Acre and had made some whiskey brags about a train robbery. Just before the robbery he and his gang disappeared. Laughlin said Indian Jack was very familiar with the area around Llano, Fredericksburg, Lampasas and the hill country in general. Then said, "Indian Jack will probably hide out for several weeks." He could well be in a predetermined cave along the river. He's an outlaw, but when pursued he reverts back to his Indian teachings; so think like an Indian when you're searching for him." Laughlin took a breath before continuing, "Jerry Jack, Boots, this is your first trip out as Rangers. Are y'all ready?" "Yes sir, we're ready, ain't we Jerry Jack," said Boots. Jerry Jack nodded in the affirmative as Laughlin said, "Good, get with Glen Ray and the three of you get on your way to Fredericksburg in the morning. Glen Ray, you'll work your way from Fredericksburg to Llano and Lampasas; just follow your nose and look for leads."

In the bunkhouse listening to the briefing being given by Laughlin, JoJo said, "Excuse me sir, I'm very familiar with the area around Brady. I also worked on ranches in Lampasas and Llano; wherever there was work to be found. I know the range and the location of quite a few caves along the bluffs. Old Indian caves that Indian Jack probably knows about. There's plenty of water available with deer for food and numerous vantage points where you can see anyone coming for miles. I would be glad to ride with y'all, but after what I done to Nathan; I can see why you might refuse my offer." Laughlin said, "I have no problem with you, we covered that, it's up to these three Rangers here." Laughlin looked at the Rangers and asked, "What do you boys think? Want him along as a deputy?" Glen Ray said, "What do you boys say, it's up to y'all." "We want him," they both said. Boots and Jerry Jack had already taken a liking to JoJo. Laughlin smiled and said, "What's the Rangers coming to; a man serving out his sentence building fences and y'all make him a deputy. I'll swear him in as a deputy, that'll help 'cause I need to leave Nathan in Uvalde, Oral is feeling poorly."

The next morning was a typical south Texas fall day. It was overcast with a light northeast wind, a good day for traveling on horseback. Glen Ray informed everyone of his plan, ride to Fredericksburg, ask a lot of questions, then follow the Pedernales toward Austin. JoJo said, "There are a number of caves east of Fredericksburg big enough for several people to live in at once."

On the morning of the third day the foursome rode in to Fredericksburg. Glen Ray and Boots went to the General Store to see if any unusual purchases had been made. Jerry Jack and JoJo visited the saloon and inquired about strangers in town or any talk of a train robbery. The owner of the store said, "A man came to town two days ago with a couple of pack horses. He bought enough provisions to last several men two or three weeks. I remember him paying in cash with large bills." Jerry Jack and JoJo had spoken with a rancher from Doss about twenty five miles north of Fredericksburg. His name was Welge. He had retired as a Ranger and was currently ranching in the area. He had told them there were several caves on his ranch near Squaw Creek and he would check them out. Said if he found or heard anything he'd wire Ranger headquarters in Waco.

The three Rangers and JoJo set up camp on the south bank of the Pedernales River just south of Fredericksburg. It was a beautiful area with good grass for the horses as well as fresh water. They built a fire and put on the coffee pot. Supper would consist of dried turkey and deer jerky. JoJo poured himself a cup of coffee, sat down on his saddle and said, "Who would believe it, me, a deputy and riding with the Rangers." "Well, how do you like it," asked Boots. "I love it," said JoJo, "wish it could be permanent," Glen Ray looked at him and said, "Stay with it and maybe you can if you practice like Jerry Jack and Boots have. But remember, always practice well; it takes more skill to face a man with a gun." JoJo stood up quickly and said, "I just remembered, as a boy I was told about a cave here outside Fredericksburg, it's a big cave full of bats. It's no more than a mile or so from here. It's not on the river; it's more like the mouth to a cavern. It's a really big cave. Glen Ray said, "Good, we'll find it tomorrow. I think Indian Jack will hole up around here and then make their run into Mexico at Eagle Pass.

The next day they were up early and searching for the cave. Glen Ray picked up tracks of three horses. He said, "These tracks were made yesterday." "How do you know?" asked JoJo. "The tracks have dew in them, dew from last night," replied Glen Ray rather astutely. They carefully and quietly began following the trail; constantly on the alert for any guard that may be watching the approach to the cave. If the cave is big enough, they knew the horses would also be in the cave and out of sight.

They were continuing on slowly when Glen Ray signaled them to stop and whispered, "There's a guard up there on that rock about two hundred yards away. He's sitting propped against some other rocks, looks like he's asleep. Glen Ray thought for a minute to figure out a plan of attack, then, speaking softly, said, "Keep the horses quiet and stay here. I'm gonna walk in and get 'em; cover me with your rifles." He started his stalk, moving from bush to bush carefully selecting where he stepped. He was creeping low and staying in the shady spots. After about twenty minutes of careful stalking, he reached the rock. The Rangers could see him as he climbed up the backside. Once on top, he crept slowly to the sleeping man, drew his pistol and with a hard blow to the head, knocked him out. The others advanced and gagged the man then tied his hands and feet securely to a tree.

Knowing they were near the hideout, they quietly led their horses and continued walking till they saw the mouth of the cave. It had a huge opening, maybe 30 feet across. Glen Ray said, "I'm sure their horses are in there with them. Let's get a rope stretched across the opening about a foot and a half off the ground. If we pull it taught and tie it around some tree trunks it'll trip the horses as they ride out." Once this had been done, they backed up about thirty yards from the cave opening and Glen Ray hollered out 'Texas Rangers, come out with your hands high in the air!' No response, Glen Ray said, "Fire two shots in the mouth of the cave." They did and they could hear horses fighting their ropes in response. Glen Ray said calmly, "They'll come out riding hard, let 'em hit the rope and try to take 'em alive in case they've hidden the money." All of a sudden four riders burst out of the cave their pistols shooting in all directions as the horses hit the rope. Down went the horses falling over each other and the downed riders. One horse and rider had made it over the rope and was trying to get away. As he rode by, Boots aimed his pistol and fired. The rider was knocked to the ground. The other three men, including Indian Jack, were on the ground unable to get up. The Rangers quickly disarmed them. The only dead bandit was the one that tried to ride off. Glen Ray and his crew rode towards Fredericksburg with one dead man across his saddle; and four others tied to theirs. They had the stolen money in the saddle bags, minus four hundred.

When they arrived in Fredericksburg they placed the four outlaws in jail.

Glen Ray wired Laughlin and received instructions to leave the four men in jail and he was to turn the fourth one over to the local undertaker for burial. Laughlin said they might be tried in Fredericksburg or possibly taken to Austin for trial. When Glen Ray saw that Laughlin had ended the wire with 'Good job, what took you so long,' he smiled knowing they would still be searching if it hadn't been for JoJo's input.

Back in Abilene Mr. Fox was enjoying his new venture as a horse breeder. Word had gotten out all over Texas about Whiskey and he was receiving stud service inquiries almost daily. He had been doing some thinking about the future and asked Fred to ready the buggy and take him to town. As they were riding to town, Mr. Fox asked Fred what he thought about Glen Ray. Fred said, "I like him very much, good Ranger and a good man. Someday he may be my brother-in-law." "Could you and him work together in a business venture?" asked Fox. "Yes sir," said Fred, "we get along fine and respect each other." When they reached Abilene he told Fred to drop him off at Stewart Coffee's office before going to the hardware store for a keg of Pittsburg square nails; they would be needed to build new stalls.

When Mr. Fox opened the door and entered Stewart's office, Coffee said, "Hello Mr. Fox, how are you?" "Fine, fine, thank you," said Fox. "What can I do for you?" asked Stewart rather curiously. "I've been doing some thinking," answered Fox, "and I want to revise my will." Stewart told Mr. Fox he could do that, then said, "Tell me what you want, I'll redo it and carry it out to the ranch in a few days for you to sign it." "That'll be fine," Fox said, "here's what I want. Take the property that I gave Fred and split it 50/50 between him and Glen Ray Porter." Stewart said that was no problem and he'd take care of it then run it out to the ranch. Then he added, with a smile, "You can cook me a steak, then sign the new will, how's that." "We can do that," replied Fox, "thanks Stewart and you're on for the steak." Fred was waiting in the buggy so they headed for the ranch. As they rode Mr. Fox said, "Fred, I've been making some drawings for twenty custom stalls. When we get back, come on in the ranch house. I want to go over the drawings with you so we can get the building started.

Indian Jack and his gang had been transferred to Austin for trial. The circuit judge arrived in town one evening, conducted the trial and sentenced the four desperados to die by hanging the next day. The gallows were built so all four men could swing at the same time. A large crowd was gathering to watch the multiple hangings. People came in wagons and lived in them. Riders came in ten or fifteen at a time, slept out then claimed areas close to the gallows. Vendors were also preparing for the crowd.

Glen Ray, Boots, Jerry Jack and JoJo were in attendance, they had testified at the trial. A crowd of about a thousand had been gathering for over ten days waiting for the trial and inevitable hangings. Stories were circulating about all the doomed men. It was said Indian Jack was a half breed and had been banished from his Indian camp when he was five or six years old. People claimed he took to living like a wolf and survived. Later he formed a gang of outlaws and ruffians and lived a life of violence. It was said he would kill you for a stale drink of water. His last call for survival was robbing trains, now he's come to his reward, death by hanging. The hangman was waiting at the gallows atop the platform. Several Rangers stood guard around the men as they were led to the gallows by the Austin sheriff and his deputies. The ropes had been measured and drop weights calculated for each man. They climbed the thirteen steps leading up to the floor of the gallows, turned and faced the crowd. All of them, except Indian Jack, wanted hoods over their heads. The noose was placed around their necks with their hands bound behind them. Indian Jack looked at the crowd and said, "I'm going to my reward, the one God in the sky welcomes me, death to all white eyes." The hangman tripped the lever and they all fell thru the floor dangling, quivering, gasping for air and then, silence. The silent sound of death was deafening. The crowd stood and watched without speaking a word. Then, after a moment, they turned and started walking away silently as if to show respect to the dead.

The Rangers and JoJo mounted up and rode toward Uvalde. Boots said, "Fellas, I'm glad I'm on the right side of this Ranger badge and not facing it." "Me too," said Jerry Jack. JoJo said, "I'm going to ask Laughlin if he'll swear me in, after what I saw today, all my trails will be straight."

The fall and winter months had passed rapidly. It was a beautiful spring evening; Laughlin and Melissa were sitting in the swing looking out over the ranch. Suddenly Melissa jerked with pain. Laughlin said, "Are you alright? Is it time?" "Yes, it's time," answered Melissa. "Get me in the house and call Maria." Laughlin helped her lay down, then ran to the porch and fired his pistol in the air. Candido came running out of the foreman's house as Laughlin hollered "Get Maria up here, someone go get Doc Milles, Melissa's having the baby!"

Chapter 30

Maria was boiling water when Doc Milles arrived. Laughlin paced the floor and after about three hours, Doc Milles said, "Laughlin, you can come in now." Laughlin walked over to the bed and sat down. Melissa was holding the baby and as she pulled back the sheet she said, "Laughlin, say hello to your son, Sam."

Time passed quickly; Jim had resigned from the Rangers. He and Linda went to Albuquerque, married and honeymooned. JoJo was now a Ranger riding with Boots and Jerry Jack who, by now, were seasoned Rangers. Sterling was completing his law school and would soon be an attorney. He was engaged to Emily and had met some powerful politicians with plans for him after law school.

In Abilene, Mr. Fox, Glen Ray and Fred were doing well with the race horses. Fred was making all the races, riding Three Paws and winning and Whiskey was happily producing quality horses.

Glen Ray was still going on Ranger patrols but Laughlin kept him close to Abilene and Lubbock. That way he could still be involved in the horse business with Mr. Fox.

It was noon. Mr. Fox, Glen Ray and Fred had just repaired a gate on the horse lot for the mares when Mr. Fox walked over to a tree, sat down in the shade, leaned back on the tree trunk and said, "Set down boys, take a load off your feet." They did and it felt good. It was hot and the southwest breeze was a welcome comfort to their faces. Mr. Fox said, "Boys," as he looked out over the ranch, "I'm proud of this ole ranch. Maude and me started it and we shared some good times here. I don't want this ranch to die when I do. You two boys are like the children Maude and I never had. Y'all are like sons to me and I want you boys to always consider yourselves brothers, I want your word on that. They both said they already considered themselves brothers and he had their word. Fox nodded his approval and said, "Well, one of y'all give me a hand, pull me up, I think I'll go in and take a little nap."

When he got up and started walking to the house, it seemed like he stood taller and straighter than before. Fred and Glen Ray looked at him as he walked away. What a picture he was, knee high leather boots, long sleeve blousy shirt, gallowses' over each shoulder, tall crowned brown Stetson, kicked in a little in the front with the brim rolled a little on each side. Gray hair was hanging to his shoulders. He had a full moustache, weather beaten face and eyes that had suddenly softened. Fox was thinking to himself, all this surrounded by rolling hills behind the house, cattle and horse pens, beautiful blue skies and Knob Hill. What more could a man ask for. He reached the house climbed the steps, opened the screen door, looked at the boys who had never quit watching, nodded his head and tipped the front of his hat with his fingers.

Three hours passed, neither Glen Ray nor Fred had said anything; they kept watching the ranch house, hoping to see Mr. Fox returning. Finally Fred said, "I can't take it any longer amigo, I'm gonna go check on him." "Yea, I'm going with you," said Glen Ray. As they walked to the house they prayed nothing was wrong. They entered the house and there he was, lying back across the bed with his feet on the floor. It appeared he had gone to the kitchen and picked up a biscuit, broke it in half and put a piece of bacon on it before going to bed. He must have sat down to eat it then passed out falling backward on the bed. He was breathing but it was shallow. Manuel was sent to town after the doctor and Rosa came immediately to pray and help make him comfortable.

A wire was sent to Laughlin advising him of the situation. When he received it, he immediately told Jerry Jack, JoJo, Boots and Nathan to saddle up, they would be riding hard for Abilene. The doctor had said Fox was in a coma and there was nothing he could do for him. On the fourth day, Fred, Glen Ray and Rosa were at his bedside. Rosa was bathing his face and wetting his lips with a wet rag while she prayed.

Suddenly his eyes opened, he raised his arms toward heaven and said, "Maude, I see you, I'm coming home," and with that his arms fell and his eyes closed – JJ Fox was dead.

A casket was built in Abilene and brought to the ranch. Mr. Fox's body was placed in the casket and put in the parlor. He was dressed in his boots, jeans, white shirt, vest, and coat. His hat was turned down on his chest with his hands holding the brim. His hair and moustache were neatly trimmed; he had a contented look on his face.

Everyone was waiting for Laughlin and the Rangers to arrive. The pall bearers would all be Rangers: Laughlin, Glen Ray, Fred, Boots, Jerry Jack and Nathan.

People were coming from everywhere: Abe Silas, townspeople, retired lawmen and Indians, he had been well known and well respected.

Stewart came out, paid his respects and then asked Fred and Glen Ray if he could visit with them in private. They entered the next room and Stewart said, "Gentlemen, Mr. Fox had a will and Laughlin is the Executor. I want to make you aware you both own half the ranch; the part that includes the ranch house and corrals, etc. The other half is owned by his brothers, Oral and Herman. Upon their deaths, their half goes equally to both of you; they're not allowed to sell it."

Laughlin and the Rangers had arrived with the burial scheduled for the next day. The casket was moved out to the front porch with everyone gathered in the yard for the services. After the service, the casket was loaded in a wagon and taken to the base of Knob Hill. It was then carried by the pall bearers to the grave site at the top of the hill. Once the pall bearers carried the casket to the grave, the preacher read from the Bible, the casket was lowered into the ground and covered with dirt.

All the Rangers were left standing alone on top of the hill. Laughlin stood in front of Glen Ray, Fred, Nathan, Boots, Jerry Jack and JoJo.

He was holding his hat in his hands and said, "Boys, lets all join hands and circle the grave." They did, as Laughlin said, "Let's bow our heads, while I pray." Then with a softness in his voice the Rangers had never heard, Laughlin began,

> "God watched as you helped tame and
> cultivate this State of Texas.
>
> He gently closed your weary eyes and
> took you in his care.
>
> God saw you were getting tired, so he
> put his arms around you and whis-
> pered 'come with me'.
>
> With tearful eyes we watched you sur-
> render and saw you fade away.
> Although we love you dearly, we could
> not make you stay.
>
> A golden heart stopped beating, hard
> working hands at rest
>
> God broke our hearts to prove to us he
> only takes the best.

Then Laughlin slowly raised his head, looked towards the heavens, and said, "Mr. Fox, you were the best and all your friends will miss you until the day we meet on God's ranges in heaven and once again, 'Ride the Ranger Winds'."

The End.

ABOUT THE AUTHOR

by Richard "Dick" Guidry

It has been my extreme privilege to have known the author, E. Richard Womack for over 20 years. We met in the mid-80s through our shared love of the sport of Target Archery and became friends immediately. He is a strong-willed person with courage to overcome the many hardships he experienced both in his childhood and as an adult.

Born Emmett Richard McFarland, July 20, 1940 in Bowie, Montague County, Texas, his last name, due to an adoption, was changed to Womack. He lived with his Great Grand-dad, John Joseph Fox until he was nine years old. He was raised in the country in an old home place with no running water. It had outside facilities and lanterns were used in the house after dark. John Joseph was born in 1872 and cowboyed most of his younger life. His many tales of the cowboy days exposed Richard to the ways and honor of the western cowboy that Richard never forgot.

His Grand-dad, Laughlin Fox, owned a team of mules and worked on the railroad with a Fresno building track. Laughlin died when he was twenty-one years old. His body was loaded in a wagon and his team of mules pulled the wagon nine miles to his burial cite in the Montague County Cemetery.

Richard moved to Fort Worth, Texas after the death of his Grand-dad and was reunited with his mother. They lived on Fort Worth's north side where the stockyards were still active; much of his time was spent in the area. Shortly after moving to Forth Worth, Richard was stricken with the dreaded disease of the time, Polio. Through tough determination learned as a boy, he fought and then overcame that setback. Later, after graduating from high school, Richard started to work as a helper with an outdoor advertising company. Working through the ranks, and learning the trade, he left the company and started his own outdoor advertising service company, Media Display, servicing billboard advertising companies throughout South Texas. Under Richard's guidance and knowledge, the company flourished and is still operating today.

Perhaps, due to his respect for Native Americans, Richard's favorite pastime is the aforementioned sport of archery. As a hunter, Richard has harvested over 200 game animals and varmints. In the realm of competitive archery, Richard has acquired twenty-five State, National or World Championship titles in indoor and outdoor venues, and presently holds the U.S. National Field Archery Association's record for the outdoor "Animal Round" in the Senior Male Barebow Division.

Richard has written, and continues to write, accounts of stories from his lifetime adventures for his high school newsletter.

This literary work is Richard's first novel and reflects and encompasses the essence of the Texas Rangers during the early years of Texas' long and illustrious history.

Rangers continue to play an effective, valiant and honorable role in Texas today, but that was even more-so before and during the state's early years as a member of the United States.

It has been my distinct pleasure and honor to have been a part of this writing. Thank you Richard.

ACKNOWLEDEMENTS

It is with grateful acknowledgement that I express my gratitude to the following contributors who made this book possible.

To Donnie Rae Cage (Fox), David Wood, Sr. and Jim Weaver, who graciously provided me with significant information and facts.

To Richard "Dick" Guidry for his enthusiastic dedication in the editing of this project as well as his guidance and suggestions in relation to the structure of the story lines.

Without these credits I could not have completed this novel. I am forever indebted.

The Ranger prayer is dedicated to my dearest friend, the late Bobby Hunt.

E. Richard Womack

Disclaimer

Although the names of some of the characters were taken from family, relatives, and friends, all the action is fiction and any resemblance to any other persons, living or dead, is purely coincidental.